DYING GRASS MOON

DYING GRASS MOON

Hennessey Reed Mystery series (Book 2)

Andrea Jacka

Published by Red River Pony Publishing

Website: www.andreajackaauthor.com

The main characters, incidents, and dialogue in this book are fictional and drawn from the author's imagination. References to real people, organizations, establishments, events, or locales are intended only to provide authenticity and are used fictitiously.

A catalogue record for this book is available
from the National Library of New Zealand.

Cover design: Jeroen ten Berge
Author photograph: Amy Cronhelm

Also by Andrea Jacka

Hennessey Reed Mystery series

One For Another (Book 1)

ONE

Each bird loves to hear himself sing.
—Arapaho proverb

To the best of my knowledge, Evangeline Muir harbored no suspicion in her thirteen-year-old head that I was her mother. On the morning of her bawling, miraculous entry into this world, those destined to become most important to her agreed to withhold this information from her as long as possible—in a perfect situation, forever. Amongst manifold, pressing reasons we decided it was unfair and ultimately even cruel to foist upon her the burden that the woman who birthed her was a bordello madam: a woman ruinously dependent on the false-hope promises of laudanum and Irish whiskey; a woman harangued by ghosts real and imagined; a woman who, notwithstanding this, drank in the sight of her and rejoiced in her companionship on all available occasions.

Not long since, Evangeline near died at the hands of Jedidiah Cannon, an iniquitous creature whose essence haunted me still. Many a night I bolted upright in bed, confused by what must be determined fantasy, and what reality, when Cannon and his demons wreaked havoc with my tormented mind.

While under Cannon's governance Evie was mostly delirious, for which I remained eternally grateful, although this proved both blessing and curse. Her physical scars healed, including the nub left glossy and pink where Cannon had cut off her finger which he then mailed me as a warning—this a constant, shocking reminder of her abduction.

Never by nature a fearless child, despite her lineage, this ordeal spun her inward, wounds undetectable by the naked eye persecuting her spirit. Evie was loath to stray from the skirts of my dear friend Lizzie who, in partnership with her husband Clay, performed the role of her parent, but I trusted one fine day she might develop a measure of independence, of bravery. Until that day, those privy to our secret pledged to fight until the last breath to protect her, to assuage our guilt and atone for what we perceived gross negligence of our collective duty in the recent past.

Evie caught me staring at her so, musing interrupted, I sought to allay worriment she might experience with my single-minded observation, plucking a benign avenue of conversation out of a basket holding rationed supplies, and said: "I believe I neglected to pay compliment on your pretty dress, Evie."

"Thank you, Miss Reed." She loosened a rare, shy smile, and ran a palm down her cotton pinafore dress, unconscious mimicry of a habit Lizzie demonstrated when steeling her nerves.

Lizzie, the girl's foundation stone, rested a hand on Evie's arm and bestowed a reassuring pat.

After Evangeline's rescue, convinced a divine entity stood guard over her daughter for the duration of her abduction—and, fundamentally, this was the practicable explanation of how and why Evie survived—Lizzie started attending church. She feasted on the Bible, working stolidly through it cover to cover, returning to the beginning directly on completion. Owing to this scrutiny her clothing and cosmetic favors transformed, crossing the border into austerity, the unadorned pinafore and bonnet Evie wore visual manifestation of her mother's newfound probity, as Lizzie cast aside gewgaws and indecorous living with vigorous, unrelenting purpose.

In garish contrast to Lizzie and Evie, my attire consisted of an emerald-green satin dress that glowed with a rich, luxurious sheen. Lace frothed at my wrists. Perhaps not of equal status to the latest fashion practices of those who cut a dash in more populous centers of the country—disciples certified at the forefront of prevailing taste—with hair pinned in a chignon I was exceptionally presentable, all the same. A French parasol, tassels of knotted silk dangling, lent itself to my ensemble more as an indulgence than an object of practical usage, and reflected particular attention spent on my appearance that morning.

I stroked the head of my giant wolfhound, Raven, stationed as usual at my hip, and returned to the festivities spread before me.

I held no recollection of who proposed the residents of Melancholy should take it upon themselves to play host to the inaugural county fair, this seen as a joint endeavor, heralded as a celebration and reclamation of normalcy.

Following the discovery of four young girls defiled then murdered the previous spring, emotional trauma endured, brash and offensive, scabs worried as a child picks a grazed knee. Hardened to threats furnished by outside forces, townsfolk were left reeling on finding these atrocities originated with a member of our community.

Memories were starting to dull, to blur, with the fair being seen as wiping a slate clean, a show of solidarity to make clear—to ourselves as much as anything—that although we may have suffered the whims of insanity we had survived, a little battered and bruised but quite a ways from broken. Along this vein I chose to believe those folks around me who laughed and chattered, a rout of blue jays, did not agonize to preserve normality or present a valiant façade; that their enjoyment was heartfelt.

Behind me, dressed like a celebration turkey, Main Street complemented those garbed in church-going finery. An industrious minion had cobbled together cerise triangles of bunting, in support of what organizers intended an annual fixture, and painted a welcome sign on an oblong stretch of canvas that was then hoisted across the street. Unfortunately, not only did the person in charge of the sign inadvertently misplace the 'h' in Melancholy, they ran out of room toward the right-hand edge, so the town's name required condensing, its last three letters squashed, accordion-style, to fit.

When these jarring mistakes were pointed out to the appropriate supervisors few took exception; besides, it was too late to remedy them. Nevertheless, in such cases there is invariably a minority who cannot be pacified, who refuse to sanction blatant inaccuracies. Mrs. Coltrane, an enthusiast of rules and self-proclaimed expert on correct procedure—her specialties running the gamut from how to tie a bow through to English language regulations and the limitless vagaries of grammar that lay within its perimeters—led dissenters.

Fierce in her determination to uphold linguistic standards she had dallied in the center of Main Street, tutting, and it was here, due to the reflexes of her nimble-witted companion, that she narrowly avoided being mown down by Henry Tippet's buckboard, requisitioned by the fair overseer to cart tents and tables to land delegated the fairground at the southern end of town.

My gaze fell upon a wooden sign propped against a pole supporting a nearby tent. The image painted on the sign depicted a fortune-teller swathed in purple fabric, bejeweled hands hovering above an unnaturally luminous crystal ball. This portrayed that with the unsurpassed spiritual powers in her possession, those close-held secrets gullible patrons tried their darndest to conceal might be revealed like magic, to corroborate her authenticity, and that a wonderful future awaited, undetermined without her valuable and well-priced assistance.

Below this disingenuous portrait twirling script declared:

Madam Beauleux
can see you now.

A gentleman posted out front of the tent paced with the contained steps of a captive bear in a futile attempt to disguise a pronounced limp. He passed out handbills, broadcasting Madam Beaulieux's prowess in a booming voice that battled for dominance over the cacophony of the fairground. When Lizzie and I made to go by him, my pointed dismissal saw him indolently withdraw an offered bill, expression deadpan. Lizzie accepted the bill instead, firing stern admonition my way, her caution to my rudeness. She should be well-accustomed to it by now.

An image similar to although not an exact replica of that gracing the board decorated the handbill, the element of skill evident in this rendition flying close to crude or, poetically, naïve in execution.

A woman rotund as a harvest pumpkin, outfitted in clothing better suited to a person half her age and size, exited the tent. Her obsequious manner saw her do everything save genuflect to a shadowed figure glimpsed past the flap, on whom she piled effusive thanks.

When she leaped back as though branded to avoid collision with me, a display of enviable agility, I did nothing to mask my amusement, gratified to see this noticeably flustered her. I walked a step ahead of Lizzie, but Mrs. Humphrys—for I recognized this eddy of dust after observing her waddle around town—subjected me to the decidedly peevish arrogance of the righteous then spurned me.

I remained indifferent to this impertinence. I owned the Fleur-de-lis saloon and cathouse, so her attitude toward me was not a rarity; it was rife amongst the parsimonious flock domiciled in Melancholy. If Mrs. Humphrys ever learned of Lizzie having shared my profession when younger, I toyed with how her face might contort in distaste before she ran as speedily as her short fat legs consented to carry her in the opposite direction.

"I thoroughly recommend a sitting with Madam Beaulieux if you are debating whether to do so, Mrs. Muir," she said to Lizzie. "It's sure to bring comfort. Can you believe she channeled my beloved Charles, who disappeared without a trace? She beheld his death as well, which she assured me was quick and painless, this of marvelous benefit for heartsease."

"I understood Mrs. Humphrys married a wainwright named Harold, now deceased," I said, once the elderly lady had left us, mincing steps taking her to the refreshment area. "Who is Charles?"

"Charles was her pet hog. Wretched beast kept breakin' outta her yard and runnin' wild causin' all sorts of mischief."

"I wondered to whom that animal belonged. I frequently spied it being chased along Main Street which, admittedly, I found enormously entertaining." I looked after the stout woman who dabbed tears dry with a kerchief stitched with royal blue thread, while awaiting a mug filled with a bracing medicinal potation. "When I think on it, that explains why I have not seen him for some time."

"I'd heard he vanished, as Mrs. Humphrys says. I'm bettin' Charles ran into the wrong yard and got himself made into a pork dinner, never to be seen again. Except on a plate."

"You have no intelligence of the whereabouts of this boisterous missing hog, Lizzie?"

"Not a smidge." Lizzie licked her lips, winked, then studied the colorful representation of Madam Beaulieux on the handbill. "Well, this could be interestin'. You wanna come too, Ness?"

An arched brow conveyed my answer.

"Ah. 'Course, you see ghosts enough without huntin' 'em out."

"Does this spiritual diversion not fly in the teeth of your new beliefs?"

"Maybe. Though I'm doin' it in fun—and remember, I've seen the truth behind *your* gift."

"You seriously intend to waste money and precious time on a soothsayer who will fabricate all manner of airy predictions, which can then be manipulated and interpreted so they fit any puzzling happenchance you experience later?"

"Might reply in kind if I could make sense of anythin' you just said." Lizzie drew her daughter closer. "Meantime, can you watch Evie?"

"Naturally."

"I shan't be long, darlin'," she said to the girl inclined to stick to her like a limpet. "You'll be fine here with Miss Reed."

Required to duck when entering the tent, Lizzie paused and waved to us before the man with the crippled leg lowered the flap to deliver privacy for Madam Beaulieux and her latest customer. Nary a word nor warmth befriended his taciturn, bewhiskered features as he secured the tent and resumed distributing handbills.

Her mother distracted, Evie forfeited allegiance posthaste and hurried to my side, an indescribable, extrinsic joy consuming me when she slotted her hand into mine.

Next to the fortune-teller, a strongman contraption garnered who knew where taunted and beckoned. The game required the participant wield a mallet with all the power he could dredge and wallop a pad at its base, to send a metal globe skyrocketing to strike a bell high above our heads.

Evie stood enthralled, fascinated by the spectacle of men who, one after another, pitted their strength against a machine I conjectured, with normative cynicism, cannily weighted against them succeeding to their true ability. Even so, never averse to an exhibition of masculine superiority and disported by their showboating, I was content watching them, too, until the event touted the fair's main event.

Within the hour my stallion, Samson, was to challenge several worthy opponents on an oval racecourse pegged out on flat land near the river. Expected by most to ride him myself, I pretended to bow to persuasion, consenting to repose elegantly on the sidelines to allow a man appointed by the fledgling Melancholy Race Committee to perform service as jockey. A week ago, I also commandeered a neutral go-between to covertly broker a wager on Samson's placing before his odds shortened, thereby rendering it a next-to-pointless exercise.

Until the horse race, crowds gathered to champion favorite contestants at the wood-chopping competition, exultant cheers resounding above hordes of onlookers when the dull *thunk* of ax meeting stump ceased and a sweat-drenched, jubilant axman raised his fist in triumph. Others chose genteel pursuits, wringing hands and jiggling in place, tracking progress of those in the pivotal office of judge as they tasted and prodded, circling tables smothered in home produce and baking.

Endued with glorious weather—to describe it as heated afforded more credit than it deserved—the fair was a last celebration, the uncontested harbinger to fall, and to snow and ice that before a body could say 'Jack Robinson' would sheathe Melancholy and the outlying county in ermine white.

A batch of horses, mules and a single donkey saddled or, more commonly, arriving in the traces of buggies and wagons, were divested of harness leather then tethered or corralled in rope pens. Youths seconded to patrol the animals strutted in their midst, chests puffed with importance and responsibility, their duty to supply pails of water to the thirsty and ensure scuffles pioneered by the bored, or feisty, were dealt with swiftly.

Families spread rugs or canvas in shade beneath ancient cottonwood boughs, where they unpacked comestibles, beverages, and relevant dining utensils. The air chimed with noise; musicians tuned screeching fiddles, a backdrop to children who giggled and squealed as they played chase, giddy with indulging in activity that did not involve arithmetic or endless chores.

When Lizzie's consultation with Madam Beaulieux ended and she stepped from the tent's dim interior into sunlight, Evie decamped, resuming her customary post near her mother.

"So, tell me, Lizzie. What pearls of wisdom did Madam Beaulieux relate?" I asked. "Is a handsome stranger going to gallop into town and sweep you off your feet? Your husband must respond to this with proprietorial vigor. Or are you to be wary of wolves in sheep's clothing?"

"She said nothin' like that." Lizzie could not meet my eyes. "Didn't tell me much. You were right, Ness. Might as well've thrown my money to the four winds."

"You appear upset."

"Got nothin' more to say."

"You are certain?"

"I told you. Come." She made a fuss of retrieving Evie's hand and tucked unruly strands of hair behind the girl's ear. Evie's braid, which reached her waist, was boot-black and shiny as obsidian. Inherited from my family, the color startled me anew, for in this detail Evie favored me rather than her father. "Samson's race is gonna start soon. Let's go find a good spot to watch it."

⫸⫷

Samson ran a gallant race, however to the disappointment of his legion of backers he galloped across the finish line in second place. I patted his neck, ribbed with froth, and praised the efforts of his jockey. When Lizzie and I encountered the owner of the triumphant horse Zeus in the makeshift winner's circle, it took all my willpower to act courteously toward him.

Clearly on the lookout for me, Joshua Hughes stood immovable as a pillar of bedrock, a wealthy, successful landowner who, in my opinion, reveled childishly in coercing me to come to him. On our approach his eyes crinkled, his mouth bowed, creasing freckled cheeks, and the closest relation to a grin I had ever witnessed on him rose then burst on his thin lips.

Hughes's wife, Charlotte, killed four defenseless girls, their bodies stumbled upon the spring just gone, the means by which they met their deaths primeval and disconcerting. By her actions Charlotte subjected the inhabitants of Melancholy and vicinage to months linked by fear and suspicion. In the tumultuous afterclaps of the murders she also tried her utmost to remove me from the land of the living which, understandably, was an ambition to which I took grave exception. During a showdown I preferred not to re-examine, Charlotte died in my presence and this, I presumed, neither sat well with nor endeared me to her husband.

The rational part of me, typically blindingly conspicuous by its absence, acknowledged it preposterous to visit the sins of the wife against the husband. The irrational, maverick side of my nature did not allow this to muddy the waters of pre-existing low regard of Hughes.

Two people, and two alone, knew the sequence of events that preceded what transpired at the Sweet Venus Too mine the day Charlotte died: I being one, the second being dead. Could Charlotte's death have been avoided? Must I shoulder a tittle of accountability for aggravations that surrounded it? When all aspects were pared to a skeleton she chose her destructive course without encouragement. Her memory and family left behind must ever carry her shame; her step-children reconciled to tolerating residual fury spat at them by a community fractured by deceit.

Ever since that period, deep and dank as the coyote hole Charlotte fell into, I had spent considerable energy observing a generous distance between Joshua and myself unless unavoidable, wanting to circumvent interaction with him that had potential to become ... problematic. Until now he, most assuredly, had endorsed the sentiment.

"Good afternoon, Joshua." I inhaled an emboldening breath and tried not to choke on my good wishes when freeing them into air. "Allow me to extend congratulations on Zeus's win."

"Thank you, Hennessey." Hughes took my words at face value and responded accordingly, magnanimous in victory. "Samson ran a commendable race although, to my advantage, that wasn't enough."

"The faster, better horse won."

"Yes, he did."

Hailed by an ale-infused well-wisher Joshua bid Lizzie and me farewell and dipped his chin to supplement his adieu, a chanticleer preparing to bask in further glory.

"Well, that was a surprisingly cordial exchange. Considerin'," Lizzie said when we resumed maundering, her equilibrium restored. "You sickenin' from somethin'?"

"I strive to always be graceful in defeat, Lizzie."

"That's utter claptrap, Hennessey Reed," she said. Her brows knitted when I turned to her, my expression exaggerated innocence. "Don't you go lookin' at me with those big blue eyes, all harmless as a kitten. You're up to your elbows in some kinda skullduggery."

"Whatever gives you that impression?"

"Years of association, that's what."

"My tutors taught it mannerly to give due credit. Zeus ran a blue-ribbon race."

She snorted.

"I gather with that eloquent response you remain unconvinced."

"You must've lost a bundle with Samson comin' in on Zeus's heels, yet there you are actin' like all you lost was a measly fistful of bits."

"Ah, but there you make a fundamental error, Lizzie. You assume my winnings depended on Samson beating Joshua's stallion. And the other horses, of course." I dangled the clue under her nose, intrigued how long it would take my percipient friend to figure to what I alluded. It seemed I must shunt her in the right direction. "If nothing else, Samson's second placing makes for an exciting rematch, with him at considerably better odds to win, do you not agree?"

Lizzie cast about us to make sure no one lingered within hearing then, with affected casualness, squeezed out the corner of her mouth: "Did you order that unsuspectin' jockey fella to hold Samson in?"

"Can you appreciate a rider unused to Samson's idiosyncrasies would find that beyond his skills? Besides, that sort of behavior is frowned upon—and if brought to light, repercussions are far-reaching—and is not terribly sportsman-like."

"You don't normally care about those things, 'specially with Joshua Hughes. You never took to him and he's no more hoodwinked by your polite congratulations than me." I went to reply but she barged in with: "No! Don't tell me. 'Round you, ignorance is best."

"As you wish."

We wandered a dozen or so yards, Lizzie feigning disinterestedness until her craving for details got the better of her, as we both knew all along it would.

"Don't know why I'm askin' this, and Lord knows I'm gonna regret it. What did you do?"

"Imagine, if you will, Samson became thirsty prior to the race."

"What's bein' thirsty got to do with it?"

I held passing acquaintance with the jockey, so felt it judicious to neither count on nor trust his aptitude to weave and duck around the truth while under pressure if an inquiry were requested by a disgruntled mob unhappy with the race results.

"Withholding water from him then giving the horse a drink just before he races is an old horseman's trick my uncle taught me. It slows him down." We paused to greet a cluster of men cockeyed drunk, valued clients of the Fleur sown amongst them, continuing our discourse when well out of earshot. "I will leave it there, for the less you are sentient of, the more peaceful your conscience shall be."

"May that go straight from your mouth to God's ear."

We wound through stalls and games. Clear for all to see, townsfolk were enjoying themselves and I grew pleased, for despite my misgivings it demonstrated they were coming to terms with the horrors of the deaths at the Sweet Venus Too, expressing positivity in looking forward, not behind them. If parsing on what those girls endured at the mine I was vulnerable to disintegrating into flakes, for was existence not tough and dangerous enough without a child forced to submit to the loathsome penchants of murderous individuals?

"What are you thinkin'?" Lizzie relinquished calculation of an impressive array of biscuits and bottled fruit, green eyes studying me from her superior height; her countenance revealed the question a formality—she divined on what I ruminated.

"I am sure you can guess. It is never far from my mind."

"Nor any of ours," she chided, not without empathy. "I know it ain't easy but put it aside, please do, for yours and all our sakes."

"I shall try." My glaring, barefaced untruth lacked conviction. Even so, I did not fret over expanding it.

Farther on, Lizzie elbowed me in the ribs. Hard.

"Ouch! Dash it, what the deuce has gotten into you?"

"Marshal's headin' this way."

"I can see that for myself. There is no need to bruise my ribcage to bring it to my notice."

Inexplicably, after everything that happened last spring, Marshal Rafael Cooper persisted in behaving markedly ill-disposed toward me. I had expected our apprehending Jedidiah Cannon, who abducted Evie and assisted Charlotte in killing girls at the mine, would bind us closer together. Regrettably, the opposite occurred, continued to be the case, and exhibited no sign of abatement in the foreseeable future.

Couched in an addendum to his crowded song sheet with regard to me, during our investigation I was railroaded into telling Raff—until then, in the dark—that Evie was my daughter and naming her father, a famous politician recognized across America. When thrown into the titanic, rocky mix of our relationship, this did not sit well with him.

Irrespective of approach, Raff's and my coupling prior to the deaths at the Sweet Venus Too could not be gauged traditional and, true to our history, further complications bubbled to the fore once the perpetrators of those horrendous crimes were dead.

Willing to grant him the space he requested to rassle with the thunderbolt of Evie's true parentage, as weeks dragged by my frustration amplified until I raised the matter with him. He changed the subject. With patience a virtue of which I did not consider myself particularly well-endowed, and on account of his reluctance to engage in conversation to redirect us to relations beyond mere civility, I was resigned to his dealing with it in his own way, in his own time, exasperating as that, and he, was proving.

With Raff more hellacious to turn than usual, his obstinacy saw me choose not to dwell on how, if I were frank, the cause behind my sickness of being rested wholly within this unresolved malaise and pangs of sadness that riddled contact with him.

Still and all, rumors circulated about Raff's employment as upholder of the law in Melancholy. Well-advised folks ignored gossip of how Cannon met his death and what, precisely, led to his being interred in a grave left unmarked. In shooting Jedidiah Cannon, Raff relieved humanity of a man whose depraved proclivities included molesting and killing children. These factors outweighed criticisms skeptics raised with citizens of astute mind around what facilitated the madman's death; the skeptics of the ilk to pack a picnic lunch and bring extended family to watch Cannon hanged from the sturdy branches of an infamous cottonwood tree or sturdy gallows.

"Good afternoon, Marshal Cooper."

"Afternoon, Miss Reed." Raven left my side and rubbed her head against Raff's thigh in welcome. He caressed her ears. "Lizzie." Raff's tone when he spoke to my friend rang notches warmer than when he greeted me. "Interestin' horse race. Not the result some expected."

Lizzie stepped away to allow Raff and me latitude, expending actorly attentiveness on a display of quilts sewn with delicacy and precision. Her interest and proficiency in needlework were elementary, at best, and I knew her consideration for show; her ears were pricked, flapping like bedsheets in a stiff breeze to avoid missing anything of import.

"Zeus is fast, Marshal. I trained Samson to where he is near jumping out of his skin, but natural-born ability will carry him only so far. To give Joshua his due, Zeus had a decided advantage where it mattered today."

"If you say so."

"I am obliged to apologize if you backed Samson and lost money."

"Don't have to apologize." Rafael Cooper reviewed me, black eyes flat, inscrutable. "Won a nice purse on Hughes's horse."

"You did?"

"Yep." Raff leaned in to me, words fluttering past my cheek when he said: "'Cause remember, Miss Reed. I know your mind." He straightened, lip hitched, a giveaway he suspected the horse race was not all it appeared.

Raff made his leave and strolled to the shooting range.

I watched him go. It was not difficult to follow him for he stood a head taller than the majority of gentlemen in the vicinity, jet-dark hair beneath his hat glossy, thick, and tied with a beaded leather thong to form a tail that swung past his shoulder blades.

"Wish you'd both get over this silly tiff or whatever you wanna call it," Lizzie posited, starched as a schoolmistress.

"I have no conception whatsoever of what you refer to, Lizzie."

"Don't give me that! Glory, the two of you need your heads banged together. It's gettin' more and more temptin' to do it myself. Might knock sense into your thick skulls. I'm at a loss to understand how you see some things clear as day but can't or plain refuse to admit others. Raff's shown his devotion over and over, yet here you are tryin' to prove somethin' that doesn't need provin'. You're pussyfootin' 'round, Ness. Forget this drawn-out, ridiculous *competition* and get on!"

"What a load of twaddle."

"No, it ain't. That man's got an extra sense about you. He can tell when you're around even if he can't see you. That's gotta count for somethin'. Apart from he goes still a moment, can't quite put my finger on it. Though, bet you can, and do."

"Lizzie!" I laughed, her innuendo a tonic. When a bee buzzed in her bloomers, distracting her felt akin to trying to divert a flooded stream to a different course with just a prospector's hammer and a shovel at my disposal. "You are incorrigible."

"Go do as you please, then. As usual." She sighed heavily, bearing the woe of the world, chasing this under her breath with: "Said it before, I'll say it again. You're stubborn as a damned mule."

"I thought on embracing your reformed, Bible-toting lifestyle, you were obliged to forgo cursing."

"It's a shame, and I'm sorry, Lord." Her pious gaze swung heavenward. "But, sometimes, nothin' else will do."

TWO

It is better to have less thunder in the mouth,
and more lightning in the hand.
—*Apache proverb*

Hiram Walsh—or, simply, Walsh, as I came to know him—blew through the doors of my saloon the following blustery afternoon. When deprived of a hat his waved hair, closely-shaved cheeks, and slender physique appareled in a wool suit the color of Scottish heather reeked of power and money—a pulsing, incandescent corona that encircled him spoke of big cities, big dreams, and big ambition.

Turbulence swirled behind cerulean-blue eyes and encouraged men he walked by to sit or stand a little taller, the amoral glint that flecked those eyes underpinning an argument it would take minor persuasion to tempt even a fine, upstanding woman to step willingly out of her britches.

I sipped whiskey from a heavy tumbler and observed him in the mirror behind the bar as he crossed the floor, convinced he was aware of enquiring glances that leaped about him. Raven, wedged between a cuspidor and my stool, raised her snout to test air that drifted in with him to skulk like morning mist in the foothills, then scrambled to her feet. Satisfied he posed no threat she did not growl, instead dropped into the sawdust strewn throughout the public area of the Fleur-de-lis and rested her head on her forepaws.

Seated next to me, Fatfoot Harry Janes, similarly indiscreet with his appraisal, twisted to stare at the man with total disregard for polite exchange. He grinned his loose, foolish grin when the newcomer halted within a yard of us, awarded simple-minded Fatfoot a tolerant smile, then fixed on Nathan, my barman.

"Good afternoon. I'm here to see Miss Hennessey Reed."

"That right?"

Without taking his eyes off the visitor Nate brought forth a rag kept under the bar lip and began wiping the shiny wooden bar top clean, even though I had watched him polish it not a minute before.

"I'd appreciate if you can tell me where to find her."

"Depends what business you're bringin'."

"That, sir, is private to the lady."

"Uh-huh."

Nathan crossed his arms. Muscles tested the fealty of his work shirt stitching, his squashed-nosed face lending validation he mastered character that gave no quarter.

In his right hand the newcomer toted a calfskin satchel. Unconcerned with Nate's belligerence, he flexed his free hand and rocked on the heels of an expensive pair of tooled boots giving the impression he was blessed with all the time he desired to wait upon the barman.

Nathan prepared to extend his reply, with the purpose of adding to his less-than-welcoming address—no doubt to encourage the man to continue walking in a loop and straight back out the way he came in.

"Don't trouble yourself further, barkeep." The newcomer caught my eye in the mirror. "I believe she is found."

Doctor Jonas Tolliger, mass draped over his stool, reposed the other side of Fatfoot. Doc's best friend, Shakey, fiercely bearded and swamped by items of clothing chosen at random then thrown onto his person, to land every which where, decorated the next perch along. The visitor's voice struck a chord and as a single entity, without conference, they left off their subject of discussion—on any given day this could include the exorbitant price of a meal in Washington, D.C., or which of them commanded the strongest grip—and waited for the entertainment to commence.

"Hiram Walsh, Miss Reed. It's my pleasure to make your acquaintance." He bent at the waist, performing a regal, formal bow. "Is there someplace we may speak without an audience?"

"If we must." I appraised him, submitting him to analysis fit to discourage a lesser man then got off my stool, blue satin dress rustling, collected my drink plus an extra glass, and gestured Nate to pass the whiskey bottle lodged on the shelf behind him. Raven rose too, and pressed against my thigh. "Come with me, Mr. Walsh."

My wolfhound's size and appearance routinely intimidated even those in control of shatterproof nerves—the reaction of folks in possession of a delicate constitution provided merriment that never lost appeal—so I was disarmed when the man who trailed the dog and me along the hallway to my office seemed genuinely at ease in her presence, displaying no signs of nervousness.

Raven repaid the courtesy, relaxation in his company speedily attained, this most unusual. In the office I sat at my oak desk where, once her ritual of awkward turns were concluded, Raven collapsed with a grunt beside my chair.

Hiram Walsh hesitated in the doorway, evaluating the room, observing a deficiency of appurtenances to miss. On spying the colorful painting hanging to the left of the door he froze, then, mesmerized, moved toward it, which inferred he was a fellow enthusiast.

"This is much like the work of an artist who belongs to a group active in Europe. Yes, it is a well-executed example of their genre. I'll go further, chance my hat, and say it was created by the brush of Monsieur Monet." He was clearly thinking aloud, with no expectation of this supposition being confirmed by me as he inched closer to the painting, reeled in by its beauty. Then, with inflection to attest his own cleverness, he said: "And there is his signature."

"You are an admirer of Claude Monet?" Hiram Walsh could not have surprised me more upon declaring he exchanged regular correspondence with Queen Victoria.

He did not answer. After minutes spent in contemplation, during which I concentrated on the onerous task of reducing the level of Irish whiskey in my glass then poured another, he breathed: "Now *this* is illustration of pure genius."

"I must agree."

He started, for I suspected he had forgotten I was there, enthralled by the innovative handling of the piece he analyzed, those astonishing eyes unblinking.

"Art captivates me and, by extension, so do those who paint, Miss Reed. I take pleasure keeping abreast of emerging talent." He released study of the painting with perceptible reluctance. "Keeping apprised of rising stars from my corner of this vast land can pose a challenge, but it is a challenge I am prepared to meet and accept."

His consideration strayed to an artwork on the wall behind me.

"There is passable aptitude evident in that piece, Miss Reed. I am unable to make the artist from here. Who is it by?"

"She did not feel it worthy of a signature while hanging in the same room as an 'illustration of pure genius'," I replied.

"Ah. It is your work? If so, please forgive me."

Although professing contrition Hiram Walsh did not seem the

least chastened, and I wondered if he had prior knowledge of my pastime, already informed I had painted the mountain scene. I brushed off his apology and poured him a shot of whiskey.

He angled the chair on the far side of the desk to suit, hitched his pants at the knee and sat, his movements fluid, elegant.

I lifted the lid of the decorated wooden box that housed my cigarettes, offered them to him—he declined—selected one, and waited on him to state his reason for being here.

He did not hasten to enlighten me, left his drink untouched, and this saw me ask: "May I send for an alternative libation to quench your thirst?"

"Thank you, no."

"I consider it goes against the grain, so to speak, to trust someone who does not imbibe." I poured a generous slug of whiskey into my glass to underscore this. "Do you take offense at being served alcohol, Mr. Walsh?"

"Not at all. I do not partake of hard liquor while conducting business, Miss Reed. Belated insight shows it can lead to ... anomalies."

"Anomalies?"

He chose not to clarify his choice of word, switching to a different branch of conversation instead—why he had traveled to Melancholy.

"I practice law, Miss Reed, and am here on behalf of a gentleman client. Mr. Jakob Diederich."

"Yes? I am unfamiliar with that name."

"He is also known as Jakob Kingsley."

"Oh, I see."

"I hoped to meet with him."

"You will find that somewhat difficult. Impossible, actually."

"Ah." Hiram Walsh pursed his lips, a heavy pause advocating he listened to inner counsel. "He is dead?"

"Why do you automatically presume Jakob dead?"

"My offices in Tynbridge Hills, Nevada, hold the last will and testament of Jakob Diederich. Before he relocated here, Mr. Diederich and I decided on a simple line of communication. Aware how his decision to live in the wilderness might impact in the negative aspect to the length of his existence on God's Earth, we settled on his wiring a message each quarter to assure me he was alive. A plan not without flaws, we thought this the easiest system to employ given Melancholy's remoteness.

"In the event of Mr. Diederich's extended silence and that, subsequently, of his friend Hans Voight, at the behest of my client I was to contact Miss Hennessey Reed, proprietress of the Fleur-de-lis Saloon."

"It would have been commonsensical to give notice of your intention to visit or circumvent the journey altogether, and send a telegram or letter stating your business."

"I first wired you some weeks ago. I received no reply to that message, or a second one, so felt it remiss if I didn't come to Melancholy as soon as my schedule allowed."

This prompted vague recollection of Nate handing me a telegram around when Hiram Walsh specified. Dispatches of that nature were few and far between; however, busy at the time I had placed it aside, meaning to return to it later. Suffice to say, it had slipped my mind and I was unaware of the location of the original correspondence and held no memory of a follow-up telegram.

"Besides," he said, "I prefer to conduct important transactions face to face."

Had I imagined the double entendre? A concurrent, roguish

twitch of his cheek convinced me it was fully intended and the statuesque lawyer indulged what I gathered by his suit and comportment an interdependent, noteworthy trait: use of wordplay for amusement, at the expense of the person with whom he bartered dialogue.

"I regret to inform you in this case your presumption is correct," I said, neutrally, to keep our meeting on an official footing, for I did not wish to veer from the core reason for his visit or engage in his silliness. "Jakob and his companion, Hans, were killed in April. They died during a raid by rogue Indians who decided to relieve them of livestock, and their lives. The invaders then set fire to Jakob's house."

"I am sorry to learn of their deaths, for my suspicions to be confirmed." The lawyer tapped a hand on the chair arm, a seal ring inset with bloodstone worn on his little finger drumming a staccato beat. "I had the privilege to meet with Mr. Diederich on several occasions, so appreciate your diplomacy regarding Mr. Voight. I should say, I am aware of their living arrangements."

Jakob and Hans had shared more than friendship, they had shared a bed. When they moved to the county rumors and speculation abounded, a contagion carried by gossipmongers. Mammoth bank deposits afforded privacy, a golden buffer against cruel taunts or aspersions of the socially damaging kind so, rarely seen in Melancholy, in effect they were absorbed into the fabric of the landscape and the gossipmongers found alternate pariahs on whom to fixate.

"My instructions are explicit, Miss Reed. If Mr. Diederich were to predecease Mr. Voight, the latter inherited my client's estate. Since both are dead and there are no surviving relatives, everything is transferred to Mr. Diederich's cherished friend."

"Why are you telling me this, Mr. Walsh?"

"The estate is of considerable value and passes in entirety to an individual." He leaned back in his chair. "You, Miss Reed, are recorded as Mr. Diederich's 'cherished friend', which means, if I may be permitted an impertinence, *you* are the extraordinarily blessed individual."

"Oh." My response was inadequate, but it proved all I could muster. I gulped a mouthful of whiskey and lit a cigarette while Hiram Walsh lounged, waiting on me to continue. "Well, I am flabbergasted by this news, I must confess. I considered we three had a rapport, although not necessarily to the extent Jakob remember me in his will. I never dreamed . . ."

"I understand."

"I am not entirely sure you do, Mr. Walsh." I drew on the cigarette, trapped smoke in my lungs long as I could without coughing, then blew a neat cone of smoke rings toward the ceiling. "When you say Jakob's estate is considerable, what, exactly, is involved?"

"Here." The lawyer bent to retrieve his satchel from the floor and placed it on the desk. As he unbuckled the straps that secured it, he said: "It's easier I show you."

He withdrew a thick ledger with Jakob's full name embossed on the leather cover, rested it on the satchel, then leafed through a number of pages. "Much of this is legalese, or records of transactions, but these figures comprise a breakdown of assets giving an overall, accurate summary of your inheritance."

He flipped the ledger around, moved it to the desk blotter and pushed it toward me with a slim forefinger, which brought the last page into focus.

"Goodness." Buying time—evidence on the page in front of me intimated there might well be unlimited reserves with which to purchase it—I stubbed out my half-smoked cigarette, selected a fresh one, and took an extended moment to light it, grappling to comprehend the extent of properties and funds here and abroad set in regimented columns on thin, expensive parchment, and the enormity of the final total. A swig of whiskey did nothing to regulate my thumping heart, its pounding emblematic of my shock. I downed another. "There were indications Jakob possessed sizeable wealth. Still, I never entertained thoughts of affluence close to this."

"Even if financially independent before today you are now a rich woman, Miss Reed. A stupendously rich woman. The offices of Parley, Dunn and Walsh would be delighted to continue administering Mr. Diederich's estate when in your control, though once you peruse this—" he gestured to the ledger "—you may want to appoint a suitably qualified person nearer Melancholy. If you do choose to assign management to a local man I can recommend one and am at your disposal to make the transfer as straightforward as I can."

"Thank you. I am sure you can appreciate this will take a while to assimilate."

"That's fine." He left the ledger in the center of the desk, buckled the satchel then set it on his lap, hands clasping the handle. "I suggest it worthwhile to ask a trustworthy professional conversant in the letter of the law to go over these papers and provide their opinion. Now we have met, after our next consultation I shall catch a return stage home and attend the paperwork."

If lacking a horse or horse-drawn vehicle, entry to Melancholy could be attained on foot or by Concord, the latter a filthy, hair-raising method of transportation. On arrival in Melancholy I had witnessed passengers literally fall out of the stagecoach in their eagerness to be rid of the bone-rattling contraption and fellow detainees, ecstatic to reintroduce their travel-soiled selves to solid ground.

"You came here by stage? The southern Concord passes through Melancholy on Friday."

"Guess I'm here till Friday, then."

"As you will have perceived Melancholy does not offer boundless attractions like those to which you are undoubtedly accustomed in Tynbridge Hills. You may struggle to find diversions while awaiting passage."

"I'm sure I'll find plenty of *diversions* to entertain me." A charming smile highlighted the salacious bent I deduced in his personality, so my rejoinder was gracious, yet non-committal.

We vacated my office and reconvened to the bar where he said he had a yen to pay his respects to Jakob and Hans, with the caveat I escort him. It came to mind this was to confirm what I told him as true; he required proof other than my word, for legal purposes, that they were dead. Or did he honestly mean to say goodbye to those he had known and respected, a friend wanting to see where they rested? Perhaps, I conceded, it was a combination of the two.

The day I galloped from the ruins of Jakob's house where, along with their neighbors I discovered Jakob's and Hans's bodies, I vowed never to set afoot the property again. The slaying of Jakob and Hans compounded with the deaths of my family when a youngster, and those since of people I loved, became a catalyst that hurled me into a state of crazed grief. Faith I held in human nature, scant during the ordinary run of things, had skittered close to crossing the dead line, past salvation.

All these months later I still had no yearning whatsoever to return to Jakob's and, if left alone, could not summon any pretext for doing so. A portion of common sense convinced me it best to forget that terrible episode—if out of sight, it was also out of mind—equipoise threatening to splinter, fragments scattering like seed pods dispersed by a zephyr if anyone touched on their deaths.

However, after Hiram Walsh's torturous, wearying trek to Melancholy, I felt honor-bound to squire him to the farmstead; it was the least I could do. Regardless of my ruling who was to administer Jakob's estate when it transferred to me, the lawyer and I would need to communicate amicably until such time it was formalized to the satisfaction of each party.

I directed Nathan go across to the livery barn when the Fleur's business hit a lull, order Hiram Walsh a horse for the morning, and ask that Samson also be saddled.

"When you wantin' 'em?" Nate asked.

"Around nine suits me," the lawyer said, applying his charming smile to Nate when the barman glowered at him.

"And around eleven o'clock is acceptable to me."

"Then we shall meet at eleven." Hiram Walsh set his hat upon auburn waves. "Until tomorrow, Miss Reed."

Fatfoot, Doc Tolliger and Shakey, backsides still attached to their stools, observed this exchange unabashedly, as if they had purchased concession tickets to watch a vaudeville production and fostered no inclination to waste a moment of a lauded performance.

Multiple pairs of eyes tracked Hiram Walsh until the batwings snapped closed on the hem of his tailor-made suit.

"Peacock," Nate muttered.

"Won't be gettin' no argument outta me," Shakey said. "Sure is a nice-smellin' peacock, though."

Jonas Tolliger maneuvered his chunky form to address his friend, this a demanding feat, throaty chuckle flittering through his jowls. "Have you taken an unnatural fancy to Mr. Walsh, Shake?" he asked.

"Nah, jest sayin'."

"It wouldn't do you harm to adopt his bathing habits."

"Hey! What do ya mean?"

Doc Tolliger ignored him and Shakey returned to his ale, indignation already consigned to history.

"Do you feel all right, Hennessey? If you don't mind me saying, you are rather pale."

"I am perfectly well, Jonas. Leastways, I shall be, given breathing space." Until Hiram Walsh's arrival on my doorstep, I considered my financial position upward of ample for my needs and the needs of those for whom I cared most. Never a spendthrift, excepting when patronizing outfitters to the feminine figure—milliners, specifically—unbeknownst to all but Nathan the currency and silver and gold that lined my coffers pronounced me richer than virtually everyone in Idaho Territory, including Joshua Hughes: not that I wished this to ever become public knowledge. "Mr. Walsh brought unforeseen news."

"May I ask, was it good news, or bad news?"

"That remains to be seen."

"Like that lunatic gallivantin' about town with a pet snake wrapped around 'im like a slippery kinda diamond necklace," Shakey said.

"For pity's sake, what are you rambling about, Shakey?" This change to a totally unrelated topic put me on the back foot, for in my mind's eye all I saw in black and white was the inconceivable sum that constituted my recent windfall, and it cast a shadow over everything.

"You ain't seen 'im, Ness?" Shakey asked.

"I met him earlier." Jonas signaled Nate his glass needed replenishment. "He was coming out of the General Store when I headed in. Had to look twice since I couldn't believe what I was seeing. What kind of madman willingly drapes a snake around his neck? He has to be tempting fate."

"He's prob'ly a friend of that lady with the crystal ball. Madam Bovary," Shakey said.

"Madam Beaulieux," Jonas Tolliger corrected, rising to the bait and then some.

"Madam *Beaulieux*, then." Although much of Shakey's face was shrouded, his extravagant, tangled beard a thicket of hair, it was obvious to those familiar with his character—and by the set of his shoulders—he smirked into his chest. He knew, precisely, the distinction between Madam Bovary and Madam Beaulieux.

An avid bookworm, as well-read as any Boston matron who coveted then greedily devoured the latest controversial novel on the sly, when notified a new edition had arrived for him Shakey visited the General Store to collect it then went home, with no deviations, parcel wedged in the armpit of his missing arm. No one, not even Doc Tolliger, saw him or heard a whistle out of him while he consumed it.

"Get a bearded lady like that oddity at the fair yest'day—" Shakey continued "—and one of 'em dwarf fellas, toss in a two-headed calf and they can start their own freak show."

"You realize the bearded lady was Bo Handley dressed up like his mama, don't you, Shake?" Jonas asked. "Organizers roped him in after the real bearded lady fell ill. They didn't want children, big and small, disappointed. I bumped into Bo behind the tent they assigned him where he was scratching like a flea-ridden hound. He wasn't given enough notice to grow a full set of whiskers, so Ray Wilde helped stick hair they'd chopped off Bo's mare's tail, to his chin. Told me it itched like the devil. Drove him to distraction."

"That's as may be, I'd pay good money to see a bunch of 'em freaks in one place."

"You'd pay good money to watch Mrs. Dickson dig her vegetable garden if starved for something to do," Jonas said.

"Got me there," Shakey admitted.

"Anyhow, Madam Beaulieux is no freak," Jonas said. "Struck by lightning when a child, she has scars running from her hands right on up to her chin. She is self-conscious and humiliated by her injury and that's why you'll never see her without gloves and a scarf or shawl. Fortuitously they are also part of her vocational costume. Apropos to that, she told me that weeks after the lightning strike she found she'd gained physic abilities." Jonas's cynicism was palpable.

"She has lived in Melancholy a matter of months, yet you are well-acquainted with considerable details about her, Jonas."

"We got to talking, Hennessey. When I mentioned my years as a physician she confided in me, guessing, I suppose, I'd comprehend her difficulties more than the average citizen. She's a pleasant woman."

"What about her eyes, Doc?" Shakey asked. "What's wrong with 'em? They remind me of a dead person."

"Probably by virtue of her being hit by lightning they are affected by cataracts, which is not uncommon. The cataracts appeared soon after the incident."

"She's a pretty lady. Shame about those eyes."

"We all have our crosses to bear." Jonas stared pointedly at Shakey who was blithely impervious to his friend's inspection. "Her family has had their fair share of adversity."

"How about the fella givin' out her handbills? He waddles like a duck. When I come across him had to look about me, wonderin' what's clankin'."

"That is her husband, Ezekiel."

"Husband?" Crestfallen, Shakey swirled his ale, mouth downturned.

"Yes, husband. You missed your chance, Shake. Ezekiel suffered a childhood disease of some description so wears metal calipers to support an ankle and knee."

In actuality, it came as no surprise Jonas knew the history of the newest residents in Melancholy—it was supremely difficult for him to extract his nose from everyone's business. If his subject demonstrated unwillingness to indulge his often less than subtle exploration into their affairs, he accepted their reluctance and, periodically, pointed redirection with dignity and self-deprecating humor.

"Bad luck sure dogs some people close as night follows day, don't it?"

"Are you wandering your philosophical path again, Shake?"

"Jest tryin' it on for size. See if it sticks."

"You have expectations it will?"

"Here's hopin', Doc." Shakey stroked the motley animal pelt strapped where his arm used to be attached, something he did without aforethought nowadays then, with finesse at odds with his appearance of a homeless scapegrace, drained his ale and asked for more.

⟫⟪

That evening I sat on the balcony outside my bedroom engrossed in a raft of memories, whiskey bottle and tobacco within easy reach. Raven was stretched flat by the railing where, having fallen into a light doze, she twitched and grumbled low in her chest.

Hours passed in a haze as I reminisced, grief memories brought unsolicited, the level in the bottle steadily decreasing until around an inch dressed its base. Thoughts of Jakob, Hans, and the friendship they extended the instant we met arrived, refusing, like an uninvited guest, to pay heed to broad hints their welcome had worn thin and they should depart. A collage of images, a visual calliope, spun and glowed brighter with each shot of whiskey or laudanum ration.

I missed my friends sorely, with grating sadness that nibbled my bones like minnows, it troublesome to reconcile the indisputable fact the fortune recently dropped into my lap was due to the deaths of people I cared for intensely.

The moon dipped behind mountains west of the saloon. The door to the kitchen below squawked, and I listened as Cookie selected logs off the pile stacked under the eaves, preparing for the day ahead, returning, arms laden, to his stove.

By now, vision blurred, I saw double or triple of everything, my movements deliberate, labored. Any notion I might receive company was ridiculous, so when Lizzie appeared at the top of the steps leading from the yard she scared the daylights out of me.

"Sorry, Ness. Didn't mean to startle you." She had spent no care selecting her clothing, trusting she would not meet anyone at this hour between her living quarters behind the store and the Fleur. She clasped a woolen shawl tight at her neck and sunk onto a chair. "I can't sleep. Thought you'd be awake."

My lack of sleep combined with uncounted glasses of whiskey provoked annoyance at being disturbed, even by her. Lizzie realized this, unequivocally, but paid me no mind, my irritation of no consequence.

To interact with her I had to concentrate on enunciation, tongue swollen, the effort grueling. I tried not to slur when telling her of Jakob's legacy, mindful that despite the words I uttered ringing clear as a mountain stream to my ears, my sentences were jumbled, all higgledy-piggledy. Used to enduring similar conversations over the years, Lizzie was resigned to inserting her own words, paraphrasing asinine gibberish I often spouted.

"Gracious," she said after a protracted silence where she tussled with the financial connotations of my inheritance. "Ain't that somethin'?"

"I am going with Hiram Walsh to Jakob's property in the morning." Lizzie did not make the observation morning was already upon us. "He wants to see the farmstead and pay his respects at Jakob's and Hans's gravesites. So he told me. I would rather not."

"That's hardly surprisin'. Say you ain't goin'. Tell him how to get there and let him go by himself."

"He came all the way to Melancholy purely to inform me of Jakob's will, so refusing to guide him would be churlish. All he asks is a harmless favor."

"Well, it's your decision." Lizzie opened her mouth, closed it again, glanced at me then fixed on an object past her boots. "You know, when I think on it, maybe this legacy is timely."

"How did you arrive at that diagnosis?"

"You seek refuge in this." Her wave encompassed my glass, cigarettes, and the blue bottle she knew was secreted in my skirts. "Makes hard things go away. But hard things have a nose like a bloodhound for findin' a person's weak spots, even if that person thinks they're well hidden."

I found myself nodding agreement. Monumentally reckless, I accepted unspoken dares and took physical gambles that left those dear to me no alternative than to shake their heads or, if inclined, like Lizzie, drop to their knees to pray for a solution. Little separated bravery and stupidity. If consulted to determine my leaning, those

I considered friends—the number of whom, already in single digits, were decreasing at an alarming rate—would, straightaway and unanimously, agree upon the latter.

"What's stoppin' you grabbin' this chance, Ness? Why not rebuild Jakob's house? You've got plenty of money now to do whatever you wanna do."

"I had that luxury already, Lizzie. It is too early to make decisions of importance. Besides, if I were to move to Jakob's, what should I do with the Fleur?"

"Things are changin' 'round here, Ness. Melancholy's growin' at such a rate the school's gettin' another teacher! It's gonna be a different place to what it is now. Maybe Jakob's legacy is a sign."

Lizzie's verdict on Melancholy rang true. Our town sat poised, rocking on a razor's edge where it could tip forward and slide down the face of respectability, or tip backward, back to the depravity from whence it originated.

Through various channels I had learned my main rival in trade sought to relocate, searching for premises farther west of where Lizzie and I were seated. It must be said, no matter how much I anticipated the departure of Faith Conway and her raggedy band of girls, her quitting Melancholy spelled reckoning day near for the Fleur-de-lis.

"You'll have so much money you can go anywhere and do anythin' you want. You needn't stay in Melancholy, Ness."

"Of course I need to stay here!" This came out harsher than I intended but Lizzie took it in her stride, accepting my mumbled apology. She knew I wished to be close to Evangeline, to watch her grow, and this could not be done if I was a global nomad with a grandiose lifestyle that once appealed, but no longer held me in thrall.

"Then keep the saloon 'cause people always wanna drink, and make upstairs into a boardin' house or hotel. If you don't wanna run the Fleur I'll do it, or let Nate and Annie take charge."

"As a proselyte of Jesus, what you propose with managing the Fleur-de-lis goes against your—how shall I express this delicately—new-found religious fervor, Lizzie."

"If the girls move on or change employment there's no issue, though the store does keep me busy. Could you gift the Fleur to Nate and Annie as a weddin' present?"

My bartender and Annie Coal, who had worked for me more years than I cared to remember, were to marry in two days.

"It would help to expand, too. Why not buy that burned-out place next door? It'll take a potful of money to make it habitable, but you've loads of that. It'll increase your takin's."

"I purchased that property months ago."

"Well then, why not do it?"

"We can discuss this another time."

It was too late in the evening—or too early in the morning—to compare advantages and disadvantages of her proposals. I aspired to pacify her; launching a hotel an idea of merit which, as I told her, was already set in motion. No matter, what little desire I had to engage with a visitor was exhausted, the endurance of my addled brain, weak.

A fleck of movement by the entrance to the alleyway that ran behind the saloon got our attention. Early for anyone other than those with felonious intent to be abroad, I relaxed on recognizing Viola Sargeson, a woman of advanced age whose memory played tricks on her. Sometimes I saw her roaming the streets in the dead of night as if it were the middle of the day and she believed herself amidst residents going about their business.

Attired in a nightgown, feet bare, wearing no cape or coat to keep chilly air at bay, and with tousled hair standing on end, this morning she appeared to dance with a solicitous beau in an assembly ballroom that resided solely in her head. She flirted with her imaginary partner, tittering in girlish fashion, dreaming, I suspected, herself young, fancy-free, and beautiful once more.

Viola had fled the closely guarded confines of the house she shared with Eli, her unmarried son and custodian, who was plain of feature and nondescript in character. Eli's redeeming quality, generally acknowledged, was the devotion he showed toward his mother.

Anticipating his monthly visit to the Fleur, if unable to find a neighbor to superintend Mrs. Sargeson while he 'went to the store for supplies', and reluctant to leave her at home without supervision, Eli brought her with him. Before carousing upstairs he deposited her in the kitchen. There, she chatted to herself, upheld both ends of conversations none made head or tail of, offered tips on how to procure the most tender stew and drank cup after cup of hot, strong coffee. She remained impervious to, and unflustered by Cookie's silence and the confusion of those who wandered into the kitchen where they were hailed midway through obscure rants as though long-lost friends.

Lizzie made to rise, to rush to the elderly woman's aid. My hand on her forearm stayed her when Eli darted along the shadow-cloaked boardwalk. He placed an arm around his mother and tenderly assisted her to their safe, warm abode.

"I'll be goin', too."

I raised no objection, which did not go unnoticed.

"Go to bed, Ness. You've gotta sleep. Even a coupla hours. You can't go on like this, drinkin' and . . . whatever."

"As always, I appreciate your concern, Lizzie," I said, words supine, thick on my tongue. My eyelids drooped. "Please tell me why you really came here. Do you have a problem you would like to discuss?"

"Told you. Couldn't sleep."

"Are you sure?"

"It'll wait. Should've known . . . Never mind."

I turned from her, overpowered by a fit of pique, for the pity mixed with love I read in her eyes embarrassed and shamed me. Thrown on the mercy of her kindness, I accepted myself sorely lacking. She was a much better friend to me than I to her, and that would be the case in perpetuity.

THREE

Listen, or your tongue will make you deaf.
—*Native American proverb*

I awoke, disoriented, what felt a minute after I staggered to bed once Lizzie went home, to pounding on my bedroom door. To the tender contents of my skull, it sounded as if a tenacious buffalo butted the door with his massive, bony forehead. Raven stirred but did not move off her blanket.

"Go away!" I rolled onto my stomach, felt blindly for the pillow laying on the far side of the bed and dragged it over my head, knuckles pressing it against my ears.

The attack continued, unabated.

I cleared my throat and tried again, protest muffled. "Leave me be!"

The knocking gained volume.

I groaned for dramatic effect, reappropriated my legs from tangled bedsheets and quilt, shambled across the floor and yanked the door handle with unwarranted force to reveal Nate filling the doorway. He handed me a steaming mug of coffee and made a performance of inspecting my person, tousled hair to clenched toes.

He refrained from passing comment on my attire, which was not a nightgown, as one might suppose. I still wore lawn undergarments, having gotten partway through undressing before deciding the task too fiddly to complete and the situation could be remedied upon waking.

"

I accepted the mug, grumbled thanks, and trundled back to bed, plumped the pillows, and propped myself against the bedhead.

"Better get goin' if you're meetin' the peacock."

"I shall." I sipped the coffee and grimaced, the quantity of liquor Nate had poured into the tin mug with a liberal hand shocking even my seasoned constitution. "Momentarily."

"Be surprised if he's been straight about what he's doin' here, Ness. Heard he checked a real nice revolver with the marshal's office." He cut to information he deemed most important. "Pearl grip. Interestin' a lawyer's carryin' such pretty tool-ware."

"Distinguished sidearms are not exclusive to the card-sharp or gunslinger, Nate. Mr. Walsh is a man who appreciates and, I expect, elects quality above all else."

Experience taught me it was easier on my nerves, and sanity, to allow Nate to speak and get whatever bothered him off his chest, for he was never reticent to formulate an opinion and let it air before cooling. Sometimes this strategy worked. Others, it entailed active participation on my part if I were at all disposed to expend the energy.

"Get your Winchester on the way out." He did not frame this as an option.

"I fully intend to collect it once we have the horses. Make sure Raven is ready, also."

"Yes, ma'am. Keep to mind, you can't rely on pearl handles." He worried suspicion of Hiram Walsh as a lion with a Christian. "Prissy shooter's prob'ly just for show."

"Instinct tells me Hiram Walsh is a man who does not promote his strengths without a slew of means, or aptitude, to support them." Reminded of suggestive comments with which the lawyer took the liberty to pester me during our meeting inspired me to add: "With regard to anything, and everything."

"Man does a lotta promotin', and a gun's helpful only if it's fired true. Shouldn't have to tell you that."

"Yet you do. Repeatedly." I faked umbrage at Nate's reference to my less-than-proficient skills where firearms were concerned, for regardless of what I said he was correct, and my handling of any weapon other than the Bowie strapped to my calf left great room for improvement. "Do you carry misgivings Hiram Walsh is not as he appears?"

"Yep. Don't trust 'im."

This sealed his parting advice, for when I braved another sip of coffee then looked up he was gone; Nate moved swiftly and soundlessly for a man of his stature. Frequently our conversations ended with his exiting the room without my noticing, interchange abridged with the realization he had walked off in despair or, more commonly, resignation, leaving me conversing with myself.

Dressed in wide-legged trousers, plaid shirt and boots, I tied a bandana at my neck. Hunting for a favorite belt not on its hook in my closet, I came upon it, a leather snake, curled through the legs of a chair by my bedroom fireplace. Choosing not to examine scenarios that might explain its abandonment, I threaded it through my belt loops, securing it a notch tighter than usual, gulped dregs of lukewarm coffee, and put the mug on the mantelpiece.

Pinned above my right eye, my headache moved in with a vengeance, assuming the cadence of a beating Indian drum. Agonizing stabs of pain triggered clouded vision that had me wishing it would not offend anyone's sensibilities, including my own, if I were to forgo the chamber pot and throw up where I stood.

Despite dillydallying I reached the livery barn ahead of Hiram Walsh and saw him emerge from Cullen's barbershop and bathhouse a distance along Main Street. Beneath the fashionable wool suit of the previous day he wore an embroidered waistcoat and a fresh linen shirt, its collar so white I averted my eyes in misdirected dread of being smote by snow blindness. Anointed by the wand of a jack-a-dandy he cut a fine figure and, if unschooled in his profession, had I seen him strolling along the street *lawyer* would not have been the main contender to spring to mind.

"Good morning, Miss Reed," he said, walking up to me.

"Good morning, Mr. Walsh."

Samson was tied to the hitching rail outside the livery, eyelids flicking as he dozed, chestnut coat burning gold under late-morning sunlight. Hearing my voice, he swung his head toward us and whickered a greeting. A white mule secured along the rail stretched its neck, friendly, to nuzzle my stallion, lipping the big horse's shiny chest.

Bron Prentiss, the livery owner, came out of the barn toting a pitchfork, lone eye squinched against a fulgent sun, rugged features corrugated, rocky terrain. He jabbed the pitchfork into the ground and rested a sparsely-whiskered chin on his hands, atop the handle, elbows stuck out, a loon prepared to take flight.

"Tell me why the mule is saddled, Bron."

"Nate wanted a sturdy mount for a fat, pintsized, greenhorn."

My companion gave vent to volcanic bursts of laughter.

"Well, it may have come to your attention Mr. Walsh is neither fat nor pintsized. As for equine-related skills, I am in no position to comment. Even so, it is plain as can be this beast is not at all suitable. Get Mouse to throw a saddle over an animal that will not find Mr.

Walsh with his knees around his ears so his boots do not drag on the ground."

"Be a minute," Bron said. He propped the pitchfork against the barn siding, unhitched the mule and led it back to its stall.

"Your barkeep doesn't believe in understatement." Hiram Walsh, not the least offended, made no effort to screen continued amusement.

"Nate and I share extended association, and down the years his protective tendencies with regard to me have grown exponentially."

On more occasions than I could mention Nate kept me moving forward, redirecting me to the pathway of morality and virtue if an impulse of unsavory origin took ahold, or troublous temptation wafted under my nose offering enticements to stray.

Aversion to accepting help or advice even when the situation leveraged heavily toward demanding it, was embedded in my nature. As my self-elected caretaker—a daunting, thankless post I would stand first in line to admit—Nathan proved his worth whenever I found myself in a bind and was an invaluable ally, which was just as well, for no queue of applicants clamored to take his place.

"You must appreciate his loyalty," the lawyer said. "In saying that, perhaps you could tell him subtlety is a virtue."

"Nate is a man who gives free rein to a caustic disposition, exacerbated at present because he is suffering toothache."

"There is nowhere in Melancholy for him to seek medical treatment? The barber's for instance?"

"Cullen cannot abide the sight of blood." I rubbed the star-swirl of hair between Samson's eyes when the horse nosed my belly. "A retired doctor lives here, although by dint of being retired he does not practice. There is also an undertaker. They are available in emergencies. Other than them, the sole active practitioner on live bodies is Huwson Prendergast. He is the local authority on animal husbandry, but I suspect Huw's qualifications are authentic as a five-legged jackrabbit."

"A mystical creation?"

"Precisely. Besides, Nate refuses to entertain thoughts of getting rid of the offending molar."

Funning with him, I had proffered to tie a string around the tooth, attach the string's other end to a door handle then slam the door, laughter bubbling when Nate acquired a sheen to infer a painter had taken to him with a white-wash brush.

Hiram Walsh soon forked a horse comparable to Samson in height, if not spirit. When he swung onto the paint mare that replaced the mule I glimpsed the revolver with the mother-of-pearl grip, of which Nate spoke. I relied upon him knowing how to use it; braggadocio, whether vocal or visual, was a sure-fire way for a person to find themselves up to their chin in scorpions if they broadcast capability they could not support with affirmative action.

He sat easily in the saddle, a competent horseman, and before long we gained a steady pace beneath which miles dissolved.

⋙⋘

An hour into our journey I brought Samson back to a walk. There was, categorically, no way in Hades I could fend off the inevitable, and I had no intention of providing more of a spectacle of myself than necessary in the presence of a man uninformed of my habits.

"You must excuse me, Mr. Walsh," I said when his mare slowed with Samson.

I neck-reined the stallion off the hard dirt road, into the trees, leaving Hiram Walsh to conclude I was overcome by an unavoidable need to relieve myself. My horse weaved through serried firs thick as my waist, sure-footed, calm. When a suitable barricade of trees lay between my riding companion and myself I drew Samson to an untidy halt. I did not trouble to dismount, emptying my stomach of its meager contents onto pine needles and other litter shed by branches that rustled in a languorous breeze above.

Accustomed to diversions into the woods, Samson moved to stand square and waited until I regained composure. The taste of bile acrid on my tongue, I wiped my mouth with the underside of my bandana, inhaled several deep breaths, called Raven who nosed in a patch of underbrush then pushed my horse back to the road.

There, the lawyer talked with a clot of men atop wiry ponies, their mounts' lean flanks matted, prickly with dried sweat. At sight of Raven the quartet exchanged glances and after cursory greetings fleeced off smirking lips, continued toward Melancholy.

Hiram Walsh booted his mare and fell in beside Samson. "I trust you feel better, Miss Reed?"

"Considerably." I fixed on the road ahead, providing no encouragement to carry the conversation farther.

"Excellent."

I detected the pitch of sincerity in his reply, and that he guessed the true reason for my sojourn into the trees; as a gentleman he must refrain from comment and allow my tacit excuse to remain undisputed. A divergent conviction, that he was inordinately cheered to gain secret knowledge of me, radiated off his person. This impressed upon me the need to exercise caution, as a feeling pervaded that if advantageous to him he would have no qualms about utilizing this knowledge.

"I am well-disposed as the next man to trading salutations, but those boys examined me disproportionately to simple courtesy." He clicked his mare and we resumed a sluggardly jog. "Did you recognize them?"

"No, but that comes as no surprise. A few months gone, a chain of murders came to light in Melancholy. They culminated in the deaths of a brother and sister, conspirators in crimes such as you could not envisage. After the murders, residents of this county are more wary of strangers than they were, hence extended dialogue, probes that may border on uncivil asked of those whom we do not know."

In pursuit of the villains who carried out those murders, my reckless behavior put everyone I cared for in jeopardy, principally Evie. Ignorance and, if I dared confess, arrogance, promoted certitude I was exempt from danger and its foot soldiers. Jedidiah Cannon, with unflinching purpose, put paid to that misconception. Did I learn my lesson from that ill-advised adventure? Time would tell.

"I arrived in Melancholy less than a day ago, but I've heard about the deaths of those girls at the mine. Hell, for all concerned."

"The horrors endured can, at the very least, be described thus."

"I was told you played a starring role in a satisfactory resolution."

"Events of last spring must be neither brushed aside nor compared to something fatuous, something *trite* as a form of theatre, Mr. Walsh." Fired to offense by his offhand reflection, my anger burned hot as a blacksmith's furnace.

"You are right. Please, accept my apology. I meant no disrespect."

Intercourse effectively terminated we rode in silence until, bounden to initiate peacemaking, he asked: "Will peace here be restored?"

"This, I cannot say. Perhaps. The murders drew everyone in and around Melancholy together with joint purpose, uniting us to apprehend a mutual enemy." I shrugged. "Now, anyone observed where it is considered they have no cause to be, or those deemed out of place in our community, are treated with suspicion. Some of these folks are questioned with less sensitivity than others, as I said."

Hiram Walsh listened, attentive, over-compensating for his earlier flippancy. When I finished speaking he nodded, solemn, then urged his mare to a lope.

⟫⟪

As miles disappeared beneath Samson's hooves I felt progressively worse, a frenzy of butterflies in the pit of my stomach keen and able to derail me given the merest encouragement, this malady not wholly physical.

At the junction ahead, the river forged past the near fork, where the road split, then bowed to flow into a fertile valley that fanned out before us, a wide, golden blanket. Stands of hemlock and stunning bursts of red and yellow that foreran autumnal days towered, clumped amongst less glamorous pine and fir that encircled the valley. This display of Nature's diversity rose into the hills, contrasting with cultivated pastures in the foreground.

"This is Utopia, isn't it?" Hiram Walsh drew the mare in, spellbound by the majesty of the vista.

"Many consider it so."

A boy sat on the riverbank a couple hundred yards away. Raven caught his scent and stopped in her tracks, nose aquiver, then raced toward the child who petted her with unbridled enthusiasm, my guess at his identity confirmed. Searching for me, he waved, then without further ado retrieved his pole and resumed fishing, Raven at his side.

"Who is the child?"

"That is Thomas, although he is addressed—with exception of me, and probably his mother—by the sobriquet Fishbait."

"Should he be this far out by himself?"

"Not in my opinion, but no one has been successful in dissuading him from venturing into the wilderness on his own and believe me, they have tried. And yes, that includes me. I have broached the perils associated with wandering into the great unknown until hoarse."

I nudged Samson to the right-hand fork. Raven would follow when ready or rejoin us when we came through the junction on our return home.

In due course we started to gain altitude, the roadway, always rudimentary, suffering neglect through lack of use and maintenance after Jakob's death. The lawyer's exclamations on the beauty of the countryside punctuated swathes of silence until we rode through gates that indicated we had reached our destination.

I led him upward still, to the barn, untouched by fire and the single building left standing after the Indian raid. As we jogged past it I dismissed the picture seared into my brain of Callie, Jakob's maid, left wrecked in the lee of the rear wall.

Mother Nature had begun her reclamation work, the weight and importance of her remit assumed with great seriousness and dedication; creeping vegetation softened the carcass of the flame-ravaged ranch house, smothering it inch by steady inch. I wished a similar technique existed to erase images seen the morning I found my friends dead.

I visualized Hans's pain if he could see the condition of the gardens he slaved so hard to create and nurture, and Jakob's devastation at the loss of priceless artwork, Turkish carpets, and antiquities shipped across the Atlantic at outrageous expense.

I sent my stallion round back of the ruins, where Jakob and Hans were buried, and pulled him up, unintentionally harsh on his mouth. Mastered instantly by remorse, I dismounted and patted his neck. A garter snake disturbed by the horses decanted like quicksilver from a flat rock and slithered into the grass, not a swaying blade to mark its passage.

Hiram Walsh reined his horse after mine, slid off her and came to stand beside me. Shoulder to shoulder we contemplated the burial plot. Smaller rocks stacked on the graves when newly dug were displaced, boosted by inclement weather or animals in search of food, drawn by rotting flesh discerned by sensitive, finely-tuned noses.

Neither Jakob nor Hans lingered at the site, and for that I gave profound thanks, although a striking woman with curly blonde hair monitored each move my companion made. Her dress, of the fashion popular a decade ago, was expensive, cut with benefit of a superb eye. When she saw I watched her, a prolonged, aching smile marred by a faint scar that ran from her hairline to a corner of her mouth alighted upon her face, then she evanesced.

Oblivious to the specter's presence the lawyer picked up a rock and balanced it atop the mound covering Jakob, murmuring words I could not decrypt. I pretended I did not hear him, allowed him a private moment, and directed excess concentration on a hawk that coasted on light winds above the home paddock. The raptor tilted side-to-side, capitalizing on the updraft, and I wondered if it might be Jakob's goshawk, Julia, freed by the raiders after they mounted the sneak attack on the farmstead.

I withdrew my engraved cigarette case from a shirt pocket, selected a cigarette, spent time firing its tip then drew the smoke into my lungs, this preliminary inhalation cosseted as a newborn. I exhaled, strands of vapor translucent as fairy wings hanging, suspended, before drifting skyward to disperse into blue.

"How did you recognize me, Mr. Walsh?" My voice was piercing in the comparative silence of the countryside.

"Jakob's holdings are extensive." He joined me and dedicated attention to the panorama, his shoulders not quite so square as they were on arrival. "Long-lost relatives and charlatans in plenteous incarnations swarm when news of a will distributing assets of a rich man—or woman—comes into the public domain. As insurance against dealing with a case of misrepresentation, Jakob filed a daguerreotype of you, for reference."

"I believe you refer to one taken in Culver City."

"He never spoke of the location." He turned to me, mouth crooked with a wispy smile that did not erase memories delineated in his eyes. "You wore, if I recall correctly, a fantastic hat adorned with the plumage of what appeared a jungle-worth of exotic birds."

My work practices involved reading people. It was far, far easier to decipher others' motivation and passion, yet baffling to dissect one's own, which is precisely why I did not do so. We inhabitants of Earth are plebeians who think we are unique, but our emotions are universal—less special, or revolutionary than we comprehend. In the years preceding Caesar, during intervening centuries, across language differences, physical barriers and continents, each citizen regardless of creed, gender or color careened along their course, transitory creatures in a cast of billions.

This preoccupation Hiram Walsh had with Jakob and the sorrow heavy about him, no matter what he expended toward disguising it, did not seem purely of a professional nature. It also did not escape my notice he had referred to Jakob by his Christian name and this, to my mind, added fuel to his affiliation with my friend outspreading his capacity as Jakob's lawyer.

"You refer to Jakob by his given name. You knew him."

"I did. He was my client."

"No, I mean, you *knew* him."

"Remind me to recommend neither your barkeep nor you, Miss Reed, for lessons in delicacy," he said, with no sign my maladroit insinuation perturbed or offended him. A heartbeat later, he asked: "Whose is the third grave?"

"Callie's. Jakob's maid."

"Sweet girl? With colorless hair and eyelashes and buttermilk skin?"

"Why, yes." Astonished, I examined him and discerned added sorrow with this news. An inflammatory demon, nails clawing my collarbone urged me to poke, to prod, to make light of a connection that should be treated with respect. "Did you *know* her, too?"

His pitying glance at this proved admonition enough.

"It is my turn to apologize." Chastened, I attempted to absolve my cruel barb and perhaps evoke sympathy as a foil to my rudeness. "I am feeling unwell. Please, excuse my discourtesy." Deciding it best to move on, I looked back to the hawk. "Jakob owned a raptor. Well, as much as a human being owns a wild creature. He named her Julia. Realistically, she has flown away, yet I fancy that is her."

"Maybe it is. It must be a wrench to leave this haven, and I can see the draw to settling here." The lawyer crouched, scraped a patch of bare soil with the edge of his hand to loosen enough to form a plum-sized ball, then closed his fist, squeezing it, knuckles white. "This farm is now yours, naturally, as part of *Mr. Diederich's* estate. Do you know what you will do with it?"

"I am yet to make a decision on that score. Until you came to

Melancholy I never expected and, indeed, never foresaw ever setting foot on this land again."

"If you decide to sell, I'd appreciate if you contact me with the price ahead of other prospective buyers."

It struck me then, cutting, and real as a meteor exploding from the firmament to hit me square in the chest. I would not sell Jakob's farmstead. Lizzie was right, as often the case.

Jakob's farm represented an opportunity to refashion my way of living and begin anew. If I rebuilt the house or constructed a new one to my specifications on an adjacent hill, the building could be a suitable monument—if that were not too grand an ambition—to my friends. They would never be forgotten, whether or not a house replaced theirs, but the idea contained an element of symmetry.

Never dreaming myself a pivot to domestic bliss with a husband, and children frolicking at my skirts, I acknowledged that the older I grew—and the fact I had reached middle years was a phenomenon in itself—this formerly untenable lifestyle held inexplicable allure. Even as I marveled at this revelation, I accepted it as an attractive proposition only if a certain marshal consented to stand at my side.

FOUR

Marshal Rafael Cooper: *Melancholy, Idaho Territory.*

Raff counted two, four, six, eight bodies. No, there were ten, stripped of clothing, waxen mounds amongst grasses on a sun-stippled plat. He couldn't tell yet if they were male, female, adult, or child.

Raff's deputy, Daniel, brought his horse alongside Raff's gelding. The boy blew an angst-ridden sigh.

Raff dismounted, took a couple steps, and surveyed the strangely peaceful tableau. His horse shifted behind him, then settled.

"We'd been in Montgomery Butte." Tall, slender as a sapling, the man who spoke tried to sound matter-of-fact. His eyes jumped earth to sky, skimming over everything bar the dead. Raff thought in a different setting it might take a lot to rattle him. In this instance his jaw worked like a cross-saw. This, understandably, rattled him. "Sam, my son here, spotted the horse grazing, hitched to an empty wagon, no one about. There was blood on the tray, so we had a look around and that's when we came across them. Nothing can be seen from the road because the ground rises, off to the side there, then slopes down. Well, you can see yourself."

Daniel sneezed, louder than he anticipated which startled everybody, including him. He grimaced an apology, honked enthusiastically into a faded red square of material, then arranged his mismatched face in a study of concentration.

"You recognize any of 'em?" Raff asked the man.

"Can't say that I do."

"Where am I gonna find your tracks, Ibsen?"

"Came off the road there." Ibsen pointed. "Left my horse by that cottonwood and pretty much took a straight line to check if any of them were breathing. All were past saving and been like that hours, I reckon. Sent the boy to fetch you and here we are," he said, words tapering off.

"Yeah. Here we are. Again." Raff didn't elaborate. He didn't have to; the men got his meaning.

"Saw the girl behind the adults is . . . was . . . expecting." Ibsen's gaze shot to his son.

A mirror-image of his father in stance and mannerisms, Sam made a show their discovery hadn't knocked him sideways. He wasn't convincing anybody. Daniel, roughly of an age, pretended he'd seen it all before, reluctant to display weakness to a compeer. His ordinarily ruddy features were drained of color and betrayed he hung by his eyelids, scrabbling to appear unaffected.

"How about you, son. You know 'em?" Raff asked.

Sam shook his head. He had barely spoken since skulking into the marshal's office where he used scaled-back language to give a bare description of what he and his father had found. He deferred to his father now, letting him do all the talking. Raff predicted he'd have nightmares for years.

"Where do you live, Ibsen?"

"On a ways. East of Melancholy."

"Why don't you get your boy home."

"Gladly."

"Go with 'em, Daniel. Ready Amos for the dead but don't give particulars. Say there's been an accident and I'll tell him about it later. Get Skeeter to round up helpers to start diggin' ten holes.

Gotta get these folks buried. When you've done that, get blankets and bring 'em back with you."

"Yes, Marshal Cooper."

"Be easier burying them where they are," Ibsen said.

"Hmm." Raff wasn't obliged to explain himself. He did, anyway. "But I'm wantin' the undertaker to take a look at 'em."

Raff asked Ibsen and Samuel to keep quiet for a bit about what they'd found to give him and Daniel time to get the wagon loaded and to Amos Adams's premises. The undertaker sure had a challenge ahead of him. Despite asking father and son to keep their mouths shut word was sure to spread, sending Melancholy's occupants into panic.

Once Daniel and the Ibsens had gone, occasional rustling leaves or a twittering bird was all to disturb him, the place hushed, noises oddly muted. A whisper—of this world or the next, Raff wasn't sure—trifled with him, a pinch out of reach. He hadn't kept company with Hennessey of late, but maybe her second sight had rubbed off on him during their alliance because he couldn't shake the feeling he was being watched.

He went over and introduced himself to the docile roan gelding hitched to the buckboard. As Ibsen said, fingers and not gallons of blood had steeped into the tray, which meant the victims were dead when brought here. Who did the buckboard and roan belong to, the victims or the killers?

He tied the horse to a tree and walked, unhurried, down the knoll.

The dead comprised paired females and males, facing each other. All wore a single bullet wound to the chest, a kill-shot fired close in. Inspecting the bodies, if asked he'd say a .45 caliber like his Peacemaker was used on the women and children, with the oldest male the single victim to meet death from a rifle. Maybe a Bardon Sharps. It made a mess of him.

All but those at the head of the line were young, two years old to around seventeen or eighteen by his estimation. The private parts of each pair were pressed together, wrists fastened behind their partner—for want of a kinder word—the love act implied with a gruesome hug. Their ankles were also tied, the rope flimsy, knotted without skill and the knots weren't tight. They might have gotten loose if alive, so were bound afterward.

Around a yard lay between each couple. Were they a human arrow, pointed toward an object or place? No, he could make nothing out, nothing of note past the adults to support that thinking.

He kneeled beside the probable husband and father, whose face he'd caught before in passing, although a name didn't leap at him. Used to be Raff knew everybody who lived in or near Melancholy, if just by sight; the color of their horse, name of their wife, even those of their offspring. The county was growing, changing.

He retraced his steps to the children in the middle of the row, their ages equal to his daughter born to Hennessey had she survived. Raff pushed mournful intrusions aside. He must devote himself to the souls lying in the grass.

He brushed flies away from eyes, noses, and mouths. Drawn by blood and fluids, buzzing angrily when disturbed, they were another sign the dead had not long lain there. If thanks could be given for anything it was the Ibsens found the bodies before more destructive hunters partnered the flies at their feast.

Raff applied himself to footprints.

Other than the Ibsens' sets, Daniel's, and Raff's own, evidence told two people participated in this brutal crime. Two people to carry and arrange the bodies. Kindred spirits.

Until the murders at the Sweet Venus Too mine Raff wouldn't have considered a woman might be part of such horrors: he shouldn't take it as given the killers here were male. But did a woman have strength enough to help ferry a body into the wagon, or the mental grit to do what was done here? Further to that, the size of the prints indicated if a woman were involved, she had mighty big feet. A sorry state of affairs whichever way you came at it.

Raff circuited the area and found that the saddlehorses—one ridden, one led—and the buckboard had rolled in off a minor track on the plat's western side. The bodies were positioned out of sight of passersby, then one man drove the buckboard close to the road where it would be seen, his partner staying in a grove of pines on lookout duty. Both saddlehorses were being ridden judging by the hoofprints Raff found that curved to meet the road after exiting the pine shelter.

Their options were limited—they could go north to Montgomery Butte or south, to Melancholy. Melancholy was closer, and sure enough the tracks merged with a host of others headed that way. He'd check those recently arrived in town. There had been a lot of coming and going in the district, particularly people who attended the fair then stayed to visit afterward, so Raff foretold he wouldn't gain much from enquiries. The killers didn't go to all this effort without devising a well-thought-out escape route.

He switched to the location.

The road between Montgomery Butte and Melancholy was well-patronized, the spot where he now stood too conspicuous to execute a bunch of people. This amount of gunshots fired in succession was sure to be heard, the curious drawn, so the killings happened elsewhere.

Space was needed to corral ten people beforehand, risks taken by the murderers accelerating with the task of then conveying the bodies here. The placement of them required time, but the killers were concealed so need not rush. They could do what they wanted then complete their disappearing act. What Raff drew from this and felt with every bone in his body was the victims were meant to be found.

He trudged back up the knoll.

There, he gazed across treetops, to the hills and mountains beyond. Along with smallholdings sequestered in valleys and along the river, there were countless fastnesses in tracts of land going from can't see to can't see, pockets untouched by human hand, any number of them conceivably where these people died. Were they killed in the same place, or different places? Were they members of the same family, or chosen from different families?

He sifted his reflections. If they were killed somewhere else then carted here, a message was being sent. But to whom? Was this affront meant to serve fear to a single person, a group of people, or residents of Melancholy as a whole? If the killings were intended as a threat to a single person, would this person necessarily recognize it as such? Were they supposed to be found by Ibsen specifically? If a general threat, whatever the reason behind it, folks were sure to get dithery and abandon the province in droves.

It had taken the fair to lift the lid off a black temper that infested town after the girls were found at the Sweet Venus Too. A step toward recovery, it went some way to reminding Melancholy's citizenry their town had a future, but Raff wondered if that, alone, would be enough to convince them to stay.

Ibsen's mention of the cottonwood here had Raff drifting back to when the Praga brothers were lynched from the granddaddy cottonwood south of town, and he tossed over whether the tree was relevant.

The Praga brothers were strung up but were found innocent after the fact. If this were a revenge killing maybe the killers stood a greater chance of being captured if they'd left these bodies by the original tree, so replaced this cottonwood for the other because it was nearer to where the family were killed. Ten years was overly long to hold a grudge and do nothing about it, so Raff ruled out the Pragas' kin seeking justice laying at the center of this. He couldn't remember if the brothers even had kin.

Above that how the bodies were left demonstrated controlled rage with a whole lot of hate seasoning the dish, but he couldn't recall if this piece of land held significance even as the site of a minor skirmish.

With their unerring nose for a story, the fourth estate would report the incident so thousands, if not tens of thousands, would hear of it. Exposing the victims, literally, in this formation made it clear the killers wanted to humiliate and shame them. Newspaper coverage worsened humiliation and shame, which he figured the point. Not much to be done about that.

Thunderheads conferred in mountains to the north, grumbles rolling peak to peak, reaching him in cracking waves. As a boy, he thought this natural marvel a spirit clearing their throat to warn rain was coming. He and Daniel would have to get moving to stow the bodies under cover before the clouds burst.

A passel of men came by, demonstrably curious what the marshal was doing on foot, to all appearances wandering aimlessly while squinting into the distance. When he signaled there was no cause for alarm, they rode on.

Raff walked over to the buckskin and looked back at the bodies, brain jumping like a grasshopper. The horse dipped his head and rested his muzzle in the small of Raff's back. They remained like this until Daniel rode up leading Bron's white mule laden with blankets. The boy ground-tied the mule and his mare then joined the marshal. Minutes passed. Daniel sent animated peeks at Raff then, unable to contain whatever he felt obliged to spout, opened his mouth.

Raff raised his hand to deflect him. Too late.

"Got any ideas, Marshal?"

"Nope."

With the interruption, a vision teasing Raff's memory vaporized.

They spread the blankets Daniel had brought on the wagon bed, untied the ropes holding the couples together, then lugged each body onto the buckboard. When they were done, Raff unfolded a square canvas stashed under the seat—going by blood splatter, used to cover the load on the way here—drew it over the victims and fastened the canvas at the sides and corners. It seemed disrespectful not to afford them this small dignity, although dignity rarely attended death and, for sure, not these deaths. The final journey of innumerable men, women and children were conducted less than ideally, or respectfully. Reverence shown by the living to those who died in appalling, tragic ways didn't affect their ending.

Dead was still dead.

FIVE

Those who have one foot in the canoe, and one foot in the boat,
are going to fall into the water.
—*Tuscarora proverb*

Our return to Melancholy was conducted predominantly in silence, Hiram Walsh content to cogitate over whatever it was he pondered without interference, so I followed his lead, headache all but gone which ensured an environment conducive to examining my recent epiphany with respect to Raff.

Outside the livery, Bron balanced near the top of a ladder propped against the barn wielding a paintbrush, filling in a blue outline of his name dabbed with a rough hand above the doors with rust-colored paint, paint tin rested precariously on the ladder's top rung.

The lawyer dismounted and looped his mare's reins around the hitching rail. I slipped off Samson but did not secure him to make it clear this was where Hiram Walsh and I parted ways: I did not want to provide him an excuse to extend our dealings.

"Thank you for coming with me, Miss Reed," he said. "It was obviously difficult for you, and I didn't appreciate how difficult when requesting your company."

"I will not say it was my pleasure, Mr. Walsh, as I found much of our visit anything but pleasurable. On a separate note, I should add that despite initial reluctance, it brought me a measure of peace."

"Well, I am glad you experienced something of benefit, and please,

Walsh will serve." He petted the mare's neck. "Close friends waive that title and my given name."

"I am neither friend nor close, and encourage you to remember that, Mr. Walsh."

"I am of a strong feeling your . . . position may change."

"If that is what you believe, I submit it would be detrimental to your state of health to hold your breath while awaiting this change. Good day, sir."

Partway down the ladder, spending care to keep the paint tin level so not to spill its contents, Bron braced himself and chuckled. Hiram Walsh ignored him and responded to my tart dismissal with a provocative, boyish smirk. He paid the mare's fee, adding a bonus that saw Bron's eyes widen in amazement and gratitude, then sauntered across the street.

"Might get to likin' that man after all," Bron said. The coins clinked when he added them to a pouch attached to his belt. "He stayin' long?"

"Until the south-bound Concord is through."

We watched Hiram Walsh greet Madam Beaulieux and her husband at the entrance to the General Store, exchange pleasantries, then continue along the boardwalk.

"If Marshal Cooper lets 'im go," Bron said.

"Whatever do you mean? What reason can the marshal possibly use to prevent Mr. Walsh leaving town?"

"There's been another murder. Murders."

Poised to lead Samson into the barn, I turned to face Bron, his statement an echo in the space between us. "Can you repeat that please, Bron?"

"Daniel told me. A fella came across a horse and wagon by the road to Montgomery Butte. Found bodies tied together, not a stitch of clothin' on 'em. Ten of 'em."

"Did you say ten?" Surely I misheard. *Surely.*

"Yep. Marshal says they've been dead maybe a day."

"There is no mistaking they were murdered?"

Bron's incredulity at this daftness flashed like a shooting star.

"You are right. That is perhaps the most ridiculous question ever to pass my lips. Put it down to shock."

"They're with Amos."

"Who are they? Have they been identified yet?"

"Not that I've heard, but reckon I know 'em." Bron put the lid on the paint tin and thumped the edges with the brush handle to seal it tight.

"You do?"

"Don't notice people much, but I notice horses." He laid the brush on the tin, eyed Raven, and casually repositioned himself by the ladder so I stood between them. "When Daniel came in with the wagon after droppin' the bodies off with the bone burier, I recognized the roan pullin' it. Belongs to a man who's been here coupla times."

"Did you inform the marshal of this?"

"'Course." He kicked at a ridge of mud. Dried hard, it broke into slivers under his boot's hefty assault. "It's funny."

"It most assuredly is not!"

"I'm not sayin' the murders are funny. I mean, it's funny your friend there hit town just before the bodies turned up."

"First of all, Hiram Walsh cannot by any stretch of imagination be termed a friend, as I made plain. Secondly, he is a lawyer from Nevada, so murdering people is not exactly considered in his line of work."

"How about Sacha Kincaid?" he adduced.

"Touché."

"Two what?"

"Never mind."

The trial of Kincaid, lawyer and first-born son of a prominent, wealthy political family, unfurled before the masses, America its platform, tortoise-slow progress broadcast in all its glory in gazettes published from the East Coast to the West. Sentenced to death after his wife and her lover were killed, even though solid proof was scarce he had done it, for the past decade he had languished in jail while his defenders campaigned for his freedom, and hidebound activists petitioned he must hang.

Bron squinted skyward when bilious storm clouds masked the sun. Damp rosettes bloomed at our feet.

"I've gotta be somewhere. Boy'll take the horses."

With that, he traced a similar route to Hiram Walsh, quickening to a run to dodge earnest raindrops that splattered the street.

"I shall tend Samson," I said when Mouse, the youngster who helped Bron with the livery, reached for Samson's reins. "If you can take the mare."

"Yes, Miss Hennessey."

⇶⇇

"Start as you mean to continue, Nate. Make sure Annie knows who's in charge."

"Do not go planting seeds of sedition in Nate's head, Jonas."

"Fair enough, Hennessey," Jonas Tolliger replied. "Who am I to espouse how a man should treat his spouse?" He elbowed Shakey, who raised his glass in appreciation of the old doctor's wit.

That evening, those close to Nate gathered at the Fleur to celebrate his forthcoming nuptials, due to take place the next afternoon. Proceedings had Nate seated on the patrons' side of the bar on the stool of honor, with my other barman, Prairie Dog, and Homer Putzenplatz—who worked part-time, in other words, on the rare day the mood struck him—assuming the groom's usual duties. Jonas, Shakey, and even Fatfoot were taking turns to pledge happiness and prosperity to the couple.

"Fill our glasses, Prairie Dog. Drinks're on Ness."

"They are?" I asked.

"It's a weddin' gift to Annie and me."

"It is?"

"Yep." Nate nodded vehemently, signifying him well on the road to inebriation.

Prairie Dog hesitated, awaiting confirmation of my munificence. When I nodded for him to go ahead men around me rushed to empty their glass, then held or pushed it within range of the barmen for replenishing.

"If that is so, I would appreciate your not drinking my cellar dry."

"That'll be easy." The width of Nate's grin rivaled the width of the Mississippi Delta. "'Cause you ain't got a cellar!"

This uncharacteristic levity summed up Nate's feelings magnificently; he was unashamedly, and overtly, happy.

"I expected your wife-to-be to drink with us, Nate." Jonas recovered his refilled glass. "Where is Annie?"

Nate shrugged, the jester's grin still on his lips.

"Did you lose her?" Jonas asked. "She pulled up stakes already?"

"Not far's I know."

"Can't say I'd blame her if she has," Jonas said. "Who in their right mind wants to go marrying an ugly brute such as you?"

"Done tryin' to figure it, Doc."

"A woman who distinguishes a man's qualities, Jonas." I toasted Nate and drained my whiskey. "She is a fortunate woman."

The assemblage was a welcome diversion, Nate and Annie's union a joyful celebration, everyone present determined to make the ceremony on the morrow about affirmation of life and love amidst the Gehenna uncovered that day.

"Heard the latest on the murders?"

It was as though my musings had left a trail bright as fireflies for Shakey to follow.

"I do not believe this an appropriate—"

"It doesn't bother me, Ness. Go ahead, Shake," Nate said.

"Do you know more about them, Shake?" Jonas asked. "How?"

"Swore not to say who told me 'cause it might put 'im in a hole," Shakey said. "He says the dead fella's one of 'em Mormons."

"They the ones with lotsa wives?" Fatfoot garnered courage to ask.

"Yep. This fella had a couple 'parently, which is on the low side accordin' to Pet—I mean, accordin' to my friend," Shakey said.

"Rumblings from the Mormon hierarchy now say the practice of plural wives goes against the teachings of God and should be frowned upon by Latter-day Saints themselves." Considered a font of all knowledge, inveterate authority universally respected, Jonas Tolliger could be relied on for facts, or statements generally considered facts—accepted as embellished, if a little, for the sake of whatever vignette he then expounded. "I've read copy about it in various periodicals."

"Our man must read diff'rent periodicals," Shakey said. "Mebbe he was in hidin' 'cause he liked havin' two wives and didn't wanna get offside of the big chief."

"Maybe," Jonas replied. "Apparently the oldest girl was with child and much younger than him, not that anything can be taken from that. Perhaps she wasn't a wife but an ungovernable daughter. There's no one to confirm either way unless a relative stumbles out of the undergrowth."

Quiet, we all scrolled through our feelings on the subject, an occasion that should have been enjoyable now considerably stifled.

"My hands are full trying to control one wife. Controlling more than one is an aspiration I don't understand how a man with a dose of sense has the bravery to pursue." Jonas Tolliger saw his conversational tangent was injurious to the festive atmosphere, close to irreparably, so this obliged him to make a doughty effort to lighten the mood.

"Do you labor under the conception you *control* Celestine, Jonas?"

The elderly doctor burst into laughter that escalated, bringing on a paroxysm of coughing. Once the coughing fit subsided, he said: "That's a bang-up point you raise, Hennessey. Many years went by before it hit me who makes the decisions in our marriage. Whenever I believed I'd scored a victory which, admittedly, is not a regular occurrence, I'd—silently—congratulate myself. I dare say I have been able to claim victory only if Celestine allows it. She steers me where she wants me to go."

"Well, Doc, I'm sure at the start who's in charge." Nathan used his shirtsleeve to wipe foam off his chin.

"Annie!" Voices united, chiming the name of Nathan's betrothed.

Nate bowed his head, accepting their raillery in good humor and near toppled off his stool. Hands shot out to arrest his fall and push him, with difficulty, back to a vertical position.

"Maybe we should go find Annie and talk her around to saneness."

"Do not dare, Jonas. Remember, Annie will come after any of you, with no exceptions, if you do or say anything to jeopardize the ceremony. Nate, you might do well to—"

"Wait. You're handin' on marriage advice, Ness?"

"I do not suffer the delusion anyone will take it, Shakey."

"Good, 'cause all this talk about gettin' hitched is makin' me nervous."

"Are you worried you might be next?" Jonas looked disturbed by the prospect.

"Stranger things have happened."

"I can't think what, straight off," Jonas said, pitch low, although not so low Shakey did not hear it.

"Hey!"

Raff appeared at my elbow, clapped Nate on the back and was granted a lopsided grin. It seemed my barman had decided to use his allocation of grins awarded him for the next twenty years in a single sitting.

"Were those poor people buried this afternoon, Marshal?" I asked.

"They were." Raff accepted the glass Prairie Dog slid across the bar. "Amos said you paid for their coffins. That's generous."

"I have unexpectedly inherited money. From Jakob," I said, careful no one else could hear me. "I might as well spend it."

"Jakob had a fair amount."

"A *ridiculous* amount, as it transpires. I am still digesting the terms of the bequest."

"I see."

"I expected you to inform me of when those folks were being interred, so I could attend." I backed the conversation up when it became plain this was to be Raff's lone response to my news.

"Didn't think of it. Had a lot to do."

"It does not feel right: them buried without a witness."

"I was there." Raff slaked his thirst, conscious of my stance that someone other than a gravedigger be in attendance to mark the passing of friend or stranger alike. He knew I held deeply-rooted fear that when it came my turn to be lowered into the ground there might be no one I cared for standing beside the grave, hat in hand, to bid farewell.

"Thank you. Did Amos give you an idea who may have done this brutish thing?"

Commentaries around us plunged into silence, all those seated within a four-stool radius awaiting Raff's reply.

"He didn't find much of use." Raff downed another whiskey. "Though Bron recognized the roan pullin' the buckboard. Goin' on that and a description of the dead man, Clay figured who he is 'cause the fella got a coupla telegrams lately. Name is Newman."

"It *was*," Shakey mumbled.

"Yardley was at the store while I was there. Told me he saw Mr. Newman turn up toward the abandoned Martin place one time. I'll go there in the mornin'. See what, if anythin', I can find."

"You are of the mind they were living at the Martin farmstead? That they were killed there?" I asked.

"It's likely."

"On the positive side, we can now refer to Mr. Newman and his family by name," I said. "If nothing else, it affords him and his kin respect."

"Suppose so," Raff said, behindhand. Morose, he stared at the floor and toed sawdust into a pyramid. "Doesn't seem much."

"You know they're religious, Marshal. That's gotta be a place to start."

"Why're you sayin' they're religious, Shakey?"

"Heard they're Mormons."

"So you reckon the women are both wives?"

"With there bein' two women and one man . . ."

"Don't know where you're gettin' information, but ain't nothin' to say they're Mormons. Shouldn't believe everythin' you hear, Shake."

The piano man chose that moment to strike a melody that danced like a Tennessee Pacer, graunching across my nerves. I usually championed his jovial pounding of the ivories for it increased liquor orders down here and the girls' takings upstairs, but I longed for the solemnity of the man who used to patronize the piano stool, once in a while, and played Mozart with the reverent fingers of a believer.

He had left town, this preordained, but he did so with more than he had in his possession on arriving in Melancholy. My girl, Polly, took a shine to the man who communicated by means of cantata rather than conversation. She declared undying love for her suitor, hugged me, waved goodbye to the Fleur and her friends then, with a skip in her step, boarded a stagecoach with her beloved to begin a virtuous life in Kansas City.

"Well, ain't this jest like old times."

"What 'old times' in particular, Shake?" Jonas asked.

"Us sittin' 'round talkin' murder."

"It's been months, not years."

"Lot can happen in a few months." Shakey saluted the groom. "Like this idiot decidin' to get hisself a wife!"

"Didn't get much say," Nate said.

Those around him laughed, familiar with Annie's determination once she set her mind on a prize. I caught Raff's eye and froze, glass halfway to my lips, transported to halcyon days when I believed I knew what he was thinking a beat before he did.

Raff raised his glass, not to Nate but me, in recognition, whereupon I experienced an intense rush of heartache, this replicated in his wry toast. What I would not give to erase past hurts and disappointment. Despite fearing I might lose Raff I had pushed him away, and in doing so alienated him, accomplishing what I dreaded most all by myself.

"You will allow sufficient time to return to Melancholy in order to attend the wedding celebration, Marshal?"

"Will do my best, Miss Reed."

SIX

Force, no matter how concealed, begets resistance.
—*Lakota wisdom*

"We about done, Miss Hennessey?"

My model was starting to fidget.

"You have sat there but an hour, Thomas."

"Feels longer," the boy grumbled.

I hid amusement, although after several minutes during which he squirmed as though a thread of fire ants trekked up his pant leg, I conceded it nonsensical to expect a lad his age and dynamism to stay motionless any length of time. I must be thankful for the hour or thereabouts he deigned sit for me as, with benefit of hindsight, it was no more than I should realistically have predicted.

Opposite to the restive child, Raven sat relaxed and compliant by Thomas's chair. She yawned, shook her head, and licked her lips. Boy and hound took to each other instantaneously on their maiden encounter, and I dabbled with a change in creative direction, my quest to encapsulate their friendship in a tolerable artwork.

"Let us finish this session if we must, Thomas." My usual subjects of mountains and bucolic scenes sidelined, the loss of Thomas's attention thwarted my foray into portraiture, wallowing in its infant stages, and also my gusto for trying a new genre; my lack of advancement in proficiency thus far did not engender enthusiasm. "Come here and tell me what you think of your likeness."

The boy leaped off the chair and, Raven at his heels, approached the easel.

"Speak your mind. I shall not take offense."

"Don't seem a lot like me," he said.

"Of course, it does! There is your earlobe, your cheekbone, your features distinguishable. See?" I traced their outline an inch or so from the canvas with the chewed tip of a sable brush. "All I need to do is fill in more of your hair and an eye, there, and there."

"If you reckon, Miss Hennessey," he dissembled, skepticism poorly disguised, although with my understanding of the boy I assumed him at pains to express diplomacy. His next comment dashed this pretense. "My face looks like a bowl of oatmeal."

Rapscallion. This time I did not conceal my amusement, laughing at his honesty. He grinned with me and I ruffled his shaggy brown hair, which he suffered with stoic forbearance, anticipating remuneration for services rendered: crucially, he did not wish to upset his benefactor further, before payment.

Thomas required no encouragement to scamper into fresh air, belting for home, the coins I had given him clenched in a fist and sure to leave grooves in his palm when he uncurled his fingers.

The process artists used to strive for perfection, mixing color and shaping a theme with the unforgiving eye of their worst critic ultimately led, if they were lucky, to personal celebration and professional acclaim. I stepped back and studied Thomas's visage, positioned in the center of a predominantly blank canvas.

"Damn it all to hell!"

Regrettably, in all fairness Thomas was correct in his assessment. I had to agree with him; his face *did* contain more than passing resemblance to a bowl of breakfast oatmeal.

Disenchanted, I felt a near irresistible urge to pull the Bowie from its sheath and rent the canvas and my pathetic attempt to capture Thomas's essence with vicious, broad strokes of destruction. Sourced through a store in San Francisco, canvasses were too precious to destroy, unnecessary wastage a luxury I could ill afford with how long an order took to arrive. To paint over the 'bowl of oatmeal' was a better alternative for the canvas when limited supplies were considered.

With my venture into portraiture shipwrecked, I decided then and there to abandon the painting of Thomas and Raven—my artistic deviation fallen flat—and return to, and concentrate on, the majestic landscape outside the window.

"Thomas is a smart boy," I said to Raven. "Strangely, although he is a child I trust his judgment, so I shall forgo completion of this pitiful effort."

I cleaned my brushes by rote, taking solace in an exercise I could do with my eyes shut. Accustomed to the smell of turpentine and linseed oil, tools of my trade—the artist's trade, needless clarification—I hardly registered their pursuant stench brigaded in pungent clouds throughout the room.

Brushes cleaned, I tidied the temporary studio set up in my living quarters—generally, indoor premises were nonessential since the great wilds of Idaho Territory were an al fresco studio—then sat with a thump in the chair recently vacated by a squirming Thomas.

Toying with a brush, a baton twisted through my fingers, I cast thoughts over the Newman family, anticipating learning of Raff's discoveries at their farmstead. It did no one good, especially the victims, to mope around towing the inequalities and cruelties of this world: constructive honoring of the family being to find their killers, then deal with the blackguards accordingly. If in pursuit of justice, Marshal Rafael Cooper would be the best lawman to have in your corner. If anyone could uncover who performed these heinous murders, it was Raff.

I reined myself in before diving too deep into soupy waters. It was Annie and Nate's wedding day, a day for promises and celebration of their future while in the presence of friends, not a day to fritter hours at will mulling over whys and wherefores, and the fate of a family of strangers.

"Come, Raven."

A stroll in the fall sunshine prior to the wedding might well dislodge all traces of murder and airy-fairy hypotheses, so I went downstairs to gather Jakob's papers. I had subjected them to thorough inspection, and though everything Hiram Walsh presented seemed all wool and a yard wide, it was wise practice to engage someone to run an expert eye over them as he suggested, to confirm I had not missed anything of major import. I considered myself reasonably competent in matters of the legal persuasion but saw no harm in securing the opinion of a qualified practitioner.

Harley O'Donohue, fulcrum of Melancholy's lawyerly requirements, fulfilled the role admirably, and his opinion should be sufficient. This would allow Hiram Walsh to congratulate himself on a job well done as he bounced, incommoded and grimy, aboard the comfortless southern Concord, home to Tynbridge Hills, Nevada.

⇥⟫⟩✕⟨⟪⇤

O'Donohue's law offices were incorporated into his house on Main Street in a room originally in service as a parlor. Raven and I were admitted by a youth of solemn countenance who performed duty as clerk. A head of blond curls and alabaster skin were suggestive of a Raphaelite cherub, however, the curve of full lips contended him possessive of sententious characteristics, not divine rapture. He wore a spartan rusty suit, material skimpy where it mattered, affecting blasé defiance toward dire straits.

The clerk failed to conceal discomfort at my proximity whether deliberately or with intent, executing praiseworthy contortions to preserve a safe margin between us, these primarily ineffective for it was a tricky undertaking in the box-like vestibule.

He announced me in a precious voice that cracked when I brushed past him—this contact deliberate, I confess, his attitude an intoxicant—and entered O'Donohue's office. The clerk backed away smartly, pulling the door to with perceptible relief.

Harley O'Donohue had once confided in me of an evening while half seas over, as my darling uncle used to say, the linchpin in a series of transgressions that led him to wash up in Melancholy. It involved acquainting himself intimately with a client and her daughter in the same bed, on the same evening. When the frisky threesome were caught *in flagrante delicto* by the husband and father, O'Donohue, fearing for his life, evaded capture by shimmying down a drainpipe, sans clothing; scrambling over an obstacle course of backyards pursued by the furious cuckold brandishing a Purdey shotgun.

O'Donohue assumed the cheeky mien of a mischievous child when admitting he referred to the incident as unfortunate purely because of how close he scraped to getting caught. This eventuated in cessation of the philandering ways of the peripatetic Romeo, which necessitated not only a hasty retreat from the ladies' boudoir, but the hasty exchange of Baton Rouge for points north.

Privation of movement saw him now confined to a self-propelled wheelchair, so with no alternative he bypassed the polite reflex of rising to greet me and remained seated at his desk, startling me when he offered his hand, clasping mine in welcome. Insofar as at what juncture during his escapades he was physically impaired and came to occupy the chair, he had never disclosed.

Withered legs were offset by an upper torso kept in muscular condition by use of barbells stowed in a reinforced cloth bag taped to the left arm of the chair. With mobility severely curtailed by his 'inconvenience', as he termed his handicap, O'Donohue treasured his freedom, whatever the method used to express it, embracing this dictum whenever chance allowed. This included venturing outside rain or shine, snow or storm in a gaudy barouche drawn by a high-stepping mahogany-bay mare.

I commanded Raven stay by the door and exchanged obligatory pleasantries with the lawyer, whose eyes lit up amidst promises of utmost confidentiality in relation to the papers I handed him. O'Donohue assured me he could, fortuitously, fit a consultation into his afternoon. Disinclined to let Jakob's last will and testament and private papers out of my sight, no matter how safe the hands to which I transferred them, O'Donohue met my offhand rejection of his brusque offer to partake of refreshments in the reception room while he perused the will with stiff, forced politeness.

I also declined his offer to take a seat, and when he pulled the ledger toward him moved away, my legs in possession of a peculiar restlessness, the origins of which I could not pinpoint.

"Jakob Diederich." O'Donohue read the embossed cover, interest piqued. "Is he late of this parish? I don't recognize the name."

"Nor did I, to begin." I picked up a delicate flower-seller figurine, antiquity undetermined, off the mantel above a fire burning a frugal wooden sacrifice and studied the maker's mark on its base.

"That belonged to my grandmother, and while she devoted her life to being a cantankerous old witch without rival, it is precious to me, Miss Reed. If you could replace it, forthwith. Carefully."

"Jakob Diederich was known in Melancholy as Jakob Kingsley,"
I said, repositioning the figurine as bid before the irascible lawyer
suffered convulsions.

"Ah. Him, I knew," he said distracted, then, perhaps to deflect
suspicion that might arise concerning the nature of their
acquaintance, expanded his statement. "Not well, I must add."

He put gold-rimmed spectacles on the veined nose of a
dipsomaniac and reviewed the ledger's index. While O'Donohue
read I resumed wandering, inspecting objects propped or sat on
various surfaces, for the treasures with which a man surrounds
himself can reveal titillating insight to his disposition.

A string of diplomas in silver frames hung across the wall opposite
the desk, the gap between each verifying a pedantic eye for spacing.
Legal terminology written in elaborate cursive and signed by persons
whose signatures occupied more than their share of the page decreed
O'Donohue's proficiency in his chosen field. Reading the diplomas
bored me in seconds.

I ran a forefinger along the handle of an ornate dagger in a jade
cradle on the occasional table below the diplomas, admiring its
intricate patterning. Magnificent, on closer inspection it appeared
chiefly ornamental, reflecting the decision by whosoever fashioned
the piece to value beauty and style over substance, and reinforced
entrusting my wellbeing to the Bowie I carried.

"I'd appreciate if you sat, Miss Reed. Your restiveness aggravates
me."

"Well, we cannot have that." I sat on a fat velvet chair, rubbed the
worn arms and amused myself by visualizing what I might paint on
the bald pate his dipped head afforded.

"I'd also appreciate silence, if you don't mind." To my query, he
said: "You're humming."

"Oh, I do apologize. I was unaware I provided that particular distraction." I lit a cigarette to occupy my mouth instead, and tried with marginal success to exercise patience, which at the best of times ran thin as workhouse gruel.

After what felt hours, although assuredly was no more than thirty minutes, O'Donohue removed his spectacles and placed them on the desk, poking them with infinitesimal nudges of a thick finger until they lay parallel to the top edge of the ledger.

"Well, Miss Reed, this is quite a legacy."

"Did you notice any loopholes, Mr. O'Donohue, that may cause problems if an opportunist decided to contest the will for a share of Jakob's property?"

"This—" O'Donohue patted the ledger "—is drawn tighter than Fergal McGinty's purse-strings." He referenced a miserly inhabitant of Melancholy who begrudged spending to such a degree, that on a famous occasion payment for goods he desired to purchase at the General Store had to be pried from his hand by Clay, Lizzie's husband. The incident thawed into town lore and was now used by everyone—including within the elderly man's admittedly inferior hearing—to denote parsimony. "A practitioner with an extraordinary legal brain constructed this, their fiduciary obligations most ably met, and I guarantee there is no loophole."

"You are certain?"

"There is no more I can say or do to reassure you. My suggestion is you accept this bonanza and enjoy it." His confidence did little to assuage misgivings I carried, and it must have showed. "Even with assurance, you still have reservations?"

"None regarding your assessment, Mr. O'Donohue. It is simply that my experience has been great wealth and happiness do not, generally, peaceably inhabit the same mesa."

"Maybe." He rested his elbows on the chair arms, steepled his fingers and blew across their tips. "You could dedicate yourself to proving yourself an exception to that rule."

I thanked O'Donohue, settled payment for his services then left, intent on returning to the Fleur to assist with readying my premises for the wedding.

Some debated the Fleur-de-lis was an unbefitting setting for Nate and Annie's nuptials, howbeit the couple thought it perfect in spite of derogatory comments overheard, uttered by misanthropes secretly envious of their love. In comparable situations the world over, multitude cruel naysayers were ever keen to poke a branding iron in a person's wagon wheel to bring their dreams to a grinding halt.

At the corner around which the Fleur was located I saw Eli Sargeson staggering down the middle of Main Street. Oblivious to curses issued by those impeded by his erratic arm gestures and sudden changes in direction, he placed one foot in front of the other with exaggerated care in a display of admirable fortitude, although perhaps ill-judged determination.

He stopped without warning and swung like a wayward compass, confused where to point his toes and, for an avowed abstainer, gave the distinct impression of being terrifically, horribly, and resoundingly drunk.

"Eli!"

Eli tottered in a circle to see who hailed him, lost his balance along with his hat, and pitched face-first into the dirt.

I cringed, feeling the impact as if I had fallen with him, and raced to help, grabbing ahold of his shoulder and with the assistance of obliging passersby, rolled him onto his back. Crouched beside him, I watched in consternation as he blinked and sniffled, his eyes flooding with tears.

"My stars, man. You are drunk as a lord!"

"Yep." His breath knocked me on my heels. "Sure am, Miss Hennessey."

With the exception of a dusky fellow whose mother incontestably dallied with a sixty-pound midget, those who came to Eli's rescue melted away. I asked the cowpoke to grab Eli's arm, we hauled him to his feet, then virtually dragged him to the boardwalk. There, my assistant helped our charge to seat himself, wedged him against an overhang support, raised his hat and mooched down the street.

"This is so out of character, Eli." I searched my reticule in vain for a kerchief then with no other recourse, brushed the skin beneath his red-rimmed eyes with gloved fingertips. Dirt particles clung to his cheeks as though he cried streams of earth, and I relinquished the task as a lost cause. "What on earth drove you to this state?"

A tragedy had clearly occurred for his tears began to flow in earnest, in no way hampered by those around us who stared without reservation, flummoxed by a full-grown man sitting effectively in the center of town, tears pouring down his face. Eli transited to loud sobbing making the spectacle more vexatious and embarrassing for all concerned. Between sobs he told me his mother had passed away.

"Viola is dead?" He and his mother were close, and of course he grieved for her, but this public, uncontained reaction to her passing struck me as overdone. "You must have expected with her advanced age this was going to happen sooner rather than later."

"When I woke this morning and checked on her, her bed was empty," he said, words broken into shards. "I found her outside Bron Prentiss's livery barn. She'd fallen and hit her head on the trough by his hitching rail."

"Oh, I see. So she died as result of an accident? Well, that is not an uncommon event, Eli. Ruinous, yes, though not uncommon."

Dreadfully ill at ease conveying sympathy in any form other than elementary condolences, I gingerly patted his arm. Once. Thankfully, his sobs stuttered and calmed, replaced by a noxious case of hiccups.

"I shall go find help to get you home where we shall fix a pot of strong coffee. Its medicinal properties are helpful in combatting whatever ails you. Sleep will do wonders as well."

He mumbled a catena of words I did not waste a moment trying to interpret as I hurried into the Fleur to commandeer an able-bodied volunteer. Everyone save Shakey was engaged in wedding preparations elsewhere. Fraternizing contentedly with his preferred barstool, while not the most able-bodied help being in possession of a single arm, since he drank on his own, he would have to do. I sweetened my request with bribery of complimentary drinks the rest of the week, and with him ambling after me returned to where my height-challenged helper had propped Eli.

He had lost his tenuous grip on an upright position and lay sprawled on his back, arms outstretched, staring with glassy despair into nothingness, pathos exemplified. Tears leaked into his hair, likely filling his ears to add to his woes. Fortunately, the gut-wrenching sobs did not resume.

"Shakey, please do the honors."

Shakey hefted Eli off the boardwalk, grabbed one of his arms, limp as rope, which he slung around his neck, then set off toward the Sargeson house.

"I assume since you are headed toward his house you know where Eli lives?"

"No, I guessed."

"Dammit." I had calculated on leaving Shakey to bundle Eli Sargeson home, but the bereft son of a woman with whom neither of us shared more than brief acquaintance was a burden with which Shakey should not be left to contend alone. "I will show you where to deposit Eli since he is in no condition to guide you. We had better hurry. The wedding is beginning soon."

"It won't start without you, Ness," Shakey said, breathing heavily. "And it's not like Nate and Annie haven't taken their time gettin' here. What's a few minutes gonna matter?"

According to in-house observations made by everyone from Annie's workmates to Cookie, observations of which I remained ignorant—by design, I discovered, when they announced their betrothal—Nate's courtship of Annie rivalled the War Between the States in longevity if fought twice in a row.

Neither basked in the glowing flush of youth, so perhaps earlier trials of love and loss dictated caution. Alternatively, as Nathan intimated, did Annie, frustrated by his caginess, stamp her foot and demand my barman make an honest woman of her? She was a force to be reckoned with, akin to a hurricane bearing down on a ramshackle hut and, if asked to place a wager, I would hold little hesitation placing money on Annie always getting what she pined for.

My attitude leaned toward seizing that which was ripe for the picking whether it be enjoying a man's company, a glass of a favored tipple, or the fellowship of one's child. Yes, therein lay my abridged philosophy on life. My flaws were also laid bare, including the damaging and damaged behavior of which I was not proud: unshuttered, for all to see.

I paid homage to my former employee for she achieved what none of Nate's erstwhile lovers had: coerced my friend to the altar. Although Annie tolerated an eight-year courtship, in the long run my barman did not stand a chance when encountering her determination. I had no intention of being late to their marriage ceremony even if immortality were presented to me on a golden platter and a fairy godmother pledged to spin my own tears into diamonds.

I led Shakey and Eli across the road, past a huddle of elderly matrons, their bias made clear when confronted with our disheveled charge. They had undoubtedly experienced worse for our fellow man did not necessarily operate within the boundaries of urbane conduct, as recent events testified, and honestly, we did not reside in a temperance zone. I suspected that behind lace curtains, in the comfort of their homes, these matrons sneaked nips from a bottle kept hidden when no one there to witness their duplicity.

"Lord have mercy on the hapless wretch," said the leader of these stalwart members of the community, formidable as a Roman citadel.

Amused to think her comment might easily apply to any of the three of us, I hurried ahead to open the door of the Sargeson house for Shakey, enabling him to maneuver Eli into the front room, collision between the door frame and Eli's forehead only a minor setback.

Seeing us with the newly bereaved a concerned neighbor, sensitive to Viola's death, bravely took upon themselves to ply Eli with successive mugs of coffee. Our contribution to his welfare finalized, Shakey and I relayed goodbyes and withdrew rapidly, not wishing to be allotted further drunk-minding duties.

Meeting Lizzie on the boardwalk, Shakey greeted her then excused himself, eager to restore his backside to his stool at the Fleur, anticipating the complimentary drinks he had earned. My friend and I followed him at a sedate pace and met Hiram Walsh about to push through the batwings.

I had requested Prairie Dog station a guard out front of the saloon to redirect anyone without an invitation to the wedding. Possessed of concentration undisciplined as a wild mustang he had crumpled beneath excitement, my instruction consigned to the ether, no guard evident.

When Lizzie was introduced to the lawyer her eyes narrowed, and I thought her tempted to make an observation that would entail remedial soothing on my part.

"The Fleur is closed for a private service, Mr. Walsh." I jumped in to head Lizzie off and divert possibility of a boisterous exchange. "It will re-open on the hour. By all means, come by then and join the party."

Notwithstanding Nathan never speaking to me again if I let 'the peacock' anywhere near him during the ceremony, I considered it my prerogative as underwriter of the wedding to invite whomever I chose to celebrations afterward; if Hiram Walsh were to come back later he would be lost in the crowd. I did not inspect the whim behind my extending an invitation to him in the first instance.

"The party is to celebrate . . .?"

"A wedding."

"Who can decline rejoicing with lovers committed to each other through the entwining of hearts and minds?"

"Who indeed."

With his grandiloquent reply Lizzie's lips parted, doubtless to make an incendiary remark, but I threw her a look that begged she bite her tongue.

"Thank you, Miss Reed. I shall return later."

"Before you go, this is as suitable a moment as any to tell you I have decided to hand administration of Jakob's, or I should say *my* assets, to a lawyer here, in Melancholy."

"That's certainly your prerogative." Hiram Walsh hesitated, as though wanting to ask a question he was unsure asking. After contemplation he seemingly discarded the urge. "Then I will meet with him at his earliest convenience to see how we can expedite the process. With plans to enjoy a whiskey at your establishment postponed, I shall enquire now when he can see me."

Until I saw him I had not yet made the decision whether to transfer Jakob's estate or leave it in the hands of Parley, Dunn and Walsh, but it hit home I should limit time spent in the company of the dashing lawyer from Tynbridge Hills after he left Melancholy. I felt his confidence, fine aspect and charming manners were best avoided once the legalities of Jakob's will and testament were executed to our mutual satisfaction.

I groped in my reticule for the visiting card O'Donohue pressed upon me when I left his offices, and gave it to Hiram Walsh, who received it with a nod.

"Way that man's talkin' you'd think this a Boston society weddin', not a jumpin' the broom in the middle of nowhere," Lizzie said, after the man in question bid adieu and wandered straight-backed and courtly toward O'Donohue's chambers.

"Regardless of location, the principles are the same."

"Watch that slyboots, Ness." Disaffected, Lizzie eschewed letting her opinion stew. "He'll talk a girl outta her bloomers then toss her aside in a blink when the next comely lass sashays by."

"Despite your concerns, along with our colleagues of the female persuasion I am of no interest to him."

"How do you figure?"

"When we visited Jakob's farmstead, Mr. Walsh as well admitted he and Jakob enjoyed, ah, personal relations."

"Hmm."

"What is it?"

"I've a feelin' he's got a boot either side of the bed."

The lawyer doffed his hat to a trio of ladies who, when he continued on his way, tittered, heads together, enchanted by his personable appearance and flattered by his attention.

"Really?"

"Yes. Mind yourself there."

"There is no call to forewarn me, for I assure you I am resistant to the obvious charms of Mr. Hiram Walsh."

"If you say so. Won't believe it myself any time soon."

"Come." I hooked my arm through hers and we went inside. A mark of her distraction was she did not pass comment on my relaxing rules around the dictate she enter and exit the Fleur through the back entrance to preserve her respectability. "I am running late and must change my clothes, so it is providential we met. Your help will be invaluable. Incidentally, you look fetching today. Are you wearing a new dress?"

"I know what you're doin', Ness, changin' the subject. But heed my warnin'. That man's a disaster lookin' for a place to happen."

"Which makes him all the more attractive if I were the least desirous of gaining his respect," I teased and led her up to my rooms.

SEVEN

Marshal Rafael Cooper: *Melancholy, Idaho Territory.*

Raff left trumped-up tasks for Daniel designed to keep him busy and feeling useful so he stayed out of harm's—and Raff's—way and rode out of Melancholy at early light, pointing his buckskin's nose vaguely northward.

He followed Clay's directions to the Martin farmstead where the Newman family were thought to have been living, checking at a smallholding to confirm his destination was close. A gaunt woman drained of cordiality, a child on her hip and a gang crowding her ankles, verified him almost there.

A mile farther on he guided his horse along a rough trace that cut through lofty stands of lodgepole pine, and opened onto land hosting a cabin, small barn, and pasture, where rawboned steers grazed. The animals lifted their heads when Raff appeared. Inquisitive, they rolled in an ochre wave across the pasture and tailed the buckskin along the fence-line, passage marked by strident, grumbling bellows. A dozen chickens dotted around the yard paid him no heed; they, with the steers, were the extent of living, breathing critters in the vicinity.

No hound alive or dead lay on the porch, so no guard to raise an alarm if intruders trespassed on the property, though a hunter creeping up on human quarry would control or silence a hound first if they knew what they were doing. Maybe the Newmans had kept a dog in the barn. Did the murderers know if the family owned a dog? The type of men Raff believed them to be would know.

He reined the buckskin past the cabin where he found tracks coming from the barn that proved two men had used it as cover, to get near the dwelling.

He rode back to the yard, pulled his gelding in, and sat a bit, ribbons loose, hands rested on the saddle horn.

A man who preferred harmony, and his own company, to legions of people, noise and the bustle of city living, Raff descried a difference between near silence that excluded humans yet incorporated birdsong and the sounds of Nature, and out and out, unnatural silence.

He'd experienced the unnatural kind after battle once injured men and beasts ceased screaming, the eerie stillness that brought a cloud-woven quality to the atmosphere, an otherworldly peace spanning the dash between when the dead fell and when their souls, almost touchable entities, lifted off the ground. The cattle had gotten over his presence and quit bellowing, and Raff felt quietude akin to that here. His pulse spiked.

He got off his horse. The cabin's front door, although open, felt everything but welcoming. Entering the cabin he walked through it, careful to lift his boots as even slight scuffs jarred and set his teeth on edge. The smell of blood was absent and he didn't see it anywhere, either.

Not much effort had been taken to make the Newmans' place homely, decoration limited to beautiful carved wooden crosses on at least three walls of each room.

The sleeping areas were separated by blankets tacked to the ceiling. Easy calculating said four boys were crammed in one bed, four girls in another, with a third occupied by their parents. Raff stood at what he thought the parents' allocated corner and took in the narrow bed. Was the young woman with child, wife, or daughter? Did she sleep with the girls, or did she share this bed? Was Shakey's unsubstantiated claim they were Mormons correct? The bed was a cozy fit for two bodies, let alone three.

Blankets and quilts were hauled to the foot of each bed, children and adults hustled from dreams in the cold hour before dawn, the father taken by surprise, given no chance to use the rifle kept at his bedside. The intruders had moved with extraordinary swiftness, as men slept lightly in out-of-the-way country like this.

About to leave, Raff saw a worn copy of the Bible on a table by a rocking chair in the front room. He flipped past the cover to the flyleaf where births, marriages, and deaths of family members were listed. Idly running his finger down the page, tracing the arms of Newman history, he caught on the last entry.

Identified as Benjamin Edward, the age of this child recorded born February twenty-seven, 1881, corresponded with that of the youngest boy the Ibsens discovered. Raff skimmed back up the names and saw all entries these past eighteen years were written in the same hand, presumably Mr. Newman's. When the deaths of five children over that period were accounted for, an entry documented a birth that could be related to the age of each child victim. This included the eldest daughter, Eliza, verifying the expectant girl a daughter, not wife of the legal or common-law variety.

Something didn't add up. Raff looked to the floor, then back to the page. Their family name wasn't entered as Newman, but Netherland. Interesting.

Raff had what he called rotten luck to cross paths with men and women aflame with religion. Deaf to their preaching, he'd taken detours to avoid their reach. Although his knowledge of Mormon beliefs and practices was scanty, he knew if the Newmans had been part of that religion the Book of Mormon would have sat on the side table, not the Bible. It seemed they were fervent believers, but under what banner?

He thumbed through pages, past the family tree, and found a nameplate on which was printed:

The Church of Celestial Light and Paradise Divine.

Closing the cover Raff tapped the book and decided to take it with him. He stepped outside, pulled the door closed behind him and dropped the latch home. The buckskin twitched, flicked his tail one flank to the other to deter flies landed there and stomped a hind leg. Raff stuffed the tome into his saddlebag and made for the barn.

Happenings of the morning the Newmans died were easy to make out in the damp soil, bold as the North Star. The size and shape of the boot prints he tracked matched those he'd found by the bodies; the soles worn in the same places, the weight of the men wearing them distributed similarly.

The family were shepherded to the barn by their killers. Space in the larger structure gave the killers freedom to move, to keep their distance, not like the cabin where a brave patriarch or foolish son, or sons, might plan a charge; it tricksy to plot retaliation then execute it when in plain view of your captors.

Raff blocked the terror that would have overrun the Newmans during the march across the yard, the confusion of the younger children at being rudely awoken swelling to fear the level to induce uncontrollable shaking and loosened bowels. Hagridden by what preceded the deaths, he told himself to concentrate, blotting out the memory of the children's trammeled bodies.

The barn door was closed. He freed the plank holding it shut, dragged the door open and stepped out of the sunlight into gloom. He sniffed. There it was. Blood. Flies drawn to it whirred, hungry, voices a constant thrum.

A couple yards inside the doors nightclothes had been thrown in a heap. He lifted a nightdress and inspected it front and back. No bullet hole rent the material. He picked another off the pile. A nightshirt, also without a hole. He folded the garments and replaced them atop the others.

Raff pictured the Newmans ordered to take off their clothes, the embarrassment of children seeing their parents naked, of the parents seeing their older children naked. They were then corralled, waiting in trepidation like beeves in a slaughterhouse.

The family were not shown a sliver of compassion, because that defeated the purpose behind the bloodshed—whatever that purpose was; it defied exploration. They'd watched their closest kin die, flinching at the crack of each bullet, of the knowledge they could not avoid meeting their maker unless saved by divine intervention. A hand extended by their god.

Raff noted where each person stood, especially the killers, jinking around patches of dried blood that swarmed and festered with insects, absorbing details, the position of footprints. A story unfolded clearly and precisely as if written in a book like the ones Shakey loved to read.

The story he read told him plain the father lay at the center of this outrage, his family innocent casualties. Raff believed Newman was shot last, forced to watch his children and wife executed knowing they were dying because of him. Well, that's how he'd do it. Newman would have been powerless, paralyzed, unable to do a damned thing to avert the barbarous annihilation of his entire family.

Raff wondered about the mindset of the instigators of all . . . this.

This was personal, not a random attack. It was an act of revenge. Revenge for what, though, was unanswerable.

To get a different perspective he climbed the rails of the pen nearest him and scanned the barn floor, a trick taught him by an old friend. That's when he saw them: letters scrawled in the dirt.

CX

Were they already here when the family were brought to the barn, part of a game the children played? Did they stand for some kind of measurement? Or, fantastically, despite being gripped by mortal dread did one of the Newmans leave a clue for whomever showed at the farmstead afterward too late to save them, but maybe not too late to solve the mystery of their deaths?

Straw rustled, interrupting his thoughts. There it came again. Raff pushed off the rail and landed silently, on his toes. Clearing his head, he drew his Colt and inched down the aisle, peering into the first stall as he went. Faint squeaks came from the next stall. It didn't sound as if whatever made the noise posed a threat, but he'd learned it paid not to count on anything so swung into the stall, finger on the trigger.

An oddly-put-together speckled hound, floppy-eared with paws out of proportion to her body, was jammed in the corner, her babies sprawled weak and helpless in the straw. Napping against her while she was warm, they had wriggled away when she cooled, and flies were drawn to a fatal knife wound that split her chest. With larger prey in their sights, the person who killed the hound left the pups to die.

Raff holstered his revolver and contemplated the puppies. Recently birthed, blind and deaf, they sensed him, for their squeaking got louder. Dammit, they were the last thing he was fit to deal with, but deal with them he must.

EIGHT

Lizzie buttoned me into an indigo silk dress and, when my toilette was complete, accompanied me along the hallway and down the stairs to the saloon where we parted, my friend joining her husband, and me tittuping alongside Jonas Tolliger.

Melancholy's sole priest, the Reverend Pritchard, declined to marry Nate and Annie due, in summation, to what he labelled Annie's licentious employment, excoriation of proceedings reducing him to apoplectic rage. Increased monetary enticement offended and incited him further, convinced as he became that everyone in town was united in driving him into Lucifer's arms. He had stalked to the church over which he presided where, by accounts of parishioners, he spent hours in prayer. Brimming with magnanimous spirit, Jonas had proclaimed himself more than capable of filling the reverend's shoes.

"Remind me, Jonas," I said near his ear, anxious the most important people in the saloon did not overhear me, even though the rising foofaraw masked my words. "Are you legally qualified to conduct a wedding ceremony?"

"Absolutely!" He beamed and waved gaily at the bride when she looked over to us. "Moreover, does it matter?" he asked, when

Annie's attention was caught elsewhere. "If the couple believe the service binding, there's no harm done, is there?"

"I hold grave doubts this is a sensible idea, for you raise suspicion with your round-about, contradictory reply. What do you propose on the off-chance Annie finds you deceived her if, indeed, that is what you are doing? By the bye, in your shoes I would be fearful of *her* counter, not Nathan's."

"As I understand, your marriage to the marshal all those years ago was part of an Indian ceremony." Jonas hooked his thumbs in his waistcoat, the perfect Phiz illustration, triumphant. "You'd do well to pick your chin off the floor, Hennessey. It isn't becoming to a beautiful woman as yourself."

I stared at him, stupefied. "How did you find out about Raff's and my wedding?"

"Never you mind. To satisfy my rabid curiosity, you didn't partake in a traditional religious service but tell me, did you feel married afterward?"

"Yes, I did," I allowed. And that was true for a few blissful months until the fantasy where my bridegroom was accepted, and prejudice and venomous or snide remarks were not applied to our coupling, was blown to smithereens.

Pilloried by strangers who, seeing us together, mocked the commitment Raff and I had made, scurrilous asides barbed, speaking to me as though he were not right there, standing beside me, saw me leave Raff for *his* sake, despite his protestations. Intervening years disclosed him a man whose word and vows must not be taken lightly; he had proved this times without number.

I wrested my consideration from the past. "That is not the point, Jonas."

"If not, my dear, what is?"

He bestowed a peck upon my cheek, his skin smooth and fragrant after recent shaving, the gesture astounding me in its audacity as much as anything he had cited thus far. His lips curled softly before he turned to the crowd and clapped his hands.

"May I please have your attention," he boomed. When the raucous din continued, undiminished, he clapped again, with better results. "Let's get this ceremony started. We don't want to give bride or groom opportunity to head for the hills!"

Annie glided to the table designated a temporary altar on which I had arranged a shawl trimmed with intricate Belgian lace. Nathan awaited her there, laughing at catcalls and whistles that heralded his bride. Stomping boots pounded the floorboards, muffled slightly by fresh sawdust strewn about the bar area.

The needle controlled by a seamstress presented the gargantuan task of containing Annie's voluptuous body exercised clever tricks of the trade to give the illusion her broad beam was less robust than reality. Encased in a whalebone corset then covered in coffee-colored satin and velvet, trimmed with silk orange blossoms, the bride was mesmeric as a harvest moon.

Soon as the crowd quieted Jonas launched into the welcome address, then his adaptation of the marriage ceremony. Verbose when gifted an audience and shown little or no encouragement, he waxed lyrical until Annie took matters into her own hands and kissed her new husband with almighty passion and dedication. This initiated roars of approval and renewed stomping enough to be heard throughout the county.

Nate gleamed, euphoric, when Annie took his arm, smile stretched ear to ear when they were engulfed by well-wishers; Nate accepting back-slapping as a universal expression of congratulations dispensed by the men, and a kiss on the cheek by the female contingent.

Chairs and tables were pushed against the walls, arranged in a slapdash fashion for those overcome by the notion to sit, and the band comprising the Fleur's piano man Lincoln Maraduke, Elmore Langton on fiddle, and a banjo player of local fame, picking fingers a blur, began to play. Cheers mushroomed, even though it remained unclear to most what they played until several bars in; the tune, when identified, a surprisingly adept interpretation of 'The Flyaway Blues'.

Standing with Lizzie I perused the room, glass in one hand, cigarette in the other. My girls laughed and danced with whomever asked for the pleasure, delighted for Annie, petty jealousies forgotten although an odd stroke of wistfulness made a fleeting appearance; a desire to be fortunate as their workmate and meet a person as kind and generous as her freshly-bridled husband.

I missed Raff's arrival, for he must have entered the saloon when all were centered on the newlyweds. The esteem in which he held my barman and termagant bride was evident in his apparel. Caparisoned in a deerskin jacket, a row of tassels from shoulders to wrists and across his chest, the Stetson kept for special occasions atop his black hair, he looked handsome as I had ever seen him. My balance shifted, regret, its jaws wide, creating fissures of almost insurmountable anguish.

"Raff's sure lookin' fine, Ness," Lizzie said, not for the first time, mischief on her mind.

"'Handsome is as handsome does'." The adage popped out without forethought. With this wisdom stifled by the music, Lizzie motioned me to a table a distance from the band, then entreated I repeat myself.

"What bearin's that got on anythin'?" she asked after the quote's second outing.

"Marshal Cooper's attractive *physical* features were never in dispute. His behavior, in comparison, is a contentious issue."

Expecting remonstration for my flippant attitude, or her to spout an apposite Bible passage in the sing-song rhythm she had acquired after her recent baptism into faith, when neither was forthcoming I found she watched me, her expression full of love, mixed with acceptance, tempered by frustration.

"What are you expectin'?" she asked. "Invariably you pretend to consider my advice, then run off to do the complete opposite of whatever I suggest."

"That does not mean I do not value your counsel, Lizzie, it is—"

"Don't need to explain. 'Specially to me."

"At the moment I am unsure quite what to do."

"Go apologize to him."

"Whatever for?" The idea was preposterous, and no circumstance would see my entertaining it. "He should apologize to me! I have done nothing to warrant apologizing to *him*."

"How long did it take you to tell him Evie's your daughter and Thomas Coulson is her father? He'll think you never trusted him all these years."

"There was no reason to tell him."

I waited for Lizzie to mention the daughter I lost years ago, but she knew that a step over an undrawn line.

"You're goin' to let this drag on, all for the sake of refusin' to admit you miss him?"

"Opportunities for Raff to bring our . . . estrangement to a close have arisen but he has neglected to take advantage of them." Out the corner of my eye I saw Raff approach Katie, my youngest employee, to request the next dance. The girl blushed furiously, taking his outstretched hand nonetheless.

I wondered if Katie had made sure to fix her hairpiece securely to her scalp. To see it fly across the room like a tree squirrel during vigorous swirls and twirls, while doing no favors for her self-esteem, would prove hilarious to the guests.

Without a word Lizzie rose from her chair and started toward the dance floor.

"Wait, where are you going?"

"To tell my husband he's gotta ask me to dance," she threw over her shoulder. "Talkin' to you is sendin' me crazy."

Content to watch the celebrations from the sidelines, I gestured Raff take a seat after he handed Katie to Amos Adams, the undertaker, then crisscrossed through revelers to my table. He set a glass and tobacco pouch by mine and pulled up a chair.

"Won't ask you to dance, Miss Reed."

"Thank you, Marshal. I appreciate your thoughtfulness."

"Ain't thoughtfulness." He sat, stretched his legs, tipped a boot side to side, and studied it intently. "Kind of like my feet unbruised."

"I suppose you find yourself extraordinarily funny."

"Yep." Raven sneaked round the table and licked his hand, Raff being the one person she deigned to honor in such a manner. He rubbed a spot between her ears and was rewarded another lick. "Sure do."

I could not dance as Raff became aware the night we were introduced what must be a decade ago now. He had learned an uncomfortable lesson, as did all my dance partners over ensuing years; my fervent yearning to flit across the floor lightly as a ballerina went no way toward balancing clumsiness when in a situation that involved stepping in time to music.

A stream of townsfolk and farmers who saw Raff sit with me came by our table to shed concerns over the Newman murders, and with them happening so close to the girls' deaths at the Sweet Venus Too mine. Fidgeting and restless limbs were a giveaway to their spiraling apprehension.

"Folks've been through my office, too," Raff said when the latest handwringer moved on. "Can't reassure 'em much. They'll leave town like migratin' pronghorn if I don't get the men who killed the Newmans."

"Speaking of which, what did you learn today?"

Raff led me from when he rode onto the Martins' land, until the moment he left. The volume of noise, music and chatter combined, rose with each minute and he scooted his chair closer to me, leaning in to be heard, breath dusting my cheek.

Relaying finding the pile of nightclothes in the barn he faltered, so I simulated a great deal of interest in a hangnail and did not attend him again until he offered a cigarette.

"Do you have any idea at all what 'CX' stands for?"

"Not yet." He spent longer than needed striking a match, held it to the tip of my cigarette, then fired his own.

"Are they initials of one of the murderers?"

"Reckon the Newmans knew 'em?"

"Not necessarily." I took a pull on my cigarette and exhaled, contributing a jet of dove-white smoke to the fumid air. "If they *are* initials, perhaps whomever gouged the letters in the dirt overheard one of the men address his accomplice."

"A last name beginnin' with 'X' is unusual. You know anybody …?"

I was already shaking my head. "Just a minute." I dropped my spent cigarette on the floor and ground it beneath a heel, checking it was properly extinguished. "It may be the 'CX' are Roman numerals which, as the name implies, are ancient in origin." His blank look indicated Raff's schooling, although fairly comprehensive, did not include learning Roman counting methods. "Using that system the letter 'C' represents one hundred, and 'X' is equivalent to ten."

"You're sayin' 'CX' means one hundred ten? One hundred ten—what?"

"Alas, inspiration eludes me."

"Hmm." Raff drained his glass, cradled it and watched me roll more cigarettes, the first of which I passed to him.

"We have a possibility, albeit slim, the letters 'CX' are the initials of a killer or refer to something that is one hundred ten. This sorry list—which is hardly deserving of the title—rounds up our cogitations thus far."

"Could be they're part of a game."

"So are unrelated to the murders?"

"Uh-huh."

I shuffled back in my seat feeling guilty conversation of the murders again encroached on Annie and Nate's wedding day. Drawn to the band I saw the banjo player had been usurped by a man whom I did not immediately identify, this newcomer intent on picking a route through a galloping verse of 'Sally O'Lore the Three-legged Whore'. Having successfully negotiated the complex, fiddly chorus, the banjo strummer lifted his head and revealed himself as Hiram Walsh.

He caught my eye and winked, purloined a flagon of beer off an unsuspecting drunk, guzzled it until not a drop remained, then replaced the empty glass in the drunkard's fist.

I returned to Raff, who had fallen into a brown study. "Are you struck with any bright thoughts, Marshal?"

"Workin' on it."

"What becomes of the Newmans' livestock?"

"Fed the cattle before I left. Went by the neighbors and asked they check on 'em."

The band leaned their instruments against the nearest sturdy prop and dispersed to enjoy a well-deserved break. Jonas handed his wife, Celestine, to Shakey for safekeeping and started toward Raff and me.

"Celestine is surprisingly nimble," he said on reaching our table. Flushed crimson, he collapsed onto a chair that cracked beneath his weight but, against probability, held together. He wheezed, breath rattling in his chest. Jittery he might suffer physical arrest after cavorting around the dance floor in a spry display to match his wife's, I decided him best kept under observation until his breathing regulated and his florid cheeks subsided to their usual color. "It's hard to keep up with her."

"Made fine work of formalities, Doc." Raff pumped Tolliger's hand. "Didn't know you're a chaplain."

"It was a revelation to Jonas, also," I said.

The men laughed, Jonas embarrassed, although his expression of contrition proved itself of temporary disposition.

"By the way, I have a crow to pluck with you, Marshal," Jonas said.

"That right?"

"You know what I'm talking about."

"You're outnumbered, Doc," Raff said. "Those pups weren't goin' anywhere after the girls spied 'em."

"To what do you refer, Jonas?"

"Out where the Newmans were staying Marshal Cooper here found pups birthed no more than a couple of days, their mother dead. Sentimental fool didn't do what a normal person would do, oh no, sirree. He tucked them all nice and cozy in his saddlebags and brought them straight to my door."

"They'd've died, Doc."

"That's as may be." After a visible struggle Tolliger's stern demeanor folded, for it tested him to hold it any period of time. "Noticed you visited while I was absent. I walked into my home expecting coffee and a delicious treat served by my delightful offspring. Instead I found the girls, Celestine included, cooing over flea-bitten puppies that bear strong resemblance to a litter of rodents. They were tripping over each other in their eagerness to fetch warm milk and blankets for the little pests."

Raff and the retired doctor knew each other well and, if their positions were reversed both Raff and I were safe in the knowledge that in the marshal's boots, Jonas Tolliger would have done the same.

Interestingly, I was under the illusion Raff was involving me in his hunt for the Newman murderers when summarizing his visit to the farmstead, yet he had made no reference to the puppies. Were there other particulars he neglected to divulge? Did he do no more than humor me?

When the band signaled they were to resume playing, Hiram Walsh materialized at our table.

"I'd like to steal Miss Reed away for the Monymusk if you don't mind, gentlemen," he said.

"Go right ahead," Raff said.

"Good luck." Jonas grinned like an idiot, versant in my lack of prowess and polish when Hiram Walsh led me, protesting, to join the dancers.

My explanation why I should not dance was dismissed. I loved to dance, I simply exhibited no aptitude in that department and this deficiency did not alter regardless how often I practiced. In addition, I did not want to make an exhibition of myself in front of half the town, but it appeared I had no say in the matter. Hiram Walsh learned of my failing, at the expense of his fine boots, but this did not deter him.

After a second graceless spin around the floor—he proved a glutton for punishment—he ushered me back to Raff and Jonas, executed another of his unusual bows, navigated the thinning crowd, and pushed through the doors, into the night. Much recovered, Jonas levered himself out of his chair and waddled over to Celestine and Shakey.

Tunes became erratic as the musical talent seesawed, original musicians supplemented by guests who flattered themselves they were piano or fiddle players of equal merit as those hired for the festivities; a free-for-all, though at no point did violence erupt, everyone gregarious and non-confrontational.

The Morning Star was blinking when the stragglers dispersed, stumbling out of the Fleur supported by friends much in need of support themselves.

Nathan and Annie, the last enthusiasts to vacate the dance floor, sweating and tired, arm in arm, went to their 'bridal suite' as the girls joked, referring to Nathan's accommodation adjacent to the kitchen.

When Raff stood, I also rose, beset equally by a surge of awkwardness and stirrings of expectancy, of new beginnings. For much of the evening it felt history repeated itself; Raff and I exchanging views, mulling over and modifying theories around every subject under the sun and moon, arguments and pain forgotten. A marked difference between then and now being that in happier days Raff did not, generally, leave.

After a brief visitation, the trappings of reinstated closeness played their fickle game and deserted us at the door. When I reached for him Raff held my hand, kissed my wrist, then released me.

"Good night, Miss Reed," he said formally, then strode across

Main Street and into the livery, adhering to his routine of checking the buckskin, irrespective of the hour, before turning in.

As he disappeared into the barn I castigated myself for my forward behavior, for it revealed weakness usually hidden. If a hair shirt were readily available I might have put it on then and walked through town, misguided and betrayed by my need for him.

I left Prairie Dog and Homer to clear rubble scattered throughout the Fleur, and climbed the stairs to my quarters, alone except for my dog, a loyal shadow at my heels.

⤜⟫⟫⟫⟪⟪⟪⤛

My earlier deception regarding Hiram Walsh when talking with Lizzie was sent to haunt me. Seated on the balcony outside my room where I had taken myself after Raff had gone, as a lantern flickered beside my chair and wolves howled, a figure strolled along the alleyway that ran behind the Fleur. Hiram Walsh took the path that wound past the privies to the kitchen below, his appearance inevitable despite my emphatic denial to Lizzie his bewitchment of me was reciprocated.

In a deliberate show of reluctance I had agreed with Lizzie's summation of Hiram Walsh's relationship preferences, suspecting if I told her I concurred she would continue to ply me with warnings to avoid him, and I had been in no mood to deal with a barrage of advice.

Sick to the core of my existence, dizzy after imbibing too much liquor, cigarettes smoked in quick succession and sips of the numbing contents of the bottle set beside the whiskey, I did not say a word when the lawyer breached the top of the steps. He removed his hat and hung it off a chair arm.

He sat without invitation, picked up my drink, took a swallow then put the glass down and crossed his legs, maintaining eye contact all the while.

Mr. Hiram Walsh, resident of Tynbridge Hills, Nevada, had shown no compunction about being amenable to sharing my bed, and since Rafael Cooper made it abundantly clear he did not desire my company, by my standards that left me available to consort with someone who did. Subsumed by hurt, snagged in a web of rejection, this formed self-serving justification for not dismissing my visitor at once.

"You said you do not drink while conducting business, Mr. Walsh."

"Who said anything about business?"

"Then I shall procure a glass all your own."

I retrieved a glass from my room and poured him a whiskey. It was left untouched.

⤞⤝

"Who is the woman with the scar on her cheek?" The ghost I saw at Jakob's came to me, not in her ethereal form, but through a persistent esoteric voice without inflection.

Hand raised to brush aside my hair, a tumble of black across his chest, Hiram Walsh stilled, the stiffening of his body evident since mine lay so close to his.

"Why do you ask?"

"Who is she?"

He took so long to answer I thought he had chosen not to.

"My wife." He slid his arm from beneath my neck, the first move to strike distance between us, threw back the covers and swung his legs to the floor. Seated on the edge of the bed he rested his elbows on his thighs, hands clasped.

I always thought this was when a man was at his most vulnerable, almost like a boy with pale skin and knobbed backbone, sometimes self-conscious, often ashamed. Hiram Walsh was of slim build, the antithesis to Raff's musculature. I trailed my fingers along the smooth white skin of his arm. He flinched, so I withdrew my hand and lay it on the coverlet.

"She passed away many years ago," he said, reaching for his pants.

"You loved her very much."

"More than I can express."

"And your child?"

"My child?" Askance, his blue eyes raked my face, but I could tell when he became convinced I knew of what I spoke. "Our son is being raised by his grandparents. Ellen's parents."

"Do you see him often?"

"They reside on the coast, a ways from me, which I believe is best."

"Best for you, or best for him?"

"Discussion of Ellen and Elijah has no place in your bedchamber, Hennessey."

"She does not blame you."

"What?" Incredulity buffeted hope, then anger overrode both. "How can you know?"

"It is inconsequential how I know. Suffice to say, I know."

"Irrespective of that I do blame myself. I'll say no more."

"Yet—"

"No, my wife and boy are no concern of yours. My recommendation is you'd do better to concentrate on restoring the status quo of your own relationship."

I did not take exception to his sardonic tone; infinite fearfulness and sadness caused this hostile response. Even so, it impelled me to respond with: "Do not spin this around and aim your frustration at me. My sole intention is to offer succor, to help ease your pain."

"I appreciate that's how you feel, however, I do not require your help." He stood, hitched his pants to his waist, buttoned them and secured his belt buckle then added, belatedly: "Thank you all the same."

"As you wish." I drew the bedsheet to my chin. "Please ensure no one sees you leave."

"Especially the marshal?" he asked, threading his arms through his shirt sleeves.

"Particularly the marshal."

"Don't worry." He shrugged on his jacket. "I'll make sure to duck out without anyone the wiser." He retrieved his hat and leaned in to kiss me chastely on my forehead, scarcely like the passion he had no shame expressing earlier.

"Goodbye, Hennessey."

"Goodbye, Walsh."

With that he smiled, patted Raven, checked the yard and stepped onto the balcony, closing the door behind him.

NINE

"I know that look, Ness. You and Raff mended your bridges?"

Furious guilt flooded me, head to toe, prickling my skin and my conscience when I met Lizzie outside her store the next afternoon.

"Hellfire. Know *that* look, too. Please tell me it was Raff in your bed."

I stayed mute, which spoke volumes. Lizzie ably published disappointment in me, which saw me want to turn tail and run to the Fleur, crawl into my bed, and stay there a week fantasizing the rest of the world did not exist.

"Lord, what were you thinkin'? What if Raff finds out?"

"He never shall unless you or Hiram Walsh informs him. Walsh has nothing to gain except the possibility of a broken nose, or worse, so unless *you* are going to tell Raff—"

"Tell Raff—what?"

The man himself appeared and looked from me, to Lizzie, back to me. Struck dumb, for there was no warning of his approach, relief overcame me when Lizzie stepped in to field his query.

"Ness was sayin' how she wants to help you find who killed the Newmans, Marshal," she lied. "Like she did with the Sweet Venus murders."

"And that went real well. Don't huff, Miss Reed."

I huffed a little more, perversely, to do the exact opposite of what he asked ingrained. To be fair, Raff telling me what he saw at the Newman farmstead was not the same as requesting I assist him. He knew I would investigate—or interfere, as he would label my inclusion—making his enquiries a tougher proposition, so probably believed if he filled me in at the outset, that might be enough to satisfy me.

"Are you gettin' anywhere, Marshal Cooper?"

"No, Lizzie." Raff seemed to discount her bare-faced untruth, and my innocent expression, letting them go.

"Despite Shakey's claim, the Newmans were not Mormons, Lizzie," I said, repeating what Raff told me last night. "But crosses were hung all through the cabin, with not much else in the way of possessions, which gives the marshal a feeling they were religious in a way that excludes everything except living their faith. The girl with child was a daughter."

"Poor dear. I've been prayin' for them," Lizzie said.

"That fella Hiram Walsh came by my office," Raff said. "He's leavin' soon on the Concord that overnights in Fancy. Didn't wanna say much in case he comes up dry, but he's gonna check somethin' there that may relate to the Newman deaths."

"I have not heard of a town called Fancy," I said.

"It's a ways east. Walsh'll send word if he confirms anythin'."

Walsh failed to mention intelligence he may have on the murders. Admittedly, we were otherwise engaged, conversation not our main priority.

"He gave you no more than that, Marshal?" I asked.

"Should he've?"

"No, not specifically." I did not petition for approbation for my liaisons—if I were blunt, they were none of Raff's business—but his attitude toward me seemed more curt than recent months. Had my tryst with Hiram Walsh been brought to Raff's notice by means as yet unidentified? I waited for the ax to fall. The blow did not come.

"I'll be gettin' on," he said.

"My offer stands if you can use support."

"Got Skeeter and Daniel."

"Nevertheless—" I said, cracking what became a painful silence "—ours is a fruitful partnership."

"Always was," he agreed. "In some things."

Raff bid us good day—well, he predominantly addressed Lizzie—then headed for his office, stride leisurely, even.

"My goodness, I had no idea he was there. That man could give lessons on stealing up on people. Thank you, Lizzie."

"Don't rely on me to keep comin' to your rescue."

"In respect to Hiram Walsh, or dalliance with any man for that matter, it will not happen again. I promise."

"What won't happen again, a dalliance, or me havin' to rescue you? Promises are easy to make. Won't be me you'll answer to."

"Do you refer to Saint Peter waiting for me at the Pearly Gates?" The misplaced humor fell like a stone down a well.

"Don't be a wiseacre, Ness," she chastened. "You're runnin' outta chances. You don't wanna go messin' with a man who'd lay down his life for you. Just 'cause he's always loved you, doesn't mean he always will."

"You are right."

"'Course I am."

Lizzie left me stranded on the boardwalk, her parting a protest of disenchantment. Self-loathing hit me with the force of a roundhouse punch to the belly.

My actions were often reprehensible, examples of obdurate selfishness decided in the heat of the moment with no regard for consequence. I defended my behavior with the postulation those who might be blindsided or angered by my decisions could never find out they occurred, so would not learn of correlative and, on occasion, sordid details.

Wherein I had no hesitation expounding this stance publicly, with confidence, if nettled and on the defensive, *I* professed to mortification however vehemently I raged in the opposition's corner. They did not leave me, those decisions I was ashamed to own, but bided their time, bastions of impenetrable darkness.

Honored with beauty and quick wit, for whatever skewered reason I believed myself undeserving, a poor object of a man's lasting desire or love, this conviction buried too deep to salvage, too deep to consider manipulation to a kinder, more lovable incarnation.

This was a crippling handicap Lizzie once had the gall to observe, unveiling my shortcomings, infuriated by this self-destructive tendency that impelled me to use whatever lay at hand to endanger opportunities for true, lasting happiness.

If he was told Walsh spent the previous night in my bed I expected Raff would find it difficult, if not impossible, to forgive me. Although large portions of the evening were lost in a fog of laudanum and quantities of whiskey best left unmeasured, in the view of most this could never be an acceptable excuse for my conduct.

I shook myself from my reverie, and instead of proceeding to the store returned to the Fleur tired, grumpy, and wishing I could roll back time in the manner of rolling up a rug, to allow scope to make productive choices; ones that would not negatively impact the man who loved me despite internecine conflicts and brick walls laid between us.

For a woman considered in possession of reasonable intelligence, evidence I left strewn about gave the impression a weather system of a scale previously unseen had torn through the county, which made it abundantly clear to anyone with vested interest that I was, in actuality, exceedingly fool-headed.

⇥⇤

I spent the remainder of the day on my balcony, sliding into a metaphorical mud hollow where I thrashed, revisiting failings of mind and deed over the course of my lifetime. Those I could recall. There were still plenty of situations from which to select, therefore a depressing afternoon ensued.

Owl light brought Eli Sargeson to the alleyway behind the Fleur. Slow as molasses in January he used the boundary fence for support, lurching from post to post which spoke he suffered dreadfully with ill-effects arising from his drinking spree. To a body unused to consumption of alcoholic beverages, the costs were assuredly catastrophic to head and stomach.

He made the corner where, after an extended breather he ventured into the street, shuffling with studied care to the entrance of a walkway catty-corner to the Fleur. I wondered where he had been and what provided motivation to oust him from his bed while so unwell. This led me to his mother.

Increasingly, circumstances surrounding Viola Sargeson's death did not sit square with me, and my unease multiplied. Failing to untangle the nature of this cankerworm, if considering how she died, a persistent niggle brought me full circle to facts as explained by her son.

Each time I almost convinced myself her death was accidental, as Eli said, a whisper that refused to be quelled insisted I not let reservations go. Did the deaths of the Newman family fuel my suspicion Viola was murdered? If not already sensitive to irregularities, after their deaths, would I have accepted Viola's death as an accident suffered during a mad woman's ramble, like everyone else appeared to have done?

Nyx threw her cloak upon the earth and time was lost to me, minutes unaccounted for that stretched to hours. Surfacing wide-eyed to an issuable state of clarity, I filed unsettling lapses in memory as occurring while consumed by maudlin thoughts, to reassure myself I was in control of my faculties. The bottle on the oval table at my elbow housed a thimbleful of liquor at most, attesting this deduction erroneous.

Closer to dawn than dusk, Raven and I ventured downstairs to procure another bottle of whiskey from a crate in the storeroom behind the bar. Unsteady, I missed a step, flailed wildly to grab the newel post, and narrowly circumvented an undignified mishap.

Bottle retrieved I stood at the foot of the stairs, boot rested on the bottom tread and decided there was something I could do to set my mind at ease. Going to where Viola Sargeson died might be in order if I were to dispel my doubts around her passing or, determining further investigation was called for, gather evidence, if it existed.

Decision made, despite the lateness of the hour I went to the kitchen to select a lantern off a shelf in the pantry, since mine had begun to splutter, and crept into the yard leaving the door ajar for I did not want to rouse Cookie, whose quarters shared a wall with the kitchen. A light sleeper, inclined to bird-dog me as a person does a wayward charge—in permanent expectation they are on the verge of misbehaving—if Cookie heard me he would insist I tell him where I was going then accompany me or wake Nathan and Annie, whose bed abutted the other kitchen wall, and ask Nathan to do so in his stead.

Raven padded beside me down the path to the alleyway along which Eli Sargeson staggered earlier. Clear of the Fleur I relaxed, comfortable in the dark—and dark it certainly was—attuned to unusual noises, thankful the sun-yellow ring of light my lantern emitted allayed the possibility of tripping and falling as I had done, I am ashamed to admit, in the course of previous night-time junkets.

I made the alleyway mouth, startled when Raven let out a guttural *woof* and hurtled after an animal sensed and seen by her alone. Whatever she pursued scampered under vacant premises across the street, so with monkeyshines unlikely to disturb an occupant there from slumber I left her: when the scent of prey entered her nostrils no one contained power enough to dissuade her from the hunt.

I pressed on to Main Street then cut a diagonal path to the livery. There, I glanced about to confirm I was alone, then centered on the purpose behind my standing by a water trough in the wee hours of the morning on what I was sure to concede—with a clear head, and lucidity re-established—a wild goose chase.

Lowering the hurricane lantern I went along the trough's length, end to end, nose near as close to its rough exterior as fine dust on a moth's wing. My eyes grew heavier, the effects of whiskey and liberal swigs from the blue bottle taking a firm grip.

Just there, was that blood? I blinked rapidly to dispel a haze that marred my vision, squinted at a mark that stood out against the pine, reached without thought to rub it and gained a splinter in my finger for my troubles.

Cursing enthusiastically, employing terms unheard in societies frequented by my titled forebears—forsooth, words foreign to even the most cosmopolitan relative—I removed the splinter with my teeth and sucked my injured finger distracted, and fascinated, by my distorted reflection that shimmered on the surface of the water.

In two minds whether the substance was, indeed, blood, I examined the short edge of the trough. Nothing. Upon inspection of the other long side I saw strands of gray hair snared by a knot in the wood. Did they belong to horse or human? Lifting the lantern to provide more advantageous light I scrutinized them, and in a timespan too small to quantify went from inhaling crisp mountain air to water.

My flagging brain strained to comprehend this dramatic turn, wasting time that would have been better spent fighting the hands around my neck that were holding my head beneath the water. Somewhat belatedly, I began to struggle against their grip.

It quickly became obvious resistance was unproductive use of my reserves, for whomever was behind me determined to see me dead had a height, weight, and definite strength advantage. I could not think, I could not breathe, I could not implement a plan to extricate myself from the assault even if one deigned reveal itself.

Seconds ticked by, the appeal of letting go, to give up and drift into unconsciousness, into oblivion, near crushing me, until my thoughts drifted to Evie, where a decided shift took place.

Damn it all to hell! My life story was *not* going to climax with me drowned like an unwanted animal in the murky waters of a horse trough.

I released hold of the trough and slumped to my knees, arms at my sides, pretending my attacker had attained what he strived for and I was dead. When he straddled me I towed the hem of my dress high enough to access the Bowie strapped to my calf, praying he was too focused on determining whether I was still alive—or not—to notice.

He hoisted me off my knees by my hair. It took all my wits not to groan, for it felt he tore clumps of hair free by the roots. I imagined he was testing to see if I was gone, but did not dwell on this, instead, I guessed where his thigh was and thrust.

My attacker yelped and let go my hair when the Bowie hit bone. I cracked my forehead on the trough as I fell, then folded onto my back, legs twisted beneath my hips.

He loomed over me, darker than the skies, fumbling for my hand in search of the knife I had let go after stabbing him. Although with nothing left with which to defend myself, I prepared to fight. He chuntered gruffly, diverted by something I neither saw nor heard, froze, then stepped away and was gone, silent as a teardrop.

Who knows how long I stared into the night sky, unsure which of the stars studded above were domiciled in the heavens, and which were manufactured by my spinning brain.

At length, having abandoned pursuit of whatever animal she had chased, Raven trotted up to me and sniffed my chin, curious why I lay prostrate in the street.

I felt sick as anything. Driven by increasing nausea I rolled onto my stomach and pressed my upper body off the ground, arms quaking. Arcs of vomit sprayed my hands. Wet hair worked loose of its tie clung to my cheeks and I suspected vomit did not miss the black tresses altogether. Clambering to my feet I swayed, chest heaving.

Tentative exploration found a raised lump the shape of a mountain range on my forehead. I bent to retrieve the lantern, thankful to see it did not shatter on impact when I dropped it. Blood rushed to my head and I braced myself against the trough rim.

The effort to stay upright proved exhausting. I sank to a crouch and fell against the trough, Raven, my centurion, standing guard.

TEN

A man must make his own arrows.
—*Winnebago proverb*

The door to the marshal's office opened and light spilled onto the boardwalk, blinding me while, lantern held aloft, Raff identified his late-night visitor. Although making time to don pants he wore no shirt, his thick ebony hair, loose.

"Funny hour to take a bath, Miss Reed," he said, absorbing my rat-tail locks and dress saturated to the waist.

"Someone tried to drown me, Marshal." I wrenched my gaze upward, past his smooth, brown chest.

"That right?"

"Yes. You find the idea amusing?"

"'Course not." His mouth curled. "Though I get why they were tempted."

"Damnation! I came here to report an attempt on my life. I guess I should not have bothered." I parroted the phrases I used just months ago after Jedidiah Cannon made an impressive attempt to strangle me.

"Simmer down, Lady Aline." Use of the title and name awarded me at birth brought me up midstride. Raff used it to rile me or wrangle me to sense, depending on the context and tone of our conversation. "We've done this afore, remember? Ain't like it's the first time somebody's tried to kill you, and I'd stake money it ain't gonna be the last. Should've gotten used to it."

"Is that all you have to say? Put on a shirt and I shall take you to where it happened."

"Can't it wait till mornin'? Won't see a lot . . ."

I glared at him until he put the lantern on the window sill, beckoned me step inside then disappeared into the room where he set up a cot in the evening, returning within seconds buttoning a navy-blue overshirt.

"Better?" he asked, arms stretched wide.

No, I thought. Eminently sensible in the circumstances, it certainly was not 'better'. I had nuzzled his chest many a time and felt desperate to do so again, longing for the solid warmth and security he provided to maybe grasp a moment, in the safety of his embrace, to weep a little.

"Let's go. Move your tail, girl," he told Raven. "Don't wanna jam it in the door."

After failing earlier in her designated function as protector, Raven now stayed close to my side. Raff leaned across me to close the door, his unique smell which I likened to moon and sand, upon him, stirring memories that even after the trials of the night saw me disposed to smile.

"Where we goin'?"

"This way."

He strode alongside me and posed no further enquiries until presented with the trough outside Bron's barn.

"Here?"

I nodded, chewing my cheek.

Raff squatted, set his lantern down, and studied imprints in the damp earth where I had fought for breath.

"Well, I'd say his boots're made outta snakeskin," he said, after a while. "Mite smaller than mine. Low heel. Made by that fella Rigby in El Paso famous for his stitchin'."

"You deduced all that from an impression?"

He looked up at me, and I could see he was trying not to laugh.

"Ah, you are fooling."

"Part of a toe showin' here, bit of heel there." He pointed to the corresponding prints. "Could be any of a hundred men." He straightened and rubbed the small of his back. "Nothin' stands out. Where was Raven durin' all this?"

"She caught sight of an animal on the way here. A dog, or rat: I did not see. She flew after it and did not reappear until my attacker was gone."

Raff went around the trough. He stroked the tuft of hair caught on a knot.

"Is that hair human or horse?"

"Horse."

"And what looks like blood just there?"

He licked a finger and tested it. "Not blood. Paint, maybe. What were you doin' at Bron's this hour?" He walked measuredly to the boardwalk, scanning the ground. Without raising his head, he added: "Go on, I'm listenin'."

"Well, I have an idea."

"That's gotta mean trouble." He pointed down the street. "Your man went thataway. Didn't get a lotta muck on his boots so it's hard to tell where he went." He thought aloud, more to put things in order than with the purpose to include me in his theorizing. "So, what's this idea of yours?"

"You heard Viola Sargeson died here?" It would be strange if he were ignorant of her death since his placing entailed keeping abreast of happenings in Melancholy, and his nod confirmed he had heard about her passing away. "I started thinking and wondered if perhaps her death was not an accident."

"How do you figure?"

"Viola wandered. She wandered at night, to enjoy a quantity of freedom, I suppose, while Eli slept. I saw her frequently over the last few years."

"Do—"

"Hold your tongue and listen, Marshal. What if she noticed something while coming by the livery barn? Something that struck even in her muddled state as unusual. Or did she notice some*one*? Someone where they had no cause to be at an hour when God-fearing citizens are burrowed in their beds, sound asleep. She did not have to understand what she witnessed as suspicious. It is common knowledge that when she started talking she waffled about all sorts of unrelated subjects. If a person with villainy on their mind feared Viola might have seen him doing whatever it was he believed she saw him doing, he may have decided it prudent to silence her. Forevermore."

"Ever thought of takin' up amateur dramatics?" Unaffected by my scowl he carried on: "The Newman murders have gotten you readin' more into the old lady's death than you should."

"That brings me to my next point. What if they are connected?"

"Why would they be? They were killed miles apart. The Newman murders didn't even happen in town."

"The killers had to stay somewhere. Why not Melancholy?"

"Did you ever consider Mrs. Sargeson just lost her balance and banged her head?"

"Why did someone then try to kill me, in the same place?"

"As I said, there's a wagonload of reasons."

"Well, if you are unable to tell much by his boot print, know he might have acquired a limp. Perhaps you could apprehend him now you are aware of *that*."

"What did you do?"

"I may have stuck him in the leg." Although I felt enervated, awfully battered and bruised, the person I stabbed was inconvenienced also, which gave me immense pleasure. "He was trying to drown me."

"Ain't gonna take you to task. You've the right to defend yourself."

"I most certainly do."

"You stuck him in the leg then he up and ran, or limped, off?"

"Yes . . . er, no." I recalled the man's intention to uplift the Bowie. "He sought to relieve me of my knife until given pause. Eli Sargeson was lollygagging round earlier, so if he is still about perhaps he frightened off my attacker. If not Eli, another nightcrawler."

"Why didn't they come help you?"

"Maybe he saw them, but they did not see him or me."

"Seems you got lucky, Miss Reed. Again. I'm goin' back to my cot. Come on." He started for the Fleur. "I'll see you home first."

"Thank you."

"Gotta be sure he doesn't have another try."

I lifted a foot weighted heavy as an anchor to go after Raff, unsure if I could make it to the Fleur, vacillating between summoning the strength to get to my bed, and the thought it might be easier to sink into the ordure of Main Street and stay there till dawn.

Raff berated Raven as a useless, no-good mutt for not being present in my hour of need, lowering his voice when I held a finger to my lips then, assured I was capable of climbing the stairs on my own, said goodbye at the kitchen door. I propped myself against the door frame until he passed the privies, retrieved the whiskey bottle from the bench beside the stove and tackled the stairs.

In my quarters I peeled off my clothes, left them on the floor, dabbed myself dry with a cloth and pulled on a nightdress. I rinsed my hair in the washbowl kept on a table in the corner of my room then let it alone, the thick, tangled mass too daunting a challenge to attend in my exhausted state.

Bruises already darkened my forearms where my attacker pinned me like a specimen insect as he searched for the Bowie, and when I explored the base of my neck for similar damage, probing of sore spots suggested my skin would be mottled a charming shade of purple. I dared not present myself before the looking glass by the washbowl, as what reflected there would be unmitigated wreckage. That could wait until the morrow when I might be better placed to disguise my injuries, exploiting a treasure trove of experience.

I dragged the quilt off my bed, wrapped it tight around my torso and went out to the balcony. Head less muzzy—it is remarkable how thought processes become clear as crystal glass after one is dunked in the freezing contents of a horse trough—I took the lid off the whiskey bottle and fired a cigarette.

Why did someone try to kill me? Casting my mind over the last months two or three candidates sprung to the forefront of an astonishingly light number of suspects—people I had annoyed, or inconvenienced—but were they disadvantaged to the extent they decided a fine solution was to drown me? And when it came to Viola Sargeson, why kill an old woman whose abilities had deserted her? *Did* she witness something or did I, drawn into fathomless depths by a mind sodden with liquor and laudanum, fabricate events so distanced from truth, Raff did not consider my theory feasible? No, feathers of certainty tickled the recesses of my brain; over the years

I had learned to trust this feeling when it begged me please stick to your guns.

Disoriented, when the sun rose so did I, moving from my chair where I had fallen asleep to my bed, muscles aching, neck sore when I cautiously tested range of movement. Snugged under my quilt I drifted into dreams where I floated above fields of wildflowers of such beauty they caused my eyes, and heart, to ache.

⯈⯈⯈⯇⯇⯇

On awaking at noon I decided to go see Raff so, after extended preparation, covering the bruise on my forehead and those on my neck, I ducked across the street to the marshal's office.

The hard light of day enforced my conviction that the Newman murders and Viola Sargeson's death were connected, even with no base of substance to explain why I believed this through and through. Raven and I marched into the office to find the place empty, although a mug sat on Raff's desk, the aroma of hot coffee bleaching the air.

"Hello, Marshal? Daniel?"

With no reply forthcoming I decided to return later. As I made to leave I spotted a telegram on the desk allocated to Daniel. Curious, I sidled closer, ears pricked for the approach of a lawman entitled, unlike me, to read the telegram's contents. It had been sent through Fancy around eight o'clock that morning, but my itch to read more was dashed when Daniel appeared from the jail cell carrying remnants of a meal on a tin tray.

"Help you, Miss Reed?" He strode to his desk and flipped the telegram, justified in his mistrust.

"Please tell me where I can find Marshal Cooper, Daniel."

"He ain't here."

"I can see that for myself. Where is he, then, if he 'ain't here'?"

"Ah, someplace else?"

I fixed on him. Prepared to stare him down if it took all the livelong day, I could tell by the extent of his jiggling I would not be obliged to do so.

"Marshal said if you came sniffin' 'round I weren't to say nothin'," he admitted.

"Did he?"

"Yes, ma'am."

"Very well. I shall find his whereabouts via a different source," I said mendaciously so he would relax his guard.

"I'd 'preciate it."

"I have one more question. That telegram." I nodded to the piece of paper he shielded with focus akin to thinking it had designs to fly out the window. "Does it, perchance, contain information Marshal Cooper expected to receive from Hiram Walsh? What does it say?"

"That's two quest—hmm. Not sure I'm s'posed to let on about that, neither."

"Now, Daniel, the whole town knows I was instrumental in helping Marshal Cooper solve the mystery of the deaths at the Sweet Venus Too mine. In fact, he went so far to say such a tidy outcome would not have been celebrated if, indeed, I had not become involved."

"You and Evie almost died!"

"Yet we did not."

"It weren't for want of tryin'." His knee jigged; he was desperate to escape. "And Marshal Cooper said . . ."

This was taking too long.

"Do you wish to be held responsible for misfortune befalling the marshal?"

"What misfortune?"

"Tell me, Daniel."

"Well . . ."

"I shall tell Marshal Cooper I threatened you with my Bowie."

"He won't believe that. Actually he prob'ly—"

"Tell me, Daniel."

A nice boy, if impressionable, his struggle to tell or not to tell, the ethics of going against Raff's order to keep the content of the telegram private patently disturbed him. I counted beneath my breath, sure he would soon reveal all. Nerviness around me when by himself impelled him to honesty—eventually—purely to be rid of me.

"Marshal Cooper says his gut tells 'im somethin' is goin' on. Somethin' big."

"Did he really say that, Daniel? Is he aware of more than he is prepared to tell you?"

"Usually if he doesn't pass everythin' on he says it's for my own good."

"I am intimate with his lines of defense, misconceived as they usually are. I suppose the marshal has gone to this town, Fancy, based on information supplied by Mr. Walsh."

"I didn't say he's goin' to Fancy! Or Mr. Walsh!"

The telegram Daniel now folded lengthways with trembling fingers had to originate with Hiram Walsh, since the likelihood Raff anticipated messages out of Fancy sent by different people pushed the boundaries of probability.

"I presume since you are here, and I saw Skeeter going into Cullen's barbershop, that Marshal Cooper went alone?"

"Yes, ma'am."

"When did he leave?"

"This mornin', right after he got the telegram."

"He intends on going straight to Fancy?"

"Yes, ma'am."

Hiram Walsh had left Melancholy around twenty-four hours earlier on the Concord, which moved at a greater speed than Raff could set the buckskin without taking the starch out of him.

"How long will it take the marshal to get there?"

"Maybe a day and a half, goin' steady."

"Thank you, Daniel. I shall not breathe a word about you telling me this to Marshal Cooper, or anyone else."

I swept from the room leaving Daniel resigned, and staring gloomily into the coffee mug he lifted off Raff's desk. Twinges of guilt concerning my treatment of him—bullying, in stark language—nagged me as I hurried to the Fleur, but kindly absented themselves by the time I made the saloon. I had the information I sought, and that was all that mattered.

ELEVEN

Marshal Rafael Cooper: *Fancy, Idaho Territory.*

Raff surrendered his weapons in Fancy, asked where the newspaper was located then cajoled his tired gelding on. To begin, all he wanted was to put flesh on the bones of Hiram Walsh's telegram, to come and go from Fancy with residents none the wiser about his motive for being here. To this end he'd taken the precaution of removing the badge pinned to his vest. He saw no advantage to stirring the pot unless it might get him farther along in his enquiries.

He dismounted outside the shopfront the sociable lawman directed him to. Written in elaborate black script trimmed with gold, 'The Fancy Weekly' scrolled across a large glass pane stippled by dust and rain. Raff peered through the window, palm cupped against his cheek. A one-man operation by the looks. The door chimed when Raff pushed against the frame, and that one man glanced up from his work.

"Be right with you." Brow a fault line, the proprietor resumed fiddling with a lever on the printing press that dominated the room.

Raff nodded an unseen reply, interest netted by a wall smothered in front pages of editions of the newspaper in whose offices he stood. He browsed, while waiting.

"Now, what can I be doing for you, sir?" The man pressed through a thigh-high swing door that separated the working area of the press and public access.

A scholarly type, thinning hair combed back off an aristocratic forehead, strands slick and shiny with hair oil, his movements were measured, as though he walked underwater, close-set brown eyes inquisitive and all-seeing in contrast.

"That's quite a machine." Raff eyed the cumbrous press.

"Most around here deemed her purchase ludicrous, but Fancy will grow, and our readership will grow with it." The man brushed ink-stained hands on his leather apron. "Clive Parkinson, at your service."

"Rafael Cooper. Wondered if you've time for a few questions, Mr. Parkinson."

"Fire ahead."

"A gentleman came through here coupla days ago on the Concord."

"Ah, Mr. Walsh. He mentioned you would probably call by. That's if you're the marshal."

"I am." There went Raff's stealthy approach. "How long you been operatin', Mr. Parkinson?"

"We came to Fancy in '77, the year of the inaugural edition of this paper. My wife suggested *The Fancy Weekly* sounded better than *The Weekly Fancy*. The latter was at risk of misinterpretation, she said. I took her advice, as I always do." Raff managed an acceptable lip twitch to Parkinson's well-worn humor. "Might've gotten away with that banner elsewhere, a town less straitlaced. In Fancy? No.

"This beauty cost me my bank savings and first born." Parkinson wore an indulgent smile as he surveyed the monolith. "Well, finagled the truth about my bank savings: not about my first born. My daughter, Collette, spied the carrier hired to transport the press from California and recklessness blinded her. Never frivolous and of even temperament, until then, when she locked on Booker Henderson there was no one else for her. Love at first sight. Never believed in it till I saw for myself. Now we're five years and five grandchildren later." Raff tried to contain his impatience, but Parkinson read the change in him. "Anyhow, you've no interest in that. How may I help you, Marshal Cooper?"

"Did Mr. Walsh ask you anythin' in particular?"

"We chatted about this and that but no, nothing in particular. Pleasant fellow. He said he was marking time before the Concord left. Complimented me on Miss Betsy here. He was literally walking out the door when he told me to expect you."

Hiram Walsh's telegram brought Raff to Fancy, then Walsh cast Raff adrift to figure the next step himself. There must be a snippet important to his investigation in the newspaper office. Raff looked around to see if this snippet might leap out and grab him.

A fairly new addition was tacked to the wall and he indicated the heading, bold and tremendously sad:

Entire Family SLAIN in Horrifying Circumstances.

"Sensationalism sells papers, Marshal." Parkinson didn't sound convinced by the hackneyed platitude. "Fascination with the ghoulish is a human condition."

"Who were these people?"

"The Wards. Gracious sakes, that was a tragedy." Parkinson removed spectacles from a breast pocket, held them to the light, then rubbed the lens with a pale blue kerchief extracted from the same pocket. Raff felt the newspaperman did this more to steady himself than any great need to clean his spectacles. "Not much was known about them. They kept to themselves." He balanced the spectacles on a bulbous nose eminently qualified for the purpose. "Ansel Jarden found them dead near on two years ago."

"Whole lot of 'em?"

"As it says. All twelve. None spared, not even infants. I'm surprised you didn't read about it. Where did you say you're from again, Marshal?"

"I didn't."

"Mr. Ward's boys weren't of the size to assist with really heavy chores yet." Clive Parkinson carried on minus a definitive response from Raff. "He'd hired Ansel to help with stump clearing. The day he was to start Ansel went to the Ward farmstead and found each member of the family with a bullet through them, dead as doornails. Ansel hasn't been the same man since and I, for one, can't blame him."

"This Ansel Jarden must've seen bodies before. Folks who didn't die peacefully in their sleep. What's different or special about the Wards?" Raff asked.

"He'd seen naught like this. None of us in Fancy knew of anything to compare." Parkinson inhaled audibly through his nose, then exhaled out his mouth. "It still makes me sick to the stomach. They were tied together, facing each other. Male and female, girl and boy, where they could."

"No clothin'?"

"Not a swatch." Brown eyes appraised Raff. "How did you guess?"

"Any clues 'round their place?" When Raff ignored him the newspaperman did not push it. "Suspects?"

"That's an unqualified 'No' to both questions. As I said, the Wards kept to themselves, the father rarely in town except to purchase items they could neither grow nor make. The children didn't attend school and the family weren't part of the local congregation, although we heard ... later ... there were multitude crosses throughout their house."

Was there more here? Raff moved along the wall. Articles

commended adventurers for daring exploits, citizens for growing the territory's largest vegetables, and recorded social occasions. Daguerreotypes showed luminaries stood stiff as totem poles, unsmiling, picnics, horse races, and other subjects modeled for those starved for news, keen to read stories regardless how trivial. He skimmed over them.

Farther along he came to a row of headlining features that got his attention, *The Calamity Bay Bugle* banner in the shape of a flapping pennant the top of each page, Parkinson's byline beneath it. Pictures associated with the articles were also credited to Clive Parkinson. All covered an ambush at the Chandelier Creek Crossing.

"I rode there soon as news came in. It was a nightmarish sight. Do you remember Chandelier Creek, Marshal?" Parkinson asked. "Admittedly, it was overshadowed by coverage of the massacre at Mountain Meadows and growing unrest across the country."

"I remember Mountain Meadows." Raff turned seventeen years old the year that massacre was reported. Mere survival had consumed his waking hours, but even living in the backwoods details trickled through to him. He had followed reportage of that atrocity and later the trials of John D. Lee with disbelief and a weeping heart. "Hard to forget."

"The aftershocks of that act of savagery were an example of the law supposedly meting out justice. A pale imitation of the process in that instance, it has to be said." Parkinson snorted. "You'll recall the controversy surrounding that farce, Marshal. Recall the pressure put on certain people to keep certain other people out of the courts. The result? Not as many as should paid the ultimate price for that bloodbath."

The newspaperman's passionate stance had not dimmed with the passage of time. Although Raff shared Parkinson's view, all he said was: "Sure were dark days."

"Yes, they were. But I'm veering off course. Chandelier Creek happened down in Nevada, just before the war. Great friends Cyrus Finnegan and Peter David Porter had established a church." Parkinson as good as screwed up his nose. "The Church of Celestial Light and Paradise Divine. Finnegan was—"

"Celestial Light and Paradise Divine . . .?"

"Quite the mouthful, don't you agree? So often fanatics seem to vie to see how many letters of the alphabet they can insert into their church's name. Finnegan was, or I should say *is*, charismatic, well-favored, perfect for his role of pastor. Porter was the workhorse. He did all the planning, organizing, and gathering of tithes or *donations*.

"Peter David, his wife and children, his sisters and their families were coming home from a gathering in Brandsville, some fifty miles from where they lived in Tynbridge Hills. Never got there. They were ambushed, gunned down while fording the waterway at the Chandelier Creek Crossing. All of them were undressed, stripped of anything portable or of value, then left where they fell. Some of those in wagons crossing at the time tipped into the water and were caught in the wheels or got swept downriver. In all, forty-odd souls perished."

"They must've returned fire."

"Yes, they must've. It made no difference to the outcome. Rumor was the Porter party toted a lot of money, donations from fellow worshipers in Brandsville. The culprits were never found, nor was the stolen money. Then the war began and there were bigger worries to deal with."

"Who is he?" Raff pointed to a picture, at a corpulent figure center of a large group.

"*That* is Cyrus Finnegan."

"He's an imposin' man. Where was this taken?"

"Winsome Valley. Also Nevada. That was '75, sixteen years after the ambush. An unnamed source took that long to knock up the law about a father and son, the Cowans. Said he'd had business in Brandsville and was riding the same road as Porter the day Porter and his family were murdered. Saw ten men coming from the direction of Chandelier Creek and he recognized Alfred Cowan, the father, amongst them—he'd sold him livestock the previous year."

"Cowan the only man he recognized?"

"Apparently."

"This source let on why he didn't report it at the time?"

"You reckon he was one of the ten, Marshal?" Parkinson was quick on the uptake.

"Maybe. Maybe his conscience finally got the better of him. What happened in Winsome Valley for Finnegan to get on the front page?"

"The Cowans were tracked to a farm outside Winsome Valley township. When the Sheriff from Winsome visited to get their take on why they were in the Chandelier Creek area the day of the ambush, he was told by Cowan the source was mistaken. This source had died, so couldn't be consulted again."

"This person die of natural causes?"

"Not unless you count a jackknife through the lungs a natural cause."

"Seems convenient."

"Decidedly. Winsome Valley was a day's ride from *The Bugle*, and at request of Cyrus Finnegan my editor, Edward Theodore, sent me there when word got out of the Cowans' location. Finnegan was a personal friend of Edward and an immensely powerful man by then. *The Bugle* ran on a shoestring, there wasn't money to support a photographer and a writer, so I had learned to use a camera. A picture is worth a thousand words, so they say. I was excited as a bull in a pen full of heifers. When I arrived in Winsome I learned the Cowans were also dead."

"Lotta dyin' goin' on. How'd they die?"

"Drank poisoned liquor. Scuttlebutt was they knew they were going to be unmasked as the murderers at Chandelier Creek so, to avoid facing a trial and hanging, they killed themselves."

"Why not cut out?"

"Why indeed? Asked myself the very same."

"You hold their deaths were suspicious?"

"You're a smart man, Marshal. Draw your own conclusion."

"That's when you took Finnegan's picture? After they died?"

"Yes, sir."

"He got word fast about where the Cowans were to get there quick as he did?"

"Cyrus Finnegan has tentacles that stretch over mountains and across seas."

"What did he want with the Cowans if there was no evidence they were guilty?"

"He believed the source. He declared the Cowans liars, said they *were* involved in the ambush. They were dead, couldn't defend themselves. Most thought he was on a false trail. There was no proof—none the public was aware of at any rate. But he could've had a spy telling him different. Finnegan said he'd traveled to Winsome Valley to look the killers of the man he considered a brother in the eye and ask why they'd done it, and just because the Cowans were dead it didn't mean he'd quit searching for their accomplices.

"Since the reasons for my going to Winsome Valley had *expired*, I decided to refresh the memories of our readers and write a series covering Chandelier Creek and The Church of Celestial Light and Paradise Divine, hoping it might lead to a new angle for those seeking justice. Edward thought it a grand idea—if accomplished in my spare time. Before I got stuck into the project he called me to his office and instructed I must 'cease and desist'." Parkinson briskly saluted his invisible editor. "Those were his exact words. My protestations were dismissed. I've always maintained this abrupt turnaround was coerced, Theodore forced to curtail my publications. It doesn't say much for freedom of the press."

"Theodore didn't explain his instruction?"

"No. After that things became . . . trying for me. But life goes on."

"Not for the victims of Chandelier Creek."

"You'll get no argument here."

Raff stood before the candid shot of Finnegan and hunted for a thread that gifted itself to unraveling.

"Mr. Walsh spent time studying that picture too."

"Who's this?" The young man stationed behind Finnegan's right shoulder was vaguely familiar. Raff tapped the man's face. "You get his name?"

"Don't recall a given name." Parkinson stepped closer to the picture. "I *do* remember he was Peter David Porter's son. The youngster was ill, too ill to travel to Brandsville with the rest of his family, so was left at home in the charge of his grandmother. That boy lost everyone close to him except that grandmother. I recorded the names of the dead and their extended families for reference later. I can get them if you're not in a hurry or feel it's of use to you."

"If you could."

"Happy to."

"Did Mr. Walsh say anythin' about Chandelier Creek?"

"No. He expressed interest in my involvement, though nothing other than the usual fascination shown when someone who was there can supply first-hand insight of a tragic or controversial event."

Raff didn't understand why prying into morbid happenings delighted folks. Maybe they had nothing better to do than prey on other folks' misery.

"I file a copy of every edition of this newspaper, and the broadsheets that publish my work. I can pull additional images and features for you. Feel free to take a look at what I wrote about the Ward family as well. There's a table in the stock room you're welcome to use. Come, I'll show you."

Parkinson pressed through the gate and stroked an oblong metal plate screwed to Miss Betsy, etched with the manufacturer's name, as though petting a beloved animal. He led Raff past the machine into a room crammed with wooden cabinets fitted with narrow drawers in which documents could be laid flat, a gate-legged table, several mismatched chairs and, inexplicably, a Singer sewing machine.

"Will you begin with Chandelier Creek, Marshal?"

"Sure."

Parkinson opened a drawer set about knee height, and carefully transferred a stack of pages to the table. "My, I haven't looked at these in years. All the papers are in order by date, so if you start here, when news came in about the ambuscade, there's background copy if you want details. What I wrote, in entirety, is in the drawers below where I got these."

"And the Wards?"

"In that cabinet left of the window you'll find editions pertaining to them." Parkinson fossicked in yet another drawer and placed a sheet of paper on top of the others. "Here's that list of those who died at Chandelier Creek, and their kin. There he is—the boy. Ferrington Porter. Holler if there's anything else you need, Marshal Cooper."

Raff started reading, taking particular note of pictures that accompanied text, to give him a sense of the massacre site and its layout.

Later, astonished to find he'd whiled away more than an hour and a half, Raff thanked Mr. Parkinson for the access to his archives.

"The anniversary for Chandelier Creek is on the twentieth of this month," the newsman said. "Cyrus Finnegan is leading a commemoration service at the site. If obligations didn't hold me here I would go. Now, if you require future assistance don't hesitate to contact me, Marshal. I'll do whatever I can to accommodate you."

"Thanks."

Raff had one foot out the door when Parkinson asked: "Why the interest in the Wards, Marshal Cooper?"

"No special reason."

"It's happened again, hasn't it? Up your neck of the woods, wherever your neck of the woods may be. Ah. Your reticence confirms it. How many dead?"

"Ten," Raff admitted after a lengthy pause.

"And what is your interest in Chandelier Creek and young Porter?"

"Don't know what to tell you, Mr. Parkinson. Not yet."

"Fair enough." Parkinson wiped a smudge off the window, then inspected the pane, as though loath to see the marshal leave just yet. "Before you go . . ." He withdrew a notebook from his apron and tore out a page. "Here, take this."

It was another list of names. All were male.

"Who are these men?"

"A time after the Cowans died a woman approached my wife Suzannah. This woman stressed she toyed with danger when she took Suzannah aside and told her the Cowans had been part of a brigade who 'made problems go away'. She encouraged my wife to take down the names she recited, those of the ten men in this brigade; the brigade who attacked Porter at Chandelier Creek. She said all in this select group belonged to The Church of Celestial Light and Paradise Divine."

"They followed the Lord and Jesus Christ but killed their own?"

"They wouldn't be the first, nor the last. Despite Edward Theodore telling me I must forget writing about Chandelier Creek Crossing, the mystery woman's information prompted me to secretly continue my research. It would have been a huge story to break and would've made my career.

"One of the first things I did was check the census taken for Tynbridge Hills, where the church is based, prior to Chandelier Creek. The names given to Suzannah—the ten men including the Cowans that the unnamed source saw riding from the creek—were in that census. At the next census all ten were missing. They'd disappeared."

"If they moved to a new city or territory—"

"A coincidence, Marshal? I'm for truth and justice, which is why being a newsman was my calling. But I love my family more. Not long after visiting the census office—where on entering I used my grandfather's name, in case of repercussions—my youngest daughter, Elodie, was snatched while playing in our garden. Whoever took her was showing they knew who I really was, where I lived, where my vulnerabilities lay." Parkinson's face paled. "Elodie was returned to us after a week. I was directed to a derelict sod house along the river. She was huddled just inside the door. Her eyes and lips were stitched closed. She never spoke again. Needless to say, I stopped my investigation."

"You think Finnegan directed the Cowans and their associates to carry out the massacre at Chandelier Creek? That he was behind your daughter's abduction?"

"I feel it's a distinct probability. No one in that church blows their nose without notifying Finnegan."

"If Finnegan directed the Cowan brigade to kill Porter and his family, why did he go to Winsome Valley and make a fuss about gettin' a confession from the Cowans and say he was determined to find out the identity of the other men? He'd already know who they were. The biggest issue is—"

"If Finnegan was behind Chandelier Creek, why did he have Porter killed? Why was his partner a problem that had to be resolved? That is what someone needs to find out, Marshal. Power can and does send men crazy, it corrupts. Did the Cowans work independently at Chandelier Creek, or were they run by Finnegan or a member in the echelons of The Church of Celestial Light and Paradise Divine? If it was Finnegan, he'd need to be seen to do what was expected in order to put the law off his scent, so he vowed and declared he wasn't going to give up the hunt for the killers to garner sympathy and backing.

"Cyrus Finnegan is lionized by his congregation, his hold over them is mythical; they would do anything for him, for their church. And in the case of a brigade member being tempted or bribed to give him up to authorities, they couldn't do so without implicating themselves."

"If anythin' comes of this, can it be traced to you?"

"Elodie is dead, Marshal. I was too frightened to act then. They scared me off most successfully. Whoever 'they' may be. I feel you are not debilitated by the same cowardice."

"Cowardice isn't fair."

"Please find whoever is responsible," Parkinson said. "In both cases."

"I'll try."

⟫⟪

Raff lingered on the boardwalk after he left Clive Parkinson. Riffling through their conversation it took a while before he became aware a clutch of men across the way observed him, talking amongst themselves. Liquored-up, he figured they spoiled for a fight, looking for an excuse to bully somebody with darker skin than theirs. He sought to diffuse their narrow-hearted cruelty by offering no spur to play mean; he unhitched the buckskin nice and easy and swung aboard.

His color and size were oftentimes read a challenge, tin star or no tin star. He'd ridden into a town unfamiliar to him, or with him, mingling with folks who might feel threatened by an Indian in their midst. The combative group were a reminder to keep his wits sharpened.

He settled the buckskin in a tidy livery barn, ensured the animal comfortable, his water bucket full and his sweat-infused coat brushed clean, and left him munching grain.

Raff had a hankering for a decent meal himself, so went the opposite direction to the men het up over him, into an eating house as far from them as he could get. He ate at a table near the door, making quick work of a dish of stew he wasn't sure tasted good because it was well-cooked—he'd have chewed on a moose's ear he was so damned hungry.

Chowing down, he kept an eye on those entering and exiting the premises, drifting over what he'd read at *The Fancy Weekly*. He mopped dregs of stew off his plate with the last hunk of cornbread and, hunger appeased, pushed the plate away and stretched his legs their full length. He got his tobacco pouch out and watched a youth come through the door favoring his right leg, in the raucous company of workmates who informed patrons between ear-splitting guffaws that he'd tumbled off a broomtail his gramma could have ridden.

They ordered and clustered round a table. The injured man positioned his chair and tentatively lowered his rump onto it, taking the badinage in his stride, and it came to Raff where he'd seen the man who bore striking resemblance to young Ferrington Porter. A man who walked with a limp. Mr. Ferrington Porter who lost near his entire family at Chandelier Creek nowadays went by the handle Ezekiel Beaulieux.

What led Porter to Melancholy where he and his wife lived under a different name? Mind, living under a name you weren't born to meant nowt. Crikey, at birth the firebrand known as Hennessey Reed was registered as Lady Aline Rafferty Cole, so best not read too much into the change of moniker.

Raff smoked a cigarette then shoved his chair back, pushed to his feet, left the eating house, and went to the livery where he'd left the buckskin.

He interrupted the hostler who forked manure out of a vacant stall into a barrow. The man leaned on his pitchfork, hair plastered to a forehead clammy with sweat, grateful to take a break.

"There a telegraph office close?" Raff asked.

"At the Mercantile. This side of the street. Can't miss it."

Raff thanked the hostler. It couldn't hurt to get Daniel to wander past the Beaulieuxs' house. He trusted his gut, and his gut told him they were involved in the Newman deaths. Somehow. Could be they were in it up to their necks. Could be happenstance brought Zeke

and his wife to Melancholy. Could be everything, could be nothing
in it at all.

⟫⟪

He awoke early, fell out of a cheap cot in a cheap hotel and went
to the Mercantile, read the message Daniel had sent, then dictated a
reply to the wizened character who manned the telegraph system. He
asked to be notified as soon the response came through.

The Beaulieuxs were still in Melancholy. The buckskin wasn't as
rested as he'd have liked, but he'd give Daniel time to respond, then
head home.

With the arrival of a telegram from Daniel late afternoon, Raff's
ponderings, and destination, changed.

Noticing Clive Parkinson at work he went over to *The Fancy
Weekly*.

"We'll soon be close as brothers, Marshal," formed Parkinson's
greeting.

"Is there a shortcut south outta here, Mr. Parkinson?"

"There is, though it's a misnomer to call it a shortcut. It isn't as
far length-wise, but a body needs a horse that's a tightrope walker.
It's less bothersome to head north ten miles or thereabouts then turn
west and go through a place called Hollow Oak Falls."

"I know it."

"Then head on south. That's my recommendation. There's better
odds against taking an unscheduled flying lesson off a bluff and
finding yourself being measured for a wooden overcoat if you go
through Hollow Oak."

"Thanks for the tip."

"Any time."

Raff unhitched the buckskin, lost in thought, ignorant of

townsfolk whose steps quickened when they came upon him, to slow again once past.

The Church of Celestial Light and Paradise Divine was the common element here; the plate in the Bible Raff took from the Newman cabin showed they worshipped under Finnegan. Similarly, crosses at the Ward home indicated the family were fervent believers. Did they also follow Finnegan's guidance? They were killed the same way as the Newmans and left in the same configuration, so he reckoned they did.

Lump Chandelier Creek with young Porter, or Beaulieux, losing his family there, and his being at Winsome Valley with Cyrus Finnegan together, and this supported Raff's idea that everything was interconnected.

Added to this, Hiram Walsh hailed from Tynbridge Hills, where the Paradise Divine church was based. Raff hadn't taken to the arrogant lawyer, but if he were honest that could be attributed to Hiram Walsh's captivation with Hennessey. Walsh sent the telegram that put Raff on to Parkinson, which led him to Porter and Chandelier Creek, and the Wards, so it didn't work if Walsh was mixed up in the Newman deaths that he would help Raff.

Raff wasn't sure of a lot, but there was one thing he could guarantee. No matter which way he looked at it, up, down, or sideways, he knew things were about to get complicated.

TWELVE

Be still, and the earth will speak to you.
—*Navajo wisdom*

Speculating if Raff was still in Fancy or on his way home to Melancholy, it did not exhaust my persuasive wiles to engineer his present whereabouts from Daniel. The deputy slumped in his chair when Raven and I walked into the marshal's office and wordlessly handed me a strip of telegraph paper on which I read:

IN FANCY. STOP. KEEP EYES ON BEAULIEUXS. STOP.
R. COOPER.

This raised more questions than it answered, and my brain started to gallop at the speed of a runaway horse.

"When did this come in, Daniel?"

"Yesterday."

"Has Marshal Cooper elaborated since why he wants you to monitor the Beaulieuxs? What relevance can they have to our situation?"

"Didn't say, Miss Hennessey." He relieved me of Raff's telegram and threw it on his desk, visibly glad of interruption when a newcomer poked his head through the door.

Built lanky and lean, the type of wiry that bends like a willow branch but halts shy of snapping, the outlander wore an extraordinary mustache, thick and sleek as a pair of beavers meeting.

It covered a large section of a weather-harassed face and contrasted remarkably with bushy eyebrows white and thick as hoarfrost.

He exuded calmness, security, a man on whom one might unburden all worries with confidence knowing he possessed the wherewithal to make them disappear—without a ripple. The badge on his chest negated explanation of his occupation; our visitor labored in the employ of the famed Pinkerton Detective Agency.

Raven growled and the agent skipped backward, arms thrown up, palms outward in a defensive gesture. "Whoa, there."

I patted the dog's head and she quieted, bright gaze tracing his every move.

"Help you?" Daniel asked.

"Marshal about?" The Pinkerton reluctantly lifted a major portion of care off Raven, though he continued to shoot nervous glances toward her.

"No. I'm Deputy Marshal Daniel Hawthorne." Daniel grew inches before my eyes. "I'm in charge while he's gone."

"Gone where? And for how long?"

"Outta town. Coupla days."

The Pinkerton removed his hat, ruffling sprouts of gray hair, and rubbed his crown in a way that spoke of entrenched weariness.

"May I enquire why you wish to see Marshal Cooper?" I asked.

"Sure." He ran consideration past the delightful, ribboned hat atop my primped hair, burnt-rose silk dress, to the pointed toes of my favorite buttoned boots, then drawled: "You can enquire all you like."

"Although you may not, necessarily, tell me?"

"I'd be better disposed if we were properly introduced." He matched my tone, a twinkle of humor infiltrating exhaustion. "You are?"

"Just leavin'." This was an inopportune moment for Daniel to assert himself and, quivering under my glare, he swiftly added: "Or, maybe not."

"My name is Hennessey Reed. Please oblige me, sir, and return the courtesy."

"McFarley. Kip. Call me Agent McFarley if you're angling to make things official."

"Consider us properly introduced, Agent McFarley."

"Guess there's no harm in Miss Reed staying if you're happy with her being here, Deputy?"

"Not so sure about happy," Daniel grumbled. "Got no choice, more like."

McFarley's mustache twitched. "Came by to ask if you've seen this couple." He reached into his jacket and withdrew a creased square of paper he unfolded, then passed to Daniel.

The boy spent intense concentration on it. "If this likeness ain't bad, it's close to Mr. Beaulieux and his wife."

When he made to return the paper to the lawman I held out a hand and he relinquished it with a distinct lack of enthusiasm. I studied the simple line drawings, my inclination to agree with Daniel.

"I believe Deputy Hawthorne correct. This is the Beaulieuxs. This lady goes by 'Madam'." I ran my forefinger over the slim nose depicted in the female portrait. "She reads palms and uses a crystal ball to tell the future." I gave the sheet to the Pinkerton.

"Beaulieux? You positive?"

"She's real pretty and wears scarves 'cause she got hit by lightnin'," Daniel said.

"You do know them." McFarley lost all semblance of fatigue; a light sparked and glowed behind his mask.

"Sure. They've been a while in Melancholy."

"They're here, in town?" The Pinkerton could not help himself, exhilaration with hearing this obvious although he tried to downplay it. He forgot about Raven and focused on Daniel.

"That's what I said."

"Have you seen them recently?"

"Marshal had me go by their house last night. Didn't see 'em as such, but the place was lit up and a body went past the window."

"What day we got today?"

"Monday," I said, unsure of the relevance of McFarley's dislocated query.

"Why did the marshal ask you to check on the Beaulieuxs, Deputy?"

"Didn't say."

"I have to speak with them." McFarley blew out a long breath.

"I'm gonna ask: about what?" Daniel placed his hands on his hips then dropped them, snappily, grasping his posturing absurd.

McFarley wandered to a board nailed above Raff's desk that displayed *Wanted* bills of assorted lawbreaking individuals. Unlike the drawings of the Beaulieuxs, I would have banked on them owning scant relationship to the men—and a single woman, mad of eye—they purported to represent. "Just need to confirm some things."

"That all?"

"For now." McFarley's casual deportment was a ruse: he wanted to jump up and down like an excited pup. This detail waltzed straight by Daniel and executed a modest pirouette, purely to make a statement. "Where are they living?"

"Can show you," Daniel said.

"Right." McFarley studied me again. Contrary to his manner this did not connote rudeness, he merely calculated how he could incorporate me in whatever plan he was hiding up his shirt sleeve; how I might serve his needs. "You keen to help us, Miss Reed?"

"That depends entirely on what you suggest I do."

"How about you come too. I don't want to spook these Beaulieuxs. If they see you at the door rather than me or Deputy Hawthorne here, they're less likely to bolt."

"That alone gives a strong impression you may be putting me—us—in danger."

"You'll be safe."

"Where am I goin' to be?" Daniel asked.

"Out back in case they decide to run for it."

"Do they have cause to?" I asked.

"It's a possibility," McFarley admitted.

"Before Daniel and I commit ourselves to the potentiality of endangering our lives to assist a man with whom we are not acquainted, it would increase my confidence if we were informed of the Beaulieuxs' background. As you know it."

"In ordinary language, you won't do this until you know why I want to talk to them."

"Precisely."

"That's fair." McFarley rubbed a bristled chin. "Kept plain, it goes something like this: they are fraudsters of the top order and have made considerable nuisance of themselves."

"Is tracking fraudsters an unusual job for a Pinkerton agent? I was of the understanding your agency is hired for security guarding or to go after bank robbers and those accused of unlawful killings."

"Our purview is a wide and colorful document, Miss Reed. In this case the aunt and uncle of a high-ranking functionary were duped of a fortune. As a personal favor I was assigned to find and arrest the culprits who did the duping."

"I see." And I did—he lied. "Do you not at least work in groups or pairs? Where is your partner?"

"He's . . . catching me up."

I felt a degree of responsibility for Daniel's wellbeing, even while abdicating concern for my own. The boy tended to rush ahead with no thought except how his actions, his bravery, might impress the marshal. With Raff absented from his post I fostered the hope Daniel not be injured, particularly with a wound of a terminal nature, while in my company.

Tolerated by Raff when left to posture and prance within Melancholy's borders, in the arena of our big continent Daniel's naïveté shone bright as a lantern, akin to those plunderers lit to trick ships laden with precious cargo to sail onto jagged rocks—a beacon impossible to miss.

"Can you assure me, honestly, the Beaulieuxs pose no danger, Agent McFarley?"

"They won't be as dumb to try anything violent, Miss Reed. If things get hairy for them they'll try to bluff their way out of a bind, not shoot their way out. Sounds like they haven't tried to hide here, and up till now there's no evidence they've got business with anyone other than their chosen targets."

"Who on earth is a target for fraudsters here, in Melancholy?"

"You, perhaps?" he said, acknowledging the quality of my attire.

"That is a ridiculous conjecture."

"Got no notion who is next. If you're why they're here, have to say I don't rate their chances."

"Are you being truthful about our safety?"

"As best I can." Impatient to be going, McFarley edged toward the egress.

"I suppose that is all I can expect."

"Clock's ticking. You in?"

"Yes," I said, curiosity aroused.

"Good. Is there a place to conceal yourself at the rear of the property, Deputy?"

"Maybe a stable."

"We'll wait till Deputy Hawthorne is in position then you can approach the house and knock on their door, Miss Reed."

"Where will you be?"

"Close."

"What do you require I say or do to whomever answers my knock?"

"I'm sure you'll conjure up a fitting conversation starter on the walk over. Now, if you're ready, let's go. Deputy, lead the way." He sized up my wolfhound. "It's best the dog stays here."

"It will be more suspicious, not less, if she does not accompany me."

With a *humph* I took as a signal he acquiesced, McFarley made for the door, giving Raven sea room.

I paraded along Main Street as though it were perfectly normal to be flanked by the marshal's deputy on my left side, and a Pinkerton agent on my right. Those whose interest nudged impolite were fixed with a stare that met and confronted theirs and which, unsurprisingly, influenced redirection of their attention.

Daniel led us along an alley and through the narrow thoroughfare behind the bakehouse and barber's shop, which brought us to the street on which the Beaulieuxs resided.

"They live where that yella cur's layin'."

"They cannot hear us, Daniel," I said. "There is no call to whisper."

"Sorry."

"Cut dirt, lad. I'll give you time to get in place."

"Yes, sir." Daniel left us, his interpretation of relaxed deportment to blend with his environment allowing generous margins for enhancement.

"Boy's got a ten-dollar hat on a five-cent head." McFarley muttered something else beneath his handlebar mustache, by example derogatory in nature, then raised his voice. "You ready, Miss Reed?"

He started up the road neither too fast nor too slow, a man with purpose on his way somewhere important, even though hidden from the sight line of anyone who happened to glance out a window of the Beaulieux home.

I scurried to catch him then regulated my pace to match his. No brilliant question or opening gambit presented itself. Panic took a hold; I faced ruining the Pinkerton's strategy, whatever it was, before it had gotten past the starting post.

As we neared the house the yellow cur whined and squeezed under the porch until a muzzle caked with mud was the only part of it visible. Raven's nostrils flared, the singular indication she knew the animal there.

A nod from McFarley was prelude to his easing his pace and snaking forward, back against the house's clapboard exterior. I walked past him and knocked, knuckles coming away stuck with specks of paint that peeled like bark from the door panels. My heart thudded in my chest, my legs primed for flight. There was no response, so I tried again, knocking harder, but discerned no footfall crossing the floor.

Hesitantly I turned the handle and went inside, Raven and the Pinkerton close behind.

"Mr. Beaulieux? Madam Beaulieux? Are you in?" My voice bounced around a pocket-sized front room. I tilted my head, to listen, an ungodly caterwauling strangling the neighbor's abode all

I heard. Astonishingly, a musician with self-assurance that over-reached their ability had blown the opening chords to 'Amazing Grace' into a set of bagpipes.

I homed in on the scene at hand. Although Daniel said the Beaulieuxs were here last evening, strong inference was the house held no memory of its latest occupants, that they had abandoned it not hours, but days ago.

"They are gone."

"Yep." Kip McFarley brushed by me, now with no requirement for anonymity or furtiveness. "Dammit! Please excuse the cussing, Miss Reed."

"There is . . ." I did not tax myself with finishing, for McFarley had clomped through to the adjoining room. I trailed in his footsteps as he barged room to room, which took no time. Furnished with bare necessities for day-to-day living, these were spread thin throughout the residence. I suspected most of the fittings, if not all, were permanent fixtures. Scratches and scars attested the furniture grew increasingly battered when each tenant sat or leaned or slept upon them. A side-table the concession, perhaps decorated with a treasured kickshaw or daguerreotype of a relative or love, these wrapped carefully in a scrap of muslin when the house was vacated.

"They lit out real quick," McFarley said when we completed our search and stood again in the cramped living space. Set by an ancient Franklin fireplace about to fall through the floor, was a table and chairs. McFarley kicked at the chair nearest him, nose wrinkling when it disintegrated beneath his anger. "They took what they could carry, left the rest." He ran a jaded eye over the contents of the room. "Didn't have a whole lot to start."

"'Travel light, travel fast'." I quoted Raff out loud without realizing

I had done so, pretending I did not notice McFarley's clandestine interest.

"They done cut and run?" Daniel piped from the doorway.

"Something or somebody must've tipped them off." McFarley gave the shattered chair another kick. "Are you sure they didn't see you last night, Deputy?"

"Acted natural." Mortification sluiced Daniel's crooked features. "Though I s'pose they might've spotted me."

"Do not apportion blame of the Beaulieuxs' disappearance on Daniel's shoulders, Agent McFarley. I shall not tolerate it." I did not examine what Daniel's idea of acting naturally entailed but felt it unfair to allow the Pinkerton to vent his frustration on the boy. "Take your disappointment elsewhere."

"I'll take it to the nearest saloon and buy it a whiskey, then, before hitting my bunk. I'd go after the Beaulieuxs if I knew where they'd taken themselves and my horse wasn't done in. He'd topple over if he saw me coming at him with a saddle right now. It's been a tough day and I've a feeling tomorrow's going to be worse. Stand you a drink, Deputy?"

"Sure." Daniel did not play down his pleasure at the offer. "Better send Marshal Cooper a message first tellin' him the Beaulieuxs're gone."

"Will you join us, Miss Reed?" the Pinkerton asked.

"I shall see you at the Fleur-de-lis, where you are welcome to whatever you prefer—to drink—gratis."

"Too tired for anything else," he said. "You're associated with this Fleur-de-lis, I take it?"

"Your sensitivity is appreciated, Agent McFarley, however there is no need to extend consideration toward my feelings. It is clear-cut to all but a blind man I am neither postmistress nor schoolteacher, and you discerned that soon as we met."

"With respect, it wasn't all that hard."

"Tell my barman you may choose your poison," I said, laughing at his candor.

"Much obliged."

"I shall be there presently."

"Meet you at the saloon when you've sent your telegram, Hawthorne," McFarley said.

I watched them depart, Daniel full to the brim with responsibility and eagerness, and McFarley demonstrably abstracted, ambages a mystery.

"What do you suppose that Pinkerton is up to, Raven? There is definitely more to his chasing the Beaulieuxs than he divulged."

Raven proved less than helpful, not troubling to listen to my reflection. She leaped off the porch, ignoring the yellow dog crouched in its meager hide, this misdirection; she crept in a wide semicircle, shoulders dropped, to approach the mutt from the side. My experience with her behavior predicted any moment tufts of fur were sure to fly.

"Raven, no!"

Intent on her prey, Raven turned a deaf ear.

I knew better than to physically intervene, for when cornered or forced to break concentration Raven reverted to her wild self, retaliation fierce and redirected on the person or animal who displayed incalculable stupidity by interfering.

Only once had I imprudently tried to distract her when she was fixated on a hapless quarry after initiating a fight to prove her superiority. Never again. Injuries sustained that day left a puckered scar that tattooed my arm, an ugly reminder that to put myself between fighting animals, although well-intentioned, cannot be regarded amongst sensible impulses a person should entertain.

Prepared to witness an attack the yellow dog would be fortunate to survive, apprehension flipped to astonishment. Instead of her customary bellicose ambuscade Raven eased to a crouch and adjusted position, forelegs stretched in front of her, eyes latched on the other dog. It showed no intention of picking up the gauntlet my wolfhound threw down—a wise decision—and remained where it lay, whimpering almost inaudibly.

Relieved by this bloodless outcome, I took advantage of the lull in negotiations and called Raven. In a typical show of independence she did not acknowledge my command, but in time rose, turned tail on the animal and, dawdling, came to me, steps exaggerated.

I strode toward the Fleur before Raven decided to readdress her magnanimous attitude. Worried the yellow dog might follow us I glanced back at the house, but a dirty muzzle was all to indicate it still cowered under the porch.

THIRTEEN

All dreams spin out from the same web.

—Hopi proverb

I hurried into the livery. Carrying a tin pail in each hand, Bron readied to exit the barn by the rear doors.

"Bron, wait up." The brisk pace I elected from the Beaulieux house had winded me, so I spent a moment to catch my breath. Impatient to plough on with his chores, the hostler inched backward. "You mentioned the other day you do not remember people so much as what they ride, or drive. Are you acquainted with that fellow Zeke Beaulieux?"

Bron contemplated the rafters, ruminating. "He got a limp? Wife has them funny eyes?"

"Yes, that is him. Can you recall the mounts they own, if any?"

"He bought Smokey off me when they got here." Bron set the buckets at his feet. "You'd have seen her. Flea-bitten gray. Keeps her in a stable where they're stayin'. If the wife wants to ride out with him she takes that bay." When he pointed, it appeared the mare he indicated picked we discussed her, for she dipped her coffin-shaped head decorated with a broad blaze and whickered. "Or they hire the buggy."

"Thank you, Bron." I made to leave, then hesitated. "Did they hire either mount or buggy recently?"

"No." He grabbed the bucket handles. "Just as well."

"What do you mean?"

"I'm a horse light and Blaze there pulled up lame, so ain't a lot to choose from."

"Has one of your horses died?"

Bron's attachment to his horses was legendary, it not unheard of for him to mope for weeks on losing an animal. He once withdrew to his cot for three days using a bout of dysentery as an excuse when a lovely chestnut mare he owned went down with colic, twisting her bowel. He did everything within his power to save her, to no avail. Folks in Melancholy went along with the charade, of the combined view empathy in genuine circumstances ought to be applauded, not mocked.

"No, she's missin'."

Ah, that explained his loquacity. Despite natural inclination of the opposite habitude, Bron wished to distract himself from the probability he would never see his horse again.

"When did she go missing?"

"Last night. Had her in the last stall." With his hands occupied, he indicated the rear doors with his nose. "Got up this mornin' and she'd gone."

"You did not hear noises or—"

"I'd been at the Fleur. Don't remember gettin' to bed, but the young 'un was on duty. He stays in where the feed's kept. He's gone, too, so reckon he's pinched my horse and taken off."

"Is that out of character for Mouse?"

"Would've said so before he stole the mare. Thought he's a good lad."

"So in your opinion Mouse had no cause to sneak off in the dead of night without a by your leave?"

"Not far's I know."

If someone were in desperate straits, in need of a horse they had no intention of paying for and the boy heard or saw something best left alone, did they dispatch him to give themselves time to get away? I looked into the hay loft, then about the barn, for nooks and crannies where a body might be secreted, the premise abhorrent. Or did they take Mouse with them, planning to dispose of him when well shot of town? I had a dreadful premonition he was dumped in a ditch or grove of trees along the road. With no family to speak of, it fell to Bron to report the boy's disappearance.

"Have you notified the marshal's office Mouse and your horse are missing?"

"Went across first thing and told Skeeter. He said ain't a lot they can do 'cause a bay mare with white socks ain't rare, so askin' folks to keep a lookout for her's gonna get nowhere."

"Be that as it may, a bay mare with white socks topped by an eleven-year-old boy without a caretaker is going to trigger a memory."

"Ain't gonna hang my hat on it."

Bron made no attempt to disguise the fact he gave more importance to his mare than the boy. A foundling, the child had little to his name and after last night, maybe not even life itself.

Miserable, Bron still bemoaned his lost mare, chin around his ankles when I left the barn, unsure if he noticed me absent myself. Bron was renowned as a tremendously sound sleeper, even when sober, and his friends made use of every opportunity to tease him about the volume of his snoring and how maddening it was to try to wake him. On a night in March when straw in his barn caught alight, he had slept through being dragged into the snow, to safety, and awoke disoriented and confused when the fire was controlled, the excitement a memory. Last night, if this and his typical consumption of liquor were taken into account, it did not surprise me Bron did not wake.

If Mouse heard whomever it was sneaking into the barn and went to investigate, perhaps the thief saw no alternative than to silence him. McFarley said the Beaulieuxs were fraudsters; were they horse rustlers and murderers, too?

Perhaps they saw Daniel stroll past their house and believed he, or Raff, were suspicious of the reason behind their staying in Melancholy. They already owned the gray mare but required another mount: stealing Bron's horse would give them a head start on a chancer with the notion to chase them.

And if Mouse recognized them, it may well have become the last thing the boy did.

For argument's sake, if a thief intended to steal a horse the night Viola died they should not have cared if she saw them or revealed their identity—to her son for example—for they would be in the next county before anyone could act. Also, there was the probability no one would believe what she told them anyway.

Possessed by desperation of a level to kill an old lady who showed up inconveniently, would the thief not then continue with his objective to appropriate a horse that night? This brought me around again to Viola's death having no link with anyone or anything else.

Yet if Mrs. Sargeson's death *was* murder, did the killer return to the livery last night figuring his way clear since he had killed one person who stumbled across his shenanigans, and only a woman with a death wish—me—would revisit the scene where she nearly died the previous evening? Did he strike it lucky on his third attempt?

The Beaulieuxs were gone, yet I should not jump to conclusions. It could be happenchance they left when they did, and I heaped blame upon people innocent of that particular crime.

And if the lad in Bron's employ stole the mare, Viola's death may have been a calamitous accident after all—this the simple, preferable explanation.

Hither and thither I went.

My head began to spin, this soliloquizing overexerting my brain, a brain that determined to tie itself into an intricate mare's nest braided with increasing concern for Mouse's welfare.

Daniel cut in front of me when I walked out of the livery.

"Sorry, Miss Hennessey," he said, ducking out of my way.

"You must be in dire want of a drink to be hurrying so, Daniel. Did you send your telegram to Marshal Cooper?"

"Yep. Says he's goin' to Hollow Oak Falls tomorrow and the telegraph system ain't workin' there, so just as well I wrote him."

"He has replied already?"

"Must've been waitin'."

"Where is this Hollow Oak Falls?"

"Down and across. Marshal's gotta backtrack partway to Melancholy then go west."

"In his telegram did he say what impels him to go there?"

"Said there was folks killed same way as the Newmans. In Fancy." This burst out of his mouth in such a rush it melted into a single word. He resumed control of his diction and the rest was much easier to interpret. "They were religious, too. Twelve of 'em. Might have somethin' to do with that."

"I dare say it does, although if they died in Fancy, why is he going to Hollow Oak Falls?" I chased an untamable herd of suppositions around and around in my head until I came back to Earth and found Daniel staring at me. I supposed he was waiting to be dismissed. "You go on, Daniel. I shall see you at the Fleur. Soon."

After visiting the privy I entered the Fleur via the kitchen, fed Raven, then went through to the bar where Daniel and Agent McFarley sat, heads together. A modest gap separated them and the Fleur's gallery of rogues—Doc Tolliger, Shakey and Fatfoot—who carried on their discourse while shooting what in their judgment amounted to furtive glances toward Agent McFarley.

On seeing me Daniel's face flushed, then he hopped his stool along the bar, keen to put air between himself and the Pinkerton. McFarley sipped his whiskey, unperturbed by Daniel's desertion. Since I planned to inveigle whatever they discussed from Daniel later I arranged my rear on a barstool, drink in hand, and relayed what I had learned during the exchange with Bron.

"So, according to this Bron fella the Beaulieuxs own a gray mare, and if they had a hand in stealing his horse—which is quite the coincidence if they didn't—one of them is now on a bay with white socks. And somewhere in the melee there's a lost boy. How old did you say he was, Miss Reed?"

"I made no mention of his age." I noted McFarley referred to Mouse in the past tense, thus reinforcing my apprehension about the lad's state of breathing. "He might be eleven years."

"Not really grown enough to be an accomplice, then. Did you notice a horse in the Beaulieux stable tonight, Deputy?"

"Nope," Daniel said.

"'Nope', you didn't notice, or 'nope', there wasn't a horse in the stable?"

"The second bit."

"Right. Sadly, I share your misgivings, Miss Reed. If the boy happened on issues that didn't concern him the Beaulieuxs might've silenced him." He read my expression. "*If* the Beaulieuxs were involved."

"You told Daniel and me it improbable they would harm a person unassociated with their target."

McFarley adopted a pose intimating he searched the cuspidor for inspiration, then said: "True, I did. If it's them, things might've . . . escalated. Anyhow, we won't find what became of the child unless we catch the Beaulieuxs *if* it was them, and if they're disposed to tell."

"'We' will not find what became of Mouse?"

"Figure of speech." He drained his glass and nudged it across the bar, blocking the bottle neck when Nate went to refill it. "I'm turning in. Got an early start."

"Thought you men don't sleep," said Shakey.

Reference to the Pinkerton dictum saw McFarley raise an exhausted smile. "You'll have to excuse me while I roll around in this sawdust laughing. Never heard that before." He patted Shakey on a bony shoulder to offset any offensive quality to his spikiness.

"Where do you intend to go from here, Agent McFarley?" I asked, to maintain the fabrication that the Beaulieuxs were thieves of money, not lives, so I might remain conversant with his whereabouts.

"Gotta think that through." The Pinkerton grinned, recognizing my ineptly disguised probe where he rode on the morrow. "Thanks for your help this evening and your hospitality, Miss Reed. Night, all."

"Good night, Agent McFarley. I wish you success with your commission." That, at least, I could offer with sincerity.

He picked his hat off his lap and left. Daniel felt it advisable to shift to another stool and ingratiate himself in a heated debate between Shakey and Doc Tolliger who, once McFarley had gone, taking the novelty of his presence, resumed their argument as to whether Slim

Joe Peckin or Tally-ho Chesterton was the quicker draw. Neither was able to claim ultimate victory when, against strong odds, Peckin and Chesterton traded lead and shot each other dead in the main street of Kirkwood, Alabama, not a month later.

Nate abandoned the pretense he did not eavesdrop on my conversation with Kip McFarley, watched the Pinkerton go through the batwings, then charged my glass.

"When we leavin'?"

"Sunrise, reputedly, although you are not going anywhere. You have been married but a minute. What will Annie say if you inform her of your desire to go gallivanting around the countryside so soon after your nuptials? Excuse me, Nate. Daniel!" The deputy jumped, features awash with guilt. When I crooked a finger he placed his drink carefully on the polished bar top, slid off his stool and came to stand in front of me like a naughty schoolboy caught in an act of revolt. "Of what did you and Agent McFarley speak before I arrived?"

He hemmed and hawed. "He asked me somethin' is all."

"What did he ask, Deputy?"

"Where the marshal's headed." Daniel's eyes romped around the Fleur. He was desperate for rescue, but no one was kind enough to oblige him.

"And how did you respond?"

"That Marshal Cooper's goin' to Hollow Oak Falls."

"Any more than that?"

"I might've told him about the Newmans and the dead family in Fancy." He looked again to Doc and Shakey for assistance, still unforthcoming. "You mad I told him, Miss Hennessey?"

I opened my mouth, but before I could speak Nathan said: "No, she ain't, Dan." Then he glared at me, which meant I better support him, or else.

"Nate is correct," I said. "There is no cause for me to be angry with you, Daniel."

"He's the law, Miss Hennessey."

"Yes, I suppose he is." Irrespective of my struggle to explain or justify my reluctance to pass information to McFarley, Daniel should not suffer under my confusion. "You may return to your friends."

Daniel repossessed the seat beside Shakey and emptied his glass.

"You playin' with the Pinkerton? Do you agree with him the Beaulieuxs're tied to Bron's missin' nag?" Nate asked.

"I do."

"Reckon the Pinkerton's goin' to Hollow Oak?"

"I do."

"Ain't no way you're goin' there by yourself, Ness." Nathan retrieved our previous topic. "The marshal's gonna need help. Besides, could use a break."

"Already?"

"Didn't see marriage bein' so . . . tirin'."

"You and Annie have been wed a matter of days, Nate. How do you expect to survive the next forty years?"

He blanched. "Forty years?"

"Do not panic. Look at it this way. You may be killed or catch the fever before then."

"God willin'," he grumbled.

Nate adored Annie; however, I appreciated at his age learning to cohabit with a person whom he loved was a double-edged sword. As a grown, mature man, Nathan reserved entitlement to do whatever he wanted to do, whenever he wanted to do it. That said, it required herculean daring to even consider telling Annie he intended traveling with me to who knew where, for who knew how long. I foresaw a commotion of biblical magnitude ensuing.

"If you insist on coming with me, Nate, go tell Bron we shall be at the livery before sunup to ready our horses. I do not want to startle him and be introduced to the dangerous end of his Sharps if he suspects more of his animals are being stolen."

"I'll go now."

"While there, see if McFarley mentioned when he is leaving and confirm, if you can, that he is going to Hollow Oak Falls. There is a slim chance he may go elsewhere. Oh, and get a description of McFarley's horse and find which stall he is in." I lowered my voice further. "Additionally, make sure Daniel does not get wind that we are going after Raff or he will want to come with us, and I am not the least disposed to childmind."

"Then leave off talkin' and let me get on."

⊱──────⊰

Since Raff had ignored decency guidelines and neglected to tell me where he intended to go and why when he rode for Fancy, I presumed he worked off information Hiram Walsh sent in his telegram, the mission predominantly a fishing expedition. Raff's subsequent telegram, saying he was not coming home but rode for Hollow Oak Falls, published loudly that he had dug up material he felt obliged to investigate.

My assailant's near-successful attempt to drown me, and the appearance in town of the Pinkerton Agent McFarley, whom I thought lied to us, brought the need to advise Raff there was more to the Beaulieuxs than how they presented themselves. I was also convinced that whatever McFarley divulged to Raff, when or if he caught up with him, would be an impoverished relation to the truth. Raff conceivably headed toward disaster, and with the telegraph system in Hollow Oak Falls out of commission, I saw no other course than to go there myself, to warn him.

I told Cookie that Nate and I were going to be absent an indefinite period, no more than a week. Maybe two. Used to short notice of my travel arrangements, a solemn nod meant he accepted last-minute instruction.

Denied convenience of basic articulation courtesy of an Indian's knife, which sliced his tongue from his mouth fifteen years ago, Cookie was adept at communicating much with an edited shake of his head or nod.

When I requested he keep Raven with him at the Fleur incertitude stained his face. Nate and I had to ride at speed to catch Raff. Above and beyond this, I had learned it senseful to dodge towns where inhabitants might take exception to a strange-looking dog of appearance akin to a wolf. Raven had shaved close to being done away with more than once, and I did not wish to tempt fate amongst those scared by a beast they could not identify as a domestic creature—or hunters who saw her as a trophy.

Raven and Cookie rubbed along fine during the normal everyday, but with my absence containing her and her remaining in that favorable condition would be a trial.

Other than his initial expression of ambivalence Cookie posed no resistance to what I asked of him and continued preparing our evening meal. The notepaper and pencil tied to his belt, which he utilized if needing to convey anything that warranted more than a head or hand signal, were left unused.

Cookie was capable of running a kitchen, but if a fight broke out in the saloon where negotiation was vital, where an argument or misunderstanding demanded tact, or brute force before fists swung and furniture and bottles were collared for use as weapons, reliable backup had to be set in place.

If exhorted to ride farther than Montgomery Butte, Raff appointed himself my travel companion whether I agreed to his accompanying me or not. While we were gone Nathan assumed my duties at the Fleur. Nathan was coming with me to Hollow Oak—apparently—so I had to appoint an alternate manager, a person I could trust.

Leaving Prairie Dog and Homer to their own devices gave rise to them helping themselves to the Fleur's products, or handing liquor out willy-nilly, for free—the inconvenience of charging customers a mire of quicksand to their addled brains. Therefore, I wanted to check if Lizzie—or her husband Clay if Lizzie decided my appeal bucked against fundamental Christian values to which she now subscribed—could assume the position until our return.

In serviceable rooms behind the General Store I laid down my suspicions and fears. Like Cookie, Lizzie listened but did not contribute until I finished. When she spoke, what she said was not what I expected.

"You remember sayin' I was actin' strange after my readin' with Madam Beaulieux at the fair?" At my cautious assentation, she continued: "Well, she said somebody close to me best be extra careful 'cause they're in grave danger."

I waited, intuiting what was coming next.

"I'm sure she was talkin' about you, Ness."

"Lizzie, with all due respect to your belief in the powers of Madam Beaulieux, she and her husband are fraudsters." This atypical authority with which my friend bequeathed the necromancer clashed with her usually canny insight of character. "The Beaulieuxs show no compunction about tricking money out of law-abiding citizens, they prey on those begging for favorable news, for a miracle.

Everything they seek is paved by chicanery. It is unimportant to them whether the price paid is for quarter of an hour with Madam Beaulieux in a fairground tent, or riches swindled by husband and wife out of the pocketbook of a wealthy, gullible victim."

"Just 'cause she's crooked doesn't mean she ain't got second sight." Fretful, Lizzie plucked at her skirts, fingers busy as a bee swarm.

"Put her prediction in context, Lizzie. Take a look around you, at where we live and the hazards we regularly face. Her prediction might easily apply to anyone. *Any one* of your acquaintances may be in danger on any given day."

"You said you've got doubts about why the Pinkerton's trackin' the Beaulieuxs, that the truth's more serious."

"If I am wrong, which, as a friend of long standing, you will recognize does not happen often . . ." My clumsy attempt to lighten her mood landed flat as the prairie. "If it allays your unease, Madam Beaulieux's prophecy may have merit. An assailant held my head underwater in Bron's trough the other night so that prophecy is now dealt with and can be forgotten. I survived, Lizzie. I am right here, safe and sound."

"For how long? You didn't see fit to confide in me you almost drowned. I heard of the trough incident 'cause Katie told me. And Madam Beaulieux didn't specify *how many* attempts were gonna be made to kill my friend. Could be more than one."

I prayed by allowing Lizzie to vent her fears she might then calm and attend my logic. When she paused I inserted: "*If* she has foreseen me in the running as victim. But time and time again I have proved annoyingly difficult to kill."

My added foray into humor, to placate her, resulted in the opposite effect.

"My Lord, Ness! People are always shootin' at you or tryin' to strangle or drown you. Don't you dare make light of my worries."

"I apologize if you see me dismissive of your feelings, Lizzie. Even knowing of this premonition of doom I still cannot—indeed, *will* not—countenance staying here to let Raff ride headlong into a situation he is unprepared for simply because a fairground prophetess cautioned I could die."

"You think seein' ghosts is normal, yet balk at a fortune-teller's warnin'?"

"They are different entities." Our debate was going in circles, chasing its tail. "I have to go. Does this mean I should find someone else to oversee the Fleur?"

"'Course not. Clay will help out."

"Thank you."

"Scat, before I change my mind."

I enveloped her in what I forecast a brief hug, but when I made to pull away she clasped me against her chest. When she released me I saw she fought tears, self-conscious of her display of emotion; as rare an occurrence as Shakey refusing a complimentary shot of liquor.

"Nathan will be with me until we reach Raff. No one would be thickheaded enough to engage either of them in hostilities, much less take them on together. I shall be well protected, Lizzie."

"Lord willin' and the creek don't rise," she replied, then shooed me out the door.

⫸⫷

Daniel waylaid me in the hallway that led to my rooms, his countenance sharing much with Lizzie's.

"What is it, Deputy?"

"Got this feelin', Miss Hennessey. A real bad feelin'," he gushed, shifting his weight, foot to foot.

"Yes?"

"Reckon Marshal Cooper's headin' for trouble."

Daniel idolized Raff, and if anything extreme were to befall the man who could do no wrong in his deputy's eyes, the boy would be inconsolable.

"I appreciate your concern." I turned from him, then turned back. "At any period did you visit Madam Beaulieux for a reading, Dan?"

"No."

"Very well. Leave this with me."

FOURTEEN

"Hungry?"

"A little."

Nathan foraged in his saddlebag, extracted an item enfolded in a spotless length of muslin, brought his mare in line with Samson and handed the parcel to me. "Chew on this."

I unwrapped the material to find Cookie's renowned pemmican. My cook added a secret ingredient to the mixing process, one he refused to divulge even when pledged recompense that ranged from monetary to promises of companionship on a cold and lonely night. I was mistrustful of his avowal, suspicious the secret ingredient a myth, that he bathed in considerable enjoyment as devotees hypothesized what it might be, frustration growing when their outlandish guesses were discarded with a sorrowful waggle of his bald, scarred head.

I nibbled at the meaty concoction then stowed the remainder. Samson's ears swiveled. A hand rested on the cantle, I twisted in the saddle, searching for whatever had caught his attention. What I learned did not please me in the slightest. I called to Nate and drew my horse in.

Raven loped toward us at a speed she could maintain all day. She dropped to a trot, deposited her hindquarters in Samson's shadow and stared up at me, as if in expectation of praise.

"Dammit! I told Cookie to shut her in the kitchen with him until we were well and truly gone. Several hours I said. Minimum. He knows she is ingenious at absconding. What are we to do with her?"

"Got no choice."

"No, but—"

"They're here now."

"They?"

"Got a friend with 'er."

"What friend?"

Nathan pointed. The scruffy yellow dog from the Beaulieuxs lagged behind my wolfhound, bright-pink tongue lolling. It reached us, collapsed, rolled onto its back then proceeded to pump its legs like it was running upside down, rubbing what I dared not imagine through its coat.

"A *man* friend," Nate said.

"Goddammit it all to hell!"

"Wanna take 'em home?"

"Of course not! We cannot afford a detour."

"Then quit with your moanin'."

"I am not moaning, Nathan," I said in a cool tone that spelled he better watch himself.

"If you say so," he mumbled, then added, quieter still: "Sure sounded like moanin' to me."

"What shall we do with them?" I ignored his prodding, exasperation already on the wane.

"Let 'em tag along."

"As you said, we do not have much choice." I chirped my stallion, presuming the dogs would fall in line. "Come on, you two."

A quick glance confirmed they trotted side by side along the trail. In spite of the inconvenience they presented, I chuckled. Raven had found a mate.

⇒⟫⟨⇐

On the outskirts of the next settlement the dogs loped nearer Samson. I arranged my hair, already braided in a thick rope, beneath my hat, shrugged on my rain slicker and fastened the toggles to my neck to imply that if not male, I was a nondescript female.

Contrariwise to my custom of dressing in apparel that displayed my assets to advantage, it was imprudent to attract unwanted attention while passing through. This reservedness, which Nate and I had deployed numerous times in the course of our travels, was foiled somewhat with the presence of Raven and the cur; they were drawcards we could have well done without.

"What is the name of this town, Nate?"

"That important?"

"No. Do you suppose we should check our guns with the lawman's office?" We rode past a stream of men who flaunted their preferred firearm on hip, thigh, or thrust through their belt. "Never mind."

Nate asked directions to the nearest livery barn and we reined our mounts down the rutted central thoroughfare, past wagons and mules loaded with supplies, saddlehorses hitched outside saloons, then into an offshoot no less quiet. Great tides of humanity surged along the boardwalk and street as residents and visitors alike went about their business.

By appearance, a goodly proportion tidied business of the previous night, eyes bloodshot, pockets empty, malodorous bodies hounded by a stink that rivaled a carcass left to rot under a broiling sun; a stink I imagined reached me atop Samson.

A number of roisterers singled me out, my bearing perhaps disclosing my gender. Some took pains to hide inquisitiveness, others were brazen. Not unexpectedly, to a man they picked another object to study when Nate fixed them with a stone-cold stare.

Amongst the throng a man of Celestial descent, eyes downcast, left a shop that sold smallgoods. I watched him glide across the uneven boardwalk. Nate happened to catch me and tracked my gaze to see what mesmerized me so. When he realized his expression darkened, although he resisted commenting. The Chinaman slid along the boardwalk and was swallowed by the crowd.

Temperate, the weather did not attain the level of warmth to induce sweat that bubbled along Nate's hairline, coursing through grooves pain had gouged into his cheeks. He wiped his forehead, surreptitiously, when he thought I did not observe him.

"I suggest you have your toothache seen to if there is a qualified practitioner hereabouts, Nate."

"Suggest all ya want."

"Let me put it like this. We are not traveling any farther until you attend that tooth. I doubt extensive treatment or surgery is required. And there, oh joyful day, is a dentist next building along."

"Accordin' to the sign he shares space with the undertaker. Tells me all I need to know."

"This is lunacy! Your face is puffed as though you have been stung by a yellow jacket. An army of yellow jackets, in fact. It must ache like crazy."

"Worse."

"Then do something about it!"

"Ness, you nag more than Annie, but I'll go see the man if it'll shut your trap."

"I am elated to hear it. At last." Nate had to feel as bad as he looked to agree to an appointment, his words thick and fat as if his tongue were swollen. "First, let us stable the horses and organize accommodation. There is a saloon by the dentist's rooms where I shall wait for you."

"Why not go to the haberdashers, or sweet shop? I'll meet ya after and get a drink. Be wantin' one."

"You do not believe it advisable to frequent saloons if on my own? I managed just fine before I met you. Besides, they are here to defend my honor." I indicated the dogs with a broad wave. "How often must I reiterate I am capable of taking care of myself?"

"Then you've a funny take what capable means."

"We can resume this discussion after your tooth is extracted."

"Can't say how much I'm lookin' forward to that."

"Which, in particular?"

"Both," he grumbled. "The same."

I decided it politic to shift our conversation to a topic of mutual concern. When we rode from Melancholy the stall where Kip McFarley's horse had billeted was empty. "Is McFarley close by, or do you think he has pushed on?"

"If him, wouldn't rest till I had to."

That made sense to me, too. Gambling on the reason behind Raff going to Hollow Oak Falls being to find the Beaulieuxs, Nate and I felt McFarley was headed there as well, compliments of Daniel spilling the contents of the marshal's telegrams. McFarley had missed the Beaulieuxs in Melancholy by the slimmest margin. Having been within sniffing distance of his quarry must have him gnashing his teeth.

The tenacity the Pinkerton had shown tracking the Beaulieuxs to lead him, ideally, to their capture, would be rewarded with gold and silver; pecuniary success combined with plaudits awarded by his peers. So the pressure to find the Beaulieuxs was likely a great burden to McFarley.

Samson and Nate's mare ensconced in their stalls, Nate and I stood in the barn entrance, weighing our next move.

"After a bed?" the hostler asked Nathan.

Solid as a locomotive engine and half as pretty, breath fetid, he reeked to high heavens of horse sweat, a smell I was not averse to but combined with stale whiskey and the consequence of hygiene practices harmful to nasal passages, it proved unbearable. I retreated a couple of steps, with no excuse, and his face hardened.

"Can you make a recommendation?" I asked.

"Rosie's. Go left, to the end of this stretch." He sketched sentiment disparate to helpfulness his mouth supplied. "Not the best rooms in the county. Not the worst."

Nate thanked him, brusquely, and we booked into accommodation that gave the impression our rooms had been ransacked by a short-sighted raccoon, then emerged into late-afternoon sunlight.

Nate's pace eased the closer we came to the dentist's premises.

"What do I see here? A grown man scared of a simple dental procedure?" I asked when he faltered outside the dentist's door, script across a transom window announcing the practitioner L.R. Sibley. "Wait until I tell the boys at the Fleur that our Nathan, pride of the fighting Irish and bare-knuckle maestro who knocked champion of the world Barnaby 'The Lion' Cortez out cold, struggled to find courage for a molar extraction."

"Stop."

"You will thank me later and accede you should have taken my advice much earlier. When this is over and done, I promise you shall drink whiskey to your heart's content." Not for the life of me could I allow a final chance to goad him pass. "To dull the pain."

"I'm warnin' you, Ness."

"You will be fine. Imagine how much better you shall feel afterward."

Nate did not appear the least convinced by my optimism, slapping my hand away when I gave him a bracing shove.

Subsequent to Nate's hesitant knock the door flung open. Tipped off-stride, Nate looked about in vain for whomever opened it, eyes soon drawn earthward.

There, he found a minute woman deserving of a berth on Shakey's list for an ideal troupe of carnival misfits. He reversed hastily and promptly stood on a foot I did not remove with sufficient speed.

"Goddammit!"

"Sorry, Ness."

The woman's limbs were plucked from the pages of a mail-order catalogue from which body parts were chosen with no thought given, or concern shown, to suitability. No limb matched its counterpart, this apparent when she hobbled to a dentist's chair bolted to the floor in the center of the room, each leg revealed a different length. Her arms shared this curse. The miniature woman lifted her skirts and climbed a wooden stepladder near the chair, thereby giving her the height and pertinent ability to see into the mouths of her patients.

"You're a lady!" Nate said.

"You may have problems with your teeth, sir, but there's nothing wrong with your powers of observation."

"You the undertaker, too?" Nate appraised a tidy store of coffins stacked against the wall.

"Currently, yes. There isn't work enough to keep busy doing one or tother," she said. "Until I have custom to fully engage in a single occupation, I must do whatever is necessary to stay solvent. Anyway, having the undertaking premises next door means it's a quick trip for those who don't make it through their treatment here. All I do is switch aprons."

Nate threw me a look of such despair I laughed, immoderately. Temper flaring he did not take kindly to this and scowled at me, then directed his scowl upon the tooth doctor. Immune to manners that loitered at the bottom of the politeness scale she ignored him. In fact, her smile broadened.

"She is fooling with you, you great clown," I said, growing annoyed with Nate's daft behavior.

The woman beckoned. "Come! Come!"

Nate hoisted himself onto the chair, soothing words of encouragement offered by L.R. Sibley and me making no dent whatsoever in his state of anguish, fear a tempest that consumed him.

"Don't worry." The woman petted Nate's arm. "A big strong man like you will be up hearty as a buck in no time."

She looked to me across Nate's chest, which rose and fell with disconcerting rapidity. "Will you wait for him?"

"No. I relinquish him to your capable hands."

Leaving the dentist's rooms I retraced my steps to the livery where Samson and the mare boarded. The mealymouthed hostler met me with a smarmy grin. I sought information from him, no more.

"I saw a Chinaman on the main street. Do they operate a laundry?"

"There's a bunch of 'em live by the river. They'll clean your clothes for a price or get you whatever else you're after."

"There is laundry I wish done."

He sized me up a beat. "If you say so."

Without Nathan's protective bulk there to deter him, the hostler's attitude skated near insolence. Bonhomie he cast about earlier, what he had presented as friendliness, was replaced with calculation that made it feel like spiders danced across my skin. I deemed it felicitous to extract myself from his company quickly as I could.

"Which is the fastest route to the river?" I asked.

"Can take you."

"That is not necessary."

"It's easy done."

"And I repeat, is not necessary."

"Don't get snitchy, lady. Just bein' polite."

"Your offer is duly noted," I replied sweetly, resisting the urge to punch him soundly on the nose to signal it a stellar plan to realign his 'polite' thoughts on me. "And duly declined. I shall find my own way."

Refusing the hostler meant getting to the river was circuitous and time-consuming, the town a rabbit warren of structures; rickety, temporary huts built with scraps, bits and pieces salvaged from trash and Nature jumbled together, with solid, respectable homes scattered in-between.

I sailed confidently down multiple side streets to find myself in a dead end, eventually compelled to interrupt rowdy pleasantries exchanged by women of dubious conduct outside a blacksmith's shop. Set right, I reoriented myself and found the Chinamen's camp.

Here, Celestials were employed taking in laundry and attending crops. Women attired in shapeless garments hoed a patch of land, turning soil in preparation for vegetables bought by patrons grateful to receive fresh produce to supplement their diet; although those who resided in town did not extend their appreciation by allowing the immigrants entry to their society.

The river coursed in a lazy arc, lending itself to diversion of gallons of water, procured by the Celestials to irrigate their gardens by implementation of ingeniously constructed channeling and dams.

Accustomed to individuals who exhibited nonchalance then crept into a miner's tent pitched beside the river, none of those toiling in the fields bothered to raise their head when I walked toward the tent.

Part of me screamed silently, begging I go order a drink before it was too late. Nathan needed me. *Raff* needed me. It was all for naught. Despite the reasonable side of my character warning I was poised to make the worst decision I had made in an awfully long while—this a declaration with significant competition, for several questionable decisions lined up vying for the honor—my feet remained precisely where they were. Raven sat, the yellow hound happy to take her lead.

The sound of water flowing over stones became less a comforting trickle to my ears, collusion with my anxious brain raising it to a pitch incommensurate with its origin. This manifestation threatened to deafen me until I dreaded falling into a faint.

I shook this sensation loose when a man dressed in a tunic and loose pants appeared. His lips did not part to emit superfluous words of welcome. Diffidence tangible, he moved aside, the tent flap swept behind him, and gestured I should enter.

I inhaled a deep breath, then exhaled with an audible *whoosh*. I could still refuse his invitation, although sensible arguments for my not entering the tent were overruled by my craving to chase the freedom sheathed by its canvas walls. Long enslaved to the source of the distinct smell that leaked through the seams and curled into the atmosphere I fooled no one, least of all myself, with falsified reluctance.

The Chinaman remained expressionless.

I could stay a while then withdraw to the saloon beside L.R. Sibley's rooms to wait on Nate. Yes, there was the perfect compromise. When ordered, Raven dropped to the ground. Unused to any form of command the cur dithered then, again, took her lead. I glanced over my shoulder, almost in expectation of finding Nate storming down the slope behind me, then stepped across the threshold.

⤜⤛⤚

Minutes later, or hours—there was no timepiece with which to tell—I heard Nathan growl outside the tent, precursor to his thrusting the flap aside to stand tall as a redwood, blocking the entryway. Once his eyes adjusted to the dim light he raked each figure that sprawled in a stupor on a cot-bed or blanket thrown on the floor—the requirement for comfort, as far as anyone present was concerned, irrelevant after the initial mind-numbing inhalation of opium vapor.

Nate stepped over a well-dressed gentleman who sucked a pipe with languid contentment, knocked the pipe I held out of my limp hand, placed an arm beneath my neck and slid the other behind my knees. He scooped me off the straw mattress on which I reclined, my head lolling, blood rushing to cloud my vision as he stepped back over the prone man, clipping his hip.

"Hey." The protest, feeble and hushed, made no mark.

The tent flap drew tight behind us. Nathan called the dogs, adjusted his hold to support my head and strode into the dark, the air fresh and vibrant, alive with currents that glinted and hissed like a lightning storm. I shivered at its touch, scatter-gun prickles harsh as bites on my exposed skin.

I stared past Nate's profile, discernible against the sky, marveling at the dense mat of stars pitched like sparkling rock crystals against the infinite cosmos. Goosebumps arose on every square inch of my body, each hair and particle dancing.

"How is your mouth, Nate?" That was what I intended to say, but was uncertain I managed to enunciate anything whatsoever.

Disinclined to answer me if, indeed, I had spoken aloud, he continued up the hill, anger fueling his legs.

I ran a forefinger down his nose, across his cheek, along his jawline. His skin felt hot as though he burned with fever, flesh puffier than when he eased onto L.R. Sibley's chair. I quailed at the thought I may have exacerbated his problems by insisting he see her while here, as there seemed little improvement after the dentist's ministrations. Perhaps he might naturally take a turn for the worse before getting better. Perhaps.

"Why, Ness?" The oft-repeated question whenever he found me in this condition whirred in the night, stern and pleading, both.

We reached the apex of the hill, the big man's stride now controlled. He paused, then I misplaced uncountable minutes as my mind wandered to a destination fabricated by my heightened senses, during which I had no conception where we were. I came to Earth when lowered onto my bed at the rooming house. Nate tugged off my boots and threw them on the floor, the sound amplified to such an extent I thought my eardrums were going to explode.

A maelstrom of light prisms brought images of people dead and buried who caressed my face, tracing the ridge of my cheekbones, running cold, spindly fingers through my hair. The dominant figure dipped her chin, thick auburn waves shielding her profile whenever I sought to identify her, and crooned a soft lullaby I recognized, although not to an end where I could place it.

Little by little the furious torrent of color calmed to form a pool that gradually separated into distinct bands, a rainbow that rose above the bed, a curved banner after heavy weather. The storm of noise that roared in my ears at a pitch and volume akin to a battlefield lessened, shifting to music played on fanciful stringed instruments, synchronized with a choir that dulled to a murmur: voices I could not detach or differentiate from each other.

I gave in to unconsciousness that beckoned, friendly, relaying promises of never-ending dreams of wellness and love, then fell down and down and down into a flooded canyon lined with slippery black rocks, water raging and unforgiving.

⟩⟩⟩⟨⟨⟨

At breakfast Nate appeared decidedly ill, a mug of coffee cooling before him. His hand would move toward the handle, hover while he considered the advisability of drinking a hot beverage before he clearly thought better of it and returned the hand to his lap.

His cheek was round and hard as an apple. When I enquired of his health and proffered it advisable he seek medical assistance, he brushed off my concern as mollycoddling, said he was capable of sitting atop a horse, and told me to leave him be because look where it got him last time he took my advice.

The state of my own health left much to be desired. Dense, low-lying fog filled my head and it required constant labor to sweet-talk my conscious mind into order, to curb its wandering.

With Nathan incapacitated, regardless how loud his assertion of fitness—once he decided on action nothing short of hogtying could dissuade him from it—for the first time in living memory, responsibility fell on me to set our day in motion.

Nate put on a brave show when we left for the livery barn, though I sensed each step giant hardship for him, and I stayed glued to his elbow in case he decided to relinquish his illusory hold on gravity and keel over to plant himself, in reflection of Eli Sargeson, in the middle of the street.

The hostler saddled Nate's mare and brought her out then he and I watched, bemused, as Nate put his foot in the stirrup, launched onto the horse, neglected to grasp the horn, and continued up and over, sliding off the far side of the mare to land heavily in the dirt. Dust billowed about him like cotton bolls, which made him sneeze, then yowl with pain.

Terse negotiations saw Nate deposited in a dung-encrusted barrow then, propelled by the belligerent hostler and his employee who each grasped a handle, he was conveyed to the rooming house amongst garbled protestations at the ignominious method of transportation. From the sidelines ribald and unflattering comments pertaining to Nate's drinking prowess, or lack thereof, provided light relief to those crowding the boardwalk.

Thankfully, Nate did not have to be wheeled far, however the goal to arrive at Rosie's with minimal discomfort to the injured party was not successful; in the street ridges and hollows were dried bone hard, and evidence—and Nate—proclaimed the hostler and his colleague did their darndest to hit every one of them.

At the rooming house onlookers helped lug Nate up the stairs to his recently vacated room. There, I settled him on the bed, where his feet hung off the end since the length of the bed did not match the length of Nate, and piled blankets on him, toes to ears, to combat his shivering.

Our hostess had traipsed after us, so I ushered her into the hallway where she agreed to minister to Nathan, her remuneration extortionate. At this juncture, I assured her in precise language if Nate was not well on the way to recovery when I came to collect him, she must anticipate my Bowie taking a morbid interest in her most valued appendages.

Calling by the physician's practice I organized the gentleman there who nursed a hangover the size of Canada to see Nathan within the hour, and succeeded when I undertook a second time to leave town—the name of which still evaded me—with just the dogs and Samson for company.

I missed Nathan terribly, for I could not remember when I last ventured anywhere without him or Raff, but a feeling of liberation stole upon me as I rode toward Hollow Oak Falls, the reassurance of the Bowie and the Derringer on the opposing calf giving me peace of mind and a sense of security that should, respectfully, be tempered by reality.

FIFTEEN

Marshal Rafael Cooper: *Hollow Oak Falls, Idaho Territory.*

Raff clapped eyes on the sheriff's office in Hollow Oak Falls, cut across the street and set the buckskin at the rack. Contrary to his approach in Fancy he figured it wise to check in here as a marshal, letting them know he'd arrived in *this* town. If an untoward . . . event . . . occurred during his stay his defense could say this showed he'd put his cards on the table.

About to dismount, he snagged on a brawny figure lolling on a chair beside the entrance to the building which, like his office in Melancholy, saw double duty as jailhouse. Recognizing the man's Stetson, its crown trimmed with beaver fur, he cussed beneath his breath, and decided against getting off his horse. His hope to talk with a deputy and avoid the man under the beaver-trimmed hat flew west. His gelding sensed his mood change and skittered sideways. Raff calmed him with low reassurances and a rub of the horse's wither.

"Rafael Cooper." The man rose and came at a lazy beat to the edge of the boardwalk. He ran a connoisseur's eye over the buckskin. "Got a nice piece of horseflesh there. Did you steal him, too?"

"Could say it's good seein' you, Kent, but Mama taught me not to lie. And I told you, I didn't steal—"

"It's Sheriff Kent to you, Cooper."

"And it's Marshal Cooper to you, Kent."

"Heard you took a pay cut and you're now town marshal of a

place the size of a mustard seed. A one-shack boil with a name like Sadness. Or is it Wretched? Sorrowful?"

Raff waited on Kent to finish his barbed jesting.

Raff had been a U.S. Marshal, where he mostly sat at a desk, but that taskwork quickly lost its shine; he wanted to be out amongst troublemakers, lawbreakers, and scalawags. When he tracked Hennessey to Idaho Territory his supporters did not want him to leave for the wilds, but in the end they let him go to Melancholy where he became town marshal. Having depended on Raff seeing the error of his ways—bait dangled to lure him back to civilization was rejected—they finally conceded defeat, filled in the paperwork, and he was cross sworn as a Deputy U.S. Marshal. Being town marshal gave him a little more standing, but titles weren't important to him, never had been unless he was proving a point.

"Won this office by the book." Kent dropped his smirk and false cheerfulness. "Didn't rely on friendships to get ahead. What are you doing in Hollow Oak?"

"I'm lookin' for a fella travelin' with a lady. Odds are they're makin' for Nevada."

"What they do?"

"Nothin' much. Just wanna chat."

"Quite the ride for a chat." Kent rearranged a wad of tobacco jammed under his lip. A stream of brown juice squirted from between stained teeth and landed by the buckskin's front hooves. "What do you want from me?"

"Checkin' if they've been here last coupla days. I see there's lots of comin' and goin' here, but they stand out. He's lame, has a brace on his leg. She's a beauty, even with her eyes all cloudy."

"Can't say I recollect anybody like that."

In a previous life, before jealousy turned his gaze green and rage took a hold of Kent's character and brain, he and Raff played games of chance together; Faro, their preference. When on a winning streak—or lying—the sheriff displayed a distinctive tick, and Raff recognized it straight away. Kent had seen the Beaulieuxs.

Frustration with Kent's fakery met jubilation. The Beaulieuxs had come through Hollow Oak, which added weight they were going where Raff suspected.

"Are you forgetting we had a war?" Kent asked. "There's a bushel of deformed men hereabouts. And my deputies are busy if this is you wanting a hand."

"Ain't askin' for help. Askin' if you saw 'em."

"What difference does it make whether I saw them or not? Guess you'll have to do this on your lonesome. As I remember, that's how you prefer to work anyway."

"Came to check my guns and tell you I'm here the night 'cause it's the civil thing to do. I'll be outta here early tomorrow."

"Glad to hear it." Sheriff Kent waved to a portly gentleman riding by on a stately blooded mare, fulfilling obligations of his position. "I'll tell you what I'm going to do. I trust you, Cooper, so I'll let you keep your weapons. You never know. You might need them."

Was Kent's offer to test Raff's nerve, with no intention behind it, said to keep him awake tonight? Or was it a threat?

"Say, isn't your town where that hellcat runs a saloon? Reece? Reeve? First name reminds me of a liquor drink."

"Reed. Hennessey."

Kent slapped his thigh. "That's it."

"She'd like bein' called a hellcat." Raff gathered his ribbons.

"So, that's how it is."

"How what is?" Raff asked, even as pride begged him not to.

Elbows rested on the guard rail, Kent tut-tutted, as though disappointed.

Raff reined his gelding into the street, the sheriff's eyes drilling holes in his back. He pulled in his horse though didn't turn when Kent called after him: "And, *Marshal*. Drusilla's gone because of you and I'm not going to go forgetting that any time soon. Deny it till you're rotting in your grave, I'll never believe you're innocent of her death."

Alive to Kent's thinking, Raff knew sure as lightning preceded thunder the sheriff aimed to light a fire under him, then use Raff's retaliatory anger as the excuse he'd shot in self-defense when Raff drew his gun. He took a steadying breath, berated his pride for not disregarding the provocation and kicked his horse around. "Drusilla was a nice lady, Kent. Can argue all you like, but truth is she's dead 'cause you beat her. You're the meanest sorta coward and I ain't gonna go forgettin' *that* any time soon."

He reined the buckskin about on its haunches, counting on Kent not having the straight-out gumption to shoot him in the back as he rode away, witnesses be damned. As he did so, a squat man casually pushed off the wall of the sheriff's office where he'd leaned, knee raised, boot against the siding. Raff relaxed when the man swung into an alleyway that ran past the jailhouse, taking his business elsewhere.

⟫⟩⟨⟨

Raff had not long taken his horse into the livery when the same fellow fired a glance over his shoulder, snuck through the barn doors, then walked briskly to where Raff readied to unsaddle the buckskin.

His visitor hooked a heel over the stall's bottom rail and leaned on the center plank, that about as far as he could reach for he was shorter than Raff's first estimation, broad as he was tall, his nose of altitude to say "Howdy" to Raff's mid-section. A wide leather belt nipped brown denim workpants in at the waist to give the notion a jokester had snaffled him in a lasso then jerked like a calf roper.

Raff returned his greeting and released the gelding's cinch.

"Overheard you talking to the sheriff." The man bumped his hat brim up his forehead with a knuckle, sizing Raff up through intelligent eyes set in a pudgy, friendly face.

"You weren't alone."

"Sheriff Kent doesn't like you."

"Don't like him much neither, so guess that makes us even."

"I'll tell you free that man's a curly wolf. A cruel, vindictive son of a bitch."

"Knew that already." Raff slipped the buckskin's bridle off and the horse dropped the bit, tongue working.

"If he's not sat outside the jailhouse watching goings on like a hawk, you'll find him in the Dusty Rose Saloon drinking and whoring while his men do his dirty work. Except the real nasty stuff. Prefers to do that himself. Kent saw those people you're after because he doesn't miss a thing."

"Knew that already, too." The gelding rubbed his sweaty cheek on Raff's thigh. Gaze trained on the buckskin's ears, Raff scratched the matted fur at their base. "If the sheriff's bad as all that, why you hangin' 'round him?"

"I've heard said it's good practice to keep your friends close, and your enemies closer. You see, Marshal, from where I'm standing it seems you could use assistance. Somebody familiar with the lay of the land. Somebody to point you the right way."

"That'd be you?"

"If you'll have me along." Despite maintaining his casual stance,

Raff saw the man's near uncontainable passion to be involved. "Not got much else to do."

"What's your name?"

"Ellington. Cam Ellington. I may not be your ideal sidekick, however I rode with McClellan." He smiled a captivating smile supported by unexpectedly white teeth. "Yep, Young Napoleon himself. I should confess my marksmanship isn't one of my better qualities. Passable probably describes it best, so if it comes to the crunch I'm amenable to standing aside so you can get on with any shooting or whatever thorny … duties you're called on to do. In my favor, my sight and hearing are miles ahead of everybody else's. During the war they used me to complement the scouts. Even the top fellows in my division weren't clever as me."

"Not sure what we're gettin' into if we find these two, so got no right askin' a man whose office it ain't to ride with me."

"You're not asking, I'm volunteering. Besides, I'm all for a bit of excitement."

"What if you hop the last rattler?"

"That sits fine with me. Got no family to cry at my funeral."

Raff studied Cam Ellington. Cam Ellington studied him right back. Assessing whether to let this stranger ride with him against taking the Beaulieuxs on by himself, if that's what it boiled down to, Raff went with his instinct. "Bring supplies. You got a horse?"

"Of sorts."

"Be here at dawn."

"Yes, sir." Ellington hesitated. "For the record, word is after the last sheriff's election closed, a box of voting slips went missing."

"That right?"

"It's common knowledge, although as you'd probably gather nobody has the courage or stupidity to bring it up with Kent. Most folks do their best to avoid having their noggin used for target practice."

"Understandable."

"Anyway, I'll see you tomorrow, Marshal." Cam Ellington doffed his hat, took stock of those strolling past the livery, then eased into the street.

⫸⫷

Raff led the buckskin out of the barn at daybreak, turning to greet his traveling companion when a horse approached. He did a double take.

"What in the blue blazes do you call that?" he asked.

"I'll ask you not insult Dasher in his hearing." Cam patted the scrawny, bow-necked, black pony he forked. "Most judge him how you are, and while I admit he's not a prepossessing specimen, his heart's the size of the Sahara Desert and he'll out-stay any animal on four legs."

Raff walked across to Ellington and blew softly into fur on the pony's neck.

"Is that some kind of Indian blessing before we head out?"

"Nope." Raff scrubbed the whiskered chin that nudged his elbow, his reward a rally of snorts that sent mucus flying and sprayed him, waist to knee. "Just seein' if he's goin' to blow over."

"Speaking on behalf of Dasher, he'd appreciate an apology for that slur."

"He'd best like waitin', then." Raff took in the pony's prominent rib cage. "You starve him, Ellington?"

"This pony eats better than a king. He'll prove his worth."

"If he can't keep up you'll have to get yourself home."

"Yes, sir."

Raff organized his ribbons and swung aboard the buckskin. Ellington brought his pony forward and they started out.

"You said Kent saw the couple I'm after. Did you see 'em too?"

"Set eyes on the lady. There's no denying she's a fetching woman. Other than her eyes, that is."

"They went south?"

"Can say for definite. Saw them go thataway myself."

"My thinkin' is they're goin' to the bottom corner of Nevada by way of Salt Lake City."

"If they're doing that, they'll turn about five miles on."

"Behind the hill shaped like a cougar's head?"

"You're familiar with this county, Marshal?"

They rode past the last house on the fringe of Hollow Oak Falls and Raff tapped his horse to a rhythmic jog. He ignored the question.

"Anyway, there's a cutoff." Ellington set his prying aside. "Shaves off a fair amount of time. If our couple know about it they'll get off the road and go up the hills over there, through Howling Wolf Pass. If they're unaware of it we'll be dodging their shadows in no time. Well, that's if the mountain man who lives up there doesn't take exception to us ambling through his front yard."

"He dangerous?"

"Opinions differ. He's a lump-head named de La Salle. Abraham de La Salle. His brain got spun wrong-side-up by the war. He considers the mountain his domain and his alone. Doesn't view anybody kindly who takes liberties and uses it as a thoroughfare. Likes to shoot at people. He's never hit anybody, so he doesn't shoot great, which is a saving grace."

"Could be he wants to scare 'em, not kill 'em."

"Maybe." Ellington sounded polite, if unconvinced. "Hal Panchez was dry-gulched coming over the pass on return from Trinity last year. Rumor has it Hal got such a fright when de La Salle fired a shot at him he pressed the trigger before getting his pistol fully out of his holster. Put a bullet clean through his leg. Careless. He never was handy with a gun.

"Come to think on it, he's never been handy at anything much. When young, if a kid was to suffer an accident, it was always going to be Hal. If a simple process could be made difficult, Hal found a way. Why, I remember when we were, oh, eight, nine years old, we sneaked onto Old Man Peddart's property because Mathew Lowery dared us to retrieve Hal's slingshot. Mathew had thrown it into a tree in retaliation for . . ." He fielded Raff's expression. "Well, that version's a long story."

"You sayin' this one ain't?"

"I'd gone with Hal for support." Ellington forged ahead. "We'd have gotten away with it, too, if that damned fool Hal hadn't fallen out of the tree and broken his dang leg. Snapped like a turtle. My word, I haven't thought of that since I don't know when. Funny, isn't it, how revisiting an incident prompts all sorts of other memories?"

"Tell me, Ellington. Ever give that jaw of yours a rest?"

"When I'm asleep." Ellington grinned. "Though, saying that, I've been informed even then it isn't guaranteed."

"So you know, just 'cause you're talkin', doesn't mean I'm listenin'."

"I'll bear that in mind."

⇛⇚

The sweltering sun blazed, a dazzling ball overhead, when Ellington hauled in his pony.

"The trail to Howling Wolf Pass starts over there, Marshal."

"Wait here."

Raff sent the buckskin on, sweeping the area for signs horses had peeled off the road in the last while. No tracks led into thick stands of pine lining the trail to the pass and his stomach clenched. If all went well, they should catch up to the Beaulieuxs before too long.

He waved Ellington over and they chirruped their mounts into the woods.

⫸⫷

"Stay right where you are."

The command rang out of nowhere.

"Oh wow," Cam said.

"Get off your horses, gentlemen. Or, rather, your horse and whatever the hell you call that sorry excuse for an animal." A cultured British accent polished as a monocle, rubbed to softness round the edges, wound through the trees. "And stick your paws in the air."

Raff and Cam did as asked, movements stepwise, deliberate.

An unkempt individual quit the shelter of a gnarly pine they had passed some yards back. Tall as Raff he wore a bearskin tunic—the grizzly's head still attached—a wolf pelt used as one sleeve, a cougar skin the other, breechclout and beaded moccasins. Hair plaited in a braid hung past his chest. Raff reckoned it fortuitous he and Ellington stood upwind, for he imagined the stench rolling off the man equaled that of the den where the bear once spent its winters.

"Where's these famous senses you told me about?" Raff muttered.

"Might be a jot out of practice," Ellington replied.

The sandbagger subjected them to intense scrutiny then lowered his Remington.

"I had suspicions it was you, Tala." He came forward until nose to nose with Raff. "I wanted to be sure before doing anything . . . rash."

"That why you've been with us the last mile?"

"Hah! You knew I was there? Here I am thinking you were getting old and losing your faculties."

"Can we put our *paws* down?"

"By all means!"

"Good to see you, Abe," Raff said, lowering his hands. "Wondered where you took yourself."

"Now you know, we can both rest easy."

An off-kilter grin sprung to Abe's face when he clasped Raff's upper arms inside an iron-hard grip.

Ellington lowered his hands, too, worried the bear-clad man might reconsider his directive and shoot them. "Are you friends?"

"We marked each other's dance cards once upon a time." Abe took a good look at Cam. "Who are you?"

"Cam Ellington." Cam thrust out his hand. When Abraham disregarded it, Cam rubbed at a nonexistent mark on his pants as if that were his intention all along.

"Ellington here's ridin' with me a stretch, Abe. Told me about this trail. Said there's a lump—"

"I'm sure Abe isn't interested in minor details, are you, Abe?"

"It's Abraham to you, youngster." De La Salle slipped the Remington's sling over his shoulder. "Let's get ourselves a mug in our fists and you can enlighten me why you're here."

A whistle shrilled, so close to Cam's ear it deafened him, momentarily. He tapped his ear in an attempt to dislodge echoes that reverberated around his skull.

"Come on, Harriet," Abraham called.

A speckled fawn emerged from the woods and trotted to the men on dainty hooves.

"Harriet?" Raff asked.

"Yes. Harriet. I found her beside her dead mama and named her for my wife. Can't remember my reasoning behind that now because this girl is a far more genial soul." Abraham petted the fawn's head. "Also prettier than my wife when I consider it. That woman resembled a retreating organ grinder's monkey. In fact, put the rear end of a monkey and Harriet—my wife—side by side, she'd make the monkey seem appealing."

"She can't've been all bad," Raff said. "You married her."

"Well, that's what she told me. Had to take her word for it since I couldn't recall meeting her, let alone partaking in any kind of ceremony. Struck pan loads of color on a claim I'd been working at Tucker's Creek, and after celebrating into the night was liquored to my eyeballs. Woke up next morning with a thumping headache, an unhappy stomach, and a wife I didn't recognize." Abraham noticed Cam's attention had wandered and he stood, head tilted, fixed on the trail he and Raff had ridden. "What do you hear, young man?"

"Somebody's coming."

SIXTEEN

Even a small mouse has anger.
—*Native American proverb*

Samson began to favor his off-fore early afternoon. Running my hand elbow to coronet, I breathed a sigh of relief when I felt no heat in his joints. I tapped his fetlock and he lifted his hoof, exemplary manners then deserting him. He leaned on me and I staggered beneath his weight, his co-operation restored after a jab to his barrel.

His shoe was working loose. To continue riding him could see my horse pull up lame, and I carried no implement with which to either hammer the nails back in or remove the shoe.

My reliance on Nathan and Raff extended to them being prepared for any eventuality, their saddlebags packed with food, coffee, and a handy tool that performed many and varied functions that included rectifying loose shoe disasters.

I released Samson's fetlock and straightened, spine clicking. Despite my fatigued state I had tossed and turned the previous night, the bed assigned me so uncomfortable I transferred the pillow and thin quilt provided to a bedroom chair not a lot less accommodating. Sleep had been neither rapid in approach nor committed to longevity and now, amongst additional desires, I yearned for sleep, preferably in my own bed.

Stood at the roadside I wondered what to do. Samson spied vegetation that appealed and, taking advantage of my distraction, tugged me over to it, snatching clumps of grass when not met by my usual resistance to his eating with the bit in his mouth. Raven and the yellow dog drafted a shadow-dipped hollow for a resting spot, lying flat on the warm, dry earth.

The benefit of a well-traveled route was—depending on whether you were riding toward or away from something—it generally did not take long until help trotted over the horizon. My rescuer forked a splendid gray stallion that took an immediate dislike to Samson and showed commitment to engaging him in a hoofed duel, so his rider and I did not speak until a workable gap separated our horses. The gray pranced, tail high, unwilling to keep still.

His near monosyllabic owner—as plain and dull as his horse was handsome—offered his services on learning my predicament. I held the gray while the man took a complicated instrument from his kit and soon held Samson's offending shoe.

"There's a fort on a bit with a blacksmith's shop," he said and put the shoe in my saddlebag, came to where I held his stallion and retrieved the gray's reins.

"I am beholden to you, sir."

With a bare, sharp dip of his chin he mounted, wheeled his horse, and continued down the trail.

I clambered onto Samson and with the dogs at his heels arrived at the fort less than ten minutes later.

We took a well-marked path to a rectangle-shaped stone building with a courtyard in the middle. Huge wooden gates out front turned it in to an impenetrable fortress if under attack, but with the gates open it presented a welcoming façade to all comers.

Sent around a corner by a rugged journeyman, I rode onto an expansive yard where people and animals mingled. A clean-cut young gent brought a shay drawn by a mare the color of clay out of a barn, also with doors opened to the sunny day, to where a woman of similar age waited. He handed his sweetheart into the shay, leaped in beside her then weaved through milling livestock and past me, transmitting a sociable greeting.

To the right, crammed in a well-ordered garden, row upon row of vegetables grew. Women toiled there, one of whom placed a wooden tray in the furrow at her feet and massaged her lower back. She stepped carefully over fluffy growth into the neighboring row where, on seeing I observed her, she raised a hand to wave most affably. Embarrassed when caught staring I returned her wave and slipped off my horse.

Ahead was a low-slung structure, a row of horseshoes of varying sizes nailed to a support beam running the length of the building. It did not take capacious imagination to figure this the blacksmith's shop. Nearby stood a hulking, ugly ox, belly supported by a sling, rear hoof clenched between the knees of a hefty man who finished hammering and dropped the hoof when I stepped around the ox's head.

"We shoe oxen who'll be carting over volcanic ground as its particularly wearing on their hooves. If you happened to be curious." Of craggy features and indeterminate age, when his sooty eyes—set beneath bushy brows to rival those of the Pinkerton agent, McFarley—landed on me they shone with the sweetest light a human being can emit. He withdrew a square cloth from baggy tan pants, wiped his brow then folded the cloth, precisely, and put it back into his pocket. "There are two pieces to the shoe because, as a young lady like you will be aware, these fellows have cloven hooves."

"May I enquire of the reason behind the sling?" I asked.

"They can't balance," he said.

"Is that a fact?"

"Yes. The silly creatures can't balance on three legs." He walked around the rear end of the ox, slapping the beast's rump as he went, this done more out of affection than to discipline the animal.

"Did you ever hear such a thing?" A voice brushed my shoulder. The speaker moved to stand at my hip, her profile revealing the woman who waved to me across the garden. "It seems when Earth's creatures were attributed peculiarities, their creator exhibited a delightful sense of humor." She smiled. "I am Sister Reem." Her smile grew wider if that were possible, jocundity transferred to the blacksmith. "And this is my husband."

Ah, my Good Samaritan neglected to inform me the fort was a Latter-day Saint stronghold. This did not bother me unless neglect of my religious education and practices became a topic to prompt reversal of their largesse. Although, would that not grate against principles held of import to them?

"I see your horse is missing a shoe."

"He is, but I have it in my saddlebag. A gentleman who providentially appeared on the trail removed it."

Brother Reem proffered a chapped hand and I passed him the shoe.

"That's an impressive horse you've got there."

"Thank you."

"How about them?" He nodded to Raven and the cur. "There's livestock here we don't want pestered. Must we worry those dogs could misbehave?"

"I shall tether them, if you prefer."

"Please, do."

I retrieved the lasso tied to my saddle and strung Raven and the yellow cur together. Unpracticed in restraint the wolfhound shook her head repeatedly and chewed on sections of leather she could reach. Her friend plopped on his hindquarters, content to watch activities around the yard.

Brother Reem proved quick and efficient. Sister Reem stayed to monitor her husband, taking as much delight in his economy of movement as he took enjoyment in a service well done. In no time, after liberal thanks to Brother Reem, I was leading my animals to the gate, cautioned to release the dogs when past the fort boundary, no earlier.

Whether in budding sistership or to make sure I left the premises and did not double back to steal items of worth, Sister Reem accompanied me, delivering a stream of chatter that provided interesting but nonessential information about the fort. She petted the dogs when I bid farewell, although gave no indication of leaving me to resume my journey. Were there not chores that needed attending?

That attitude was uncharitable so I quashed it at once, spurning a pressing urge to jump on Samson and kick him to a gallop soon as I could graciously do so. Increasingly suspicious Sister Reem judged me a subject worthy of her cause, I had no wish to partake in difficult conversation that would tarnish our interaction.

I held Samson and the dogs in place to allow three Indians to cross in front of me. They did not enter the gates but were met there by a middle-aged woman who spoke briefly to the taller of the three then handed him a bulging hessian sack.

"Many Indians have developed a taste for coffee, amongst other provisions," Sister Reem supplied, noting the transaction. "We distribute what we can."

Raff had spoken of Indian wars of the past, mentioning in that context settlers whose lives were spared, their property left untouched because of an alliance with the Native combatants.

The Indians thanked their benefactor and wandered toward the barn, at home in the fort environs. I watched them go, filled with sorrow how their lives had changed so, against their will and within a generation.

"We adhere to the dictate of our predecessors who vowed it better to feed them, not fight them," Sister Reem added as the men went into the barn.

If we did not fight them in the beginning, there would be no requirement to feed them. I caught myself before the necessity to vocalize my opinion triumphed, for it would be the height of rudeness and inexcusable when my welcome was extended with generous, open arms. However, this did not preclude freedom to think it.

※

Exhausted made no dent in describing my condition when Hollow Oak Falls came within range. The dogs were plain tuckered out, especially the yellow cur, and I had reined Samson to a walk so they could keep up with him. Samson's rhythmic gait relaxed me as well as a soothing melody played close to my ear might do and, chin on my chest I dozed, coming to with a start and a crick in my neck.

The sun began to descend behind tree-covered hills, commencing her voyage to the other side of the world to bring light and sparkle to countries and islands spawned in wild blue oceans I would never see. Shadows lengthened, and dream-induced visions anchored in fantasy that evoked forests dark, impenetrable, and home to mythical creatures peppered my brain.

Travelers in the opposite direction were sparse, a recent band of men yipping their horses on, keyed up to make their destination before nightfall. A solitary rider rode our tail, far enough behind not to be bothersome, but close enough my horse's ears flicked intermittently; the dogs would pause to note where the rider was in relation to us, then resume a lackluster trot.

Turbulent falls thumped, a ferocious noise that rose with each step Samson took, sinking into cadence with dull throbbing at the center of my forehead that graduated to full-blown thunderous applause when the Hollow Oak Falls came into view.

I nudged my horse to the water a safe distance from eddies and foam that churned and blossomed at the base of the waterfall. He snorted, dropped his head and buried his muzzle. The dogs caught us up and waded into the river to drink also, belly deep, tongues lapping a mile a minute.

A pair of bearded French trappers paddled around the bend ahead, guiding their bark canoe against the current. They stared through me as though I were a specter of light, a product of fertile imagination. They drove into the far bank and leaped nimbly out of the vessel, dragged it to flat ground where they flipped it over to enable portage, hiked it above their heads then vanished into the woods.

Ghosts who placed no demands on me were a rarity, my pleasure at being left alone, snubbed by the trappers, matched by all too uncommon relief.

Dismounting I crouched by Samson, lucent water spinning in pinwheels at my feet, cupped my hands and splashed the cold river water onto my forearms, to my elbows, then sat on my heels and closed my eyes, spray misting my face.

When I opened my eyes Raven and the cur, thirsts satiated, had waded deeper and now swam parallel to the riverbank, downriver. I called them, insistent when their reluctance to make shore became apparent. I did not put it above Raven—patently the ringleader—doing this deliberately, to test my patience.

In time the rebellious canines swam in a perfect semicircle and returned to the bank. I skipped backward with a second to spare, tripping in my haste to avoid their rigorous shaking that sent multitude skeins of water into the air.

The rider on my heels rode out of the dusk. He did not acknowledge me, perhaps deaf from weariness; he urged his flagging horse to a pace munificently described a jog and pointed it toward Hollow Oak Falls township. When man and horse were gone, I realized I had fully expected the horseman to be Agent Kip McFarley. Where had the man gotten to?

I tugged absently at a reed growing in a bunch of scraggly plants by the river's edge. It resisted my efforts, so I hitched a trouser leg, withdrew the Bowie from its custom sheath and sliced through the stem. I brought it to my eye, recalling a time when Raff and I watered our horses near marshes many miles from here. He had procured a knife and done what I had just done, then gave me the reed and told me to look through it. Indulging him, I did as asked, to discover it hollow.

"Hold your nose, put it between your lips and breathe," he directed.

Battling disquiet with the thought of restricted air flow I had followed his instruction, surprised how easy it was to sustain even breaths.

"There was a well-known soldier and scout called Captain Samuel Brady, famous for leapin' a gorge across the Cuyahoga River," Raff said.

"He did this because . . ."

"Sandusky Indians were chasin' him."

"A grand incentive. There were too many to fight?"

"Hard to do when they'd taken his clothes and guns."

"Goodness, he was in a tight spot."

"They'd captured him originally and were gonna celebrate by torturin' him to death. He escaped from 'em but they gave chase and had gotten him cornered. He'd no chance to get away except by leapin' over the river, which he did, a distance it's said was thirty feet. He landed the other side with a leg wound.

"Made it to a lake where he hid beneath a submerged log. It's said he breathed through a reed till his pursuers gave up searchin' for him." Raff had plucked the reed from my grip and rolled it between thumb and forefinger. "Did that happen? It'd be real difficult to do. Others say the log was hollow so he could keep his head above the water and breathe fine. Heard the Indians walkin' on the log. Makes a good yarn."

I stashed the reed in my breast pocket, wiped my hands dry on my trousers, hauled myself into the saddle and guided Samson to the road.

⫸⫷

At the entrance to Hollow Oak proper, places of worship stood as sentries. Were they built across from each other as a last offer of redemption before heathens barged through the gates of Hell? Were they a frontage behind which warring factions planned domination over their rival, who held an opposing interpretation of the Bible, as well as an opposing side of the street? I imagined two wizened religious fanatics drawn to this town and its residents, each ablaze with lust to bring the word of the Lord to the masses whether they were predisposed to listen or not.

My surmising gained full flight, fatigue and remnants of opium that stuck with grim determination to the least assertive droplets of blood in my body contributing to these phantasms.

Did these men dismantle invisible barriers that separated their orders of belief, confer, then agree to divide slim pickings, a 'One for you, one for me' system to divvy up the sinful? Good luck to you, I thought, their mission folly, unobtainable as the glowing, phosphorous moon.

Handing my Winchester to an official in a building with barred windows, I made sure he would be there early next morning so I could retrieve it then ducked and dodged to where the animals were tethered.

Compared with Melancholy the township of Hollow Oak Falls was a conurbation. It spread like a disease, running rampant, bursting with delights unbound and paper promises it had neither motivation nor intelligence to uphold. Everything appeared in abundance, particularly drinking establishments. Streams of men jostled to get into saloons, raucous with anticipation or calm for the moment, affairs, whatever these entailed, concluded for the day, or postponed until the morrow.

If I had held even a thumbnail of interest where the two clergymen were, that interest would not have remained unsatisfied. They had staked claims outside neighboring watering holes, fain to educate an apathetic tide of humankind. Dismissed by the majority, heckled by those who condescended to react to their preaching, their voices clashed while each sought to do the impossible—drown the crowd, and the other, out.

"'Know ye not that the unrighteous shall not inherit the kingdom of God?'" Of striking bearing, the closer of these men attained the height of Nathan, possessed an iron-gray beard to his sternum, and was dressed top to toe in black. He boomed, his voice a match for his size: "'Be not deceived: neither fornicators, nor idolaters, nor adulterers, nor effeminate, nor abusers of themselves with mankind.

Nor thieves, nor covetous, nor drunkards, nor revilers, nor extortioners, shall inherit the kingdom of God.'"

He put forth a compelling argument. Arms flung above a shock of white hair, Bible held prisoner in a beefy fist, he kept his eyes shut until he finished reciting the passage. Perhaps given divine forewarning his eyes snapped open, locked on me, and traced my progress their shrewd, unblinking gaze predatory. Nostrils flared he twitched, catching the musk of fresh prey on the breeze.

Too far down the road for redemption to be considered practicable, even if coveted, I refused to heed a man seeking to annul whatever pleasure the general populace managed to scrimp out of tough, spare lives—a man determined to replace hard-fought-for joy with rules upholding God-loving ways that included wearing clothing bland as milk and, worst of all to my mind, no liquor of which to speak.

"Right there, Samson, is a prime example of being wise in one's own conceit," I murmured.

The other minister stuttered partway through similar discourse, unsure why his competitor had fallen silent until he saw me and stared, too, a maniacal tint to his expression. Did they strip me bare of my piteous disguise, recognizing who and what I was, conspiring to intimidate, united in loathing and distrust? Often, all it took to rile a zealot was to prod, to agitate what they held dear. I lifted my chin, blew each a kiss, and rode straight on past.

I checked the dogs, fretting they might stray into the path of a wagon or suffer injury from the hoof of a saddlehorse, or obstreperous mule. His haunches tense, the yellow dog's tail grazed the street, the sheer number of people, animals, and the racket of the seething town upsetting him. Keen to find lodgings I chirked Samson on.

To accommodate those staying here or visiting from farther afield, I presumed there were maybe four liveries in Hollow Oak, if not more. If my calculations of his progress were correct, Raff had arrived that day. Riding from Fancy, situated to the southeast, I figured him to overnight the buckskin in the first livery he came to by Hollow Oak's southern entrance, so I lodged Samson at the first barn I saw by the northern entrance. Raff had no call to go into a livery that did not house his gelding, so the likelihood of his stumbling across my stallion should be minimized.

On the off-chance Raff defied logic I requested a stall near the rear egress of the barn, refusing a mustachioed Mexican's offer to supervise Samson's comfort, although I accepted his proposal to send a boy to fetch grain and an armful of hay. I led my horse down the aisle to a vacant stall, joined there by the boy who juggled Samson's victuals in thin ropey arms, trying not to drop them.

He deposited his load in the appropriate containers, ran off, then came back with a bucket of fresh water which he slotted into a bracket on the wall. This accomplished, he loitered, watching me curry the stallion.

Samson groomed and comfortable, I beckoned the boy. His reticence to comply tweaked sympathy, his age and build reminiscent of Mouse, the missing youngster who worked for Bron. Leaving Samson with his nose in the feed trough I latched the stall behind me. The child backed away, with tear-jerking caution.

"Come over here. I mean you no harm." When he stood before me I stooped to be eye-level with him. "What is your name, young man?"

"Will, miss."

"How are you at keeping secrets, Will?"

"Good, miss." He brightened and ceased fidgeting.

"May I charge you with a task and request you not tell anyone I asked you to do it?" At his wary nod, I said: "Please go to the livery barn nearest the southern end of town."

"Mr. Lafferty's?"

"If that is the name of the person who runs it, yes. See if a tall buckskin is lodged there. He has a snip on his nose like a swish of white paint and a stocking on his right hind leg. Try not to be seen. I shall wait here."

"What if Mr. Sanchez wants me, miss?"

"Is he the man who owns these stables?"

"Yes, miss."

"If he should ask your whereabouts I shall explain to Mr. Sanchez you are running an errand for me. Do not worry on that score."

Twenty minutes later the boy hared into the barn.

"Horse is there, miss. A big Indian's brushin' him."

"Thank you, Will. You were marvelous." I handed him a cartwheel dollar which he bit on, hard, then slipped into a pocket, loath to leave hold of this unexpected bounty.

If Raff headed out he would do so at first light, it being positively idiotic to set off in the dark. As consequence of this, my rising early was imperative for I could not risk waking at leisure, to sunlight, to find my quarry gone. Samson must be saddled and ready at daybreak if I were to stand a ghost's chance of keeping track of Raff.

With no idea where Raff was going from here I had to stay concealed and follow him best I could. Once Hollow Oak Falls was a distant memory, and on making my presence known to him—which indeed I must to raise my concerns regarding McFarley, and the unspecified threat posed by the Beaulieuxs—he would have no option than to take me with him whether amenable or otherwise. Intimacy with his qualities suggested he would lean decisively toward *otherwise*.

Meantime, if he were to chance upon me I held no doubt he would insist I either return to Melancholy or cool my heels in Hollow Oak Falls, to await his finishing whatever involved him, after which he would chaperone me home.

Events in our checkered past saw him obliged to manipulate my involvement in certain adventures, going to extraordinary lengths to keep me safe, for my own good. Needless to say, that was his terminology, not of my choosing.

Years ago, in a situation fraught with danger, this necessitated Raff luring me to a sublime hotel where he locked me in a bedroom and stationed an accomplice, who had been given strict instruction to allow no one entry or exit, outside the door. He went so far to warn this guard if he valued his life, any attempt by me to decamp must be squashed or the guard would suffer consequences.

As ill luck would have it, another man with similar instruction was posted beneath the window I slithered out of at the first opportunity. He had bundled me, protesting at the top of my lungs, to my room, impervious to my outrage and bribes that soared the closer we came to the sumptuous prison cell I had recently fled.

Now, my venturing outside held potential of my meeting Raff or McFarley, wherever the Pinkerton might have taken himself, so I reserved a bed and evening meal at a rooming house near where Samson was stabled.

The woman who ran the accommodation proposed an excessive fee for the dogs to stay with me. Hungry, at the end of my tether and disinclined to argue after observation they were sure to make less mess than many of the human beings who walked through her doors, I paid the amount asked, drawing the line when she told me to lock the dogs in the laundry while we ate. After much fussing, she bowed to my immovable stance on the matter, and said they could stay outside an alcove off the passageway bequeathed the grand and mis-designated title 'dining hall'.

I fed Raven and her mate in the fenced yard before supper, an excuse to shake prying eyes and guzzle whiskey out of the flask replenished from bottles stashed in my saddlebags, wrapped in items of clothing to lessen possibility of breakage. I smoked four cigarettes, nose to tail, while the dogs ate their meal, completed ablutions then investigated the property, snouts rarely lifted off the ground, the cur marking the territory his while he explored.

Summoned to supper by the landlady who employed a strident tone, I did not rush, but in my own time called the dogs and repaired to the dining hall. Directed to sit, I faced an unidentified and unidentifiable cut of meat congealing in a porridge of fat on a chipped china plate at my place setting.

Our hostess protected a serving dish of potatoes like a card dealer protects their deck, distributing stingy portions to each diner as if the Irish potato famine were ongoing and each scrap of food must be accounted for at close of the evening. My appetite dwindled when confronted by the unappetizing meal, and all I could bring myself to ingest was a solitary, over-cooked potato.

Five women were seated at table. A blend of colors and chronicles, three were subdued and circumspect, the balance quick to relate their history, plotting to ingratiate themselves as friends, amity brittle. All who sat around the oval walnut table appeared intimate with the dining ritual and our landlady's quirks, inquisitiveness about me outstripping any I held of them. With no delay, when the landlady and her slatternly maid cleared the gelatinous ruins of our meal, I disengaged myself and walked the dogs to the livery to check on Samson.

I had also paid the rooming house cook a ridiculous sum of money to wake me when she arose a half hour before dawn so, half asleep, I retrieved my rifle and threw my saddle onto Samson, thankful he showed no adverse effects after his exertion of previous days: his training regime preceding the Melancholy fair holding him in excellent stead.

Reins bunched in my fist, I led him to the rear door of the livery and onto the adjoining street, past shuttered houses, store fronts, and saloons emptied of revelers and rabble. Windows gleamed with lanternlight to guide early risers, or those expected to lurch home after a late night spent drinking, or in the arms of an accommodative painted cat. Attuned to my mood, the dogs picked the need for silence and padded by my side.

Near where Will told me Raff had stabled his gelding, I rested a hand on Raven's head to indicate she must stay close, peeped round the corner of the Mercantile and, breath shallow, focused on the barn doors across the way.

After a few minutes Raff came out of the barn and conversed with a plump gentleman astride a pony that looked in no condition to attain the end of the street without toppling, much less venture past town boundaries. Raff mounted his buckskin and the men turned south, leaving me to wonder what gave Raff cause to go in the direction from which he had just ridden.

I waited until they were swallowed by early-morning mist, shoved my foot in the stirrup, and climbed aboard Samson.

Luck continued to ride alongside my canine allies and me, the sun eager to repose in a sky the indigo hue of a new bruise. The number of travelers I encountered increased as the morning wore on, Hollow Oak Falls a thriving community, in a thriving area, and although drawing a strip of ribald attention from wagon driver to cowboy I was, by and large, left unmolested.

Early afternoon I started to panic, thinking I might have lost Raff and his porcine friend. Cursing, I booted Samson to a canter then pulled him in, sharply.

There is a particular curve to a horse's neck, a unique set to its tail. How a rider sits in the saddle, the angle of his body completes a puzzle in the unconscious mind. If familiar to a person, these characteristics can be recognized from afar, which is why I realized it was Raff and the round man who guided their horses to a stretch of grass that bordered the road near three hundred yards ahead. If I had come along a minute later I would have missed the marshal and his companion—whomever he was—going into the trees.

Where they left the road I saw an enshrouded trailhead a stone's throw away. When feeling benevolent and in possession of the required stoicism, Raff had deigned instruct me in rudimentary tracking, so after scanning the area between the road and where the men vanished, I was certain no other riders had entered the woods at that point. Even so, I practiced caution when nudging Samson forward.

Forests were often arduous to navigate for me and caused varying levels of distress. There were relatively quiet tracts, home to a lackadaisical phantom, but with others it seemed the dead of a small county resided in their spiritual form in trees and undergrowth adjoining the trails. This heightened awareness of my surroundings kept me on tenterhooks.

Samson performed a crabwise jig, my anxiety at what might lie ahead transferring to the big horse beneath me. I smoothed his neck to relay confidence, sure I did not fool him, doing my darndest to control apprehension and emotion but failing, miserably.

I called Raven, wanting the dogs to stick close by the stallion, feeling disproportionate relief when she and the cur fell in either side of Samson. Their presence offered nothing in respect to protecting me from insistent ghosts, but the security Raven and her besotted acolyte afforded went toward maintaining a semblance of calm.

Interested where the trail headed and to what purpose Raff took it, I clucked my horse and started him up the slope, into the pines.

SEVENTEEN

A frog does not drink up the pond in which he lives.
—*Sioux proverb*

An hour after entering the forest stealth no longer reigned priority, for I rounded a bend and came face to face with Raff, the man with the skeletal pony, and an apparition cloaked in animal skins, beside whom skittered a young doe.

Raff gloomed, brows scrunched, hands braced on his hips; the lumpy fellow considered me with undisguised fascination; the loose-jointed figure dressed like a tumble of wild beasts walked across to Samson and stroked his muzzle.

Raven's nose twitched when she caught the doe's scent. She executed a series of warning growls when the man approached but lay down when instructed, although continued to invest unhealthy interest in both of them. The yellow dog sat beside her, panting.

"Aren't you a welcome sight, Hennessey," the apparition said. Initially at a loss to identify him, his voice joggled familiar strings. "Must be the loveliest woman I've laid eyes on in years."

"Abraham?" I jerked my feet free of stirrups and slid off Samson. "As I live and breathe, is that you under all that fur?"

"It is." His contagious grin broadened when he pulled me to him, enveloping me in a hug that went a fair way to crushing my ribcage. "Let me take a proper look at you." He released me, though left his hands rested on my shoulders. "My eyes didn't deceive me. You're as pretty as ever, if not prettier."

"You were ever an exponent of flattery. Now, if I were able to reply in kind . . ." I saw a charge, enigmatic, flash in his brown eyes. "You are not what is commonly described pretty, Abraham, but you appear well. *Are* you well?"

"Extremely, my dear, and I thank you for asking." His grin faltered, but he reclaimed it before turning to Raff. "Let's adjourn to my abode and you can tell me why you are all here."

"Ain't got time, Abe—"

"Nonsense, Tala. Have a cup of coffee with me then you can be on your way. After all, I may be in a position to assist you."

"Better be quick." Raff's gaze rippled over me to the track. "Where's Nate, Miss Reed?"

"He stayed in the town prior to Hollow Oak Falls, Marshal Cooper." Clearly, according to Raff, we were still on formal terms. "He had a tooth extracted there but developed an infection and was so deathly ill staying atop his horse was beyond him."

"Must be real sick to let you come on by yourself."

"He was not consulted in the matter."

"Doesn't surprise me."

"Now, before we go any farther, are you not overlooking the custom of introducing associates, gentlemen? Who, may I ask—" I signaled the pale-faced man who absentmindedly rubbed the chest of his skinny pony "—is this?"

"Cam Ellington, Miss Reed. It's sure great to meet you."

"And what is a personable fellow as yourself doing in this prodigious company, Mr. Ellington?"

"Mindin' his business," Raff said, sidestepping the worst of a geyser of hair that ballooned about us when the cur, hind leg put to vigorous use, attended a sudden itch. "Where'd you get this mangy critter?"

"He sheltered under the house where the Beaulieuxs were living in Melancholy. I think he may have belonged to them. Raven has developed a fondness for him."

"It's a wonder she didn't rip out his throat," Raff said.

"That is what I would have expected also."

"Do you know who he reminds me of with all that yellow fur?" Ellington asked.

"This'll be interestin'," Raff said.

"General Custer."

"Hope he doesn't come to as bad an end." Abraham bent to fondle the dog's ears.

And, just like that, Custer, the stray mutt became.

"If everybody's introduced to your satisfaction, Miss Reed, can we get goin'?"

"Of course, Marshal. Lead on, Abraham."

⟫⟪

The three of us mounted up and trooped after Abe and the fawn, the dogs bringing up the rear. Abraham soon guided us off the trail to a sun-speckled clearing.

A basic cabin built with care, its builder commander of a perfectionist's eye, backed on to trees at the far side of the clearing. I imagined the dim interior of this humble retreat, fusty air entrapped in a protective timber womb, a haven for a sad, damaged man.

How did it feel to dwell in this minikin cabin over winter months when the snows came? Nauseous at the idea, fear of confined spaces injected my veins, black dots afflicting my vision.

On meeting Abraham de La Salle I read in him despondency,

profound disenchantment with the world and plundering vicissitudes of those who roamed its continents demanding all upon them as their prize. This, I could relate to.

Raff had sketched an outline of Abraham's past, enough to explain his friend's behavior. Abraham was always kind and respectful with me, but these tales added another dimension to his nature and complexities. I prayed never to be in a position to witness his tortured depths or how they manifested in action.

We hobbled our horses to let them graze. The doe tottered on legs thin as spindles to lip at branches and leaves at the clearing edge, neck stretched, ears fluttering. Raven lay beside me, tracing her movements.

A sweet smell permeated the air, however, I could not detect whence the aroma originated, nor which aromatic plant Abraham burned. Moving around his camp at home, and at peace, he propped the cabin door open with an old saddle that had graced a horse of which there was no other sign, and retrieved coffee off a shelf inside, requesting Raff fill the coffee pot atop a water barrel he would find behind the cabin.

"You see anythin' unusual in these parts, Abe?" Raff asked, once we were seated on segments of a tree trunk chopped to different heights set beside the fire, coffee poured and in hand. He sipped his drink and grimaced, then placed the steaming mug by his boot. Raff preferred his coffee lukewarm for some inscrutable reason, the brew too hot for him at present. "Last few days?"

"Not seen much of anything or anyone, let alone something you'd consider suspicious. Why?"

Raff retrieved his mug and considered its contents awhile, possibly killing time while he decided what might be disclosed without prejudice, and to whom.

"There's a husband and wife. Don't know for sure if or how they're involved in what happened 'round home. Wanna talk to 'em. Hopin' they're headed where I think they're headed. I'm listenin' to my gut, Abe. Takin' a gamble."

"Guts rarely lead a person astray in my experience."

"We'll see. Had my deputy, Daniel, go past their house in Melancholy, where we live." Raff pointed to me, then his chest. "He sent a message to Fancy, where I've just been, sayin' this husband and wife, the Beaulieuxs, have split town."

"That's not remarkable by itself. Depends what else is going on in the background . . ." Abraham checked the fawn still pottered by the trees, then swung back to the fire. "Why do you wish to speak with them?"

"A family were murdered in Melancholy last week. The Newmans. I went to Fancy goin' on information sent to me that might help get their killers," Raff said. "Was talkin' to the fella runs the newspaper in Fancy and he told me a while back, a family was killed there same way as the Newmans. Saw a daguerreotype on his wall attached to a story about a massacre in Nevada. At Chandelier Creek Crossing."

"That was an atrocious incident," Abraham said. He rested his forearms on his knees, mug already empty, forefinger looped through the handle.

"You heard of it?" Raff asked.

"I did."

"What did you notice in this daguerreotype?" Abe asked.

"It was a 'who'. Zeke Beaulieux, the husband of the couple I'm followin'. The picture was taken at a place called Winsome Valley, which is also in Nevada." Raff chanced another sip of coffee.

My, sometimes Raff dithered like an old crone and extracting details from him was like pulling teeth. I wiggled my silver hip flask out of the pouch in my waistband, poured a generous measure of whiskey into my mug, then passed the flask to Abe.

Ellington, until then soaking everything up like a dry dishcloth, decided to exercise his tonsils and ask the question on my tongue, also. "What exactly happened at Chandelier Creek, Marshal?"

"Forty-odd people goin' from Brandsville to Tynbridge Hills, in Nevada, were cut down crossin' the creek. They were members of a church started by a Cyrus Finnegan and Peter David Porter. Porter and his kin, all but a son and Porter's own mother who had stayed at home, were slaughtered. Somebody came forward a few years later givin' up those they swore were responsible. A father and son. The newspaper man in Fancy, Clive Parkinson, went to Winsome Valley where these men had been tracked. They were dead when he arrived. He took the picture of Cyrus Finnegan, who'd gone there to confront the so-called killers. Young Porter was standin' behind him."

"Porter? Who the blazes is he?" Abraham asked.

"It's Beaulieux's real name."

Abraham rewarded his mug with a second dollop of whiskey then handed the flask to Ellington. "Where do you think these Beaulieuxs are going? Where do *you* plan on going, Tala?"

"The anniversary of the massacre is comin'. Accordin' to Parkinson there's gonna be commemorations at the site. Cyrus Finnegan will be there. That's where I reckon the Beaulieuxs're goin' and it's where I'm goin'."

"You believe there's a tie-in between Porter/Beaulieux and Chandelier Creek, the church, and the recent murders of these families?"

"Seems like."

"Why is that? Are there hard facts to support the theory, or are you convinced purely because of those gut feelings of yours?"

"To start, I found a Bible at the Newmans' cabin. It has a nameplate inscribed with The Church of Celestial Light and Paradise Divine, the church Finnegan and Porter started. The Wards, the ones killed in Fancy, were religious too. They could've belonged to Finnegan's congregation. And how both families were killed shows they're connected."

"Folks killed by similar methods isn't conclusive, Tala."

"Way they died, well, it'd be strange for people who didn't know each other to kill the way they did. It took . . . imagination."

"If you come at it from a religious angle, that's a slim link. Plenty of true believers around." Raff's expression shifted and Abraham threw up his hands, to deflect the marshal's irritation. "Don't shoot. I'm playing devil's advocate here. You have to admit it's a ways to come on a hunch."

"Did you determine if the Beaulieuxs spent time in Fancy, Ra—Marshal?"

"Asked Parkinson if he'd heard the name Beaulieux. He said no."

"Did you give Mr. Parkinson a description of them?"

"You tellin' me how to do my work, Miss Reed?"

"There are times—"

"All right, you two, don't get your dander up," Abraham said.

"Parkinson remembered a woman with cloudy eyes but not her name. I didn't wanna let on Porter and Zeke Beaulieux're the same till I knew more."

An awkward silence flattened our discussion.

"Why're you here, Miss Reed?" Raff asked, his return to a civil tone primarily for the benefit of Abraham and Ellington. "You didn't come after me 'cause you missed me."

"You are correct, Marshal," I said, and left it there. Abraham spoke the truth. We were on the same side and it did not constitute a game—or sparring match—unless each antagonist committed to the fray.

Maybe I should have remained in Melancholy after all, leaving Raff to continue his quest and enter dealings with the unknown quantity that was the Beaulieuxs without interference. It would serve him right. Then again, if he were injured or worse in the course of searching for them, or *finding* them, I could never forgive myself. He appeared cognizant the Beaulieuxs may not be as they seem, but to warn him the couple was possibly dangerous lay behind my being here, so warn him was precisely what I must do.

"A Pinkerton agent arrived in Melancholy soon after you left, Marshal. McFarley is his name. Kip McFarley."

"What he want?"

"He is also looking for the Beaulieuxs."

"This McFarley say why?"

"He told Daniel and me relatives of a high-ranking person in the Pinkerton Agency were hornswoggled by Madam Beaulieux and her husband. They lost an astronomical sum of money according to Agent McFarley. He has been commissioned to find the Beaulieuxs and re-appropriate the funds with which they absconded."

"You believe him?"

"Not a doggone minute. McFarley showed us a drawing of the Beaulieuxs, but my impression was they are known to him by another name, although he did not go so far as to divulge it. He did not mention the name Porter and had no knowledge of them as Beaulieux."

Abraham would do anything for Raff, but Ellington deserved to know what he had signed on for. The latter's eyes, star bright, had widened when Raff revealed what he had uncovered, but it was not apprehension or fear of plunging into a hazardous situation I perceived in him. Ellington was excited.

"I'm going to pay my respects to the trees." Abraham rested his mug on the stump he had been sitting on and ambled into the forest. Harriet trotted after him.

Raff, Ellington, and I stared anywhere and everywhere except at each other. I paid inordinate attention to a flock of ravens that swooped in decreasing circles above us, before settling in the branches of a tall ponderosa, caws scolding. Samson shook his head, bit jingling.

"Why does Abraham call you Tala, Marshal?" Ellington caved under pressure, indulging the impulse to speak in an effort to ease tension that hummed between Raff and myself.

"Was my name."

"There was a famous scout called Tala prominent during the war. His exploits became the stuff of legends." Ellington tried to assume a casual attitude but fought a losing battle. It was probable that since hearing Abraham address Raff as Tala he had been chomping to get his suspicion off his chest. "They said if he tracked you, you'd do well to give yourself up to the nearest authorities before he found you, because he was always going to find you. Are you that Tala?"

Raff did not dispense an answer.

"Well." Cam interpreted Raff's silence as confirmation. "Apart from telling you I'm honored to be associated with such a famous figure, I can't think what else to say."

"Gotta be a first time for everythin'."

"But I'd like to ask." Ellington managed, in spite of his declaration, to find more to say. "May I call you Tala?"

"Nope."

Abraham waded through the grass, seed heads brushing his knees. "Right, friends, what are we waiting for?"

EIGHTEEN

Day and night cannot dwell together.
—*Chief Seattle, Duwamish*

We were a group of diversified makeup. Abraham brokered a tireless pace, silent on feet encased in hide, our spearhead through forest heavy and thick, the weight of the bear head coat no hindrance to him. He looked more animal than human. Was he at all concerned a hunter might, with grave consequence, mistake him for a grizzly and take a shot at him? The doe cavorted beside him, with Ellington next, the line of his pony's spine crooked and thin.

Raff guided his buckskin alongside Samson, foreshadowing my request to construct a cushion against the onslaught of those who broke cover from tree trunks, branches, and the skies. He understood my worriment of old and I sent him clipped thanks, then fixed on Samson's poll and bobbing ears. Raven and Custer were on my other side so, as a united front, we fell in behind Ellington.

Without discussion we moved as quietly as we could, although there were noises impossible to muffle; saddle leather creaked, and our mounts expelled gentle huffs in rhythm with the steady thud of their hooves on ground layered with fallen leaves and pine needles.

Birds vacated perches on our approach, animals scurried through clumps of underbrush, or became furred statues, blood pumping, activity resumed once we were safely past their nests and lairs.

Pockets of terror were embedded in the essence of the landscape.

Each fresh season it pulsed along branches into the veins of wind-blown leaves, the down of squawking nestlings that jostled for food in beds of twigs, and the blind eyes of baby animals, a relay of memory through generations of every creature that lived and breathed.

The farther we rode, the visceral weight of a bone-chilling occurrence decades, even centuries old pressed upon me, presence cloying, as though in punishment the archfiend balanced an anvil upon my shoulders. I dared not search for the roots of my malaise.

Our surrounds grew brighter, sunlight streaming through a break in the canopy overhead. Samson ducked mid-stride to avoid Ellington's pony when it jerked to a standstill.

"What in thunderation …" I pulled Samson in, ready with an armful of curses agitated by uneasiness. Ellington did not utter a word to counter my displeasure; all he did was point upward with a fat, quaking finger, jaw dropped fit to reach his knees.

When I saw what he pointed to my heart aspired to sprout wings and fly from my throat. With attention firmly on the space between my stallion's ears during most of the ride thus far, I had failed to notice the dense forest we rode through had thinned, and we were about to cross terrain dotted with trees misshapen not by fire, but insects, or fungi.

Stricken trunks lay bare, canted on angles that defied gravity. A section remained upright, although might easily be bowled, toppled by a shove. Burdened by grotesque growths resembling gargoyles, flowering limbs bulged; they reminded me of illustrations of lands beyond the pale in fairytale books of my childhood.

"I don't come through here unless in a hurry." At my exclamation Abraham had rambled back to us. "I forget the shock this—" he gestured the grove "—gives those who come across it unexpectedly."

'This' was an extraordinary sight. Skulls hung like jack-o'-lanterns from upper branches or were wedged into clefts, dressed in lichen, or bleached white as the Utah Territory salt flats. By my guess around half were human, secured by methods not immediately apparent, with arm or leg bones—sometimes both—strung together then draped or suspended by lengths of leather, rope, or intertwined plant material.

Others bore elongated profiles of animal species with split nasal bones, or horns, still complete many moons after their last meal. Captivated, despite the macabre nature of the exhibition, I began counting the skulls, which were assembled in configurations of eight. On reaching fifty-six I decided that to support serenity of mind, it would be advantageous to cease.

Raven and Custer paced back and forth, raised tails stiff, plumed, perceptive senses overwrought by the aerial graveyard.

"If trespassers are here at nighttime, up to no good, I'm not above lighting a candle in an eyeball cavity of a select number of these … attractions," Abraham said. "To give the wretches a surprise and incentive to leave."

"And tell me, sir, does it work?" Ellington posed this in a derisive manner to camouflage a tremor in his words since, although daylight out and in company, he showed symptoms of *surprise* himself.

"Oh, yes," Abraham replied in all seriousness, as if a thought-provoking Sunday sermon were under discussion. "Strangely, as a rule they hightail out of here like their britches have been set afire."

Ellington hauled his gaze from a buffalo skull hanging chest-level if one were mounted upon a standard-sized horse—it dangled far above his pony—to gawp at Abraham.

"It would pay to close your mouth, son. Never know what will get the kink to fly inside and make itself at home."

Ellington's mouth snapped shut.

"Did you put these skulls here, Abraham? Or decorate them?"

"Take a closer look, Hennessey. I have lived on this mountain these ten years. They've been here longer than that."

"Let's get on." Raff shouldered the buckskin past Ellington's pony and reined him into a stand of healthy pine.

Going by the quantity of bones there were fewer ghosts in the area than I expected. This advocated the bones were not all arranged here at a similar time, nor did they originate at a single source but were amassed over years, from different locations.

The victims were Europeans who had died as result of conflict with Indian tribes, for I glimpsed soldiers wearing faded uniforms, eyes hooded, injuries inflicted by ancient weapons; there were no casualties who looked as though they had died from wounds caused by modern firearms.

All bar one.

Amongst the bones hung the body of a man no more than eighteen or nineteen years old. What endured of him swung high, tethered to a branch of an unrecognizable tree, a deformed specimen near where the trace continued into the forest.

"Hmm." Abraham circled the tree, appraising the angular corpse. He tripped on an exposed root, steadied himself against the trunk, then said: "This fellow wasn't here when I last came by."

"How can you be sure?" Ellington asked, rediscovering his voice.

"Just am." Abraham stroked the rough bark, then he and the fawn chased Raff into the trees.

I refused to engage with specters that hovered about us, captivated—an exception being the youngster whose earthly vessel swayed ever so slightly above his ghostly self in a breeze that charted a course exclusively around that tree.

He accepted his plight and his death which, going by vibrations that pulsed through him, had been violent and bloody. One of the lucky dead, permitted to move on, he was not destined to be suspended in the realm that bridged life on Earth and the Hereafter. I nodded to acknowledge him, caught his near imperceptible nod in reply, and kicked Samson after Raff's buckskin.

Our positions behind Abe adjusted and Ellington now rode tail. Not entirely comfortable with this after what we had just seen, he kicked his pony unnecessarily, crowding our mounts until cautioned by Raff, who told him in no uncertain terms to keep his distance unless he wanted to lose a few teeth—distributed by the hoof of Samson or the marshal's gelding.

Abraham kept an even pace, refusing to ride pillion on Samson, citing his desire to remain in contact with the earth. As the sun began to set we descended Howling Wolf Pass and rejoined the road we left hours before, much farther along than if we had not met Abraham.

"You've saved plenty of time," Abraham said. He approached the buckskin and shook Raff's hand. "I'm glad to see you again, Tala. Go well."

"You, too, Abe."

Abraham then came to Samson and stroked his nose. "Take care, Hennessey."

"My aim is to do my best in that regard, Abraham." This did not ring as historic truth, but I did not wish to cause him undue worry.

"Your aim's never great," Raff muttered. "With anythin'."

"Please be extra vigilant." Abe moved to Samson's off-side where, shielded from the marshal, he stroked the stallion's neck, lowering his voice so only I might hear him: "There are rogues who'll relish getting the better of you, Hennessey, and I sense you'll come up against untold danger with pursuit of this couple. Whether they are the main threat, I'm unsure."

"Thank you for your concern, but Raff is with me so I am well-protected." I bent to kiss his stubbled cheek. "By Ellington, too," I said, close to his ear.

"I'm not convinced that should be taken in a positive light." Abe stepped back and raised his voice. "As for you, Ellington, listen to Tala. Do everything he tells you. Without question. Happy hunting, my friends. If you come through here again let me know if your mission was successful."

Harriet leaped stiff-legged around her master and I imagined, fancifully, this was how she expressed goodbye. They disappeared into the forest, Abe without a backward glance, and I pushed Samson into a jog to catch Raff and Cam, already a ways ahead.

The road was wide enough for us to ride abreast, and I squeezed Samson in-between the buckskin and Ellington's scrawny pony.

"Where will we camp, Marshal?" Ellington craned his neck, looking past me to Raff, and did not react to my rude behavior.

"Abe told me about a place. It's safe along here, still, we'll keep watch. Don't want anybody takin' a shine to our horses or rifles."

If one were partial to conserving a heartbeat, I felt it was best to err on the side of caution and not travel through the night even in an area considered safe. The Beaulieuxs, too, would surely stop until morning whether in a rooming house or by a fire.

Raff led us off the road to a platform bordered by a stream where we fed and watered the horses, picketing them at the site Raff selected. So tired I was near asleep on my feet, I rubbed Samson down, and fed the dogs a meal of Cookie's pemmican and a smoked joint of an anonymous beast Abraham supplied, divided between them. By then I was spent.

Ellington loafed off, but when crunching twigs signaled his return to camp a voice carried with Ellington's. Primed for defense, Raff drew his Colt so fast I did not catch him doing it.

Cam sauntered into the clearing, mighty pleased with himself and accompanied by the Pinkerton agent, McFarley.

"Good evening, Miss Reed. It's nice to see you again," the Pinkerton said, conviviality grating. "And I assume you're Marshal Cooper."

"You assume right." Raff issued a barely audible hiss and jabbed his .45 into its holster. "I'm guessin' you're McFarley."

"So, my name, or reputation, precedes me."

"Also guessin' you didn't walk here. Where's your horse?"

"I'll go get him." With that the Pinkerton left to retrieve his mount.

"Where'd you find him, Ellington?"

"Heard a noise while . . . seeing to business." Ellington's gallantry in my presence and consideration of my sex saw me laugh, tiredly. Embarrassed, he concentrated on Raff. "When I investigated, caught him skulking about those rocks by the road."

"Your amazin' hearin' comin' back, eh, Cam?"

The Pinkerton came out of the twilight leading a rangy bay gelding. He stripped the horse, settled him, gave him a friendly scratch behind his ear then joined us by an elementary though efficient fire.

"A gentleman doing an extraordinary impersonation of a grizzly said you spoke of me. Beneficially, as it happened, for I got the impression he wanted to test that Remington of his on a moving target. Anyhow, I wasn't far behind Miss Reed. To find you here as well, Marshal, makes this a red-letter day."

McFarley had read me like a book, believing me in possession of

Raff's exact whereabouts and that I intended to go after him. Daniel had told McFarley that Raff was headed to Hollow Oak Falls, but the Pinkerton probably left Melancholy, hid along the route until Nate and I came by, then tagged us to make sure we had not deliberately misdirected him. Raff would not waste thanks on me for leading the Pinkerton right to him.

"Sit yourself, McFarley." Raff rifled his saddlebags for ingredients to assemble a simple meal. "You hungry? Can add another bean to the pot."

"I'd be obliged."

McFarley oriented his saddle, sank to the ground and leaned against it, knees crackling. "Damn, getting old isn't fun."

"Yet preferable to the alternative, Agent McFarley."

"Can't say I disagree with you, Miss Reed." He shuffled his posterior, seeking a more hospitable position.

I prepared my bed, limbs torpid. Shaking Samson's saddle blanket out before laying my bedroll on it, I collapsed with a sigh of appreciation as though reclining atop a feather bed. The smell of horse sweat, fresh and stale, wafted with no apology into my nostrils: this, oddly, was of comfort to me. Raven rolled over and rested her chin on my ankle. I scratched her rump and she responded with a contented yip. Custer lay outside the fire's glow, unsure yet what, or who, to trust.

"You're in charge of cooking, Marshal?" McFarley asked.

"If I wanna eat. If Miss Reed was cook we'd starve."

After more shuffling, and bland getting-to-know-you, still-figuring-if-you-might-be-useful-to-my-investigation probes, the Pinkerton looked to have made a decision. Even then he took his sweet time raising the Beaulieuxs. Raff, a patient man when dealing with anyone except me—this apparent our entire acquaintance—listened intently to McFarley's putative rundown of his history with the pair.

"I thought if we met, we'd band together to find these criminals, Marshal." McFarley gave it to him straight.

"That right?"

"We have a common goal, and these Beaulieuxs are crafty, so I could use backup."

As a brand-new associate McFarley was unversed in tell-tale signs the marshal exhibited when displeased. The Pinkerton folded his arms, surety of Raff's agreeing to assist in his search lending him confidence. I waited, agog.

"Backup?" Raff asked, deathly calm.

"Wrong word." The Pinkerton rushed to amend his statement, belatedly conscious of Raff's malcontent. "I apologize, Marshal. Didn't mean to sound as if I'm demeaning your abilities or judgment, or those of your friends here. Let me rephrase my request."

"Do that."

"What I should've said is there's strength in numbers. We both want to find the Beaulieuxs, and we'd make a formidable team if we combine forces."

"You're soundin' like Miss Reed when she's butterin' me to get somethin' or do somethin' she knows I ain't gonna be happy about."

"I had already informed Marshal Cooper of what you told Daniel Hawthorne and me about why you are keen to apprehend the Beaulieuxs, Agent McFarley," I interjected before McFarley waded deeper into the sinkhole threatening to swallow him in one gulp. "I also told him I did not believe the fable with which you regaled us."

"Pappy said I never could lie worth a damn. Unhelpful in my profession, as it turns out. Shall we start over? Let's share honest information as well as our talents, Marshal."

"You first," Raff said.

"Here's the truth." McFarley accepted the tin plate he brought to the fire when Raff invited him to eat with us, now piled with beans. "Two other families lost their lives in the identical way to the Wards in Fancy. Your man said you've just been there, Marshal. You told him about them."

Raff nodded.

"These killings happened over the past five years, in different territories. I can put this husband and wife, the *Beaulieuxs*, in each area prior to the murders."

McFarley ran his spoon around the rim of his plate and scooped beans into his mouth, aware we were transfixed, hanging on his every word.

"The Beaulieuxs are being chased?"

"In each case, Miss Reed, after the murders these Beaulieuxs moved on within six months." McFarley allowed that to cure. "Then came the deaths in Melancholy."

"If they had been the targets and were worried about their safety they would not wait six months to move." My brain tried to catch what the Pinkerton mooted. "You are saying the Beaulieuxs are the instigators of all that wickedness?"

McFarley displayed admirable manners in that he did not respond until he finished chewing. I had spent months of early adulthood in the company of lawless men, and became immune to rough behavior and speech, so these did not bother me.

"Yes, ma'am," he said.

"Did you suspect this too, Marshal?"

"Had an idea."

"If this is so, how many persons do you record the Beaulieuxs murdering to date, Agent McFarley?"

"There were ten victims in Melancholy?" McFarley asked, after swallowing his mouthful.

"Yep," Raff said.

"Eleven," I said, wanting McFarley to hurry with his explanation, not draw it in a fine line for effect. "The unborn child should be included in the tally."

"That makes ..." The Pinkerton stared past me, while he calculated. "Forty-eight. Or forty-nine."

"Good gracious!"

"That's one way of putting it, Miss Reed. There are plenty of alternatives."

I played with my meal, rearranging it, our topic of conversation not conducive to digestion. Eventually I kept hold of my spoon and laid the plate on the edge of my blanket where Raven licked it clean.

"There must be a reason behind the Beaulieuxs' actions. A connection between the families," I said.

"I agree. Though whatever it is we haven't uncovered it, which makes it harder to figure who's next on their list," the Pinkerton said. "Impossible, even."

"Why are you convinced it is them carrying out these murders?"

"Apart from them being in each town? Details I'm not authorized to divulge and a feeling I can't shake."

"Gut feelings are a common affliction hereabouts. That is all you will tell us?"

"Let's say I'll tell you what you need to know if, or when, you need to know it."

"That seems a prerequisite for you lawman types."

"For now it has to be enough to get on with, Miss Reed."

"How long you been after 'em?" Raff asked.

"A while." McFarley put his plate beside his thigh and withdrew a thin cigar and tinderbox from his coat. He lit the cigar, then continued. "It's tricky since they change their handles with each new . . . project. They were the Willards in Fancy, the Simpsons up round Whittaker, and the Andersons prior to that. Who knows how they started out."

Cam Ellington opened his mouth, but censure I threw him encouraged him to slowly close it again. If Raff wanted to tell McFarley of Zeke Beaulieux's original name he would do so when it suited him.

"Up until the use of Beaulieux they chose ordinary names to blend in, so not to be memorable. Anyway, that's my reckoning behind it," McFarley said.

"That alone must be problematical when Madam Beaulieux is so attractive," I said. "Regardless how she tries to disguise her attributes she will always be noticed."

"There is truth in what you say." McFarley sucked on his cigar, then sent a gossamer stream of smoke toward the fire. "I'm wary of how to take this change in operations."

We considered the winding trails the Beaulieuxs plotted with unflagging industry. I listened to the wind speak—guttural, somber remarks that trolled over mountains, down river courses and pebbled shoals, past untamed beasts and the ears of grazing livestock to arrive without fanfare in this clearing, where we camped.

"Tell me, Agent McFarley," I said. "You arrived in Melancholy within days of the Newman family dying. How did you get word they were dead?"

"I didn't know about their deaths until your deputy told me," McFarley said, addressing Raff. "That was by accident. I wish I'd gotten to Melancholy earlier."

I wished that, too, as I guessed Raff did and, by association, Cam Ellington.

"How'd you know the Beaulieuxs were in Melancholy?" Raff asked.

"It's hard to say why—" the Pinkerton turned shifty, reluctant perhaps to reveal everything he knew "—but I got a telegram."

"Tellin' where they were?"

"Yes."

"Which means at least one other person out there is aware of what they are doing and that you are suspicious of them," I said. "Who hired your agency, Agent McFarley?"

"That's confidential."

"Then from whom was the telegram sent?"

"That's a mystery."

"From *where* was it sent?"

"That, I can answer. Nevada."

"You haven't asked why I'm goin' after the Beaulieuxs, McFarley," Raff said.

"After we found they'd scarpered, young Hawthorne told me about the Newmans and the telegrams this Hiram Walsh fellow sent from Fancy, so I took a stab. The reason behind these killings and the methods used may not make a lot of sense to those of us of rational mind, but it makes crazy sense to the Beaulieuxs. I want to hear an explanation from their own lips."

"What brought them, in particular, to your attention?" I asked.

McFarley cocked an eyebrow. "As mentioned previously, there's a limit to what I'm at liberty to tell you, Miss Reed."

"For goodness' sake. Call me Hennessey, Agent McFarley."

"If you insist, Hennessey." His mustache quivered but he did not reciprocate with his own offer. "Now it's your turn, Marshal. By the way, where we headed?"

"Reckon the Beaulieuxs are goin' to Nevada."

"Why?"

McFarley must not have made the connection between Chandelier Creek and Zeke Beaulieux—well, if he had, he did not reveal his suspicions—although those who sent him after the killers surely know more of what lay behind his assignment. Did McFarley assume the murderous Beaulieuxs were focused on their next victims, or did he ask the question to see if *we* knew where the couple were going?

"The Wards and Newmans were overly religious," Raff said. "Were the others?"

"Yes," McFarley said. "They belonged to that church run by Cyrus Finnegan."

"You know about the killin's at Chandelier Creek Crossin'?"

"Sure I do." If the switch in direction befuddled the Pinkerton, it did not show. "That's history. What's it to do with these other killings, Marshal?"

"The anniversary of Chandelier Creek's comin' up."

"When?"

"'Round a week."

"And?"

"There's a tribute organized. I think the Beaulieuxs are goin'."

"Why?"

"Reckon they've got somethin' bad planned when everybody's congregated there."

"What would they be doing that for?"

"Zeke Beaulieux's family were killed at Chandelier Creek. He was called Porter then."

"Was he now."

"My thinkin' is Beaulieux holds Cyrus Finnegan responsible."

"Where did you get this idea?"

"Couldn't say."

"A hunch?"

"Partly."

"That's it?"

"'There's a limit to what I'm at liberty to tell you'," Raff said.

McFarley choked on smoke he had involuntarily inhaled.

Raff began telling McFarley how the Ibsens called him to where the Newman family were laid out. Having heard this before, with eyelids drooping I removed my boots, put them in the bottom of my bed roll and pulled the blanket to my ears. Cam Ellington listened to the lawmen, swinging between Pinkerton and marshal, not wanting to miss a word.

Happy to share up to a point, it seemed Raff's rebellion twinned McFarley's. Raff did not disclose all he knew or suspected to the Pinkerton, choosing to keep some things to himself, his motive for this I supposed he would make clear later on. He had not said as much, but was Raff, like me, mistrustful of McFarley's motive behind making himself known to us?

A wolf howled, the spine-chilling call fluctuating in volume, dancing up and down a musical scale that echoed, bouncing off rock, tree and crag. Another wolf answered, communicating a reply that raised bumps on my arms. Raven sat up, ears stiff, and when I reached to pet her, to reassure her, I petted muscles bunched hard as marble.

What did the wolves discuss? Was a dominant male warning the others there were intruders in their midst, and to beware? For they howled a language all their own, dusk the time to seek the locale of pack members, then encouraged to return to their den. I should ask Raff of what they spoke, convinced the wolves' conversation was no-nonsense, unlike the conversation presently being conducted around our fire.

I stared at the sky. The stars, as always, filled me with veneration anew of vast galaxies that floated above inhabiting darkness with no depth. No accomplishment as human beings stood to run close to the majesty of Nature and what she had created.

I attempted to recall lessons undertaken as a child when my uncle sat my cousin, Sarah, and myself on a window seat in the drawing room of his Washington mansion, and relayed fascination of his true love, astronomy, to giggling eight-year-old girls. Sarah had admitted his undivided attention excited her most, her delight when reverence moved across her father's face like a lunar eclipse, joy in his presence having little to do with silver webs spun in the heavens.

Cold air nipped my extremities and I snuggled under my blanket, serenaded by a great horned owl who slipped on the mantle of proclaimer when the wolves desisted. A branch sawed its neighbor, a minor irritation; I grew used to it, blocking the noise as I sank closer to oblivion.

Dry grass rustled as nocturnal wanderers made forays into the meadow hunting for food, and I mumbled caution to steer clear of the owl. A horse stomped, a log clunked and hissed when added to the fire. It had been a long time since I slept under the stars and I had forgotten night-time noises traveled farther and beat louder than their daytime counterparts. Despite this, comforted by the warm bulk of my dog and knowledge Raff was near, I fell asleep.

At intervals during the night I heard murmurs when the guard changed. I had voiced no objections to my exemption from watch duty, secretly pleased to take advantage of my femininity, as I was exhausted.

In the early hours, encouraged by the frosty autumn night, Custer wavered and crept closer to the fire and, observing Raven's example, lay along my side. I stirred when he leaned against me, then succumbed to the arms of Morpheus again, fortressed by the dozing beasts.

NINETEEN

Marshal Rafael Cooper: *Southern Idaho Territory.*

Raff lay on top of his bedroll, close enough to the fire to enjoy its warmth, but not too close the heat could lull him to sleep. With night sounds backdrop chatter to his thoughts, he looked for the resident owl when it hooted, spotting it directly, an inky smudge against the sky.

The wolves howling at dusk had seen him pause while he picked individual calls, the timbre of their howls similar, which identified them all as being from the same pack. They spoke to each other, communicating to family much as humans did, though their family unit was loyal and loving the way many human families were not.

With their relations complicated as all get-out, unlike those of the wolves, Raff ached to get back to the innate understanding he used to have with Hennessey. In better times they had enjoyed each other, their squabbles quick to ignite and equally quick to die; they were drawn into neither spite nor hurt. At loggerheads after recent developments they had reached a stalemate, and he wasn't sure how to go about fixing it.

As the man in the equation he took responsibility for their relationship being in tatters, though deep down he felt, at a stretch, only a portion of blame should fall on him. Mostly, he ruled the blame Hennessey's, but Raff would forgive her. Some day. He always did.

Thinking of Hennessey, he tipped onto a hip to check on her.

Her body formed a slight lump under the blanket and if he hadn't watched her get into the bedroll he might be wondering where she'd gotten to. He'd swear she was wasting away in front of him, and there wasn't a whole lot of her to begin with. She'd hardly touched her supper, chasing beans around her plate with her spoon thinking he didn't notice when she nonchalantly put the plate within reach of Raven's snout.

Hennessey's protectors lay either side of her. The yellow cur had taken to her in record time, but Raff had seen Hennessey work her magic on animals; those vicious and untamable became meek and affectionate, ready to lay down their life for her. Raff shared this peculiarity with her four-legged conquests.

He glanced to the general vicinity where Ellington patrolled, crossed his ankles, and folded his hands behind his head. He'd learned Ellington did not leave off anything if set on it, this borne out when insisting he be included in standing watch. He did not relent in his badgering, wearing on Raff's nerves until he acquiesced just to get Ellington to damn well shut up. Raff didn't see how another person existed on the planet with the ability to irritate him as much as Hennessey. Without trying. And what about the raw deal which had that one person want to ride with him?

McFarley stirred. Raff supposed the other man lay awake, too, brain crowded with the people they were tracking and how things would play out the next couple of days. If he thought like Raff he was probably also raked by qualms of Ellington being up for the job, praying he wasn't going to have his throat cut in his sleep if Ellington got distracted.

The Pinkerton started snoring. Raff propped himself against his saddle, rescued a roll your own he'd made earlier from his jacket, and successfully lit the end without extra effort other than raising his head. Smoking always helped in the figuring process.

A crack and thump saw him and McFarley leap to their feet.

"Sorry, Marshal." Ellington's disembodied apology came loud as a trombone in a marching band. "That's just me tripping on a branch."

"Kid near got himself a new vent someplace inconvenient," McFarley said. "Somebody should take him in hand. Give him lessons on how to avoid getting shot, accidental-like."

"You offerin'?" Raff asked.

"Hell, no." Patched with firelight the Pinkerton looked horrified at the prospect. He untangled his legs from a striped blanket and pulled on his boots. "Might as well go take over from him now I'm awake."

"What was that?" Hennessey asked drowsily.

"Nothin'. Go back to sleep."

She didn't reply. Raven and Custer returned noses to paws, unruffled by the interruption. Raff knew if an attack were imminent from a person whose scent they didn't recognize they'd have been after him long before the branch snapped.

Ellington appeared rubbing his hands together, collar up against the cold. He shrugged another apology, augmented by a rueful smile, at which Raff waved a dismissive hand. Ellington dragged his rig closer to the fire, sat, and sighed with contentment.

Raff tossed the butt of the hand-rolled cigarette into the flames and stuck a log in the center of the blaze, careful not to raise sparks. Having more confidence in McFarley, he resumed pondering.

McFarley had shared his objective though shied from disclosing information which he said was of a sensitive nature. That sat fine with Raff as it made him feel better about withholding what he'd lit on. Unsure what stoked this reluctance, it suited him to think it because he was used to working on his own. If forced to work with a man he hadn't met before, first and foremost, they had to earn his trust.

After perusing the archives in the offices of *The Fancy Weekly*, Raff swore he'd remember the reports he read of the killings at Chandelier Creek the rest of his days. Add the abduction of Parkinson's daughter, Elodie, to that and . . . well. He steered himself away from that heartache.

He thought he was successful maintaining a neutral expression when it hit him the surnames McFarley revealed—of the families killed prior to the Wards in Fancy—all started with the same letter as the names of those on the list Parkinson gave him.

It was the breakthrough he needed, but it made him antsy that more victims were credibly in the Beaulieuxs' sights.

Raff had shared the church inscription he found in the Bible at the Newman farmstead but didn't tell the others the Newmans were really the Netherlands—he had noted Pretorius Netherland particularly on Parkinson's list. He'd decided to hold that nugget close for the time being.

Those implicated in riding with the Cowans *must* be aware they were being picked off and, warned they were in danger, should have gone into hiding. They could be living anywhere. Whosoever put them into play would have security measures in place, with only a select few kept up-to-date of their whereabouts. How, then, did the killers know where to find them?

Back in Melancholy, studying how the Newmans were arranged in death he'd tossed around how, maybe, they pointed toward a specific item, or place. If a tack were pinned to a map to show where the bodies were found, and one on Chandelier Creek, the family, headed by the parents, were aimed like a human arrow toward the creek. It was damned satisfying what you could deduce when you got rolling.

Raff fastened his jacket, to his neck, mesmerized by the fire. Despite riding on the trail of suspected murderers with a tiresome man who tripped over his own feet, a Pinkerton agent with secrets aplenty, and a woman who drove him *loco* with no effort, he had to say that out here in the cold and dark he was happier than he'd been in a very, very long while.

TWENTY

The weakness of our enemy makes our strength.
—*Cherokee wisdom*

"I'm getting too old for this." McFarley threw aside his blanket, and rose in increments, rubbing forearms and thighs to encourage blood to pump and circulate.

I shared the Pinkerton's attitude. On inspection the previous evening the hard-baked ground appeared relatively free of lumps, but I had felt every dip and knobble, bedroll and saddle blanket next-to-useless buffers.

"That Arbuckles I smell?" McFarley stretched arms thin as licorice straps above his head, clasping at the sky, then reached for his boots.

"Help yourself," Raff said.

I sat up, ran fingers through tangled hair with the false belief that might make a difference, then quickly braided it. Aching in parts of my body I hitherto had no notion existed, I experienced a ray of freedom from constraints of society and convention—until reminded of our purpose.

The sun poked its nose into what promised to be a beautiful morning, shafts of light diving past pine and fir, through cracks and fissures, shadow latticework bordering our camp.

The buckskin was saddled, ready to depart, Raff occupied buckling the gelding's cheek strap, face drawn, and I imagined he acquired little sleep. Habitually, he slept with an eye and both ears open, including when in his cot at the jailhouse in Melancholy. Out here, lacking a yardstick with which to measure their proficiency, relinquishing watch to strangers did not come easily to him.

Ellington waited in the clearing, Dasher on a loose rein eating grass at such a rate it suggested he held grave concerns he partook of his final meal. Ellington waved when he noticed me arise, seemingly well-rested, which made me envious of his speedy adjustment to life in the open.

Mild panic accosted me when unable to see Raven or Custer until a clump of reeds swayed by the stream. A brace of dusky grouse exploded into the crisp morning, a flurry of feathers, indignant squawks confirming the dogs entertained themselves at avian expense.

"You gonna sit 'round lookin' grumpy, Miss Reed? Got five minutes before we're outta here."

"All right, all right," I grumbled, searching for my boots. I shook them vigorously to ensure no creatures had retired there for the night, then tugged them on.

"Ellington's saddled Samson. Used his clean blanket."

"That is kind of him. *Gentlemanly.*"

"Get organized or we'll leave you here."

"Yes, sir!"

Raff's threat was empty, hot air, and we both knew it.

I rolled and bound my blankets, carried them to Samson where I strapped them behind my saddle then went back to the fire, where McFarley lingered.

"Thank you, Agent McFarley," I said, accepting the mug he handed me. "It is gratifying to know there is another gentleman amongst us."

"I gather you're not fond of mornings, Hennessey," he said.

I deployed a compressed smile, cupped the mug between my palms, relishing its heat, and walked to the stream at a sedate pace, banking on Raff observing me. There, I set the mug down and splashed water on my face in an attempt to rid myself of the groggy feeling of half-sleep attached to my eyeballs. Calling the dogs who reluctantly abandoned pestering the local fauna, I meandered to where Samson and McFarley's horse were staked.

We broke camp, Raff dousing the fire that had been allowed to die down, seeing to delinquent embers. He ran a bladed eye over the clearing and got aboard the buckskin. The Pinkerton and Ellington already forked their mounts and I, too, climbed into my saddle, muscles tight, protesting. In single file we wound through a littering of pines and spilled onto the road.

With all we had to hand, we agreed to head for the Utah Territory border. Recognizing the added safety of riding together, if any of us were incapacitated by unforeseen circumstances the balance of our group could maintain a feasible prospect to continue after the Beaulieuxs.

Raff confessed limited familiarity with the countryside we were to traverse. McFarley's employment saw him ride across lands named and uncharted, but he admitted no previous cause to visit much of the territory we rode toward. Ellington said he knew the major byways and trails that threaded southern Idaho Territory, so initially we would defer to him, in the main, and hope this would not see us ride in an almighty big circle. Whether he bolstered his capabilities, inflating prowess to earn recognition and praise, remained to be seen.

Ellington quietly told me he had a map on his person as a last resort, at which Raff, overhearing, grunted and put steel to his gelding.

Of comfort, Raff had sent a telegram from Fancy to the sheriff's office closest to Chandelier Creek telling them to prepare for trouble. If something went terribly awry our end a reception committee would be waiting for the Beaulieuxs at the commemoration.

Mid-morning I noticed the hierarchy accepted by each of us dictated our riding order. Raff's and the Pinkerton's horses trod side by side, their riders shaking down to camaraderie of sorts, brought by a common occupation and a shared goal, although they exchanged words only if a thought of import came to them—a theory aired, action proposed.

I rode next, content to leave all decision-making to the lawmen whose expertise with criminal behavior, singularly, outstripped all my other acquaintances combined. Cam Ellington lagged at the rear, buoyant with high spirits. He chatted to his pony as if conversing with a human being, asking the dogs their opinions as well, the themes on which he pontificated of contrasting seriousness.

Before long I started to feel distinctly ill. My nose dripped and my eyes watered as though a trickster had turned on an internal faucet then neglected to turn it off again, liquid in my body daring to flee by any route available. Believing my symptoms due to the gypsy wind, as the day grew boisterous as a weanling, it crossed my mind the entirety of my aches and pains might not be attributed to weather conditions alone.

"How far is it to the next town, Marshal? I require an apothecary."

"You sick?"

Raff reined in the buckskin until Samson caught him up. I did not examine whether this indicated concern for my wellbeing, or apprehension how illness might impact our progress. It proved impossible to tell.

"I have felt better."

"You've looked better. Ain't far to North's Ridge."

He sent his horse after McFarley, less than sympathetic input hinting he guessed what I wanted to hide from the other men. Last night I had gone for the bottle of laudanum I carried—purely to aid sleep—to find after my last indulgence I must have failed to replace the stopper correctly and the precious medication had leaked through my saddlebag. I rejected the pull to evaluate how this was going to influence my physical or mental state.

"When I last went through North's Ridge there wasn't much in the way of physicians and such." Ellington nudged his pony level with Samson. "You do appear unwell, Miss Reed. Will you make it there?"

"I am not about to fall off my horse, Cam, or suffer an inconvenient temper of mind." He was pleased by my use of his Christian name but in all honesty I used it because, even if my life had depended on it, his surname did not avail itself. "It is a sniffle, at most. If there is no apothecary in this North's Ridge to attend me, I shall have to bear it."

"Does the marshal know any useful Native preparations?"

"Quite possibly."

Experience of Raff's preparations meant my preference lay with alternate remedies to those his ancestors used to cure ailments that ran from a mild head cold or fever to injuries of various descriptions. Undergoing traditional European treatment for much of my childhood and adult life—while wary of concoctions applied by practitioners enamored by horrors such as leeches—I hoped if Cam took it upon himself to broach the subject with Raff, the ingredients required to concoct a suitable poultice were not to be found growing nearby.

"Would you feel better after a bite to eat?"

"I do not think so." At the thought of food my insides somersaulted in the manner of a circus aerialist.

"My landlady is a wonderful cook. Here, try this." When I did not move to accept his offering, wrapped in paper, he pressed it upon me. "Take it. It will help, I promise."

Why did men of my association feel compelled to ply me with food?

"Go on, I don't mind sharing. It's her specialty."

"May I ask, of what does her specialty consist?"

"Caribou tongue," he said.

Bile threatened to gag me. Since a child, I could not bear to consume identifiable body parts of a beast or offal of any kind, even if presented flambéed or stewed by a celebrated chef trained in the kitchens of Paris.

"Your generosity is laudable, but a cigarette shall suffice."

Ellington shrugged and deferentially buckled the precious tongue in his saddlebag.

"We are surely gaining on the Beaulieuxs by now, Marshal."

Raff acted as though he did not hear me. Relegated again to single file he was in the lead, McFarley in behind him. The Pinkerton twisted in his saddle and nodded. "Thank you," I mouthed, bored, and so ill to my stomach I feared no apothecary had resources to combat such wretchedness.

Raff glanced down the bank to our left then, interest triggered, swung the buckskin about and let him select his footing downslope. Kip McFarley did the same. To what purpose I remained ignorant, until Samson reached the spot where they left the trail.

A pool near the base of the embankment breathed gentle, steamed breaths into the air, declaring it part of a chain of hot springs found throughout the area. Elevated, water-slathered rocks trimmed the spring, the water clear and inviting. The overflow spilled onto a natural stone ladder that tumbled to earth bare of vegetation. The trail hemmed the entry to this oasis, rocky escarpments encased two sides, with the fourth side a gateway to an unrivalled, spectacular vista of land and sky.

The susurrus of leaves that graced trees behind me was all I was aware of, this replaced by roaring in my ears to rival the volume of Hollow Oak Falls, for the extraordinary beauty of the locale was marred by an object floating in the spring, which, even from where I sat atop my horse, I recognized as Madam Beaulieux.

Dead—for dead, she indisputably was—she floated face down, scarf drifting like the crossbar of the letter 't', green dress soaked to charcoal below the waterline.

Ellington kicked his pony after Samson when I sent him off-trail to join Raff and McFarley.

"Oh wow." Ellington paled. "Is that who I think it is?"

"That depends entirely on who you think it is." McFarley smacked a hand on his saddle horn. "Damn it!"

Custer chose that moment to tip his nose to the sun, releasing a plangent howl so primordial the hairs on my arms prickled, disquiet climbing my spine.

"Shut him up," Raff hissed. "Beaulieux mightn't be outta hearin'."

I got off Samson and made a fruitless attempt to entice the dog to me so I could grab his scruff, but he darted away, evading my grasp. Thankfully, he did not have the compulsion to contribute further vocal torment, pacing to and fro, just out of reach, distraught at finding his mistress in this condition.

Raff dismounted and examined the rock walls that loomed above us, section by section. Satisfied no one observed us he then inspected the ground, each footfall placed with care to avoid obliterating tracks made earlier by the husband and wife Beaulieux. Inspection complete, he leaped onto the barrier containing the spring and jumped rock to rock, until he stood opposite us, across the water.

Kneeling, he reached for Madam Beaulieux, stretching—to where I believed him perilously close to falling into the water—to grab her sleeve. He tugged her toward the spring rim, clasped the shoulder farthest from him, bunched the fabric of her skirts at her hip in the other fist and rolled her over, muscles strained, grunting as the water sucked at her, reluctant to release purchase. She now floated face-up, to the sun. Raff let go his grip and studied the body.

"Is she dead, Marshal? For definite?" Ellington had gotten off his pony but did not approach the spring. "Shouldn't you check to make sure?"

It was obvious to most everyone present Madam Beaulieux journeyed far beyond assistance the earth-bound could offer; a red mist diluted about her, bloody wisps yielded by a wound on her skull.

"No call to. She's dead." Legs braced, Raff rubbed the crease between his eyes, the stance he applied during contemplation. "Notice anythin' peculiar here?"

"Other than a dead woman floating in a hot spring with her head bashed in?"

"Yes, Ellington, apart from that."

"What do you make out, Marshal?" McFarley asked.

"McFarley, you'll see better from your perch."

"What are you getting at?" The Pinkerton soon began to nod, an unconscious response when he registered to what the marshal referred. "Ah, now I see your meaning. That's interesting."

"Now you see what meaning?" Anxious to be privy to whatever the other men had seen, Ellington hauled himself onto a boulder, huffing and puffing with the effort. Afforded a better vantage point, he revolved on Madam Beaulieux's body. "Well, that's what I'd call a kicker."

"A 'kicker', you say? Seems the lady was a mite … confused," McFarley said.

This comment and a tremble of his mustache that accompanied it stirred my interest. When the men did not advance anything further, I approached the rock Ellington balanced on and took the hand he extended, to determine to what they alluded.

Despite her death arriving unexpectedly and at an inopportune moment—as, of course, did the majority of deaths—Madam Beaulieux portrayed unusual calm, resignation, as though her demise were pre-ordained with the only detail left to be confirmed the matter of *when*. If she were in possession of a genuine gift and had been an honest to goodness soothsayer, not a pretender, did she foresee how she was going to meet her death, but not the identity of her killer? Did a hazy prophecy appear within her crystal ball?

"What astonishes you so?" I asked.

"Take note of her undergarments." Ellington blushed madly, eyes galloping from mine.

"Or her throat," McFarley added. "If you can stomach it."

"Why in the … oh! Well, that adds another dimension to their history."

Madam Beaulieux's skirts drifted above her waist, bloomers clinging like a cotton skin to her lower torso and thighs. What became apparent was the attributes outlined did not confirm her female. Instead, it made clear Madam Beaulieux was, in fact, plainly, and irrefutably—male. The scarf wound around her neck had worked loose, or been worked loose, to expose a prominent Adam's apple, if one felt disposed to argue the inarguable.

"To what purpose would a person go to such extraordinary lengths to present Monsieur Beaulieux as Madam?" I asked, thinking out loud. "What could be the motivation behind this elaborate deception? Can you imagine the demands of remembering to speak in a higher, lighter voice; to move like a woman; affect mannerisms of a woman? It must be exhausting!"

"Maybe the Beaulieuxs figured they'd be less conspicuous if they masqueraded as husband and wife rather than brothers, for instance," McFarley said. "It isn't a bad strategy."

"It must've taken a lot of planning." Riveted, Cam Ellington could not tear his gaze from the body. "She's tall. Where do you suppose she bought her dresses? And her feet are the size of the marshal's, so woman-styled boots would've had to be specially made for her."

"Half the men in Melancholy were smitten with Madam Beaulieux," I said. Like Cam, I mechanically referred to the dead man by a female title inclined, also, to use a feminine pronoun of identification. "Perhaps fondness for presenting herself of the female sex stemmed from an altogether different objective. Perhaps it was how she wanted to be. There are cultures where men live as females. The man-woman of some Indian tribes as an example, Marshal."

The men stared at me as if I had taken leave of my senses.

"You can't compare Madam with *berdache* or *winkte*, Miss Reed."

"Let us shelve that discussion for another day."

"Speakin' for myself, don't care if that 'discussion' never happens," Raff said.

"With you there, Marshal," McFarley said.

"Was she killed by her friend?" I returned to theorizing. "Or did someone else kill her?"

"There'd be two bodies if the killer was a wanderer who came upon them," McFarley said.

"Do you concur, Marshal?" I asked.

"Yep. There's another thing." Raff continued around the lip of the spring to meet Ellington and myself and bade us turn around.

"See those tracks? They show no handicap. No limp," Raff elaborated at Ellington's incomprehension. "Madam Beaulieux's *husband* had a limp, but he's fit as you or me. Well, maybe not you, Ellington."

"Is what we see here a result of an argument between thieves? A disagreement that escalated after a misjudged aside or observation?" McFarley raced through possibilities, calculating each. "Are the Beaulieuxs related, or did they meet by accident and find they had a joint cause?"

"Who'd know?" Raff leaped off the boulder, landing in a crouch. He drew to his full height, fixed on the base of the cliff. "There's slight hollows where they slept last night. Lit a fire, too. Haven't tried to cover they were here."

"So, whatever happened that ended in this—" McFarley's gesture tagged the body in the spring "—happened this morning."

"It's how I read it. Didn't sense we were trackin' 'em."

"Not then. If Beaulieux's near and can tell the difference between a coyote or wolf howl and a dog's howl, he'll suspect all right, thanks to the mutt." McFarley twirled the end of his mustache, stared at the floating corpse and solemnly mangled Benjamin Franklin: "'Two may keep a secret, if one of them is dead.'"

Ellington repeated this under his breath, inflection suggesting he filed the quote in his spacious brain for future use.

"Give me a hand, McFarley. Pool's tainted now." Raff went back to the body. "Gotta get her out."

Raff followed Cam's and my lead, referring to 'Madam' Beaulieux as female, not at all uncomfortable with *her* being *him*. Keeping their original address to differentiate between the couple known to us as Beaulieux was, all in all, easier. I expected McFarley would follow suit.

The Pinkerton dismounted and climbed a rock to stand beside

Raff. Madam Beaulieux bobbed, bumping against the spring edge. "Where do you want me?"

"Grab her ankles."

I looked away, but turned back to Raff and McFarley when I heard a thud.

"Sorry, Marshal, lost my grip. She's not light as a bird."

Raff nodded, preoccupied with trying to flick something off his hand, the pantomime vastly entertaining, though I saw nothing to warrant his frustration and violent shakes of his arm.

"He knocked her out first." Raff made a production of drawing whatever it was from around his wrist then squatted next to Madam Beaulieux. "With a rock. Then he wrapped this fishin' line 'round her neck."

"Zeke used fishing line to ensure Madam was dead? Why not shoot her, or knock her out and leave her in the spring to drown?" I asked.

"Maybe she was still alive after he hit her, so he used this to finish her off. Didn't want her comin' to and climbin' outta the water. If he shot her, would've told where they were." Raff ran the fishing line through his fingers, pausing to inspect it, then looped it several times until it resembled a bitty lasso. "This here's quality. It's made of white, or near enough, horse hair."

"If you soak that hair in linseed oil it's pretty hard to see in water," McFarley provided. "Maybe Beaulieux beat her with the rock because he felt guilty about what he was about to do, so didn't want her conscious."

The Pinkerton spoke in a dispassionate manner, words lean. He never met Madam Beaulieux, there were no personal relations between them, whereas I knew her as a vibrant creature, albeit a swindler, a mountebank. I watched him, perpending how mundane this death must be to a man of his profession, how often he found himself in a similar position.

Her death brought her collusion in this affair to a resounding halt, so did McFarley feel deflated, cheated at being denied the notoriety of bringing her to justice with her partner? There was no question they would have been brought to trial, been found guilty, and swung from the gallows. Perhaps she had gotten off lightly.

"He thought it kinder to render his victim unconscious before he garroted her?" I speculated this might be seen as humane in some quarters, considerate, after a fashion.

"What should we do with her?" Ellington asked. "Are we going to leave her? Or bury her?"

"Beaulieux's gettin' away," Raff said. "Gotta quit jabberin' and go."

"Fine with me," said Ellington, mounting his pony.

"Tracks tell he grabbed the horses and vamoosed when he'd dealt with his wife. Friend. Whoever," Raff said.

Astride his buckskin Raff set it at the slope and rejoined the trail. The rest of us spurred our mounts on, scrabbling after him.

"You hear anythin' with those magical ears of yours, Ellington?" Raff asked.

"Nothing but the wind."

In time we came upon a compact bay mare, snatching bites here and there, reins trailing; they had not yet caught on a branch or gotten wedged in a smattering of rocks. At our approach, she lifted her head.

"They did steal her, after all," I said. "That is Bron's mare. He will be pleased with her return. Oh . . ."

"What is it?" McFarley asked.

Buffeted by loss and tidal waves of insuperable powerlessness, I could not respond.

"Ah, the boy. Is the boy brought to mind, Hennessey?"

"Yes, Agent McFarley. The horse is here. Bron's stable boy, Mouse, is not."

"What's this about Mouse?" Raff asked.

"He went missing the same night as this mare," I said.

"We'll find him."

"When?"

"After." Raff pushed his horse into a jog, face grim, the missing boy adding further impetus to our chase. "Get the mare, Ellington."

I centered on Madam Beaulieux. What tipped the balance between the killers? Was it an argument, as McFarley put forward, stoked by the pressure of the scheme next on the Beaulieuxs' agenda? Were they not siblings, or friends, merely brothers in blood whose paths crossed and who, that day forth, collaborated to bring death and mayhem to those guilty of doing Beaulieux, and dozens of others, an injustice? Why kill her?

I suspected we were not far away from finding out.

⟫⟪

Raff tracked Beaulieux's horse with ease until our trail merged with a well-marked stock highway. Recent hoofprints pugged the ground; hundreds, if not thousands of them.

Raff tapped the buckskin to where the prints of Beaulieux's mount and those of the traveling herd converged. "Where does this go, Ellington?"

"That depends. There's a fork ahead," Ellington said. "The drivers can take the cattle east across the Eagle Rock bridge and on to Cheyenne, or down to Winnemucca where they're processed for San Francisco."

"It late in the year to be doin' that?"

"Not really. People have to eat, Marshal, and the money's good. It's worth the trouble in my humble opinion." Ellington's pleasure at Raff asking his view glowed like foxfire, which I found strangely endearing.

"Could be movin' to new grazin'."

"If so, they'll all go in one direction when they get to the fork," McFarley said, entering the conversation.

"We'll see." Raff kicked the buckskin on.

Heavy forest now behind us, we transited through stands of pine and fir that thinned the closer we came to the Snake River Desert. Rocky outcrops grew more common, distinctive cone-shaped hills on the horizon denotative of volcanoes and jagged terrain treacherous underfoot.

If Beaulieux hit open country, reaching the desert before we caught him, he would be easy to spot, a black figure defined, prominent amongst sun-parched grasses and wildflowers. The reverse was also true, self-preservation making him vigilant, as with a glance across miles of flat land it would be just as easy for him to pick that we rode after him.

Further to that, to pilfer Raff's favorite phrase, where in the blue blazes *was* the man?

"When did you last come by here, Cam?" I asked.

Interpreting this an invitation, Ellington clucked the mare he led to quicken her pace and brought Dasher alongside Samson. His belly jiggled above his belt, sweat sheened his brow and dripped into his eyes; frequent whispered curses attested salty water burned his eyeballs. His shirtsleeves were rolled to the elbows, folds crisp, forearms burned red. Despite these discomforts I gauged he was having the time of his life.

"It's a number of years." His mouth drooped, but he brightened in an instant, the swing to low spirits temporary. "Me and my friend Hal Panchez decided to go seek our fortune. You remember I told you about Hal, Marshal?"

Raff muttered something unintelligible. McFarley snorted.

"Anyhow, it wasn't a month before we decided there's no place like home, so home we went."

"How far did you boys get?" My engaging him in conversation sprang more out of wanting to relieve boredom and distract myself from tremors that blitzed my body than interest in his youth, or tales of exploration with his crony Hal Panchez.

"We made Eureka."

"And where, pray tell, is Eureka?"

"Just head for Boise, get on the Overland Stage there to Payne's Ferry, which takes you across the Snake then on to Kelton in Utah Territory and …" He saw my attention streeling, but instead of taking offense laughed at himself. "South of here, Miss Reed. Eureka is south."

Raff, brows a dark line, sent the message loud and clear we should desist talking.

We rode in silence. Assuming a casual pose, I rested one hand atop the other on my saddle horn, in the hope no one would notice how badly they were shaking. Samson did not let escalating plaguey symptoms of my ailment bother him; I allowed him rein to tread on the heels of the other horses, taking his steadiness for granted, as many a time he had carried me with little guidance.

"Do you have a sweetheart, Cam?" To this day I have no clue what prompted me to ignore Raff's directive. "Does a lovely young lady await your return to Hollow Oak Falls?"

"Don't encourage him," Raff said.

Cam held my eye, a conspiratorial grin spread on his boyish face, as he slowly shook his head in exaggerated denial.

Seemingly at pains to confirm himself an annoyance of the highest caliber, Cam Ellington had redeeming qualities awkward to discern amongst the wheat and chaff of his incessant blather. I appreciated his sincerity and perception of fun, there was no uncharitable bone in his body or meanness to his character. Not least of his qualities was a sense of wonderment in mankind, of the human spirit.

I smiled with him and was rewarded with a cheeky wink before, in as fine a display of shooting as I have ever witnessed even when skillful, notable shooters of popular Wild West shows were included, an unseen marksman shot Cam Ellington clean through the heart and wiped the disarming grin off his face, forever.

TWENTY-ONE

Make my enemy brave and strong,
so if defeated, I will not be ashamed.
—Plains Native American proverb

"To the rocks!" Raff called, his buckskin already halfway there, McFarley's horse at his flank.

We made shelter, bullets pinging around us, splintering chips off the boulders we hunkered behind. When Raff made sure McFarley and I were sufficiently protected, I noted a cut on his cheekbone.

"You are injured!"

"It's nothin'."

"But—"

He held up a hand and my protest fluttered then duly died on my lips.

In spite of the encouragement of scattered gunfire to do otherwise, Dasher stood by Ellington and nosed his master's hip, unflurried by bullets fired in rapid succession past his ears. Bron's mare strayed along the trail, any sense of urgency to remove herself out of shooting range low on her list of important things to be getting on with.

"If he intended to shoot, why pick Cam?" I asked no one in particular.

"Roundest target," McFarley said. Shamefaced when meeting my ire he added: "Sorry, Hennessey. Spoke out of turn."

Raff got off the buckskin, removed his hat, and hung it on his saddle. Heart in my mouth I watched him climb to the top of the boulders that were our sanctuary, boots slipping on occasion. With infinite care, he peeked over the top. He ducked a fraction of a second before a fusillade of bullets, raps of hell and fury, ricocheted near where his head had been.

"Must've gotten close to getting yourself a new parting, Marshal. You get a bead on him? Reckon he's yonder, where the trail widens," McFarley said.

"Saw that." Raff clambered back to the horses.

When twenty minutes passed with no further shots fired, Raff collected his reins and prepared to mount. I did not move.

"We are not leaving Cam here, Marshal."

"A murderer is—"

"We are *not* leaving him."

"*We* aren't. *I* am."

"I agree wholeheartedly with your decision to leave Madam Beaulieux by the spring, but unlike her, Cam was no interloper, or killer. He deserves more."

"If you've strong feelin's, stay here. We'll pick you up when we're goin' back to Melancholy. Maybe."

"I might just do that." I scowled at him, but he showed no sign of retreating, therefore, I saw no middle course. I dismounted, crept to the boulder at the edge of the pile, rested against its warm surface, and peered around it.

"You wanna lose your nose, goin' the right way about it," Raff said.

No warning shots sounded with my appearance, so I decided the person who killed Cam Ellington—surely Zeke Beaulieux—had skedaddled. Or did he wait for me to step from behind the outcrop?

I saw one option to detect if he had flown while his pursuers argued whether or not he was gone, or if he waited us out.

I ordered the dogs to stay then, presenting myself as small a target as possible, ran fast as my wobbly legs deigned carry me to Cam, skidding, falling to my knees by his head. Bullets punctuated my footsteps, Earth spitting mouthfuls of dirt that bounced off my back and thighs.

Beaulieux had not skedaddled.

"Dammit, woman!"

I hooked my forearms under Ellington's armpits and clasped my hands across his chest, but quickly realized a flaw in my plan; stymied, I lacked the wherewithal to hoist Cam onto his saddle. With no alternative, I grabbed his feet and started dragging him in fits and starts toward the rocks. Dasher matched my pace. Hesitant, with the wooden action of an animal aware there is something amiss but not at all sure what to do about it, in his bewilderment he provided an effective shield.

Raff ran after me, dipping below Dasher's wither when a bullet whizzed past his chin.

"You're gonna get yourself killed with this sorta craziness."

If not out of breath my retort would have been pithy and robust, devoid of compliment or gratitude. Raff pushed me aside with uncalled for vigor and slung the not inconsiderable weight of the dead man over Dasher's saddle in an enviable demonstration of strength.

He retrieved the pony's reins, pressed a hand to Cam's thigh to hold him steady and keep him from slithering to the ground then, hunched behind Dasher led him, and me, to safety.

"Happy now?" He transferred Dasher to McFarley's care and stalked to his horse.

"Yes, I am."

"Beaulieux knows he's bein' followed. 'Less he recognized us he mightn't figure who's doin' the followin'." Raff's voice rang flat, factual, no chink in his emotion. "But he's gotta be thinkin' it may be the law and we ain't givin' up, 'specially with one of ours dead."

"If he did not recognize us, Marshal, why shoot? For all he knew we could be normal folks heading to North's Ridge."

"Men like him make it their business to familiarize themselves with goings on. They remember things because not remembering can make a difference to whether they see tomorrow. Or not," McFarley said. "We haven't gotten close enough to see him, but he has to be checking if he's got a tail. Maybe Beaulieux saw your horse on the road, Hennessey. He doesn't fade into the background."

The relationship Raff and I shared at various times was not a well-kept secret in Melancholy. If Beaulieux became aware of my friendship with the marshal while living there, he would assume if he spotted Samson, that Raff was not far behind.

Frustrating as it was to give Beaulieux a head start, staying behind the boulders until Raff deemed it safe to venture out ensured none of us found ourselves in a similar condition to Cam Ellington. Raff assured me the delay of negligible concern, so we used the enforced rest period to discuss events of the morning, all the while avoiding the bundle secured atop the skinny pony that, seemingly conscious of the responsibility of his burden, did not move.

"Beaulieux's choices tell us about him." Although Raff pitched his voice low I had no cause to strain to hear him. "He could've run, stayed ahead of us, but he didn't. He confronted us."

"He is confident," I said.

"Yep."

"He feels he has nothing to lose. He'll fight when cornered."

McFarley tugged Dasher nearer his bay. "*If* he presumes we know who we're chasing, and why."

"When Miss Reed and I took cover behind old Dasher here, if I was Beaulieux I would've dropped the pony. That done, it'd be a turkey shoot."

"I agree, Marshal, though it's harder to hit somebody at a distance than people think. 'Specially if they're moving," McFarley said.

"He had no issue hitting Cam square in the chest," I pointed out.

"Was that good marksmanship, or a stroke of luck?" McFarley asked. "Or something different again? I hear what you're saying, Marshal. Beaulieux had the perfect opportunity to reduce our party so there was just me left. That would've made the odds much higher for him achieving whatever it is he's gotten his mind set on doing."

"Do you mean he missed us deliberately, Agent McFarley?" If so, this added another facet of dangerous to Beaulieux's character, and quadrupled the sense of urgency baying we must capture him, at all costs.

"He wants us to chase him," McFarley said. "He wants us to see what he's going to do. And that won't change unless we get real close, which is when he'll probably get the notion to deal with us by taking action that's a bit more . . . permanent."

"You give credence to him wanting us to be, in effect, his audience? Can a man behave with such arrogance?"

"None of us have spoken with him, Miss Reed, except in passin'. How can we know what he's capable of?" Raff sized up Dasher's load. "Ellington stays here."

"I told you—"

"And I heard you. He's gonna slow us down." Raff indicated a protective overhang left of where we stood. "We'll put him there and cover him with rocks since we ain't got a shovel. Bury him later when we're goin' home."

"That will do." We might not make it home, there might not be a 'later', and I guessed the men digested that prospect, also. "If it has to."

"Come on. Got to be quick," said McFarley, who had already dismounted.

Soon a cairn marked Ellington's temporary, above-ground grave.

Raff and the Pinkerton arrayed a final rock apiece atop the mound and returned to their horses. I lingered, for it felt disrespectful to enshroud the newly dead then immediately leave them, all alone. They met eternity by themselves, a kind word to send them along the crow road was not too much to ask. I bowed my head without conscious thought.

"You prayin'?" Intimate with my record pertaining to religious practice, Raff did not hide his skepticism.

"Not in the usual interpretation of the word. My version."

"You don't believe in God."

"No, I do not." I opened eyes I could not recall closing, and blinked Raff into focus. "But Cam Ellington is the type of man who probably did."

Raff, at his limit with me, abandoned our discourse and climbed the boulders again. No shots were fired, and he arrived back on solid ground with all his limbs attached. "Can't wait 'round all day for this fella. If he's smart, he's gone."

He mounted the buckskin and spurred him to the trail, reins in one hand, Sharps gripped in the other. I watched him go, his body rigid, every atom singing, and dreaded hearing the snap of a rifle shot.

It is said a person does not hear the bullet that kills them, although how anyone pitched upon this theory or volunteered to test it mystified me. I hoped for Ellington's sake this was true, that when drawing his last breath he had no premonition lead inscribed with his name flew over tussock and soil, rock, and water, aimed at his big, generous heart.

"Are you coming, Hennessey?" McFarley adjusted his hat, wound Dasher's rein about his saddle horn, collected Bron's mare and trotted after the marshal.

I fumbled for my whiskey, fortified myself, then called the dogs who were rolling in the dust, immune to the serious nature of our situation.

"Here we go, for all it is worth," I muttered to Samson, the only living being who never questioned my methods, or judgment. "Godspeed," I whispered to our fallen friend, squeezed Samson's gleaming sides, and chirped him to move along.

⇢⇢⇠⇠

Optimism McFarley raised that the cattle barreled onto the same trail at the fork proved no influence on the matter to hand.

"Dammit!"

Even with limited experience in tracking, I instantly grasped the problem that confronted us, sharing Raff's frustration.

"The herd split," McFarley said, unnecessarily.

Hoofprints juxtaposed hoofprints; those of horses ridden by drivers nursing the cattle and anyone riding through in-between. I had confidence Raff could determine which trail Beaulieux took if we were not in a hurry, but time was limited in supply.

"We've gotta split too," Raff said. "Ain't got time to figure which way Beaulieux's gone. We'd lose him."

"Two trails, three of us," the Pinkerton said.

"I'll go left with Miss Reed. You go right, McFarley."

"Why not send her with me?"

"He know you?"

"Don't see how. And if he does after our . . . altercation, not much I can do except stay out of sight."

"If Beaulieux sees you, mightn't recognize you. If Miss Reed and the dogs are taggin' along it's a whole different story."

"Sounds reasonable."

"Trust me. Be glad she's comin' with me."

"I am sitting right here, gentlemen. Do not discuss my involvement as though I hold no opinion of my own or have suddenly become invisible. Did you just roll your eyes, Rafael Cooper?"

"Ain't got time for this, neither."

"Take these spares." McFarley ignored us, not wishing to become embroiled in our dust-up, and handed me Dasher's reins. "If Beaulieux sees me following him he'll definitely recognize the mare. Gives us a half 'n' half chance."

I tugged Ellington's skinny pony to Samson. Bron's mare, tied to his saddle, plodded after him.

"If he does see you and recognizes you, McFarley, he'll know Miss Reed and me're nearby, so have to catch him before he hits the desert. Whatever happens, it'll end soon."

"How do we make contact afterward?" I asked.

"If McFarley doesn't find Beaulieux by tomorrow afternoon, latest, he'll figure we did and cut across country to meet us."

"And the other way around if all goes according to plan." McFarley wheeled his gelding. "Good luck!"

"And to you, Agent McFarley," I said.

Raff and I watched the Pinkerton's horse pick a line across the trail and disappear.

"Just you and me now, Miss Reed. Let's go."

Late afternoon the darkened sky intimated nightfall was closing in, although it hovered several hours ahead. The diaspora of a brewing storm filled my senses, and to underline the expectancy lightning punched distant mountain peaks, thunder adding its forceful opinion.

"Rain is coming, Marshal."

"And gonna be a lot of it."

The storm overtook us, rain light and intermittent, increasing until it felt like rain gods fired slivers of ice at my cheeks, the slickers we had donned plastered to our bodies, hopelessly inadequate protection. Wind and water roared, the rain aggressive, deafening when striking the hood of my slicker. I bowed my head, water streaming off my nose, entrusting Samson to stay with Raff's gelding.

When barely audible words reached me, I lifted my head to see Raff pointing to a ledge that wound up the side of a ravine we had entered. I steered Samson and the ponies after the buckskin, who tackled the incline sure-footed as a mountain goat.

Shale bounced across my path and I looked skyward, afraid I would see Beaulieux silhouetted there, rifle trained on me. All I discerned through pelting rain was the rear ends of big horn sheep as they zigzagged and kicked, then leaped nimbly over the ridge, rumps and stripes trimming their legs flashes of white in the eerie, diaphanous light.

Midway up the ravine wall Samson jerked, fighting the bit, tense and jittery. I glanced behind me and saw Dasher had missed a step and a hind leg hung off the track; he worked it, searching for purchase, walleyed, pitching like a rocking horse to maintain balance. If either pony lost their foothold, I had no desire for my stallion or myself to be dragged with them, to our deaths, so released the slip knot that secured Dasher to Samson's saddle.

Dasher teetered, and I thought I was destined to watch him topple into the ravine, reduced to crumpled bones and flesh below. Mercifully, he regained his footing, and he and the mare trudged doggedly on without further mishap.

I slid off Samson, rescued Dasher's reins, and led the horses through a cave mouth after Raff and his buckskin, relieved to walk into a spacious cavern. Anxiety at entering a confined space shimmered and died, the transition from suffering Nature's ear-splitting invasion to relative quiet, a blessing.

The cave was not discernible from the lower trail, but I did not ask Raff how he knew of its existence. His outlaw past saw him shelter with a parade of men disporting names and descriptions found in bold, fancy script on *Wanted* bills. In later years many of these men brought fame—or infamy—upon themselves and bedecked pages, even chapters in history books.

Now in the position of upholding the law, rather than fighting it, Raff redirected my attention with no care for subtlety if I ever raised his former profession.

The depths of our refuge were indistinct, difficult to determine in the gloom. I shoved the slicker hood off my forehead, gaze drawn upward to a dome suggestive of the primitive and precious; it added gravitas, intimating we stepped on hallowed ground. Odd-shaped blotches clung, spread across the ceiling and upper walls.

Bats.

I shivered, imagining them gliding into the dusk, flying past us in a tactile scream, and prayed the incessant storm would compel them to stay where they were.

The horses drooped, coats slick, drenched. Custer huddled against

Raven, taking comfort from her solid body. They were as sorry and bedraggled an assortment of creatures as I had ever seen.

We unsaddled the horses, split grain we carried into equal portions, scarcely sufficient for a mouthful per horse, and rubbed them down best we could.

Once we had attended the animals Raff transferred wood to a stone fire ring. The last person to shelter here had carted kindling and a stack of branches to the cave, enough for a fire to burn throughout the night, and I felt terrible we would not be able to replace it, accepted disbursement for usage.

"Get your wet clothes off," Raff said, arranging sticks in the shape of a teepee. "Let 'em dry overnight."

"Then please avert your eyes."

Lord, I sounded like a prim virgin with her virtue under threat. Raff did not hide a smile, a splash of brightness in the murky light, amused by the absurdity of my request for he had seen me mother-naked more times than I could count.

Still, I draped a blanket around my shoulders, turned my back to him, removed my boots then wriggled out of my trousers. They were saturated from mid-thigh where not protected by the slicker, and the fabric stuck with frustrating tenacity. They peeled off my legs, eventually, and I hung them on a knob protruding from the wall the perfect height to service as a clothes peg. I shrugged into a clean shirt and trousers, wrapped another blanket around my waist and shook my bedroll loose, laying it close as I could to the fire without it catching alight.

Raff took my boots and placed them next to his, away from the flames.

"Don't want the leather gettin' stiff and crackin'."

"Thank you." I lowered myself to the ground, crossed my legs and held my hands to the growing flames. The smoke thinned, swirling to nothingness, inhaled though an invisible fissure above us. "You are not worried Beaulieux could spot the smoke from our fire?"

"Rain'll screen it."

"What do you expect he will do? It would be madness to carry on in this weather."

"If he's got his wits about him he'll shelter till the worst passes."

"He may decide to ride through the storm, especially as he is certified not of sane mind."

"On a ways there's a cavern that's wider known. If he's ahead of us that'll be where he's holed up. That'd be dangerous."

"It might flood?" All going well, perhaps the weather would complete our business for us and drown Beaulieux. Was that too much to ask?

"No. Long time ago was in it with a friend, Alexander. Sometimes there's volcanic rumbles hereabouts. Mother Earth shifts. Had to cut coupla trees and put 'em in to support the ceiling 'cause it's unstable."

"Were you not concerned it might collapse on you?"

"Seemed the lesser evil," he said, enigmatically. "Later an old coot told me about this place, so I used here then on."

I jumped when a noise from the ill-lit depths echoed throughout the cave. "Do you think there are rattlesnakes in here?"

"If we don't go lookin' for rattlers, they won't come lookin' for us." Raff poked the fire with a stick. It flared, encouraged to bite. "Stay calm."

Words failed me. Here we sat in the company of bats and, potentially, rattlesnakes, in pursuit of a disgusting aberration of a human being, Cam Ellington lay dead in a makeshift grave and Raff was telling me to 'Stay calm'? The man was insufferable, his blasé standpoint inducement to clout him upside the head.

The fire grew, highlighting the wound that, washed clean by the rainstorm, oozed clear liquid from a scab establishing hold on his brown skin.

"I'll put salve on it." Raff pre-empted me, reading my mind.

Firelight flickered on the cave walls, and I stood and walked over to what looked random marks intrinsic to the rock. As I drew closer they evolved to assume childlike forms. I peered at a line with dashes running through it, like a simplistic centipede, bulb-shaped at the bottom.

"How old do you suppose these are?"

"Been here generations before we were born," Raff said, reverent. "Be here after we're forgotten."

"Evidence we are but 'temporary beings on a borrowed Earth'. That is what my uncle used to say."

My beloved uncle wore a rhapsodic expression when expounding his hypotheses on the universe. From a young person's perspective his observations were a maze. I would sit, spellbound, when he spoke, coddling ever-present hopefulness I might understand, piloting my intellect around obstacles to the center of the maze, calculating where an egress lay.

His twists and turns more often than not left me in the same state of incomprehension as when he began. Satisfied with an explanation he would recline in his over-stuffed armchair, hands clasped on his mountainous belly, lecture complete. I would nod, as though I cottoned on to the wisdom he imparted. Only on reaching adulthood did I appreciate what he attempted to relay to his impressionable niece.

"Native peoples believe the same," Raff said.

This brought home that yes, there were differences when those of diverse backgrounds and continents were evaluated from the outside; skin and hair color, the shape of a nose or slant of an eye, compared. But delve below the surface and Earth's population was alike in more ways than were self-explanatory; when individuals not taken, exclusively, as a measure of bone, ligament, and muscle bound in skin clothing.

"What do these mean?" I indicated a drawing that had the appearance of a more elaborate centipede, all squiggles, and dots with a truncated body. "What does this depict?"

Raff rose and brushed his hands together, patting Samson's rump, muttering reassurance when he sidled between the stallion and Dasher.

"Not sure," he offered, after intense study. "Not of the story they're tellin'. That shows water." He pointed to several indistinct shapes. "Those lines show death—they're bodies. The upside-down head? Means whoever this drawin's of is dead."

"These are fascinating."

"About all I can tell you."

Carved with painstaking care they must have taken the artist or artists hours, conceivably even days to complete. The unsophisticated figures depicted were not indicative of a dearth of talent; shapes and lines were abbreviated because they were all that was required. I admired the condensing of a tale, it whittled to its purest representation, easily read by those party to their meaning.

"Not much like your art," Raff said.

"That does not mean they are not impressive in their own right."

"Wasn't what I'm sayin'," he said, hand light on my arm.

He returned to the fire and began preparing our meal.

I walked along the wall, captivated, and wondered at the lives of the people whose legends were illustrated here. Were these figures a historical rendition of their origins? Did the artist complete them expecting someone might happen upon them in the future? Or did they not care a whit for recognition, their work an expression not necessarily executed to share?

About to go sit with Raff, I noticed a modern contribution to the wall, carved perhaps by someone sheltering in the cave, as did we, waiting for a storm to pass. This man had written:

Alexander Jackson

1867

Unlike the preceding artwork the blocky lettering jarred, a discordant note, no beauty or symmetry to its execution.

"What is your friend Alexander's family name, Marshal?"

"Jackson," he replied, after a pause.

"His name is right here! Wait, there is another. I shall see if I can . . ."

"It'll be 'Raff Cooper'. Same year."

"Indeed, it is."

"Was gonna write Rafael." Raff folded into himself. "But when I got to the 'f' was already bored. It's harder to carve that rock than you'd think. Now I'm ashamed how it disrespects these people."

"You were young, deprived of much as a child," I said, wanting to go to him, to comfort him when bleakness settled on his face. "There are many who will persecute you for reasons solely in their heads, so do not chastise yourself for what you did when no one cared to teach you better. When there was no elder to guide you and set you on the right course. I am aware this lack bothers you greatly. I am also aware you aspire to rectify past mistakes to balance what you perceive shortcomings. Tell me more of Alexander."

"He wouldn't leave things half done. Haven't known a body as stubborn." Raff smiled at a memory, then at me. "Well, maybe one person. Anyway, Alex had time to put his name there 'cause we cold-camped in this cave a week."

"Had you run afoul of the law?"

"We'd made it here but was every chance we weren't gonna get much farther." Characteristically, Raff skirted my bid for information. "Alex wanted to do somethin' that lasted, to show he'd been alive. His scratch on Earth."

"Yet, you did make it to a safe haven."

"*I did.*" Raff paid close attention to whatever canned delight he had emptied into the skillet. "Alex equaled you in determination, Ness. Determination didn't get him far. We split when we thought ourselves free of the posse after us, plannin' to meet in Montana Territory in a month. I got to our meetin' point first and waited for Alex. Then I heard he'd gotten himself killed at White Buffalo Calf on the way. Got mouthy with somebody who took offense."

It took a couple minutes, but it occurred to me Raff had addressed me as Ness, not Miss Reed as when we were in company, or Hennessey if thawing toward friendliness, or distracted. He might revert to formality on our return to Melancholy once this chase played out, however, betweenwhiles, I was happy to accept this relaxed attitude as prelude to us regaining lost intimacy.

"You never speak of Alexander. I do not recall you ever referring to anyone by this name."

"He's years gone. Lot's happened since."

"You were close?"

"Yep."

Metal plates clattered on the fire surround, signaling the discussion of that specific topic at an end. Drawn by the aroma of heating meat the dogs were settled by the fire and watched Raff dish our food. Damp, shivery, and hungry fit to eat a bear, when Raff handed me a plate I looked at the meal and struggled to control my roiling stomach, my impulse to vomit. I steeled myself, picked up my spoon and made the effort to eat. It proved beyond me. Raff devoured his meal then gestured I should pass mine over so he could finish what I could not.

I pulled my hip flask free and offered it to him. If he made mention of my shaking hand, the excuse it shook because of the cold lay at the ready to apply.

"After you, Ness."

A single mouthful was insufficient. The second proposed a hand in friendship to my gullet, tentacles of warmth radiating toward my extremities. The third had me believing it possible I might feel human again. I leaned around the flames and exchanged the flask for a cigarette.

"While studying those drawings on the walls a thought struck, Raff." I stuck a twig in the fire to use as a taper, then put it to my cigarette tip. "It is of nominal use at this late date, probably never of use even if we figured it at the beginning—"

"Just tell me." Raff reduced the contents of my flask with a long swallow, rested it on a flat stone my side of the fire, and waited on me to explain.

TWENTY-TWO

Old age is not as honorable as death,

but most people want it.

—*Crow proverb*

"I doubt the artists here were pressed for time, so that does not contribute toward the simplicity but effectiveness of these etchings," I said. "What is integral to completing this work is persistence, for the process is labor-intensive and, as you found, Raff—tedious.

"Let us examine the 'CX' a member of the Newman family toed into the dirt in their barn. Consider, if you will, that unlike the Indian here, whomever did it *was* pressed for time. Desperate to convey a message, this had to be done in the most concise form they could think of. That they came up with anything useful under such pressure was a miracle."

"I'm gettin' lost."

"Bear with me. The Newmans were going to die, all of them—there was no way around that shattering reality and they knew this—yet one of them was exceptionally brave."

Raff nodded agreement but did not contribute more.

"Last spring, when Charlotte and I were at the Sweet Venus Too mine the day she died, when not rambling like a brainsick woman she took great pleasure regaling me with her warped justification for killing those girls. Charlotte wanted to make sure I knew *what* she had done, and *why*. Consider this.

"What if the 'X' at the Newman farm was not used in its guise as a letter—it represented an action. We discussed that Zeke might enjoy an audience, essentially to grandstand and prove his cleverness. The Church of Celestial Light and Paradise Divine is too long a title to write when time is short. Did the Beaulieuxs tell the Newmans the reason behind their hunting them down, and why they were determined to kill them, and the father, mother, or sharp-witted Newman child devised a code for whomever cared to search their farmstead after their deaths? If they knew their bodies were going to be transported elsewhere, desperation saw them do it anyway."

"What kinda action you talkin' with the 'X', Ness?"

"Do you recall your school days? Arithmetic lessons, particularly?"

"Not with any sorta fondness."

"Consider for a moment that the 'X' is the multiplication sign."

I let him sit with what I had said, rolled a cigarette for each of us and lit mine, rewarded with a bark of appreciation when Raff understood what I had surmised.

"That's quick thinkin'."

"Yes, it was, and they took an enormous risk. They were restricted by time and must act without raising suspicion. Whomever drew those letters in the dirt meant 'CX' as 'C *multiplied*'. If 'C' is multiplied three times, what might those initials stand for?"

"Chandelier Creek Crossin'," Raff supplied. "That was brave and clever."

"It was all they had left to them; waiting for the inevitable without at least trying to leave a clue or mark was unthinkable. Better to leave something behind, no matter how inconsequential: much like your friend Alexander."

"Alex wasn't just my friend." Raff busied himself wiping our dishes, rubbing at grease spots visible only to him, stacked them, and went about preparing coffee. "Was my cousin."

"Oh, Raff, I am so sorry."

Why did condolences fall flat regardless how sincere the person who offered them?

"Boy had no more'n a lick of sense." Raff shrugged and set out our mugs.

"I wonder how McFarley is faring." My change of subject sounded all kinds of clumsy, even when a complimentary light shone upon it.

"No worse than us."

Raff poured the coffee and we sat, lost in cobwebs of thought. After extended quietude Raff began to speak.

"The newspaperman Parkinson has a lotta stuff about Chandelier Creek 'cause he was writin' articles on it. Got pictures, pieces he'd written, scribbles."

"So you mentioned."

"Said he hadn't looked at his notes in years. Didn't make the connection."

"What connection? Gosh-darn, just spit it out!"

"Frustratin' habit, ain't it?" He surely referred to my propensity to draw somber conversation down byroads many found difficult to stick with. His comment made no contribution toward amusing me, but I allowed him to continue without riposte. "Parkinson spent a lotta time readin' and filin' everythin' on Chandelier Creek. He sure was thorough. Then he was instructed to abandon his work. But a time after the Cowans died a list of names ended in his possession. Fired him up again."

"Who is on this list?"

"Ten men. Finnegan ran a brigade that sorted out what Parkinson called 'problems'. It was made up of those ten."

"A pastor directed men under his auspices to kill?"

"Uh-huh. Could be they're responsible for Chandelier Creek."

"Criminy." This unwinding conversation was like a snowball gathering speed and bulk as it cannonballed down a mountain side. "How did Mr. Parkinson get the list?"

"A lady gave it to Parkinson's wife, on the quiet, after the Cowans died."

Raff furnished more of why Clive Parkinson abandoned his research on the massacre.

"That poor child. Her poor parents!" What sort of person could bring themselves to stitch a child's lips and eyelids shut?

"A Henry Wilson's listed as a member of this brigade." Raff blew on his coffee, clearly expecting a reaction to the name, for me to link facts of some description or another. Like his man Parkinson, I did not.

"It has to be a common name," I said, then expanded this with: "Shared by quite a few, I suspect."

"The family killed in Fancy were called Ward. The father: Henry."

"So I believe." If Raff bargained on my pulling his loose musings together I was to fail him. I had no idea where he tried to lead me.

"Another on the list was a fella called Netherland. Pretorius Netherland. *That* ain't common."

"No, it is not."

"The Bible at the Newman farm had the Netherland family tree inside. They hadn't been in our county long—reckon Netherland was in hidin' as Newman."

I thrust my mug at the coffee pot spout. Raff refilled it then topped his own.

"Please explain."

"I'd say in the beginnin' Beaulieux, as Porter, didn't know who was behind the Chandelier Creek Crossin' massacre. He relied on the law to catch the men involved and call 'em to stand trial. That never happened."

"So when the Cowans' supposed involvement in Chandelier Creek came to light, Beaulieux suspected Finnegan ordered the massacre?" I asked.

"Beaulieux was part of the inner circle of Finnegan's church. He'd know about the brigade and the men who rode in it. He'd seen Parkinson at Winsome Valley, so I'm thinkin' later on, not wantin' to put himself in the firin' line, he set the newspaperman onto the killers through Mrs. Parkinson by givin' her their names. When Clive Parkinson was threatened, his daughter kidnapped, he gave away investigatin' Chandelier Creek, so Beaulieux went after Finnegan's troops himself.

"This Finnegan sounds an intelligent man. His offsider disappeared—somebody who'd lost relations at the creek—and his men started bitin' the ground. Doesn't take a highbrow to figure who's doin' it. He sent the remainder of the brigade into hidin' usin' aliases.

"Say Wilson and Netherland changed their last names but started the new one with the same letter, changin' Wilson for Ward, Netherland for Newman. Not wantin' to give up their forenames, they kept 'em. Folks weren't gonna find 'em out 'cause they were gonna be called Mr. Ward, or Mr. Newman—"

"And lived in isolated places where interaction with others was minimal," I said. Raff had kept more than the puppies he found at the Newman farmstead to himself. "If the Beaulieuxs started their spree by killing Cyrus Finnegan it would put everyone on high alert straight away, whereas if they began with those in the brigade, who were scattered to the winds ..." The Beaulieuxs were not indiscriminately killing followers of Cyrus Finnegan, they were killing *particular* followers. "Beaulieux and his victims were members of the same church. They would have known each other well, which begs I ask: Why did his victims not recognize Beaulieux when he moved into their town?"

"When Finnegan figured who was behind the deaths I'd say he told his men to move on since Beaulieux knew where they were, but to watch close for him. Those in hidin' rarely came to town, so it wouldn't be hard for the Beaulieuxs to avoid bein' seen. Besides, each party would be constantly on the look-out for their enemies."

"The feeling of betrayal Beaulieux must have experienced when it struck him who was behind the attack would have been unbearable."

"Or when he was told. Makes sense Beaulieux still has a contact in the church. That's how he knows where these men move to. And Finnegan's gotta know somebody's passin' on their whereabouts to Beaulieux if brigade members are dyin' in new locations."

Bron's mare let forth a seemingly endless deluge of urine that steamed in the cold air, the stench acrid, overpowering. I fanned my face with both hands, then asked: "Do you think this woman who gave the names to Mrs. Parkinson was Madam Beaulieux?"

"As like as not. The Beaulieuxs've been smart. Devious."

Raff's tone made it sound in his view the Beaulieuxs' behavior was less than repugnant—he felt more a kind of . . . brotherhood, toward them.

"Do you admire the Beaulieuxs for taking the law into their own hands? They killed women and children, Raff. A babe in its mother's womb."

"Women and children died at the creek too, Ness." He stared into the flames. "Don't 'admire' 'em. Understand 'em." He removed his gaze from the fire, to meet mine. "If somebody I loved was slaughtered, cruel vengeance would come to their killers sure as I'm sittin' here."

"Would you kill entire families and arrange them the way the Beaulieuxs did?"

"I'd look at it."

Now and again, when confident I had Raff all mapped out, he aired an opinion or insight to affirm his mind an agile, slippery beast, my grasp on corners of his character tenuous—people safely ensconced in a civilized environment might venture his attitude bordered archaic. For him to admit he would consider such violence evidenced this man I had known near a third of my years possessed dimensions unfathomable to me.

"Do you suppose the Pinkertons connected Beaulieux to Chandelier Creek Crossing from the beginning?"

"Have to ask McFarley. He knows who the Beaulieuxs've murdered, so if he didn't connect 'em whoever sent him after the Beaulieuxs did. Somebody made up the story about 'em stealin' money as cover."

"Why would Finnegan not send a church representative after Beaulieux?"

"Maybe he did. Maybe he has."

"The Pinkertons? McFarley? Did Finnegan hire the Pinkertons to go after the Beaulieuxs because he cannot find them? No. Wanting the minimum of people involved he would send his own men if he knew where they were. Then again, he may not think he can send men away for an indefinite period without the wider church community knowing the real reason why he was doing so. McFarley received a telegram from Nevada telling him the Beaulieuxs were in Melancholy so . . ."

"McFarley said he got a telegram, but what if that's a lie? And you could say Beaulieux is actually helpin' Finnigan. He's killin' off witnesses to Chandelier Creek. Anyhow, church ain't gonna want all this gettin' out."

"This is supposition, Raff." My head spun, my brain caught in a whirlpool. "So many people have died, so many innocents on the periphery from children to elderly ladies. You know, originally I felt the attempt to drown me was because Viola Sargeson was murdered. This, after her killer noticed me studying the horse trough at Bron's livery."

"Now?"

"I am still disposed to think that." I fielded his confusion. "In between, when Bron told me his horse was stolen, I wondered if I interrupted a thief scouting out the livery. Wanting to cover his tracks he subjected me to an unscheduled bath. I returned to my first theory after figuring it unlikely separate people with evil doings on their minds would be at Bron's barn during the night.

"Furthermore, the Sargesons lived along the street to the Beaulieuxs. My guess is Viola saw something to incriminate either one or both Beaulieuxs during her nocturnal wandering. Something they could not sanction coming to the attention of the law—specifically you."

"Could be you're right."

Cramps gripped my insides and I doubled over, clutching my belly. I groaned before I could tame the pain when it wracked my body.

Alarmed, Raff circumnavigated the fire ring and crouched at my side. He placed a hand between my shoulder blades, the warmth of him healing, comforting. "What is it, Ness?"

"Naught with which to concern yourself." I forced my stomach muscles to relax using diminished reserves of willpower and hitched my shoulders to encourage him to remove his hand. He did not oblige me.

I had neither courage nor discipline to look Raff in the eye without giving in and turning to him, so concentrated on the cut on his cheek and attempted to control my breathing, dreading another dose of cramp; I hated him seeing me in the low state addiction brought me to. Although difficult to hide the symptoms, I had unprecedented success in doing so when in the presence of everyone except Rafael Cooper.

He removed his hand and went to sit the other side of the fire.

"*Ward* and *Newman* and the rest of the brigade followed orders," I said and pulled myself together to divert further interest in my current state of health. "That can be said of soldiers during war."

"War's different."

"How many more victims could there be?"

"One family."

"There is more to this, Raff. Those left who we presume are in hiding will not show at the Chandelier Creek commemoration, but along with Cyrus Finnegan, High Church dignitaries are sure to attend. Will Beaulieux forgo this last family now Madam is gone and kill Finnegan in their stead?"

"Zeke's on his own now he's gotten rid of his 'wife'. That's a big task."

"A single person in a tactical spot with a selection of guns and ammunition at their disposal could inflict appalling damage on an unsuspecting crowd. If he got into position prior to the ceremony no one would know he was there. When he opened fire—well, utter pandemonium would ensue. Zeke has shown himself a person who lacks integrity or empathy in any form, and I do not foresee him holding back."

"I agree."

"However, his chances of getting away would be slim."

"He gets that far, he's expectin' he might get caught."

"Do you believe this could happen, Raff?"

"He's goin' there and feels so strongly about his mission he killed his friend. Likely his only friend." Raff rubbed his face and winced, forgetting the wound. "So, yeah, could happen."

Beyond exhausted, I shivered uncontrollably, hoping with misplaced sanguinity that during sleep the nausea coiled in my stomach would dissipate. "I am going to lie down, even though I doubt I shall sleep."

"Here, take this." Raff made to pass his blanket to me.

"No, you will need it."

"Take it."

He lobbed it across the fire ring.

"Well, if you insist," I grumbled, pleased for the added warmth it would provide.

Under the blankets, I rolled onto my side so the fire warmed my back. Raven lay at my head, Custer at my feet. Despite my declaration otherwise, I fell instantly into deep sleep.

⟫⟫⟫⟪⟪⟪

I jerked awake, my heart beating rapidly. A dog's head was outlined against the glow of the fire, the cave's close, wily air creeping to wind around me like a wheedling cat.

"What is it? Are we under attack?"

Disoriented and panicked, it took seconds to work out that Raff, tenor calm, was gently shaking me while murmuring shapeless, nonsense words. I licked lips dry as parchment.

Although my eyes were open, horrors from the nightmare retained a hold, my nemeses hale and hearty, entertaining themselves. Playlets, their characters swamp-like creatures painted in dark colors were terrifying and real, and I feared their story preordained. Did Lizzie reveal everything Madam Beaulieux prophesied?

"Here, drink this." Raff handed me his canteen, which I was required to hold with both hands they shook so hard. "You were dreamin'."

"More a nightmare," I managed.

"Lie down."

I set the canteen by my side and complied.

He sat with me, solid and reassuring, until the tremors subsided. Wedging the blanket securely under my chin, his fingers brushed my neck. They were like icicles.

"Your hands are ice-cold, Raff!"

"I'm fine." He resumed his position by the fire.

"You are not 'fine', Rafael Cooper. You will freeze to death. I insist you crawl in with me." I lifted a corner of the blanket.

"Doesn't matter how cold I am, ain't gettin' in with you, Ness."

"Why not? Are you afraid I shall corrupt you?" I profess teasing Raff added great joy to my life. Oh, how I missed it. And underlying truth was body heat was a remarkably effective method to restore one's temperature. "You know what I say makes perfect sense. It is scientifically proven."

"It's just when we share a blanket, not much sleepin' gets done."

"I am in no condition to use my feminine wiles to lure you into congress. I promise I shall keep my hands to myself. I shall keep *every part* of my body to myself."

"Heard that before. Ain't that what you said the time we got snowed in on Flintlock Mountain? Look where that got us."

"You are being ridiculous. Forget everything except how to avoid falling ill, and join me before I retract the offer and leave you to turn into a pillar of ice. Pretend I am Shakey, or Fatfoot, if it will make you more comfortable about the prospect of us in close quarters."

"Won't help 'cause you sure don't feel like Shakey or Fatfoot," he said. "Or smell like 'em."

"Praise be for small mercies." I held my breath, awaiting his decision.

He walked around the fire pit, stepped over Custer, and crouched at my hip.

"Gonna shift over?"

"What made you change your mind?" I made room for him, and he slipped beneath the blankets.

"Can't feel my nose, or my toes. Don't want you wakin' in the mornin' and findin' a stiff corpse 'cause of my pride," he said, words riffling my hair when he pulled me close. "Still think it's a bad idea."

"It makes no difference if that is how you feel, or if you are saying it to justify doing what you stress you do not wish to do." I nestled into his chest, although refrained from wrapping my arms around him, the temptation almost more than I could bear. "As you can see, this is proof I am able to hold to a promise and actually *sleep* with you."

"I'm bettin' not for long."

Gradually the heat of him, pressed against my length, spread with pertinacious intent through my limbs. I gave in, averring it would not hurt in these extenuating circumstances, to concede him one, minor victory.

TWENTY-THREE

Marshal Rafael Cooper: *Southern Idaho Territory.*

The storm eased. A weak sun displayed admirable pluck, pushing above the hills, leaden skies flaunting a temperamental bent when Raff and Hennessey brought the horses outside. Testing stability each step, they descended the path to the trail.

"Won't mount up yet."

"Why ever not? Beaulieux's tracks will not be visible after the storm."

"Weather's changed things. If he's on this trail that cavern I was tellin' you about is the only shelter to be had." It was years since he'd ridden through with Alex, but Raff remembered the cavern where they'd propped the ceiling lay a half mile from here. "If he's left it this mornin', his tracks're gonna show."

"He definitely came this way."

"You sure? Forget it. Shouldn't bother askin'."

Hennessey looked about her—wondering, Raff guessed, if Beaulieux watched them, deciding whether to shoot them stone dead.

He clucked the buckskin then cautiously and at what Hennessey called a 'maddening, snail-like pace' moved to the trail shoulder and gestured she do so, too. She tugged Samson's ribbons and called the dogs, command a hair above a whisper.

Obedient, which raised his suspicions, they fell in behind Raff and his gelding, Dasher and Bron's mare behind them.

They left the ravine, leaves strewn by wind and rain trudged into mud, ankle deep. Water dribbled off naked trees and evergreens alike, bunched together—willowy, gossiping ladies. Raff knocked a branch and cussed abstractedly as water cascaded down his arm.

"Raff, do you—"

"Quiet."

Her silence had been too good, and uncharacteristic, to last.

"But do you—"

He turned, annoyed by the interruption, which broke his concentration. She knew better. What he was going to say was lost, cut in half by the shock of an almighty punch to his middle section. A peculiar, not unfamiliar sensation came over him. As he keeled over, the sole thought that barged through his brain was: *Aw, hell, not again.*

⟫⟩⟨⟨

Raff moaned and attempted, without success, to lift his head.

Hennessey knelt at his side, fussing, as if she couldn't figure out what to do or where to put herself. She stroked his forehead, eyes huge. "Raff, Raff, can you hear me?"

"Don't yell," he breathed. "I'm right . . . here."

"I feared you were dead!"

"Not yet." Not far off, though.

"Shh. Save your strength. Oh, Lord, this is my fault." Talking to herself she mumbled reprimands, then said: "You better make damned sure you do not die on me, Rafael Cooper. I shall not allow it."

They were strong words, nice to hear, if useless when taken down to brass tacks.

"Don't worry . . . not goin' . . . anywhere."

"Do you promise me?"

He nodded, clenched his teeth, and shuddered.

"If you break your promise I shall not be responsible for my actions."

"Better stop . . . shakin' me, then."

"Oh dear, I am so, so sorry."

Even though pain throbbed through his body, Hennessey's concern heartened him. If the situation were different her distress would be cause to celebrate. Their association was tumultuous—that was understating it—but he protected a ray of hope that no matter how determined Ness was to prove he had no place with her, all would come right in the end.

"Let me get you comfortable."

"Don't touch . . . point."

"Why not? I—"

"Poison . . ." Just once could she not question him?

"Are you saying the tip is poisoned?"

"Maybe." Raff assessed his health. "Probably."

Raff took stampeding cattle, mama bears on hind legs protecting their cubs and flash floods roaring through dry washes toward him without batting an eyelid. Not much put him off his feed, but right now he wasn't keen to see a wooden stake poked through his gut.

"How do I remove this?"

"Bowie."

"You want me to *cut* it out?"

"No." Raff figured the stake the same as a knife, and amateurs shouldn't extract a knife because the wounded could bleed to death. "Take end off . . . whittle away from me. Get rid of shavings and gloves . . . after."

Well, this was a turnaround. Usually it fell to him to administer to her injuries, not her to his. He wouldn't gain a lot from Ness doing as he asked, but it would keep her busy till she steadied.

The stake had scraped his hip bone and lodged near his spine, poking out either side of him like a handle. Ness appraised it and unclipped her Bowie.

"This will hurt," she said, like he didn't know it.

She was right.

"Well done. You will be fine."

She lied. Ness could lie with the best of them.

Raff blacked out. He came around to Ness wiping the Bowie blade thoroughly. She slid it into the sheath on her calf then threw her riding gloves away.

"Look . . . in saddlebag," he said.

Face strained, she left his sight. He twisted his neck to follow her, the smell of rotting leaves and wet boggy earth, biting. Ness rummaged through food supplies and spare ammunition, uncovering the package of bandages and salve he carried in case of an emergency. They were a temporary solution, inadequate long term. He needed a surgeon's skills.

Raff tried to roll onto his knees, to stand up. He'd expected to struggle. What he didn't expect was a pathetic response from the body that had served him well these forty-some years. Muscles remained slack, instructions he gave them, ignored. Worse, he had started to shake, not a good sign.

The dogs milled around their mistress, getting underfoot. Ness shooed them, stern as he'd ever heard her. The yellow dog crawled to Samson, disturbed by the tension and smell of blood. Raven came to Raff, sat, and considered him.

Ness sensed Raff move, grabbed the salve he concocted going by his mama's recipe, and strode to where he lay helpless and vulnerable.

She was trying to keep her expression blank, but he read uneasiness there.

Raff shared it. The outlook for his recovery wasn't great.

"Ness, you've gotta ..." This difficulty he had talking also bothered him, so he gave up. Anyway, his advice was wasted on her since she mostly didn't take a blind bit of notice of it.

"Save your reserves."

Ness did her level best to dress around the stick without causing him more discomfort than necessary, but when she'd finished he felt absurdly light.

"Let us put a layer between you and this wet ground."

She untied their bedrolls, stripped the horses bar Samson of saddles, and brought horse blankets and bedding to a sturdy pine, piling them at its base. She made three trips then spread some of the blankets flat.

"Can you make it to that tree?" She kneeled, poised to steady him.

Distrustful he could take a step, Raff was willing to give it a darned good try.

With her help he wrangled his legs under him and lumbered in stages to his feet. Sort of. Hennessey staggered when she took his weight, but he had to admire her grit as she steered him to the pine and arranged him, floppy as all get-out, on the blankets. He hurt like hell. Blessedly, he blacked out again.

When he resurfaced he found himself wrapped snug as a papoose. He couldn't see where Ness had gotten to, but then she appeared, an angel. He blinked, and she became Ness again. He had to stay conscious, so forced himself to speak.

"Fishin' line?" he asked.

"Pardon me?" She squatted at his shoulder, nose near touching his, her hair, which she usually wore tied, loose across his face. He felt surrounded by a waterfall black as onyx. She brushed strands off his cheek.

"Fishin' line?" he repeated, sounding to him, at least, slightly louder.

"Yes." Ness secured her hair at her nape with a strip of leather then, for something to do, tucked the blankets firmer around him. "Beaulieux stretched it across the trail and rigged it to a slingshot contraption. Coward." Raff went to look where she pointed but his eyes didn't want to co-operate. "When you tripped the line . . ."

Beaulieux set a spring trap for them. If the buckskin had been beside him it would have dropped, the angle and height off the ground of the projectile set to penetrate behind the front leg of a horse where it met the body. Straight through the heart. Or, if a man walked in front of his horse, through his waist, side on.

If it didn't hit a major organ, the substance he felt was smeared on the stick, be it venom or sap from a poisonous plant, would be absorbed into the blood.

Raff's earliest memory of kin was a man he called Grandfather. If they shared blood, or if the title was honorific, it didn't matter. Grandfather's lessons fascinated Raff, who fostered particular aptitude with a bow and arrow. Out of bounds to a small boy was a clay vessel inside Grandfather's quiver, which Grandfather impressed upon him he mustn't touch as it contained a poisonous mixture. Arrowheads dipped in this mixture before shooting could be lethal, he told his pupil. Did Beaulieux, a white man, know enough about Indian warfare to measure the right dose to kill? Or did he miscalculate so Raff was not going die, but would be exceedingly ill?

"I am going to North's Ridge for assistance, Raff."

"No. Get . . . Zeke."

If Beaulieux planned violence at the Chandelier Creek ceremony, Raff's death was of no importance when stacked against those of folks defenseless against that lousy swine. With Raff incapacitated and McFarley elsewhere, Ness was the only weapon left in their armory. He'd venture her nerviness had worsened because her laudanum bottle was empty or had succumbed to misadventure, so sheer bloody-mindedness had better carry her a day or two longer.

"I care not a crumb for that sorry excuse of a—"

"Get him." Raff paused, breath ragged. "McFarley . . . will come."

"If Beaulieux is not at the cavern I shall be straight back and bring you to North's Ridge." Raff's reply was cut off when Hennessey butted in. "Do not argue."

He didn't listen to any more. When anxious or out of her depth her language got more flowery, more confusing than usual, and Raff often found it prickly to keep hold of what she was saying even when fighting fit. He pictured her with Beaulieux when she caught up with him, which she'd do after considering his order because she stuck like the fever when set on a course. She'd get started on Beaulieux with her roundabout language and confuse the poor bastard to death. Raff grinned, weakly.

She frustrated the hell out of him, her wanton behavior flayed his soul but damn, he loved her, always had, and he didn't see an end to his affliction any day soon. This became his last thought. A jagged steel border encircled his vision then, as if a drawstring were being pulled tight around it, his sight reduced to a pinhole, molecules within him crumpling into a measureless void.

TWENTY-FOUR

A starving man
will eat with the wolf.
—*Choctaw wisdom*

When Raff toppled like a felled oak and lay motionless, all I could do was stare, rigid with shock. On speaking I distracted him, a transgression of extreme foolishness, for which he paid dearly. Furthermore, to compound my culpability I held no recollection of the critical question that required his immediate attention.

Then his chest rose, and the relief he still breathed stole *my* breath. I never wanted to endure bleak despair or turmoil of emotion to compare ever, ever again.

After tending his wound I did as he asked. I left him there. It tore me apart; however, what he said was true. If Beaulieux planned a massacre all his own at Chandelier Creek, the loss of life could rival that of 1859. So, with every piece of my being screaming to procure assistance I abandoned him unconscious, wrapped in stinking horse blankets, and separated by what might as well have been a million miles from the medical treatment he desperately needed.

Decision made, I left his rifle and ammunition pouch within reach and resolved to leave the dogs with him; if circumstances demanded, Raven would fight to her death to protect him.

I understood what Raff tried to relay before he succumbed to unconsciousness: I must find Beaulieux. I prayed he would not kill me in the process, or, if he did, that McFarley arrived in time to get Raff to North's Ridge.

I lashed the buckskin, Dasher, and Bron's mare to adjacent trees, took Samson's reins, skirted the fishing line, and rejoined the muddy trail, deciding to adhere to Raff's original instruction to walk, not ride.

Raven and Custer, by way of canine communication, split obligations between Raff and me. The yellow dog tagged Samson, and despite firm words of encouragement to stay behind appropriated selective deafness, having learned this tiresome habit off Raven during their brief affiliation.

My porting a lasso again proved valuable. I looped it around Custer's neck when he made it clear he was going to come with me whether I endorsed what he conspired to do or not. Still an enigma, I figured he could be of use having belonged to the man in whose footsteps we trod. Custer gave the lasso no more than a tug then set off at a brisk trot, nose to the ground, and in doing so near wrenched my arm from its socket.

The dog moderated his pace influenced, granted, by persuasive yanks on the lasso, for no way in Heaven could I match him, the speed if I were to keep up with the hound beyond me when in rude health, never mind in my present state. If riding Samson was not brought into account, my lifestyle was sedentary, broken little by physical exertion, which consisted, mainly, of strolls along the boardwalk to the General Store.

We approached the half mile mark Raff spoke of, the turnoff for the cavern unmistakable. I stumbled after Custer when he switched course with an unexpectedly sharp turn. Samson, jogging beside me, overshot the turnoff, did admirable work of near pulling my other arm out of its socket then, agile as a cow pony, swiveled on powerful hindquarters and jogged after us.

If blessed with a modicum of sense Beaulieux would have sought cover rather than pushing on, braving the storm, so if he had sheltered in the cavern ahead as Custer's nose suggested, he may already be gone.

I wound Custer in and held him on a short rope. Samson flanked my other side: woman and beasts. Anxious not to reveal my presence, I scanned rocks and trees as I went. Spotting the cavern entrance ahead I scuttled into a parcel of woods, dragging the animals with me.

Tethering Samson to a spindly tree I took the dog, afraid he would get to yowling if left with the horse, and crept closer to the cavern. Beaulieux might still be inside or, pants bunched at his ankles, be crouched amongst the trees heeding the call of nature. Or did he watch me, or for me? Was he rubbing his hands together, gratified at my swanning into his clutches? Or were my amateurish stalking talents squandered by my creeping up on an empty cavern?

I dashed across the trace then, using dutiable concealment of a raggedy line of spruce, crawled over scree and stubby brush to a ledge perhaps a yard wide that gave an unobstructed view of the cavern mouth.

More accessible than Raff's and my lodgings, the ground rose in a broad sweep, flattening to an easy approach. A flea-bitten gray stood ground-tied by the entrance; it was difficult to see from here if the horse's saddlebags were packed, but a rifle was in its scabbard, indicating Beaulieux's departure imminent.

Undecided quite what to do, I gasped when cramps tortured my innards. Did Beaulieux circle undetected to where I hid while pain hammered me? Or had he used his horse as a decoy, then tramped overland to Raff, excitement building as he anticipated the efficacy of the spring trap? I pictured him drawing a knife across Raff's throat, finishing what the poisoned stake began then shoved the image aside, for a person could be sent crazy going that route.

Custer strained on the leash. When the debilitating cramps eased, I recalled Raff and McFarley opining Beaulieux might tolerate our party if we kept a reasonable distance between him and us, but if we got too close would take a different approach, sighting his rifle for an accurate shot. From whichever angle I studied the situation, I was now much too close.

As it happened, I need not have agonized over how to proceed for Zeke Beaulieux relieved me of a decision.

"Welcome, Miss Reed. Please, join me." His voice rode over hillocks and rebounded off rock formations to assault me where I huddled. Beaulieux chased his summons out of the cavern and stared in my direction. Lord knows how he knew it was just me, or where I was hiding. He yanked the rifle free of the scabbard as he passed the gray and held it in a way that said it was primed a step from firing. This provided great incentive to accept his invitation.

With no option available than to slide off the ledge, wrestle scratchy, denuded vegetation, and clamber to ground level to meet him, that is what I did. Custer's tail wagged madly when he heard his master's voice. Rapturous, he squiggled like a grub on a fish-hook, and bounced toward Beaulieux, squeaking with joy.

"Animals are oftentimes fickle with their affection," Beaulieux said. He stooped to pat the animal then caught himself, pretended that had not been his intention, and straightened.

"Yet their loyalty remains unaffected, even when ill-treated." Deserted in Melancholy when Beaulieux absconded in the middle of the night, the dog still wished to be with him. "Some creatures are not astute or are too big-hearted and cannot separate good from evil."

"Are you calling me evil, even with a gun pointed at your temple?" He laughed, which did not dispel the feeling he sought to distract me from a momentary show of weakness. "If you were any other female I'd expect a man to accompany you as a matter of course. You're different. Your reputation is formidable, Miss Reed, although your conduct is universally explained as reckless, downright dangerous even. But I've got to ask, where are your friends?"

"I beg your pardon?"

"I'm picking the marshal's injured—stabbed, at a wild guess—and you've abandoned him."

"I did not abandon him!"

"Did I touch a nerve? If Marshal Cooper isn't here—" exaggerated perplexity lit his face "—you abandoned him. Where's the third person? No, don't act stupid and tell me there isn't another man. There were three of you after I took out that fat fella."

"He shall be here soon."

"He take the other fork?"

I held his gaze, where he read the answer.

"Won't be soon enough," he said.

Beaulieux gestured I should precede him into the cavern mouth, stepping back, which left no prospect to tackle him. Admittedly, the concept of tackling a man who stood six foot tall in his stockinged feet and was twice as heavy as me was patently ridiculous.

Confronted by a natural hallway stoppered by an earthen wall, I went right, past the tree trunks Raff and his cousin erected to support the low ceiling, then to the center of a cavern around a third the size of the one where Raff and I had sheltered.

"Turn around."

I did not race to obey his command—a prisoner's petty rebellion—instead, looked about, at knobby walls, scattered clumps of earth, and accruements of transient life; striped Indian blankets, a skillet, and a metal pot without a handle.

Rushing water formed a muted, faint screen of noise, evidence a waterway ran through the hillside.

When time enough went by to make my statement, I faced Zeke Beaulieux. Custer sat by me, submissive, and did not move a muscle. A funnel of weak sunshine leached through a natural chimney in the ceiling, the dog spot-lit within this halo.

"Let go the mutt."

I did as he directed then tossed the lasso toward Beaulieux when he made his next request clear.

"I'm going to give you the once over for weapons you may have about your person. If you move the slightest bit or show resistance I'll shoot him." He aimed the rifle at Custer, obviously cognizant of the love and protective instincts I harbored toward animals—general knowledge amongst residents in Melancholy—then trained the gun on me. "Got it?"

"I understand."

I doubted Beaulieux would shoot Custer inside the cavern and risk it falling in, although was not inclined to determine this the hard way.

He placed the rifle on the ground and began to search, touch repellent. Never in all my born days could I recall feeling more violated by a man, including in a professional capacity. He took liberties that gave him cause to grin, slyly, and saw me fight to contain abhorrence to his probing, invasive fingers.

Discovering the Bowie he admired the blade, honed to perfection, how I insisted it kept. He *hymphed*, seemingly in approval and I crossed my fingers the knife would mollify him, inspiring him to cease pursuit of further weapons. This was not to be. Beaulieux was a diligent man; he tucked the Bowie through his belt then skimmed a palm across my opposite calf.

"Well, well." He made a grand production of whisking the Derringer from its custom holster. "Got to get real close if using this to make it feel more than a skeeter bite," he said, examining the shiny barrel of the compact ladies' pistol. "But it would do the job."

With a snap of his wrist he tossed the pistol toward the cavern atrium.

"You must be delighted by your recovery, Zeke."

"What?" He retrieved the lasso and started coiling it into order.

"Your limp," I said. "Your improved range of movement is remarkable. A miracle."

"By force of circumstances," he replied, ambiguously. "How's your friend the marshal? He dead yet? Is that why you abandoned him?"

"He is not dead, no thanks to you."

"Figured he'd be walking so he would be hit, not his horse. Not the tracker his reputation says he is."

"You went to a lot of trouble setting the spring trap."

"Ah, it was no trouble." He decided to take me literally, a deliberate misunderstanding. "Took but a few minutes since I had the makings. You were getting close so that called for a diversion. Your marshal tends to make his own rules when it suits, so I didn't want an *accident* to befall me while *escaping the law*." I supposed Zeke referred to the opinion the misinformed held that Raff's killing of Jedidiah Cannon was not self-defense. "Thought your attachment to him sufficient for you to go straight for a doctor, allowing me to get on. Guess you're not so friendly after all. You'd let him die, to catch me?"

"He is not 'my marshal'. You would have been better served

ignoring hyperbole associated with discussion of Marshal Cooper and me in the same sentence." I sought to deflect his focus from Raff, to put up a front he was not of significance to me. "But he will not let this rest. We know what you and your accomplice have done. He will find you."

"If he survives. We've never gotten anywhere near to being caught so who'll stop us now? Or, should I say, who'll stop *me* now? The Pinkerton who reckons he's so clever we had no notion he's tracking us?" He beheld my surprise. "You thought we didn't see him? He's your third man. Am I right?"

Again, I did not have to say a word.

"Marshal Cooper saw a picture of you with Cyrus Finnegan in Winsome Valley."

"Did he?"

"We are aware your real name is Porter."

"You figured that out, huh?"

"We also figured out you are bound for Chandelier Creek Crossing."

"I can go wherever I want. Thought I'd join the commemoration, have a bit of fun."

"What sort of fun?"

"Doubt you'll learn of it."

"Do not count on that, for I believe you underestimate Marshal Cooper."

"We'll see. Anyhow, after the commemoration I'm gone." He mimed a puff of smoke evaporating into thin air. "Marshal Cooper, if he isn't dead, and Mr. Pinkerton Agent can search high and low. They won't find me."

Our eyes locked, neither willing to secede dominance by breaking contact.

Cam Ellington lost his life pursuing the Beaulieuxs, and I did not want to die with questions unanswered. I wanted answers, *needed* answers. Beaulieux told the Newmans why they were about to die. Would pridefulness take over and see him regale me with all I asked of him?

"Tell me, why did Cyrus Finnegan kill your father? By all accounts they were like siblings. Good gracious me, your father and Cyrus Finnegan were *partners* in The Church of Celestial Light and Paradise Divine."

"Guess I owe you a tidbit for your perseverance."

I waited.

"In the early days Cyrus and my father worked well together. Complemented each other. My father was fulfilled beavering in the background letting Cyrus bask in adulation. But Cyrus sees his blessed self as the center of the universe. The church revolves around him. *Everything* revolves around him. Father wasn't after recognition or wealth; he lived to spread the word of God, a believer who'd fight for the honor to practice and preserve his faith."

"He sounds a man to admire." Truth be told, he sounded a fanatic, but I did not want to upset Zeke or discourage him from finishing his history lesson.

"He was. I worshipped him more than I worshipped the Lord. Strove to be like him."

"What went wrong between them?"

"Finnegan got too big for his boots. Father grew concerned about where Finnegan was guiding the church, particularly after Finnegan proposed to Elders that the church should form a secret brigade."

"Led by Alfred Cowan."

"Yes. This brigade was to be brought to action if disciples were needful of protection or . . . persuading."

"Strictly speaking, they operated as a threat."

"Finnegan said that's how non-believers would see it."

"It is not a terribly Christian practice, that of injuring or killing people you judge have wronged you."

"Which is why after conference with his brothers-in-law, my father was going to leave the Paradise Divine church and start anew someplace else."

"He confided in you?"

"Father let me sit in on their discussions since he said I was near a grown man. He and my uncles, Benedict and Tobias, went to Brandsville to preach and collect donations, but also to finalize details of their move at a distance from Finnegan and Tynbridge Hills."

"Your father could not discuss his concerns with Cyrus Finnegan?"

"He'd tried. Diplomatically. Cyrus had changed, and Father knew it was safer to pack up and go."

It was not, as it turned out. Beaulieux must have registered what he had said and spat, as though disgust soured his tongue.

"Cyrus Finnegan presumably hit upon what your father and uncles planned. He took extreme measures to deny them leave of the church."

"He's an extreme man." Beaulieux twisted the lasso, knuckles white. "After Chandelier Creek Finnegan took me into his home, treated me as a son, groomed me to step into my father's position. I swore to do right, to live right. To make my parents proud. The whole time I was ignorant of Finnegan's part in the massacre."

Beaulieux and I had both suffered great loss when young. My family were killed by Indians when I was six years old. He and I were spared when those closest to us were murdered, so I empathized with him, seeing how pain manifested with endeavors in his youth to be an upstanding representative of his family. I also empathized with his torment, the guilt he could not shake. Was this all we had in common?

"What age were you when you lost your family?"

"Eight, and I didn't *lose* them! They weren't a shoe, or quirt," he spluttered.

"When did you find out Cyrus Finnegan had sent Cowan and his brigade after your father?" I asked after Beaulieux brought himself under control.

"Long after Chandelier Creek. After the Cowans died that stinkard looked me in the eye and said the Cowans killed my folks but had acted on their own, that they'd been after the donation money my father carried and he'd used his influence to dig into every corner of the country to find them. I believed him, but he's a lying skunk. He acted all high and mighty at Winsome Valley, but I found out much later that Cyrus had ordered the Cowans' deaths. The law was on to them and Cyrus didn't want Alfred throwing him to the wolves."

"You confronted Finnegan?"

"No! I'm not crazy!"

Now there was a debatable point.

"This person who came forward to say the Cowans were at Chandelier Creek was the same person who told you Finnegan was behind the massacre?"

"Might've been." Rope burn surely chaffed Beaulieux's hands. "All right, yes, it was. Garfield Tanner. He'd belonged to Finnegan's brigade, but his conscience struck—late. He told me Cyrus specified everyone at Chandelier Creek must be left naked because if they were leaving *his* church they should be stripped of clothing as a symbolic gesture."

"What did you do?"

"I couldn't rely on Tanner as he'd gotten himself knifed."

I would have gambled my fortune Beaulieux wielded said knife.

"I stood at Cyrus's right hand, was privy to his secrets. The brigade members were known to me. I had somebody give a list of those men to the wife of a newsman who'd been in Winsome Valley. Nothing came of it.

"So, it was up to me. One of those murdering bastards had a smallholding on the Tynbridge Hills boundary. I started by killing him and his children. Finished them off and was home for supper. No one had an inkling it was me. The next family lived a ways from town so I killed them and kept on riding. When Cyrus sent the rest into hiding a friend wrote me where they'd gone—a friend Cyrus would never, ever suspect."

"You will kill him. Cyrus Finnegan."

"Yes."

"Chandelier Creek was an obscene tragedy. Misuse of trust cannot be rationally explained or defended, and there is no excuse for slaying innocents. You have every right to be furious and sad, to want justice for your family."

"I'm not after your approval, Miss Reed."

"I do not contest that. But what you did . . ." A cramp caught me, and Beaulieux startled when I cried out. I rode out the crimping pain then cleared my throat. "How is your behavior different to those who massacred your relations?"

"I don't expect you to understand, and whether you do or not isn't of concern to me. I have no interest in persuading you to my viewpoint."

"You and your accomplice also murdered innocents."

"We did."

"Innocent people will die at the commemoration."

"I know!" He stared through the chimney, into the past, a haunted, hollow man. Despite purporting he could not care less, the carnage he wrought was a colossal burden.

"You left your victims naked and bound together. Why did you not shoot them and be done?"

"My family were discarded like animal carcasses. They were left. Just … left. I wanted the disrespect and brutality—and more—shown my kin, shown to kin of those behind the attack."

I sighed, blisteringly saddened by his conviction he thought his actions and those of his accomplice were vindicated.

"Why did you kill your friend?"

"He was full of piss and wind to begin but dressing as a lady made him start to behave like one, too, till he got to where he had no use for his pecker." Beaulieux rubbed his thigh, nervous. "Said it was easier to stay a woman rather than switching—female to male—when with me. Had to remind him that even with growing aspirations otherwise, she was actually he. He became a weight around my neck."

"It was a clever ruse."

"It was his idea and it worked well. Too well. As I said, he'd gotten to liking it, and at times I forgot he was a man. Strange, huh?"

Perhaps revealing more than he felt he ought to, Beaulieux turned cagey, eyes darting. I studied him and wondered if, while parading as a woman, his friend exposed more than physical indicators of his role. Had he nursed an undisclosed motive, using friendship as a bulwark? Did he proposition Beaulieux, which the latter found so abhorrent the friend died under Beaulieux's revulsion and fury?

"Most of your family died, but was he related to you?"

"A ways back on Mama's side. He was adamant as me the men who got off scot-free for those deaths had to pay. Be punished," said Beaulieux, his anger a festering sore.

"What name did Madam Beaulieux answer to . . . before?"

"What's it to you?" He ran his tongue under his top lip. Seconds stretched until he said, quietly: "Charlie. His name was Charlie Fairbanks."

"He is gone, so you are not obligated to do whatever it is you have arranged for the commemoration service."

"I've come too far." Beaulieux refocused on me. "Got to finish what I started."

Forsaking conversation, he bade me lay on my stomach, utilizing the lasso to bind my hands behind my back and secure my ankles. Trussed like a hog, I wriggled my fingers, finding they were bound neither hard nor fast, as I would have expected.

"They're not tight," he said, picking my confusion. "Don't have to be. If you get free after the explosion, where are you going to go?"

"Explosion?" Oh, Lord.

He did not elaborate.

Neck straining to keep my chin off the ground, I held my head high.

"Well, here we are. It's been awful nice making your acquaintance, Miss Reed."

He bowed low, an actor's bow that mimicked the acceptance of praise after a theatrical performance while applause deafened and roses arced onto the stage, scooped up my Derringer and left. I heard the faint scuff of boots on rock but little else.

When he reappeared I wondered with naiveté born of desperation whether he had undergone a paradigm shift. The answer, I discovered, rang a resounding 'No'.

"You will hear an explosion, Miss Reed. I've put dynamite in a strategic hole which, going by calculations, will collapse the entrance, leaving no way of escape. If your uncanny luck holds, the ceiling will fall in and you'll suffocate."

"And if luck does not favor me?"

"I suppose you'll starve to death. You and the mutt. Unless he gets hungry and takes to gnawing your arm or leg. Not that there's much to gnaw on. Death by dog. It's probably not the nicest way to die."

"Why not shoot me?" I could not believe myself in a situation where this did not sound illogical, inappropriate.

"Well, an affliction of mine is I can't bring myself to kill a woman directly."

"How frightfully inconvenient. Then how do you explain the bodies of women and girls scattered across the countryside in your wake?"

"Charlie had no problem there."

"You were in charge of the rifle." Raff told me all the Newmans, except the father, were killed with a revolver. "You shot the fathers."

"I didn't want to be left out. Charlie and me, we each had our strengths so we divvied our duties accordingly."

"Duties?"

"I won't get into that. In addition to my inability to kill women outright, a vexatious fly in the ointment must disappear with you. And there I will leave it, because that's what I intend to do. Leave."

"To what do you refer when you say 'a vexatious fly'?"

"That's not your business."

"Why not untie me before you go? As you say, I shall die regardless."

He waggled his head, feigning sorrow, and went outside whistling 'When Johnny Comes Marching Home'.

"Goodbye, Miss Reed," came his muffled farewell.

Not long after, as he warned, a boom ravaged my eardrums. I tucked my chin into my chest, clumps of dirt sloughed from where they had clung overhead, hold precarious, raining upon Custer and myself, sections of the walls crumbling.

I scrunched my eyes shut, bombarded by tremors that penetrated my bones. It felt a monster clasped Earth in his massive hands and shook her as a losing gambler shakes the dice.

The hillside grumbled and rattled to a standstill, the cavern ceiling, remarkably, still intact. Draped in a cape of dirt, I tried to spit fine dust particles but, dry of saliva, my mouth did not accommodate me. Ears blocked, I worked my jaw side to side to unblock them. It was no use. Custer quivered against me, likely convinced the Apocalypse was upon us. When I lifted my head I saw he too wore a filthy topcoat.

Clods weighted my back, so I tipped onto my side, which released much of the pressure on my neck and spine and drew in my mind how Beaulieux wound the lasso that secured me.

It took some doing, but after contortions, bending of joints that did not bend willingly in the natural course of things, I freed myself. No small amount of cursing—every impassioned profane word and phrase known to me, and a plethora of new contenders tested for suitability—supplemented these manipulations.

Rallying composure, I brooded over the mindset of a man who carried poison, dynamite and blasting caps, and fishing line not used for its intended purpose in his kit. This did not augur well for the gathering at Chandelier Creek Crossing.

Beaulieux must be stopped. Regrettably, the glaring truth of the pile of rubble that now blocked my exit declared I was in no position to do the stopping. I pushed myself upright and kneaded tight muscles in my thighs.

Custer rubbed his nose on my sleeve, sneezed, then rested his chin on my arm, limpid eyes overflowing with trust near my undoing.

"We shall be all right, boy."

Fumbling in the haze of drifting particles, I fashioned a cigarette between shaking fingers, lit it, and took stock of the damage that surrounded me. Terrified the ceiling might still collapse, I jumped when a scattering of clods crashed through the chimney, caromed off the wall and landed against my foot.

I stubbed out the cigarette and clambered over debris to stand at the base of a soil pyramid that climbed the wall. Staring at the crumbly, unsteady mound, I wondered if I could shinny up to the peak, then use crevices and knobs that jutted from the wall as hand- and foot-holds to ascend to, and out of, the chimney. If I failed to haul myself to safety, dying in that dry crypt with no one I loved aware I was incarcerated there would, conclusively, be my fate.

The unavoidable, negative aspect of my venture into mountaineering meant Custer must remain in the cavern. I could not look at the dog, guilt at abandoning him as had every human of import to him almost too much to bear. Climbing through the chimney was the sole opportunity open to me. I had no choice.

I inched up the pyramid, cheek scraping gritty earth, the smell peculiar to caves, underground mines and passageways besetting my nostrils, fraught nerves pulsating with each placement of my boots. Slipping often, at risk of plummeting to land with a thud, doing calamitous damage to my person, I progressed, inch by vital inch.

On making the top of the pile I stole a moment to rest and carefully tilted my head to better inspect the chimney from this perspective. Could I climb through it, legs braced against the sides, and reach daylight? It would be devastating to make the opening to find it too narrow to wriggle through.

Shuffling to remain stable I balanced, a palm against the wall, and removed my boots and stockings. Feet bare, I stretched as far as I could, fingers working blind, searching for cracks to lever myself upward.

Over and over the wall defeated me. I would gain momentum then freeze, petrified to move any part of my body it not imperative I move. I shunned the lure to glance up, thinking that if I did I might come to the attention of an unseen deity who would scoff at my pitiable efforts and send me tumbling.

Dearest Lizzie came to mind. A fun-loving, impudent creature, when we skated so close to losing Evie her attitude shifted within each sector of her being. I had knocked back overtures to accompany her to church, responding with a glare sufficient to burn the soles off her boots, but extolled her perseverance, which originated from a place where she wished for her beloved friend the standard of happiness she enjoyed. She cached disappointment, saying rather than being offers of serious intent she invited me largely for her own amusement.

Even with differing attitudes our friendship survived, and the prospect I might never see Lizzie, Evie, or those I cared for again, that I might never sit in the Fleur-de-lis, Raven by my stool, and drink until dawn with compatriots old and new was beyond comprehension.

I gave up. Despite intense sorrow at what I stood to lose I did not possess the strength, or ability, to climb the chimney. With less care than used in the ascent, I slithered to where Custer waited, the dog's welcome suggestive my absence totaled weeks, not minutes. I ruffled the soft fur between his ears.

Posterior rested on a clay mound, I pulled my boots on, lit a cigarette, fanned the match, and ran through alternate routes out of the cavern. It did not take long. I took a swig from the hip flask Beaulieux had decided against appropriating, although not before he enjoyed a draft from it, I should add. With the absence of food of any description, did whiskey constitute my equivalent of the Last Supper? My feeble attempt at humor died a pauper's death.

Impossible.

That single word without flourish, or adornment, touted my chance of survival.

I fired another cigarette. Silence reigned. Almost. The dull, constant rush of the water course that burrowed through the hillside grew, the sound consuming, and it came to me perhaps an alternate route proposed itself.

Over smaller mountains of earth, around larger ones, I listened at intervals, ear pressed to the wall. The sound of water grew louder. Toward the rear of the cavern I clambered around a corner. Where the ceiling lowered, a fissure wide as me separated the body of the cavern and an offshoot. Did this fissure represent an escape route? Pulse surging I stuck my head into the aperture. The walls closed in. Dear Lord, it was my worst nightmare realized.

Immobilized, I shut my eyes and saw Raff's face. I took one step, then another.

Shoulders brushing the walls I concentrated on breathing.

In. Out. In. Out.

A ways in the ground ran up a slight incline, the walls angled until, hunched, I found the passage blocked. Water roared, the noise funneled through a hole the shape of an eye slot in a suit of armor. The integrity of the hillside had shifted, an ineluctable side effect of the blast being it weakened the hillside's core, its structure. Was this a way out? Could I *dig* my way out?

Unable to turn around I backed into the cavern, drenched in sweat. The paraphernalia left by successive visitors was buried, but it did not take much to disinter an implement—the skillet—to pass service as a tool.

Girding myself for a return sortie into the fissure near had me tip over, but I forced myself to take one step and then another, along the passage. I trembled, fearful intermittent grumbles were a prelude to the hillside collapsing as I scrabbled at the hole, desperation giving me strength. Behind me, Custer treated it as a game, soil flying between his legs.

I discarded the skillet, working feverishly until the gap, at a pinch, was sufficient for the dog and me to shimmy through. I fumbled for a match. It took several strikes to light one that held a flame long enough for me to see when I thrust my head into the hole. What I found did not inflate me with confidence.

I saw virtually nothing but heard that far below water gushed out of nowhere and vanished into nowhere. In a misguided attempt to gauge its depth I threw a clod into the water. Was it a river or stream? No, not a stream, for when describing a stream inevitably pictures came of a delightful bubbling waterway winding through wildflower meadows and wooded hills.

My mind went blank, going on hiatus as I struggled to appreciate what this represented. I grappled with the enormity of this next obstacle, while common sense put to me that wherever the river flowed, eventually it was spirited out of the of the hills.

Before it did, were there points where it tapered, backing up like a stopped pipe, too narrow for the volume expected of it? Along the channel did space adequate for a body to catch their breath lie between the surface of the roaring torrent and the roof beneath which it had raced, in all its embodiments, for millennia?

Blood drained from my face.

Throwing myself from a height into a confined rush of energy determined to spit me into the world or transport me deeper into the center of it brought such anxiety speckles riddled my vision.

Custer licked my ear. I pushed the dog and dread about to overwhelm me away. Perhaps I still had the reed cut from the river at Hollow Oak Falls, of use if I were shunted into a cavity where it was difficult to breathe and where the legend of Samuel Brady could be tested for authenticity. I patted my shirt. No, it had fallen out without my noticing.

I had to decide whether my preference was to starve to death or drown. When these equally atrocious ways of dying were compared, which might be considered the least horrific? Which should I choose?

Custer, much as he demonstrated growing fondness for me would—this reinforced by tales told around campfires and bar-room tables—show no hesitation to feast upon my carcass when I died or, as the wretched Zeke Beaulieux took pleasure to highlight, while I was still alive. This may well extend Custer's life by a few paltry days, but with no water or more food, to what end?

Contemplating the grisly image, expectation this chamber would become my tomb was unrealistic. After I died and Custer stripped the final bone and gobbled the last scrap of skin, there would not be an awful lot left to entomb.

Options analyzed, processed, and done, one course of action was left.

Fortified with the last mouthful of whiskey, I secured the silver flask in my clothing. Custer whined, perturbed. If he followed me into the unknown, all well and good. And if he elected not to? I left that to him. I wormed through the gap, inhaled a final, wild breath then plunged headfirst into an icy void that sucked each minuscule ounce of me into its custody and carried me on a swirling, turbulent, freezing ride to perdition.

TWENTY-FIVE

A brave man dies but once,
a coward, many times.
—*Iowa wisdom*

I suffered a lifetime of confusion, unable to make head or tail of which way was up, which down, lungs fit to burst. By and by, pounded and bruised, I drifted on clouds soft as a mother's kiss, and relinquished the agony and tribulations of my existence into the cupped hands of Destiny.

After an age I pitched toward a beam of light that grew with each twirl, and tumbled into a bright sphere where, awarded a broader course, the surging torrent calmed. My euphoria knew no bounds when I doddered out of the water and fell on my stomach, gasping, chest heaving.

Abrasions wattled my skin. Lumps, bumps and scrapes joined those received hitting Bron's trough, the pain almost sweet and definitively preferable to my inert body washing up on the same bank to be picked by crows with pointy beaks, cawing shrilly, language harsh and cruel.

Later, after inward consultation, I chose not to share I was convinced a tutelary entity guided me through pitch-black into sunlight.

A colony of ants trickled past my nose, forbidding any obstacle to interrupt their march or dictate where they could go. Up and over leaves and grass they went, endurance extraordinary, when compared to their size these barriers equivalent to climbing the Sawtooths. The smell of damp grass worked like a soothing balm, and I embraced the piece of Mother Earth on which I stretched.

Custer had placed faith in me, leaping into the torment of water. He staggered up the bank in a dismal state and cowered within arm's reach, ribcage inflating and deflating like wet blacksmith bellows. Slavering, he hawked low in his chest, water spewing out his mouth, coughing as though he tried to dislodge a blockage from his lungs.

I rolled over, reveling in the sun, which favored a lapis sky, the calm after the storm. Mental fatigue, incalculable relief I still breathed, and a physical counterforce set my skin tingling, ravaging my frayed nervous system. I did not hustle to pull myself together, instead, concentrated on how incredible it felt to be alive.

Custer bellied through the grass, his body a source of comfort against my thigh.

"We made it." I touched his forepaw, thrilled he survived the cavern death-trap.

We lay there a long while, until roused by a scream, an unholy sound that clawed, crampons extended, from the throat of a person or beast submitted to undoubted and absolute agony. The scream, repeated, broke off.

Whomever or whatever emitted that terrific noise was nearby. I clambered to my feet, legs quavery, and moved toward where the scream originated, beleaguered brain impressing upon me someone might be in need of help; although in my condition and without a weapon I was not auspiciously placed to do more than give verbal assurance.

I stepped over a rotten log, green and soft with moss, and pressed apart needles of a blackjack pine. Samson, Beaulieux's gray and a calico horse were tethered in an idyllic shaded glen, base to a tongue of sere grasses, brassy in the sunshine.

A man bereft of clothing lay spread-eagled, wrists and ankles secured to pegs hammered into the ground. He convulsed, as though carried by a landslide. I could not see his face, but it did not require more than one guess to identify the unfortunate individual. A grubby bandage above his right knee also signified him the attacker who did his deuced best to drown me in Bron's trough.

A figure crouched at Zeke Beaulieux's head. Horrified when I comprehended the activity in which he engaged I stepped back, praying I would not reveal myself to the man, intent on the deed at hand, by the inadvertent snapping of a twig caught beneath my boots. If Lady Luck kept me under her wing I might reach Samson and lead him to cover without being seen.

Custer had a different notion. He bounded toward the men, tail a whisk, gladsomeness restored. I ran toward Samson with leaden limbs, feeling I waded through a snowdrift, desperate to erase what I had witnessed clean from my memory.

"Hennessey? Wait!"

I ceased running. Dreading what awaited me I tried to compose myself, cast aside that otiose task, and slowly pivoted to confront the person beside Zeke Beaulieux.

Hiram Walsh and I stared at each other, the air between us buzzing, frenetic and charged. It took every driblet of willpower not to look at what dangled from his fist.

"You have my horse," I said at last, through chilled lips.

At the sound of my voice the man lying at Walsh's feet jerked, whimpered, then grew still.

"He assured me—" Walsh indicated Beaulieux with his chin "—you were dead."

"You took his word as gospel truth and did not feel it prudent to check?"

"The volume of the blast made it a reasonable assumption." The lawyer appeared neither unduly affected nor surprised by my being here. "I'm pleased to see you're alive, Hennessey, if the worse for wear."

"I am rather pleased with the outcome myself," I said, our tête-à-tête an oddity I had no taste for. "You should be almost home by now, so what are you doing here, Mr. Walsh? Disregard that. It is obvious what you are doing. What is not obvious is why in the Almighty's name you are doing it."

"I'm fulfilling a commission."

"Your employment guidelines include abominable conduct no humanitarian would condone?" I asked, hysteria trimming my voice. "Abominable is not the correct word. I believe barbaric is a frank comparison."

"Now and again a situation calls for methods some might say are . . . extraneous."

"Am I next?"

"You? No. Though your beautiful hair would make a fine trophy."

From the outset Hiram Walsh conducted interaction on separate levels, his words taken at face value, or laced with innuendo—toned with a flagrant undercurrent if interpreted within a different context. He made me uneasy, for I was unsure whether he must be taken seriously, or if he merely expanded the desire to tease.

All a muddle I balked at dancing attendance to this complex man, grown agitated by, and weary of, translating his exact meaning.

"Beaulieux stole my knife and gun. Where are they?" I asked, doing my best to portray a casualness counter to how I felt.

"So you can kill me?"

"I would not dare try."

The prospect of my disarming or killing him clearly titillated Hiram Walsh. I had to be close to use the knife and the Derringer was nothing better than a deterrent even if accuracy blessed my shooting. The mother-of-pearl-handled revolver would bark before my hand moved.

"If the knife is a fine Bowie—" he pointed to the horses "—you'll see it over there atop his clothes."

I went to items of clothing dumped by the calico, rescued the knife and clipped it into its scabbard. "And my gun?"

"I'm not sure the peashooter you term a gun is deserving of the name. If you mean the Derringer, it's in his pants."

I salvaged the Derringer and restored it to its holster.

"I can explain, Hennessey. If you're willing to listen."

"There is no call to explain." Desperate to go to Raff, it came to me that if Walsh cultivated thoughts of causing me bodily harm I should not draw attention to Raff being injured, therefore incapacitated. He might kill us both. "What would be the purpose?"

"Pure selfishness." His mouth tipped with this admission. "Be assured, I was after this man, and him only."

"Are you a bounty hunter, Mr. Walsh, or a hole-and-corner lawman?"

"Me, the law?" he asked, amused.

Dear me, what was I thinking? No lawman the right side of justice factored scalping the object of his hunt into arrest procedure.

"Why do you torture Zeke?"

"If you'll allow me five minutes I'll tell you."

"I do not—"

"Five." He held aloft the hand that did not hold Beaulieux's scalp, fingers splayed. "Five minutes, that's all. I'd say you're keen to confirm suspicions you have."

He was right, I was, and I did not understand his being here, standing in front of me when I expected him about to enter Tynbridge Hills.

"Are you really a lawyer, Mr. Walsh, or is the law cover for your true profession?"

"Each of the above," he said, expression flat as a tombstone.

"Did you use Jakob's will and your friendship with him as a smokescreen to cover your activities, whatever they may be?"

"I practice law, Hennessey, and you did inherit Jakob's estate. I say that in all honesty. But a sideline billet of mine incorporates . . . digressions."

"Such as killing people for a master with a pocketbook of cash money? You do not present the type of man who takes kindly to instruction. I trust you are paid a fitting stipend."

"Periodically, opposing divisions of my employment collide. I apologize if this offends you."

"Oh, by no means am I offended. I am merely interested in the degree to which you are committed to those occupations." Custer returned to me and sat on my foot. "Very well, carry on, if you must."

"Some years ago—" Walsh began to saunter widdershins around Beaulieux, who had capitulated to the siren song of insensibility "—it became apparent to a person of my acquaintance that those who rode with the Cowans and were *alleged* to have slain Peter David Porter and company during the Chandelier Creek debacle were being targeted. Murdered."

"Chandelier Creek Crossing was no 'debacle', Mr. Walsh. It is labelled a massacre because that is what it was," I said. "Devout men, women and children. Slaughtered."

His wave of dismissal said, *Have it your way, it's semantics.*

"After the second family was killed those in certain quarters felt the rest of the men implicated had best disappear. It was only supposed to be for a few months, until the matter was sorted. Although told to implement measures to protect themselves, all but one of these men have since lost their lives, and those they held most dear have lost theirs. This man and his female companion have a lot to pay for."

"His male companion."

"Pardon me?"

"Did you not pass the spring?"

"Why do you ask?"

"Never mind. Whatever the case, it appears a cycle of vicious complexity. Go on."

"This gentleman friend of mine identified the person responsible for the deaths. He sought my advice, then hired me. He has authority within his . . . organization to do whatever is appropriate to rectify a predicament, but cannot be seen to initiate conduct unbecoming or influence an outcome."

"Why did this nameless man not employ a sheriff or marshal? A Pinkerton, if flush with funds. I can recommend an agent *par excellence.*"

"He wanted the affair resolved quickly. For it to go away with minimal publicity."

"You were directed to kill whoever was doing this?"

"I see myself more an intermediary, my duty to disable the responsible party," the lawyer in him replied.

"Do I take from this you were contracted by a member of The Church of Celestial Light and Paradise Divine? Did Cyrus Finnegan himself employ you?"

"I couldn't possibly say."

"Do you belong to Finnegan's congregation, Mr. Walsh?"

"My association with Cyrus Finnegan is historical, not ecclesiastical."

His cryptic reply had me grinding my teeth. My confusion grew inchmeal. "If you work for this unnamed person, who employed the Pinkerton agent McFarley?"

"The Paradise Divine church seems to me a seedbed for salacious, underhand behavior, its members as Janus-faced as the court of the Medici."

"Mercy's sake, they are Christian!"

"Percase, there is a faction within the church with a stratagem to overthrow Cyrus Finnegan. *They* hired the Pinkertons." Hiram Walsh desisted pacing and trained his full attention on me. "Cowan's men are an increasingly rare breed, but this faction needs one of them, in person, to threaten Finnigan with exposure to the law."

"So they can depose him with a minimum of fuss? You seem wise to each side, Mr. Walsh."

I took his raised eyebrow as confirmation.

"Let us say, for purposes of discussion, that you *do* work for Cyrus Finnegan. If Finnegan identified Beaulieux as the miscreant behind the murders, why did he not send a henchman after him—them—and meanwhile relocate the Cowan brigade members until Beaulieux was captured? Let me rephrase that, for they are a gang. He presumably knew where the Cowan *gang* members were living and has resources to find Beaulieux. Why employ you?"

"The disciple my client sent after Beaulieux couldn't find a camel on a prairie littered with groundhogs. Plus, he looked for a single man, not a married couple."

"Finnegan must know there is a serpent in his network, that this person is feeding Beaulieux the whereabouts of the gang." Clay, Lizzie's husband, said Mr. Newman received an occasional telegram. Those in hiding would have kept in contact with handpicked Elders, even if it sporadic. "How else would Zeke figure where to go?"

"It's beyond me."

"Finnegan surely tried to smoke the traitor out by setting a trap . . . or . . ."

Hiram Walsh waited on my enfeebled brain to collate information.

"You. It was you!"

"You have me, Hennessey," he said, looking pleased with himself. "The trick I learned early is to lay a foundation from which people can move onward believing *they* are in control. I contrived to put a suspicious character under Finnegan's nose. Lucius Gilbert is currently in limbo awaiting Finnegan's verdict on his betrayal."

"This Lucius Gilbert is not involved, charges laid against him were based on falsified information?"

"Gilbert adheres to teachings and scripture without deviation, but is of quixotic personality, difficult to warm to." Hiram Walsh papered over framing an innocent man. "There are ramifications after every battle, in every war. He's a sacrificial lamb."

"What is your connection to Zeke Beaulieux? Did he approach you to work on his behalf, sweetening the pot with sums of money too great to refuse?"

"Money is ever seductive, but let me present a hypothetical dilemma." He resumed circling Beaulieux, this time walking sunwise. "Where is the best place to hide a haystack?"

"What has that to do with this?"

"If you'd said, 'In a hayfield', of course you would be correct."

"I have no idea what you are saying."

"Where do savvy people conceal items or dealings they don't want unearthed?"

"Mr. Walsh, I do not feel at all well. Please cut to the crux of whatever it is you wish to impress me with."

"In a hayfield a haystack is hidden in plain sight. I was being blackmailed. My blackmailer was part of Finnegan's brigade and, under the name Harper, lived in Whittaker at the time of his demise. Mr. Harper underrated me."

Dog tired, I struggled to keep up.

"And so Cyrus Finnegan presumed Harper died for no reason other than he rode with the Cowans," I said.

Fingers twined in Zeke's bloodied hair Walsh absentmindedly swung the scalp, like a pendulum. Those fingers, those hands had caressed me. Unprepared when vomit blocked my throat, I swallowed, hard.

"Why scalp Zeke?"

"This—" he held Zeke's scalp eye height "—is proof he's dead, accepted as such by my client. I take pride in being a man of my word."

"You do not consider a coat button or horse adequate confirmation?"

"They could belong to anyone. I prefer to add a personal touch to assignments."

Cookie was living proof a person did not necessarily die when relieved of their scalp. Impelled to make an obvious point, I said: "He is not yet dead."

"He will be." Walsh poked Beaulieux with the toe of his boot, contemplative.

"You distanced yourself by manipulating us." It dawned on me it was imperative for Walsh that his involvement in this counterstroke of punishment did not come to Cyrus Finnegan's attention. He was cunning, I could give him that, an unapologetic master controlling a stage of marionettes. The Beaulieuxs were collaborators alert to which strings he pulled, but they were past confirming the extent of his machinations. "You manipulated Marshal Cooper, in particular, sending that telegram when in Fancy, predicting he would visit there at once."

"Yes, I pointed Cooper to the newspaper."

"You definitely went to Fancy because you sent that telegram." I averted my eyes from Beaulieux determined, since we had gotten into this conversation, to bring it to an end. "You acquired a horse then doubled back to Melancholy, to find the Beaulieuxs had already left town after your appearance on Main Street. Unnerved, they probably believed you were there to cause them trouble. Is that anywhere near what happened?"

"Brava. You're doing well so far."

Grudgingly admiring of his double-crossing ways, I was afraid Hiram Walsh might decide I now had more insight of his enterprise than he could allow me to walk away with.

"You got what you wanted. Who you wanted," I said.

I glanced past him to Beaulieux who had regained consciousness. Fixed on the sky, Beaulieux dropped his chin and stared at me, eyes glazed, resigned.

General consensus would be he deserved everything coming to him, and more, but the Newman deaths crowded those at the Sweet Venus Too mine, and Beaulieux lying there in such a state perpetuated a lack of humane behavior to wrest sympathy from the bondage of less forgiving hearts than mine. Disenchanted by the death and destruction prevalent in Melancholy of recent months, my pistol-whipped soul ached for peace, an end to enmity dispersed like grapeshot to those who resided in the place I called home.

Off a ways a kettle of turkey vultures coasted, dots stamped black against blue. I thought of Beaulieux's victims—those with whom I was unacquainted and the one with whom I was: Cam Ellington.

"Will you leave Beaulieux to the animals and elements?"

"He's not worth more."

I approached Beaulieux and knelt beside him, studiously avoiding his bloodied scalp. After he screamed Walsh had stuffed a swatch of material in his mouth, the man's own bandana. Laid out, arms and legs extended their full length, the killer became just another man in a sequence of men convinced taking a life would obliterate the pain left after the deaths of those taken from them in tragic circumstances. "An eye for an eye" or, as Indians proclaimed, "One for another".

Beaulieux's incubuses pushed him to start his crusade, but the killings did not ease his spirit. As Lizzie proffered, we can run but bad memories have a habit of keeping pace, irrespective of how hard we try to unhitch ourselves from their harness and leave them at a crossroads.

"I ask you not touch him."

"I have no intention of doing so," I assured the lawyer, and in a literal sense I did not lie. "I am merely checking these are tied securely."

In support of this I tugged in a cursory fashion at the rope binding Beaulieux's left hand to a peg.

"Move away from him, Hennessey." Hiram Walsh spoke in a deceptively light tone.

Beaulieux stuck on me, eyes brimming with tears and a wordless plea. I squinted up at Walsh, then past him to the vultures, a prophetic swirl of doom. "Beaulieux will soon have an audience."

He must have realized to what I referred, nevertheless, perhaps as an indulgence to me he looked to the gliding birds. With his interest caught on them I pulled my trouser leg over my boot and pulled the Derringer free. There were seconds to do what I felt compelled to do while Hiram Walsh was distracted.

At this distance even I could not miss my target.

Shots fired point-blank against his ear put Ferrington Porter, now known as Ezekiel Beaulieux, out of his misery.

Walsh did not jump, in fact, he gave the impression the mercy killing was not unforeseen.

"Do you ever heed instruction, Hennessey?"

"It is regarded a rare event." I homed the Derringer in the holster and patted it. "Uncommonly rare."

"You sure are in a class of your own."

"It has been said. On numerous occasions." And by better men than you, I added silently.

"I suppose you want me to bury him."

Did he see Zeke Beaulieux shoot Ellington, and my insistence we bury him? No, Raff would have noticed him, and if he did would have mentioned the lawyer was stalking us and done something about it.

Walsh's expression was impermeable, with no hint he poked fun at my expense so, instead of witnessing Ellington's burial, maybe this was what it appeared: an enquiry, with no ulterior meaning.

"No, do not bury him." Beaulieux did not allocate his victims an iota of dignity, he showed no compassion toward their remains. Regret over the impulsive shooting swamped me. What possessed me to let a flash of sympathy—which, left unchecked, history indicated would vanish of its own volition—lead to helping a man who, by rights, should suffer until the end of his days? "That is more than he deserves. Let him stay where he is. I must go."

I hobbled toward Samson, worried Hiram Walsh had no intention of allowing me to ride from the meadow.

"To the marshal? I saw him on the way here. He is stable but needful of medical attention. He wasn't dead yet. That was all I could tell since that hound of yours wouldn't let me near him."

Of course, Walsh had followed us, therefore knew Raff and Kip McFarley had been with me. And by stable, did he mean Raff was conscious or had he dispatched Raff as I had just dispatched Beaulieux? Did he continue to trifle with me?

Criminy, not only did I lead McFarley to Raff, but I also cut a trail a mile wide for Hiram Walsh, too. We had made quite the procession with no requirement for banners or drummer boy to broadcast our location.

"Shall I help you get him to a doctor?"

"No. We do not require your help."

I retrieved Samson's reins and led him to a cut by the river bank that brought his withers level with my hip, making it easier to slide onto his saddle.

"If you change your mind, you know where I am."

Uncomfortable presenting my back as a target, I kicked my stallion out of the cut and reined him to face the lawyer. "I assure you, I shall not change my mind, Mr. Walsh."

He rubbed a thumb over the silverwork of the holster that housed his ostentatious handgun, this read as casual or threatening depending on his mood.

Catching sight of the Colt's pearl handle reminded me of Nate's assertion Hiram Walsh was not, necessarily, as he appeared.

"Nate was right," I said.

"How so?"

"He advised me not to be beguiled by your finery, for he suspected you should be kept happy. That you command depths of unplumbed dangerous."

"He's a smart man."

"Yes, he is."

Walsh's reply contained a thinly-veiled warning I should not make an enemy of him. He had revealed much to me, more than might be thought wise, but he knew I held no recourse. He was protected by a man of absonant power who had no compunction about using his authority and methods at his disposal to bring his concerns to a satisfying finale—methods that coasted on the skirts of the law or guffawed at its presumption.

"Before I go, I want to make plain nothing justifies your unconscionable acts of violence."

"There, we must disagree. One shouldn't criticize another if uninstructed in the motive behind their actions, Hennessey. Now, go to your marshal."

A fly alighted on Samson's mane. I flicked it off, thankful for a distraction regardless how minor.

"If your wife were alive, I wonder how she would view the man you have become, Mr. Walsh."

That struck home. I admired how quickly he recovered.

"Go, Hennessey." His lip crimpled, a serif, tinged with emotion, perhaps regret. "Go, before *I* change my mind."

About what? It was best I not ask. It might bode ill for my general health and wellbeing.

I whistled Custer, then, without soliciting permission, collected Beaulieux's flea-bitten gray meaning to return her to Bron, wheeled Samson about and directed him toward the trail, toward Raff.

I did not look back.

TWENTY-SIX

Ask questions from your heart
and you will be answered from your heart.
—*Omaha proverb*

Six weeks later.

The Pinkerton agent McFarley held a door open for Raff, who came into the Fleur and waited inside, this his inaugural visit to the saloon since arising from his sickbed. They made their way to the bar in companionable silence.

Raff wore the badge of prolonged illness, the core essence of him haggard, though each week he gained weight, if not a great deal, and recouped more of himself, more of his spirit.

Subsequent to our foray to the border of Idaho Territory a friendship developed between the lawmen, Raff indebted to the Pinkerton for saving his skin—along with yours truly—which forged a bond to stretch and contract as winds blew, never to break wherever either ventured.

The day of Raff's near demise McFarley, hearing the explosion that trapped me in the cavern figured, understandably, that we had caught up with Beaulieux. He rode hard toward the blast, apprehensive what he was going to find. Would we be dead, blown apart and distributed to all the corners of kingdom come? Or would he find us victorious?

He met a lone rider who denied he had seen anyone, and definitely not a man and woman with two dogs, so McFarley carried on. When I informed him the person he spoke with was likely Hiram Walsh, he said no matter who he was McFarley did not believe what the man told him, so until he saw us in the flesh was gravely concerned we had been 'taken care of'.

Never have I felt so relieved to see a person when I saw McFarley, and exhausted, with nerves threadbare, may have wept a little, the thought I might contribute anything constructive to proceedings laughable for quite some considerable time. I cried a little more when I saw Raff.

Raven did not relinquish guard duty on seeing the Pinkerton, her four-footed suitor and myself, a signal Raff lingered in a bad state. When I braved auditing the seriousness of his injury, whether he might live or die, it brought an avalanche of heartache upon me.

Beyond embarrassed by my weeping, when I began to weep anew McFarley talked me around to sense and turned to constructing a rough travois, enlisting my help largely, he admitted later, with the purpose to distract me.

We hitched the good-natured buckskin to the travois, strapped Raff on it and took him to North's Ridge. I do not wish to suffer the agony of such a journey ever again, for it tested my sanity.

The physician at North's Ridge informed us with suitable gravity that Raff was in a dire condition, a redundant observation in the circumstances—an opinion I voiced somewhat acerbically—and he did not want to encourage false hope, going so far to declare we should prepare for Raff surrendering to infection.

Afterward, Raff told McFarley that soon as he beheld me riding behind the travois he felt confident he might survive, citing my indomitable will, mulish insistence to get things done and downright refusal to accept defeat of great assurance, and this calcified the backbone of his recovery.

He said to *me* that in the numinous place where his psyche roamed, unrestricted by pain and illness, he heard my comforting murmurings and entreaties to fight and was scared witless to do anything except battle to live, spurred by fear of what I might subject him to if he died.

In spite of his jesting—and how he could jest after brushing so close to death perplexed me—his faith broke all bonds, his confidence in me near bringing me to my knees.

McFarley stayed in North's Ridge to tie loose ends after informing his superiors of the inopportune demise of the Beaulieuxs. Grateful for his support, I was also tremendously grateful for his friendship and tirelessness in helping nurse back to health someone with whom he was barely acquainted. He downplayed his heroics, self-conscious when thanked for the part he played in Raff's convalescence. I foresaw nothing that could repay this debt.

Precious days after Raff was carried into a rooming house with access to fresh water and the ability to boil it, unable to keep my eyes open, I dozed at his bedside mid-afternoon.

Shaken awake by McFarley I glanced to Raff and found him staring at me. I knew then he would recover—it was not a good day for him to die.

This marked a turning point in Raff's restoration to health which, although cheering, was lengthy. The physician, Doctor Harlow, put success down to his diagnosis and treatment and, less importantly to him, Raff's size; the poison not so concentrated to be lethal in Raff's large frame. Harlow had looked me up and down and said: "You'd have been bug food, lady."

Agent McFarley sent word to Nate who, recovered after his

indisposition, arrived to accompany us home when the doctor agreed Raff fit to travel. En route to North's Ridge Nate sheered off-trail, following McFarley's directions to the cairn, to bury Cam Ellington. It did not require a word being said that the longer Cam remained above ground, the need for internment lessened. We visited his grave on the way to Melancholy, Raff insistent he dismount by the site, standing with negligible support of my arm to pay his respects.

⊹⟫⟩⟨⟪⊹

There is nothing special about Melancholy. There are more attractive, more exciting places to reside on this huge, beautiful continent. The town's isolation was a magnet that drew folks of extremes; misfits, outcasts keen to fade into the landscape, those running from debt, the law, or themselves, a bubbling mix of the kindly and freakish. Despite these deficiencies, it was home. When we rode out of the hills and entered Main Street I took great interest in Samson's ears, tears welling.

⊹⟫⟩⟨⟪⊹

The Pinkerton accompanied us to Melancholy where discussions continued between him, Raff and me regarding what we had experienced these last weeks.

With the end of his assignment in sight, McFarley confessed he had deliberately manipulated orders, left his argumentative partner asleep at their lodgings in Rock Creek, and struck out for Melancholy. Contrary to instruction by the Pinkerton's client the Beaulieuxs were now dead, and although McFarley had no hand in the deaths the agency was displeased. He sheepishly confided his extended stay in Melancholy served the purpose of giving his superiors, and his partner, room to cool down.

Now at liberty to tell us how he came to be tracking the Beaulieuxs, McFarley said the Pinkertons were employed by an individual who said the similarities of the murders of The Church of Celestial Light and Paradise Divine families was being noticed. There was talk and reporters were comparing stories, newspapers were comparing stories, readers were comparing stories. This person did not want the monstrosity of Chandelier Creek resurrected, so asked the Pinkertons to quietly bring the killers in to forestall closer inspection of what inspired the massacre. *He* had sent the telegram telling McFarley the Newmans and, therefore, feasibly, the Beaulieuxs, were in Melancholy.

McFarley would not confirm the Pinkertons' client came from within the church—his superiors knew, categorically—but would not confute the submission, either. If McFarley's version differed from Hiram Walsh's, it was immaterial.

The daguerreotype Raff saw at *The Fancy Weekly* placed Ezekiel Beaulieux—it still easier to refer to Ferrington Porter as 'Ezekiel or Zeke Beaulieux' and his partner as 'Madam'—as a member of Finnegan's church. The rationale behind his single-minded tracking of the Paradise Divine families that culminated in the Newman deaths were backed by his own admission.

Revenge.

Raff could not recollect reference to Charlie Fairbanks in relation to Chandelier Creek, so wired Mr. Parkinson at the newspaper asking if he could search his archives for the Fairbanks name. Parkinson wired back he found nothing that tied Charlie to Zeke, or to the massacre. If Beaulieux lied about their familial relationship and Fairbanks shared Beaulieux's lust for blood and adventure, nothing more, their secret died with them.

McFarley said people were starting to connect the murders, so did Walsh decide the Beaulieuxs had served their purpose? Did he want to make sure no one caught them? If he were rid of them they would not have the opportunity to give him up to authorities. Did he sense they were going to abandon their joint project to dance with their own demons, or disappear? He was in the perfect position to inform his client of the Beaulieuxs' latest identity, presented as the fruits of a nonexistent investigator's labor, which saw this man then send Walsh to 'disable' those with whom he actually conspired.

When Walsh arrived in Melancholy and the Beaulieuxs saw him, they must have decided to head for Chandelier Creek right away. He was too clever for them.

All this was, of course, conjecture. Heeding Walsh's warning, we did not mention him tracking us, or why he did so, to anyone. If our friends were ignorant of facts they could not inadvertently disclose any part of the sordid tale, thereby negating the possibility of it filtering back to those in charge in Tynbridge Hills. With a real chance of violent repercussions.

If we chose to take things further it would be wasted breath. Links and suppositions might be confirmed in the hallowed halls of Tynbridge Hills, but we were up against a powerful organization. Hiram Walsh was protected. A blanket denial would be issued; besides, who would believe our argument? Even if they did, what could or would they do about it? It was us against them.

McFarley mooted telling a church Elder Walsh was a double-crossing reptile, trusting that information would leak to the right person, but we could prove nothing, and Hiram Walsh knew it.

Ultimately, he did not reveal his client's name to me, and he did not kill anyone.

But I did. And he was witness to it.

Our resolution? To let the whole affair die. The Beaulieuxs would have hanged, anyway. Did it matter how they died, or by whose hand? Going by the list Parkinson gave Raff a single man avoided Beaulieux's wrath: this last member of Finnegan's gang was free now to return to Tynbridge Hills where the mutinous faction within the church could use him against their leader. Let members of The Church of Celestial Light and Paradise Divine fight amongst themselves from here on. Cyrus Finnegan was sure to get his comeuppance.

⇒⟫⟪⇐

Raff removed his hat and carefully deposited himself on the stool beside mine, wound flaming if he moved impulsively, and responded to a rash of greetings extended by those crowded around us.

Nate poured McFarley and Raff a drink. Military-straight, consistently close to smiling, the earmarks of proprietorship flitted about my old friend. With the assistance of Harley O'Donohue I had gone ahead with gifting the Fleur to Nate and Annie—the official takeover was slated for the next day—and Annie had joined her husband behind the bar where she ordered Prairie Dog here and there as though born to the position of overseer.

"Do you have anything more about events leading to you near dying on us, Marshal?" Jonas Tolliger asked.

"Doubt we're gonna learn more on it," Raff said disingenuously.

According to Lizzie, when news of Raff's injury came through, Jonas, Shakey and Fatfoot declared they were going to form a posse and ride after the degenerate who hurt him until informed the man was dead. I shuddered to think what fix those boys would have gotten into, the likelihood being they would have needed rescuing themselves.

"How were we suckered in by those Beaulieuxs?" Jonas asked. "They set the scene, didn't they? Her telling me she wore a scarf to cover scars she got from lightning, and that her *husband* wore a leg brace after contracting a childhood disease."

"People see what they expect to see, Jonas. We were no different," I said. "In our defense, they were masters with sleight of hand, of manipulation."

"Any news on Mouse?" Shakey asked.

"No," Raff said.

"Heard Fishbait's bin helpin' Bron." Shakey contemplated his glass. "Seems he's got hisself permanent work."

"Poor child," Jonas said.

We knew he referred to Mouse, not Thomas. There had been no sign, hide nor hair, of the stable boy after he went missing the night the Beaulieuxs slunk out of Melancholy. Lizzie had organized an extensive search for the boy the day Nate and I rode out of town, but not a trace of him was found. His body might be discovered some day; then again, it might not. Part of me wondered if he was the 'vexatious fly in the ointment' Beaulieux spoke of, the 'vexatious fly' that must also disappear in the cavern explosion. Although it was illogical that Beaulieux had taken Mouse that far with him I prayed I had not, inadvertently, left Mouse somewhere in the cavern to die.

Skirts flouncing, making doe eyes, Katie pranced alongside Kip McFarley and bumped her hip against the Pinkerton's.

McFarley said he was also sticking around Melancholy to see Raff through his convalescence. This was an excuse. Growing affection for Katie formed the real basis for McFarley's reluctance to go home.

Old enough to be her grandfather—this of little account to Katie—they were not as ill-matched as they appeared and McFarley's affections, to his quiet delight, were reciprocated.

I had observed their courtship with the eye of a cynic and the optimism of a lapsed romantic. When it came to affairs of the heart, love was a strange and unusual country. Besides, I was in no position to pass judgment when my own relationship frequently languished in a state of flux.

I covertly watched Katie and Kip McFarley, not the only person to do so; Jonas Tolliger, a long-time customer of Katie, donned a satisfied air. If the girl decided to move on with McFarley, and with Annie now a respectable married woman, replacements for them needed to be found. With a jolt, I realized hiring girls for the Fleur was no longer my domain.

I rested a hand on my belly.

This registered in Jonas's agile, doctor's brain. It hit me the precise moment it hit Doc Tolliger. His eyes widened when he scoured my face. Oh Lord. I shook my head, the motion slight, nevertheless he caught it and tipped his glass. No one saw our exchange.

It could not be true, could it? Was an ancient sense telling me I was with child? I distracted myself from the prospect by inserting my opinion in a lively discussion between Doc Tolliger and Shakey that became more and more bizarre and tailed into the evening.

⟫⟪

Having shooed the last customer home, Raff and I stood under the overhang outside the Fleur, Raven and Custer at our feet. Raff wrapped an arm around my shoulders and drew me in, looping his other arm around my waist, to encircle me.

A full October moon shone round and huge, Melancholy

illuminated in an unaccustomed glow as though it were daytime, the grime, dilapidated boards, sidings of speedily erected homes and businesses glossed over, the town seeming awash with opportunity and potential. Even the burned-out building next to the Fleur assumed a foreign, magical grace.

This jigged an idea, germinating kernels that had been lying dormant. Making use of my fortune, could I help Melancholy fulfil this moon-gilded promise? Perhaps I could pay for a new doctor to administer to Melancholy's growing population, or employ a dentist so there were no more excuses for such a performance as Nate's. Supporting both physician and dentist would be a trifling expenditure against the total monies in my accounts, so why not do both? My mind raced. And if the burned-out building were restored and made into a safe harbor for orphans like Mouse—children brought to homelessness or near starvation through no fault of their own . . .

"It's the dying grass moon," Raff said of the pale yellow orb above us.

"You had better explain."

"It's time to ready for winter." His lips brushed my hair. "To get in supplies. Hunt animals grown fat. It's also called the hunter's moon 'cause it's easy to stalk prey at night, it bein' so bright."

"It feels like we are the sole creatures in existence."

"Yep. Us, the dogs, and Shakey."

Doc Tolliger had left before Shakey, summoned by his eldest daughter who declared her sister had sliced her thumb with a carving knife and required stitches. Shakey stayed on, was the last person to leave the Fleur, and now staggered to his surprisingly well-kept cabin—a prerequisite to the purchase of a home being that it had to be within walking, or staggering, distance of my saloon.

"Please make sure he gets home, Raff." I extricated myself from his embrace. "He may fall asleep before getting there. Remember the morning Clay unlocked the store and found Shakey propped against his hitching rail, dead to the world?"

Raff grinned and stepped off the boardwalk, forgoing leaping off it as he was wont to do, a hitch evident in his stride as he went to intercept the old soldier. He had skimmed close to vacating the planet in the past, but there was a different slant to his handling of this recent near-death experience and recovery.

Although Raff moved gingerly he caught up to Shakey—the elderly man moved at the speed of an arthritic sloth. Raff said something to him, clasped his elbow and matched his gait, setting Shakey right if he deviated off course.

I looked to the skies, at the ball Nature had painted with broad strokes.

The dying grass moon.

It was oddly fitting to be gazing at the heavens, shooting stars and clusters of glittering jewels beauties to behold, mindful this strange moon forecast not only the end of a season of weather, but a season in my life.

I knew deep down suspicion of my condition would be confirmed, the impending arrival left unannounced to keep reservations and disquiet at bay; this growing child concealed beneath thick clothing until snowmelt.

The loss of the daughter Raff and I had together was a perpetual sadness. Gone these eight years, we never spoke of her, as though our broken hearts cherished faith in mending if her name was never uttered mournfully or howled in grief.

Raff was a tremendously kind man, a good man, and I loved him with a passion that defied description. There, I had admitted my innermost feelings, if only to myself. It would take bravery of a magnitude I neither comprehended nor possessed to admit the depth of my feelings to the man concerned, which meant it may well stay unsaid forever.

How would Raff react when he heard he was to be a father? How would he cope if, God forbid, another child were taken in infancy?

Raff and Shakey disappeared around the corner of Lizzie and Clay's store.

Again, I rested a hand on my belly, wondrous, despite trepidation, birth to death a marvel, an awe-inspiring cycle.

I enjoyed the stillness and night air, the bracing temperature forerunner to coming blizzards and snow and ice, when southerners changed straw hats for felt. My thoughts roamed far and wide, encompassing Mouse, the Newman family, and the other wretches who died as consequence of Beaulieux's fixation, his roaring hatred.

Wishing to be strong for Raff during his illness I had done my best to limit my intake of laudanum in North's Ridge and on our return to Melancholy, although still drank the Irish whiskey I loved. That said, of late I had felt queasy, ill to the point that often the mere thought of an alcoholic beverage saw me excuse myself from whomever I was with and race to my chamber pot. My mind was clearer than it had been for an exceptionally long time, and this clarity brought with it insight and truth.

After Zeke Beaulieux's family died at Chandelier Creek he had turned the anger and guilt he felt outward, on others, including innocent children, demonstrating in the worst way how violence can be perpetuated if left unaddressed. I had gone in the opposite direction, turning my guilt inward, to punish myself. I trembled to think that if my situation growing up had been different I might have evolved to strike out as he had done, my guilt spun around, to twist and defile.

I saw that I needed to overcome old habits and hurdles and learn to deal with my enduring grief so I did no harm, for in a few months a small human being would be relying on me for care. My self-destructive behavior must not harm the child I nurtured; if something happened to this baby, something that could have been prevented, I could not live with myself.

Once spring came and a cabin was built on Jakob's property I planned to move there. Would Raff be joining me? I did not see him as a farmer, but time spent together during the winter months ahead would allow for discussions about our living arrangements, and our future. I looked forward to those debates, which I foresaw being heated and, without a doubt, infuriating.

Increasingly chilled I moved inside. I did not stop to lock the saloon but went straight up to my room, secure in the knowledge Raff would bolt the outer doors on his return to the Fleur, and to our bed.

AUTHOR'S NOTE

Organizations, events, establishments, and locales in Hennessey's world are a mixture of reality and invention; one example being the fort in *Dying Grass Moon* which is based on Cove Fort, Utah. If you find yourself in southern Utah heading along Interstate 15, I highly recommend you swing off and take a look. Founded in 1867, it is one of only a few Mormon forts that remain—because it was built of stone and volcanic rock, not timber—and is well worth a visit.

N.B. With regard to the relationship between the inhabitants of the fort Hennessey visits and local Native Americans, Sister Reem says her predecessors vowed 'it better to feed them, not fight them' (Chapter 16). This refers to a comment made by the Mormon leader Brigham Young. It is my understanding he said: 'It's cheaper to feed them, not fight them'.

The Bible passage in Chapter 16 is from the King James Bible—I Corinthians 6: 9-10.

If I found one of the Native American sayings or proverbs at the start of each chapter attributed to different sources or tribes, I have used a broader term like 'Native American proverb'.

ABOUT THE AUTHOR

Andrea lives in Orewa, New Zealand. When not working or writing, she can be found making her way through the works of Charles Dickens with reasonable success; learning to stand-up paddle board with fair to middling success; or attempting to limit consumption of peanut M&Ms with little to no success.

Reviews are important too and much appreciated by authors. If you enjoyed reading *Dying Grass Moon* as much as Andrea enjoyed writing it, please consider writing an honest review on your preferred platform.

If you would like to keep in touch, sign up for Andrea's newsletter.

www.andreajackaauthor.com

facebook.com/andreajackaauthor

twitter.com/andreajacka2

ACKNOWLEDGEMENTS

I owe eternal thanks to: Eva Chan for her sharp copy-editing eye, Jeroen ten Berge for his spot-on design, and Lesley Marshall for suggestions that smoothed out plot glitches. Last, but certainly by no means least, Martin Taylor, who has led me through the byways of self-publishing with infinite kindness and the patience of a saint. Any mistakes and missteps are my own.

www.ingramcontent.com/pod-product-compliance
Lightning Source LLC
Chambersburg PA
CBHW030833110726
47900CB00006B/1875